prey for the birds

book one of the sandmarches

clawson smith

CLAWSON SMITH

Also known as HYPERPHANT *(pseudonym)*

PREY FOR THE BIRDS

BOOK I OF
THE SANDMARCHES

ISBN: 979-8-218-71089-7

For Tariq, Amir, Shalsem, Antonius, and all the others who were there when my sanity was unbound in the desert, when it was a wild dervish trapped with nothing but my wit and the endless heat. You made life worth escaping from.

And of course to the puppetmaster, who shall remain nameless, for pulling the strings and offering a paradise in sand...your efforts will never be forgotten. You are the ghost that haunts these writings, always.

Thank you all.

contents

Beginning 6

Akala-Juradh 14

Qaryat al Hadid 44

The Crownlands 72

Nefara 91

The South Road 111

Nomarch's Plaza 138

Waddun-Sida 154

The Maze 181

Thieves Road 220

Shobai Hamada 256

Nomad's Camp 305

Nemset 330

Black Oasis 360

Pearl of Tyhri 383

Hemopolis 413

White Kasbah 436

al Khandaq Keep 453

Epilogue 477

"Many men would take the death-sentence
without a whimper, to escape the life-sentence
which fate carries in her other hand."

— T.E. Lawrence

Beginning

"Gharib," was the last thing the stranger wanted to hear as he was rudely dragged from his slumber.

Disorientation—where was he? Darkness and weight. He was lying down and smothered by sheer mass.

"Gharib," the slur for outsider and pale-skin was spoken again, louder. But it was muffled, like through a wall.

More conversation. Like the speaker was talking to themselves. The stranger wanted to sleep.

"Go away," he tried to slur back but was gagged.

Was that grit in his teeth?

Pain lanced suddenly and spiked his adrenaline—something pierced his flesh. As if his heart had been filled with ice. He could not scream out. That heaviness was like a lead blanket. Claustrophobia set in as even twisting his neck felt impossible.

A muffled laugh and then something swept the darkness from his eyes; a turbaned figure holding a pig sticker, coated with blood.

His blood.

The blade hovered now over the stranger's eye.

"Taa abad o-ddahr," said the turbaned man with the knife.

Agony replaced with cold recognition; this wasn't a murder, it was grave robbery. He'd been buried. The grit in his teeth and overwhelming weight was sand.

And he'd been stabbed already.

Moonlight flashed on the blade as the pig sticker flew down to his chest for a second time.

Reflexes took over.

The graverobber gurgled in shock—the buried stranger had ripped an arm free and stuck a dagger of his own in a soft place. He didn't know how. Mewing and shuddering, the robber fell like a limp bag of apples.

"I'm not dead yet, fucker," the buried man said through a mouthful of dirt.

Nearby there were discordant shadows of men and howls that disturbed the peace of the dead. Blades like pale spears of moonlight pierced the dark blue veil. Turbaned heads that floated from nowhere.

The buried man fell back and tasted something on his tongue; liquor burned his gums still.

A darker realization; he hadn't been buried without merit. He had drunk himself to death tonight. Ending the misery that was dragging himself onto these foreign shores and hating himself with every dusty step. The final moments hit him with painful clarity.

How the hell was he breathing again?

Blackness took him.

The kick that woke the man up was goddamn hard. It rocked him. Which meant he wasn't buried anymore. Or dead.

How?

He rolled to his side and creaked a dusty eyelid. An ugly orb blotted out the light; a brown face that broke into a jagged-toothed smile. Tooth doctors were apparently non-existent in this godforsaken side of the world. More of that tongue-rolling gibberish, ending with 'gharib'.

"Come to finish me off?" and he made the universal gesture of hostility, followed with, "Do your worst."

There was quiet examination.

Then the little brown man uttered fluently, "You speak the imperial Patina? If you understand me gharib, say yes."

"...yes."

That crooked smile further widened, "Yes yes! Good. I pray to Ghazparaba you would not be mute."

"Lucky for you."

Not buried anymore, however, the stranger was draped across the back of a camel, hogtied. And he didn't know who they were. Friends of the graverobber? Another party? Nothing kicked a stupor than fear. He nearly fell off the camel. And groaned; his chest was stiff and the stab wound fresh.

"You are Teridian?"

"No."

His newfound friend prodded, "Tell me gharib, what is your name? I must know!"

Answering could wait; the man was looking around.

Hills ate hills and were eaten by steeper and even meaner hills that were dwarfed by mountains that bristled with premature snowcaps. The road took them up into the thick walls of distant crags. Squads of rough-leafed trees and armies of sagebrush flanked the squabbling, poor excuse for a road. This was hill country—bandit country. He twisted his head the other way. The glimmering Jewelport of Qamar and the band of blue sea barely more than a dream.

A bad dream.

"You first; where are we and why am I not dead?"

"Akala-Juradh. To you, it would be Rat Eater. As for your death...it is an omen."

Leave it to the desert crazies and their creative nomenclature.

Impossible to ignore; the little man was scratching furiously into a leather-bound journal. Taking notes perhaps.

"Ah, you are unfamiliar. Giant rats only live here, they eat well gharib. Better than goat. You tell if you see rat."

"And why are we going into the hills where there are nothing but rats to eat?"

"It demands us to take this path of danger."

"What demands?"

"Ah the tongue of the copper lands, the Patina escapes Nereel! I say now, we have no other path but this, yes?"

This language barrier was already getting old.

"Where?"

"Kahil. We already are one with the vulture. Now gharib. You must answer me. I must know the name of the man who cannot die."

The stranger was confused—what did the little man mean?

His fingers traced up his breastbone and it caught just left of the center; the wound lay just over his heart. An ugly lump of poultice had been hastily stuffed into it.

The organ missed a few beats as his fingers traced it.

The stranger swallowed down this strange emotion.

But how?

Afternoon's undying grip brought the caravan to a halter. Judging by the camel and horse butts the man could see from his limited view, they rode with a small army. Fifty or so, maybe more. They—draped in the livery of thieves with turbans and rough coats—were watering their horses. Everyone was slow to hobble off their horses, clearly saddle sore.

Someone had told the stranger once he was a details guy. Sometimes he noticed too well for his own good. It was obvious they'd been riding hard and for some time. Judging by the bowed legs and deftness of most, the bearded desert-dwellers in the odd pajamas and turbans could have been raised in the saddle.

Gap-tooth had returned from taking a leak, "Gharib, I will translate for you."

"Uhwhuh?" he was too busy in thought to notice.

They were approached by a contrasting pair of thieves; both sun-tanned and well-armed. One tall and with a swagger. The other in a black turban, big beard, and an eyepatch. It didn't take long to figure out there was a power dynamic between them.

More desert-speak, to which his translator said, "The captain and his lieutenant wish to know if you will cause them grief."

"Tell them if they don't start explaining what's going on soon, I can guarantee it."

Big Beard Eyepatch didn't like that and his comrade chuckled.

"They say if you try to run, they'll splinter your legs like tree and let the rat finish you. Do not tempt them gharib."

Outrage filled the man but he let the others do the talking. It would help him little to lash out now. Escape could wait a moment.

Big Beard Eyepatch was talking fast and never broke eye contact.

"Darwish says you kill one of his best men, but this proved you are a ghost warrior. Hassan wanted your armor and sword. They agree on middle."

"This Darwish made a mistake then. I wasn't planning on living long."

The crooked-tooth translator paused, frowning, then relayed. Big Beard rippled in contemplation, then he uttered fast phrases.

"Darwish says you owe him doubly. One for killing a friend before his time. Another for having to settle your debts with the den master. He is impressed you did not bleed wine."

"Ah."

The tall arrogant man snickered and said something in a tongue that the stranger recognized as Medean.

No explanation was needed; memory, wicked and unreliable, stirred in the stranger's recollection. Oh, he remembered all right. Every inch and curve of a perfect, olive-skinned goddess who had practically jumped into his arms, pushing wine cup after wine cup into his hand, dancing him right into the hammock...

The suicide had seemed so fitting to his unceremonious realization that he had come to Nowhere, capital of Edge of the Map.

"How much wine?"

"Enough Darwish had to sell a camel. A barrel."

So that's what was making his brains feel like mashed beef under a butcher's mattock. The blinding sun wasn't helping the headache either.

"Goddamn. Goddamn it. Take me back to the port!" and now he really did begin to struggle to free himself.

"Darwish and Hassan. They must know your name gharib. Else they will let the men name you," the translator bristled, "Which I do not think would be wise."

Oh, the man had one of those too—one good enough to command taxes from peasant's purses, one that could demand an audience with barons and that one many would have died for. That one was burned out of the history books. Along with his estate, his lands, and everything his family had left him. A name he buried with the bones of his sons and daughters.

"Didn't they hear me? I need to go back—"

The lieutenant wound and struck him in the jaw. The stranger was hurled off the saddle, barely avoiding the spear that would have pierced his right knee. He scrambled on his butt and waited for another jab. But the lieutenant had been called off by Big Beard.

His gap-toothed translator tut-tutted, "Darwish will give you one last chance gharib. Choose your words carefully."

An invention of rivals and enemies, his nickname was not like his birthright; it was not a good one. But it was all the stranger had left, besides the rags on his back.

He muttered it.

"Speak up gharib, I could not hear you correctly."

"No you heard me right."

"Please...say it louder gharib."

When repeated, the tall man howled in laughter and the bearded cyclops continued to stare.

The translator smiled wide and dared any fly to dart between the gaps, "Welcome my friend...yes welcome, Cock."

البشر لحوم آكل
Akala-Juradh

The man who was actually called The Rooster was allowed the magnanimous privilege of walking a death march along with the other slaves. All in tow to the warband who marshaled them at an unsustainable pace across the marrow of hill country—defiles like sunken bones cut into rims of rock and yellow knolls. Nereel, his fast new friend, offered to translate the words of his captors. Rooster declined. As they walked, he winced. That dagger that barely missed his heart should have killed him—now it was just a festering nuisance.

Pain his lonely walking companion.

It would be divine intervention if the rot did not take him.

"When in Kahil, Darwish will sell them for more horses," Nereel rode alongside him at the back of the train, "And you. Always have more need for war slaves. There is talk of war."

"Isn't there always, everywhere?"

Besides the underfed excuses of slaves that were walking alongside weren't worth the wood for spears you could arm them with. Rooster doubted they would make the journey to Kahil—not with the frosty monsters of mountains that grew by the day on the horizon. Darwish—the short man in the turban and the eyepatch— drove them like whipped dogs.

Merciless and distant, he was.

Even with the other thieves.

Nereel was a man of infinite patience and was easily entertained by conversation, "No Rooster! Not for a hundred years! Now with the Ivory Queen…"

History droned on. The scenery was far more interesting. Exhausting as it was, the reward gave the

Rooster his first idea of what the land was outside the port; raw, barren, and open. Its naked and primitive vastness made him feel the mouse below the eye of the eagle. Barren mounds of tans peppered with sage bush, cloven by gray spines of dead hills that loomed over meadows of orange and yellow. Here and there, a striped stave rammed into rock cairns to indicate some indeterminable marker.

Days passed in yonder wilderness climbing into the belly of the cold sun. Into grays and yellows of boundless humps. The road was growing steeper with every day.

"Whose land is this?"

"No man's," replied Nereel.

And yet there was smoke in the hills—faint notes of civilization.

"Somebody lives here."

"Yes. A tribe called Ibgrud. We avoid them."

Little wonder why. They began to skirt pastoral villages built out of the rock if they could be called that. All torched. Blackened piles of corpses long burned—whether beast or human—were all that remained.

"Who were they?"

"Medeans. Families settling new land away," Nereel sighed, making a sound, "Look away Rooster. Bad curse here."

It was no curse. It was foolishness. By the looks of things, the villages could have been sacked by a dozen motivated thugs. They should have known better.

The warband broke into scouting parties looking for a watering hole. They came back later to report that sheep corpses had been dumped into the wells.

"Ibgrud don't play nice with their neighbors eh?"

"Gah! It's Ivory Queen. She give steel, fill pockets of raper and thief with gold. Tell them to hunt Medean. Even in White Dove peace."

No rest for the wicked and the cunning then. Using the local noose fodder to commit crimes of war while maintaining plausible deniability? Sounded like the Ivory Queen had a lot more in common with grubby northern warmongers than some exotic desert monarch. By the looks of it, she was winning.

And no sign of banditry nearby, Rooster scanned the horizon out of habit.

"You said that the White Dove made peace? Well it doesn't look like that's working out between him and the Queen eh? Why don't he march out and tan her hide?"

Nereel muttered something in his funny tongue, "It is not this simple Rooster. White Dove not like the father. He is Shah and not Caliph."

"Which means what?"

"He cannot pick up his sword ever again."

Darwish chattered and pointed up, gaining the attention of the warband and Rooster. The little one-eyed warlord even drew his bow and aimed at the sky.

"What is it?"

A brown shape darted up the steep hill and grazed their heads, wheeling into the blazing midday sun. It shrieked and left their ears ringing with bird-sound.

Darwish let loose and cursed as he missed.

Nereel exclaimed, "Shaitan, Rooster. A warlock of the enemy has given our names to Death. No doubt placed a curse on you and the other kul."

"The eagle?"

Nereel poked his tongue through the gap in his teeth, hissing, "A servant of shaitan. Your little brain at this word. Its name Shemsari. Ancient name. They are birds, see through their eye and speak as man through beak."

"Tell the captain to untie my hands and I will fight these shaitan. I can actually hit the damn thing with a bow."

Unamused, the little man made a hasty prayer by bending to press his forehead into the saddle and reciting his gibberish. Writing for the blink of an eye.

How many damn prayers could a person utter in a day? Was anyone counting to make sure they said enough?

"Perhaps their god stands invisible with a sword behind them, ready to smite the limbs off whoever misses their eleventh bow and scrape of the day..."

The quill was out and ready to record, "What god do you speak Rooster?"

"Nothing," he dusted himself off and stood, "Just more gharib nonsense."

"Aha! Good, good."

Nereel went into great detail on the demons known as Shemsari while they made camp near the village. He told Rooster about the tribals with unnaturally long lives, marked by their tattoos and ways of the horse. He said they were a creation of the now-dead gods of the forbidden sands beyond something called a 'sparkle wall'. He talked at length about their blood pact with the land that allowed them to possess creatures and live for days without water. It all sounded like superstitious horseshit but the Rooster had heard more creative in his day.

Like all things, myths grew legs the more mouths and ears were to receive them.

Tending to the fire, there was a palpable fear among the slaves but something else; hope. Dangerous thing that. Especially for one in captivity. Rooster wrapped himself in the horsehair blanket that had more holes than cloth and tried to sleep off the day's punishment. Tomorrow there'd be plenty more of it.

Whispers. Tugs. Chains strained. He was being dragged in the dark. It was still deep in the night.

Rooster creaked an eyelid; there were shadows hoisting him. The slaves were escaping. All of them were silent, moving together as one, holding their chains as to not let them clink. A moonless night—lucky for them. No better night for slipping away than this one.

There was no point in arguing—one of them had a knife. It would have been easy for them to cut his hand off and break for it without him.

Escape sounded better than a maiming, but just barely.

"Goddamn idiots," he hissed to himself.

Hope at the thought of freedom flickered in the back of his mind but Rooster didn't let it fester. This was an alien plain full of vagabonds and farmers who didn't speak his language. Escape would be as difficult as life as a slave.

They crossed the fields into the burned village if only for a short time, scavenging what wasn't already picked clean by the warband. It was too dark and the slaves were wasting time—their bold leader began to drag them out and into the hills.

Rooster was already exhausted from the grueling day before. How long he could press on like this would depend on how much longer the adrenaline would grant him. Blood blisters already covered much of his feet—they'd need draining in the morning.

Eventually they mounted enough hills that the ambience of plains was omnipresent.

A dark flapping in the night spooked the slaves, prompting a few to throw rocks.

Shut up, the bold leader was probably saying in their crude tongue, and a few more choice things.

They moved on to the hill next practically dragging their heels and letting the chains dangle.

Rooster didn't see it but knew the smell of freshly doused coals well enough. He tried to get the other slaves' attention but they pushed him away and ignored his protests. So he looked for movement among the grays and black of the horizon.

A scream from one of the slaves on the outer perimeter.

From all sides they were attacked. Shadows with spears and knives began to poke and herd them like wild cattle. The few slaves that fell became like anchors weighing them down to the dirt. Their attackers laughed blackly and deeply. Grisly sounds of hacking of flesh.

The night wasn't even over and they'd been caught again.

Whoever the gods of this land were, they sure got a kick when they made the Ibgrud.

Rooster found himself staring at the faces of his new captors; their eyes the wrong shape, foreheads protruding and wide with a jaw that could crush a rock. What else was there to eat out here anyway? Like if a toddler carved a clay frog with a spoon.

The humor of the moment vanished when the wide-headed raiders began to cut one of the slaves into pieces. Alive. Scooping the meaty remains into a crude iron cauldron. The last living half of the slave was still screaming with stumps for legs.

Bloody splash.

"Fucking savages," he ground his teeth.

Wild panic set into the rest of the slaves who began to beg and scream. Hackle-raising sounds. The chopping continued. More slaves were hauled to the cauldron. Judging by the two dozen raiders that corralled them to this pit and the starved looks on their leathery faces, who knew if any of them wouldn't go in the cauldron.

Cannibals. This wasn't the way Rooster wanted to go. That little cold hole with his blanket back at camp and a life with blood blisters sounded pretty nice right now.

Bad day not to have a god to pray to.

Only a few slaves chained between him and the chopping block. Didn't look like this would end well. He just hoped it would be over quick. A few minutes and he was all but guaranteed to become dinner.

An Ibgrud leapt up in his human-skin jacket, yelling at his companions for whatever reason. That reason was the hail of arrows that bombarded them from the darkness. A few of them went wild and actually hit the slaves too.

The scuffle that followed was more slaughter than skirmish. A few of the Ibgrud were able to lob some javelins of their own and felled a horse or two. A dead rider toppled into the fire and knocked the cauldron over, spilling grisly red paste on the dirt. Dozens of horses and camels circled the camp, cutting down any who tried to escape the onslaught.

One of the cannibals got clever and tried to pull Rooster and the remaining slaves away into the night. Couldn't blame the bastard for being hungry.

Instinct beat his exhaustion—Rooster was able to trip the Ibgrud over and smash his head in with a rock.

Rooster breathed heavy and fell back on his haunches, watching the warband reap the remaining raiders like wheat. It was over in a blink of an eye. Soon all there was to do was clean their blades and count the dead.

The lieutenant Hassan approached. It was jarring to see the man with that khud helm and foreign chainmail carrying his sword like it was his. The greatsword's blade had tasted blood and ran thick with it.

What would his family think of him, losing it to some bandit?

Rooster laughed like a madman at the dumb thought.

How funny that amongst carnage and horrors he had witnessed all he could think of was how his family—those who must have thought him long dead now—would disapprove of losing his sword. How bizarre.

"Gharib! Rooster! You live!" Nereel was hopping off his horse to approach.

He might have been sleep-deprived but he did not mistake the anger on the lieutenant's face.

Who went over and kicked over the cauldron. More than liquid came out to douse the flames.

There was no retribution for escaping—the punishment of surviving the ordeal seemed enough. Few kul were left anyway. There was little to no bandit sign the rest of the journey through the hills. Ibgrud must have gotten the message.

The giant rats, however, didn't.

It took a few dozen arrows to convince the dog-sized rodents to scurry back into the holes from which they came.

Chai wasn't just for the silk merchants and affluents of the Jewelport, Rooster pleasantly discovered. The fragrant smell mixed with cinnamon stirred his nose as Nereel passed the crude ceramic cup his way. Flakes of the spices floated like little boats on the ochre ocean within the cup.

"*Wakt behyr*," the funny little man said.

"I'll never understand you people," Rooster muttered back but accepted the gift all the same.

Pleasantly and without warning, Darwish stopped the train in one of the small valleys where a spring bubbled up. The biome was ignorant of the cold season's approach and offered its lush escape to any visitor. A fading green gem tucked above a rocky sea of tans and grays.

They'd traded colder air and heights for the cannibal plains below. Out of some mysterious generosity, the warband gifted him wool and robes to stay warm. Maybe out of pity. Or simply because there were too few slaves now to fight over them.

"Your language is backwards."

"So said Nereel! When as boy taken to holy house to learn Patina."

For a moment Rooster forgot he was a prisoner to the warband and that he was swimming in his clothes that once fit neatly. The chai warmed his stomach down to his toes.

"What did you do Nereel? Before they burned your holy house? Your profession?"

The quill hovered, "I taught words. Hill child need learn Medean. I was teacher. Good teacher!"

"And Darwish?"

Like an owl, Nereel's brows furrowed, "The student."

"Forgive me that I can't see that shrewd little warlord holding a quill."

"Forgive? What sin does Rooster hold?"

An eagle scream corrupted the tranquil moment. Their demonic watcher taunted them, flying low enough even a well-thrown rock could take it out. And it chortled, almost human-like as some of the riders did attempt with rocks. Darwish forbade the wasting of arrows after two bags had already been wasted on such occasions. Hypocrite just didn't want to be one-upped.

With grace it climbed and widened its circle but never let them out of its sight. It struggled to fly straight he realized. Something had bent its wing once, forcing it to compensate with the other. And it was missing a tailfeather.

"Bastard's been through the wringer. And he doesn't let up does he?" it was hard not to appreciate the dedication of the warlock.

"I do not have the know Rooster. Shemsari too far. Not make sense. Shaitan never come north of sparkle wall."

Ever since his sudden departure from his port of call, neither did Rooster.

On the maps he'd studied before stepping aboard the vessel that took him south of any imperial reach, the Jewelport was at the very edge. And not of all the wise men or scholars or professional fart-sniffers had spoken anything of this barbaric land of cannibals. Nor their demonic inhabitants who ate rats and took the forms of eagles.

Every day he asked a question, and his answer delivered more questions tenfold. What was the point?

They sipped their chai and Nereel began to mash some sort of flour-paste to cook over a fire when a rider shouted something from a hilltop. A lump of dough was sizzling on the hot stone top above the fire.

"What is it?"

"We spy somebody below, maybe close," Nereel murmured.

A hubbub—men and horses quickly assembled into a knot of scouts led by the lieutenant. Darwish halted their advance and dispersed the men accordingly.

The little man sprung up like a weed, "Our rest is over. Darwish wants eyes above cloud, gharib. I am to translate and paint history."

"Wonderful."

Cruel and short as their break was, the scouting party did not go far. Their position was nearly vertical to the canyon valleys below. Rungs of ill-traveled switchbacks climbed up to the road they took, where the lieutenant and his scouts assembled.

Dust was kicking up just below their feet on the rim of

the escarpments. Wind was carrying their ambience; horse sound and mail clinking. One of their scouts yelled down the valley, twisting a helm in the light; a signal.

It didn't escape Rooster's notice they had traveled out of earshot and eyesight of the rest of the warband.

The visitors came hard and fast, winding up the rock staircases with their banners and glinting mail. Little domed helms that grew in size and numbered as easily as their own party. At least twoscore warriors fully kitted to slot a group of vagabonds or cattle thieves. Which the warband very much appeared to be—sans a herd.

"Rooster...maybe you leave."

Not far away, the lieutenant Hassan was cradling a sword across his legs—his sword. Eyes glinting along the well-kept edges and then over to Rooster.

They weren't meant to be part of this meeting.

"We'll be going back then," he spoke in the Patina towards the lieutenant, who didn't so much as twitch.

Most Medeans weren't bilingual, which was proving useful.

He just wished he'd learned their tongue on the boat between rounds of puking.

After scrambling halfway up to the plateau, Rooster pulled the tiny man behind a boulder, "Come Nereel. I'm damn curious now. You can write about what you see."

"But..." a litany of excuses, but the little brown man followed suit.

Soon they peered behind a boulder that straddled the sharp rise overlooking the valley.

Each tenth rider carried a tall rectangular banner; one was a slash of sea foam green and a white bird, the other a red diamond on a yellow field divided by a black halberd, but Nereel grew excited to explain. There was no hostility amongst the visitors, despite the speed in which they rode up or their armament.

"It is the banner of Ayubin Suhrab. And they fly the White Dove of the Shah too! Aie we must be of care!"

Hassan and their leader traded words but Nereel didn't

care to illuminate on it. At the most inopportune moment, the chai made a move on the little man's bowels. He excused himself to find a large rock to squat behind and vacate breakfast.

But Rooster could put two and two together. He took everything he could mentally jot down.

Voices raised. Horses stomped hooves and their riders swayed stiffly. The dispute took legs and really gained stride. For a tense moment, any onlooker would think heads would hit dirt. Tension brewed over that little canyon. And then after what felt like hours of negotiation but likely took moments, the armored host rotated out and left whence they came.

One thing was clear barring language barriers; that Lieutenant Hassan was up to something and Darwish wasn't meant to find out. A split was formed somewhere down the middle of the warband. It was fundamental and it was tangible.

"Ah it appear I miss the end."

"No," Rooster muttered, watching as Hassan rallied his men with hushed speech. It was impossible it wasn't conspiratorial, "I fear we've only just seen the beginning."

Nereel frowned and studied the column of dust afar, writing something down.

"Tell me. Why would this party be under the scrutiny of this Ayubin Suhrab."

"No idea Rooster! It not make any logic. Ayubin Suhrab is far away. Too far land. They and Darwish fight as White Dove. With? Of? You understand me."

"And Hassan?"

"Hassan fight whoever Darwish tell him."

Not based on what he just witnessed, but the Rooster didn't need to elaborate.

Back at camp the warband was ready to take off once more, watered and rested. Bringing up the rear was the little one-eyed captain, surveying the scene of the valley just a few moments before. For a brief moment, his silent observation scanned over the Rooster and held there.

An oracle would have a bitch of a time telling what hid behind that lone ochre bulb.

Juniper trees shuddered to shed their coat of frost. Winter was coming fast. Seemingly unthinkable in a land that was supposed to be desert but old man Winter reared his ugly, ancient head and howled. Frost blanketed the backs of horses and camels in the morning, gray shrouds billowing on the horizon, and even the leaves fell from those twisted trees and bushes. On the road of the high country—taking them on exposed saddles of lower mountains before the wall of crags—there was nothing to shield them from the biting winds.

A dry chill assailed the warband, clustering behind the cover of the gnarled juniper that somehow grew between the slabs of granite and gravel of the high country. And a forsaken country it was. Even the berries on these desert conifer were inedible.

All Rooster could do was wrap his miserable excuse for a cloak about him and eye the hillman enviously.

Drooping mustaches, turban-wraps, even riding their horses differently—these were the men who clung to Darwish. Shorter and hairier. A squad-sized clique of entirely different people—whereas most of the warband were taller, dressed more colorful, and appeared more soulful. The shorter men made up for the elegance of their counterparts; their horses seemed invulnerable to the elements or the terrain and the hillmen deft on their tasseled saddles.

They made slow time and had a hell of it trying to ascend what was barely a road any longer.

A horse lost its footing and snapped a foreleg, sending its rider tumbling and his screams rang out across the gorge. Packs and gear went with it and caused a chain reaction. Another rider and his camel swayed and hit the rocks. The chaos brought the party to a grinding halt.

Everyone gathered round—save the hillmen. Apathetically they sunk into the cold gravel slope and watched cooly. And began to crawl to the rises to look ahead and provide overwatch.

"Da'wali," the little man explained and wiped his nose, "They come from mountains east. Called Ghurandaanhaa; Black Teeth. Primitive people, Da'wali. Not like Medean at all. He would eat his horse for strength."

A practical people toughing it in impractical land. Little critique would sway Rooster's opinion of them.

"Also. They do not approve of Darwish's current plan."

"What? Why?"

Nereel braced for a cough that did not come but steeled himself silent. His condition seemed to be worsening by the day.

Rooster grunted, "Speaking of mountains, we've got a problem."

Clouds darker than sin were stewing over those jagged walls of granite ahead and they were going real ugly, real quick. On the long end of an hour, that storm would hit and the warband was exposed. Badly.

"Bastards. We need to leave the body or we'll never make it off this rock," he shouted but none of the party cared, except to curse him or mutter about gharib nonsense.

A ragged fit of sputtering and wet coughing from Nereel. The man doubled over on his horse and hung there.

For a moment they were not on these untamed slopes of this uninhabited land of barbarians and devils, but back in the firelit halls of his lineage. Watching his father's father die wretchedly, choking on his own spit. Children hanging onto his liver-spotted arms like vultures, waiting to fight over the land and spoils when he croaked. Those wet rattles from the little crooked-mouthed translator were too similar and unearthed uncomfortable familiarity.

"You need a leech-man Nereel. How far are we from Kahil?"

Feebly he attempted to write but it was too much effort, "Another sundown, Rooster. But I...I cannot..."

"A day's ride? Answer me damn it. Without you, I die

Nereel."

A sad chuckle and then the little man began to ramble, incoherent. The journal fell from his grip. Rooster almost jumped out of his skin; a hillman had moved on them silently, tugging on his clothing like a child.

"*Mariz moalem*?" the hillman could not have been more than eighteen but was impassive, stone.

"He's sick. Kahil? Need to get to Kahil or he dies. Get it?"

It was impossible to tell but the hillman in the funny beaded headband did some kind of nod. Conferring amongst his own. They argued hotly. A litter of the juniper branches was crafted in wicked time and Nereel was soon being drug behind a horse.

Another tug—they wanted the Rooster to follow close by. Without any warning, the hillmen hooted and howled not unlike a pack of dogs, rode ahead of the party, and took off through the pass. Despite the holes in his boots and his frailty, Rooster decided he'd live longer if Nereel did.

They rode and he ran hot behind.

Down the treacherous switchbacks and gravel slides, they charged with frightening speed. Footing was a luxury. Rooster winced as his joints felt swollen and rolled his ankle more than once. It was all he could do to keep up with the hillmen.

The eagle crossed his periphery, sailing above their descent.

"Some guardian angel huh!"

Was it following the party or following him?

Delusion shifted into realization; that rocky abyss was darkening deeper and the air falling rapidly in temperature. Even the eagle shrieked, reeling just in time as the torrents of cold snow descended in fury upon the crevasse. White blurred and clung to Rooster's eyelashes.

"Slow down," he shouted hoarsely as the hillmen disappeared.

Panic set in as he was alone in the snowstorm. Helplessness and anger as there was nothing to accompany him in the bleak rock walls besides the white noise of the snowflakes and wind pounding the walls.

He was not equipped for these elements.

He would die in this waste.

And suddenly Rooster felt his body float and muscles strain, heels rapidly lifting to carry him into a sprint. Even the chafed skin of his feet did not weep and blood congealed by the cold. He knew the moment he stopped that death would descend among the white torrent.

Eagle cry right above his head—was it madness? Or was the demonic warlock watching with his eagle vision, waiting to pick from his bones? A shadow passed overhead but in this light, it could have been anything.

Rooster flew so fast that his eyes froze over. And ran into the side of a horse as he entered a shielded canyon. It took the wind out of him. Like phantoms, the hillmen waited.

From the ground he grunted, "You sons of whores. Don't leave me behind or I'll torment you as a ghost in this life."

Even in the dark the hillmen looked thoughtful, muttering.

That same young one approached with the lead of Nereel's horse in hand. And in the crudest Patina ever uttered in the history of the southern tongue, he said, "Ride. Fast. Quick. Alone. Kahil. Souzon. Heal."

Climbing with embarrassing weakness, Rooster didn't need to ask. It'd been a while since he'd saddled up. But familiarity set in. Yeah, a horse was still a horse here.

The bay-colored steed was sturdy and shuddered at his touch.

Hillmen hands carried Nereel and placed him in front of the Rooster on the saddle. The little man had little warmth at all. A quiet wet cough—it was barely a sign of life.

"Stay. Road. Go. Gharib. Go!"

A hand slapped the horse and it did what all mounts did; it bolted.

Daring to drive the steed as hard as it ever had, Rooster

rode as he had as a boy. As if the creature had no limits. It galloped and exhaled weakness. They nearly ran into a cornice that collapsed under the weight of the new snow. The horse teetered.

"We'll both freeze fucker. Don't stop now. Ride for your master, horse. Ride for oats and for a warm stable!"

The beast somehow listened. White and tan blurred. Gravel chewed under the hooves. Twilight light was dying.

Nereel moaned and gave his last little rattle.

Snow relented—they were in the eye of the blizzard. Illumining hope as the path they rode was a hard-packed albeit less-traveled one. A crack in the walls of stone appeared. Above the arm of old man winter was swinging down another torrent of merciless cold, blinding snow.

To Kahil, or to death.

"Hyah!" Rooster pressed into the enveloping whiteness.

Glow of lamps. Perhaps the torchbugs that waited at the crossing of Death's River. But was death this cold? That seemed cheeky.

He dared not open his eyes fully.

"Don't try to stand," accented but in a northern tongue, chastened, "Your left hand and both feet need the warm water for the hypothermia."

Getting to the tower-hut of the Souzon was a blur—Rooster didn't recall being pried off the frozen horse, nor sitting down or having his limbs doused in warm water. Or put in fresh robes either.

"Answer me. Hello. Are you with me? How many fingers am I holding up?"

"...yes."

"Yes is not a number."

Across the barren room the tall, skinny healer called Souzon sighed and squatted on a stool. Spectacled and looking forever disappointed. A tanned and lanky gharib—the first one Rooster had seen in months. Doing who knew what in this remote hole at the edge of the map.

"I should tell you. It will not be long now before your

friend goes on. He is dying. Both lungs are filling with fluid and I do not have access to healers who specialize in magical auguries. Before the morning, he will pass."

"How? Why so soon? Poison?"

"Disease, unfortunately. Many from the farms in Aduara and al Zahra suffer a similar fate and do not wax long in their years. I think it is dust from the mines."

Rooster swore.

The tall man toweled off his hands, "If it's any consolation, he should have been dead days ago. By your and his state, so should you. No one takes those mountain passes in this season."

Just his luck; the only person he'd crossed paths with and could translate would croak any minute.

"Nothing can be done?"

"Unless you happen to have a giant eagle to ride on over those mountains, there's not a true magician and healer capable of forestalling his fate. Not here in Kahil."

There had been so many deaths this last year, but this one felt the worst. No reason why, Rooster just felt attached to Nereel. It wasn't like the little man helped him escape or was related to him. Took the wind right out of his sails.

After his limbs thawed a bit, Souzon took him to the room where Nereel rested. Odd—on the table the little translator looked even smaller on the cream cloth. A single candle burned.

"I am sorry, whatever your name is. Was there any relation?"

"No, just a riding companion," Rooster grunted, "And a translator."

Souzon eyed him sideways, at the rags no doubt, "Darwish and his Duskhounds don't speak northspeech."

The thought of the loss was hollowing. Nereel had been the only soul he'd had a conversation with longer than a sentence since he'd left the ship.

"Do you take the chai?"

It was a brief and silent memorial. Letting himself get sentimental, the Rooster left a ring—the last silver he'd hidden from Darwish—and placed it on the man's chest.

"For a box and a good burial. That least he deserves."

They took their cups and sat.

Rooster was feeling acutely aware of his condition when it hurt to sit down, almost spilling the steaming chai. Everything was catching up, starting with his joints.

Shutters opened wide—the window was a portal to the snowy night. Frost topped the garden of towers that was Kahil; all its limestone and granite architecture chiseled into a steep terrace, sheltered by toothy crags barely taller than they, midgets of mountains that stood on the shoulders of granite monsters. Higher up their elders climbed to the heavens, coated in deep snow already. Perhaps they never melted.

Leaning to try to find the tops of the peaks earned him a painful bout in the chest. He fell back hard on the seat.

"Careful Rooster. You were a dead man when you fell onto my doorstep. Quite a nasty cut you had there. Almost didn't think you were worth the silk patching."

Rooster could only but grunt.

"Don't get sarky with me. That stuff costs more than the flesh of the living. But you're with the Duskhounds, so I'm contractually obligated."

"Sure."

"So how did you come into service of Darwish?" Souzon refilled his cup.

Now that he'd had a better look at him, the Rooster noticed much more of Souzon. Little peculiarities and details that had not been so apparent. A northerner. Scarred and roughly of his age.

"You first."

"Friends ask me such questions—you are a client."

With little choice, Rooster forked over the short and bloody version of his origin. Omitting the dishonorable particulars. And polished his dry throat with the chai. The surgeon took it all in, sans interruption.

"Interesting. If it is any comfort your horse will make it, so the stablemen say. Give it a day or two and he'll be fit to ride. North, if you were wise. As a thrall to hillmen, you won't likely last winter."

"Run where? North? They speak Patina in the North?"

Souzon shrugged, "No one speaks anything civilized outside the ports. Have you not learned yet? This land is not fit for men but gods. It chews you up and spits out only the bones."

"Should have been a poet, not a surgeon."

"Poets eat their own shit. Do I look like I have shit on the corners of my mouth? No, Rooster, I am a man of the knife and the science. My medicine is prized in these lands. There are none else. Not on this side of the mountains."

"From what Nereel told me, there's nothing beyond the mountains besides demons and spirits."

"He wasn't all incorrect. But he—like all his countrymen—are mostly ignorant. Beyond the Glittering Wall is a sea of dunes as large as any body of salt I know of. In it are peoples older than anywhere else on this green earth. Cities that dwarf what you and I know of as the peak of civilization."

How could any sane man believe that? The only professions it seemed anyone took up on this continent so far involved herding, throat-cutting, or a mix of the two. Thievery ran in the blood of this land as thick as religion.

"You don't believe me. This is fine. You would not make it to Nefara. You likely won't last the winter."

"Death doesn't like the taste of me, if you haven't noticed."

"Little escapes me Rooster. I've seen cadavers with less colorful scarring. The hillmen locals would call you sakshat—without death— and carve you up into trinkets of good fortune. Your fingers would fetch a pretty price."

"Lovely people, these."

For the third time, the same man-dress and white-bearded fellow rounded the corner below their stoop with his donkey. Leading the laden beast through the snows without break.

Souzon sniffed out of the corner of his eye.

Rooster asked, tracking the man's movement, "How many spies does this town have?"

"The better question is, how many here aren't spies."

Coldness hit Rooster's gut because the man in the donkey did not even make eye contact. To the untrained, they might mistake him for making multiple trips up the same road. Or lost. But to the learned, it was to confirm visual details.

"For whom?"

"Whoever is paying," the surgeon pointed at the horizon visible from the window, "On a clear day, Kahil sits above all of the Qaryat al Hadid. You can see the doors of the Iron City as well as the lakes governing the western Ghazwala Brushlands. There is no road beside the winding goat paths up to Duizmatha. That's the great mountains you see. Neither the gu-Khans of the Dawali nor even the Caliphate itself can hold Kahil. So we stand neutral and watch all that happens below. Until recently, that was very little."

"Such as?"

Draughts of cold hit the window hard, carrying with it the ambience of a disturbance. Horse and camel noise like the crowing of roosters—the sun had hours yet to rise. A lone rider had made its way into the darkened stables below.

"There is still time to slip north."

"Where do they fit into all of this?"

"How much did your friend Nereel tell you of Darwish?"

A shrug seemed fitting.

Souzon's expression exuded a deathly seriousness, "The Duskhounds are not like the other Dawali. Darwish was once a prized headsman for the Ivory Queen—back before the White Dove made peace. Her best killer. It has come at a terrible price; the Dawali people have placed the gravest of fatwas on his soul. Darwish can never return to the Ghazwala."

"History loathes a traitor."

"No Rooster. No such thing. Dawali served on both sides. The Ivory Queen sent warlocks with Darwish to find their sleeping enemy in the night. Terrible deeds were done, sometimes to women and children. I will not discuss the details further."

"Ah...so the Duskhounds..."

The surgeon stood, eyeing the advent snow falling, "It is not a name they gave themselves, no."

"Forgive me Souzon, but what the hell does their history matter?"

A few curse words in a language the Rooster did not catch, then left saying, "Didn't you smell it in the port when you arrived? War is over the horizon Rooster. An ugly one, not the kind over a river or a woman's honor. Come now. A stew is waiting for us now."

"Will it pay well?" Rooster loathed the thought of unfolding from the chair.

How his enemies would laugh at him now; a frail, emaciated creature, battling to hold up a teacup.

Winter blew the door open and admitted a devil.

Darwish arrived with a blizzard snarling at his back. He ignored Rooster and went right to stoop over Nereel's dying body. That big frosted beard and single eye glanced his way and returned. Uttering a few quiet questions in that rustic hillman tongue, to which the Souzon responded softly.

Rooster felt his knees quake by the strain but refused to sit.

So small and elderly a man, it was hard to imagine Darwish amount to the rumors of ruthlessness.

"I have another room for you to rest in," Souzon was starting to usher Rooster out of the room.

"No Guillaume. I want him to stay," that gruff voice like gravel.

The dog! Darwish spoke nearly fluent Patina! Making Nereel translate everything, feigning total ignorance for weeks? Goddamn, this bastard was playing him the fool!

Soon it was just the two of them and the little man's

struggling breaths.

Nothing came to mind as appropriate or creative so Rooster just stood there impassive.

Then the bearded man croaked, "Urustad was an oud among our people. A song of a man. He wrote all he saw. A historian among us gharib. There have been so few."

It felt like the unripe moment to mention said journal was somewhere lying in the mountains, left behind.

"He saw something in you gharib. Another student maybe," that lone eye appraised him again, sharp in scrutiny, "Urustad Nereel was like an uncle to me. Now I must respect his dying wishes. Do you wish to put a blade between my ribs?"

"A week ago maybe. Now I just want something to eat and my boots back."

Something between a grunt or a dull laugh rumbled in the bearded man's throat. Stoic and sorrowful, Darwish just continued to look at Nereel.

Hard not to get sucked into the scene.

Would he have done the same as the warlord—had a foreigner showed up on their greener shores, a half-dead mystery? Made a slave to carry a sword in some mad bastard's battles? Maybe. Rooster had done worse in his heyday. And was not proud of those either. He had more in common with the war criminal in front of him than not.

"Tell me; what will you do if I give you your freedom?"

"I imagine I'd go find a warmer place."

Darwish said, "In the south beyond the Wall, they have a saying that the sun never sets beyond Nefara."

"Sounds a place as good as any."

"You would perish trying to pass the Wall," the man stroked his beard, "Yet you are sakshat and would somehow find a way. Tell me... Rooster...you were not no one before you came here. And now you are. What will you become here?"

What was it with this guy? First he was all quiet and brooding. Now he was getting philosophical?

Rooster shrugged, "I don't know. I didn't plan on living

this long past the Jewelport."

The distant place Darwish went to as he stared vacantly at the wall was anyone's guess.

"For your freedom gharib, I would have you write of what I do in these lands. Is this a satisfying proposition? You can write, yes?"

Being a scribe was like being a shit-scraper and an udder-cleaner. But it beat being someone's house slave collecting firewood and sleeping with horses.

Guillame's voice rang distantly that the stew was growing cold. They two began to wander to find where the surgeon was calling from.

But Darwish grabbed Rooster's palm and stared at its lines at the threshold of the doorway. Screwing his dark beady eyes and peering up at the man.

"A fortune-teller as much as a warlord too, eh?"

And mysteriously as always, "Yes you will make a good historian to me, gharib. For now. For now."

Snow reminded him of home. Up north. Its slow white descent on cold draughts battering harmlessly against indifferent stone walls. How he would stare up in the courtyard of his father's father's fortress and wonder where it came from. Summoned from the ethereal to haunt the living world—a white blanket of death.

"Come now dreamer. You are dragging like a dying horse," Darwish chastened him from ahead.

The place they went to took a hike up a hill. Everywhere was somehow uphill in Kahil. Maybe that's how it got the damned name.

It was snowing as it had for days. There was no sign of the other Duskhounds. Perhaps they'd been trapped in the storm. There was no prying answers from their leader—he was a tough nut. Rooster had met rocks that were more talkative.

Old Darwish was hunting for something. There had been three other destinations—three other stoops where they dawdled and barely thawed their feet.

That big beard and eyepatch emerged from under the frosty maw of icicles, ducking and weaving back onto the street and marching without explanation.

Son of a bitch, the warlord's feet had to be frostbitten by now.

The Dawali certainly weren't built like normal men.

"Hey I can be wet or I can be cold. Can't be both."

From ahead, "What is this gharib?"

"Gharib-nonsense. Who do I have to kill to warm myself up by a fire here?"

Darwish did not find this so funny, "No one. I hold the sword, you hold the quill."

Better wait to tell the warlord he was barely literate in his native tongue. Didn't have much to bargain with at the moment as it was.

Warmth didn't need to be won with a sword—they two stepped into the belly of a wide tower-turned smoke den, complete with blackened walls and an even darker cauldron tending to the many patrons. If there was a coin earned for every brooding look, one would need a mule to carry all the silver. A quick glance around. There were thieves' dens back home that looked more inviting.

An unconcerned Darwish was shoving strangers aside, peering at their disgruntled faces. Not a single dagger was drawn. Instead, they parted for the man who stepped on their toes.

"Goddamn," Rooster was having a hell of a time trying to squeeze through the crowd.

The notoriety of the warlord didn't carry over to his cohorts apparently.

Darwish turned suddenly, shoving a coin in his hand, "Get us drink. He's not here yet."

"Who's not?"

A tyrannical, "Buy drink, gharib. Stop with fool questions."

Pushy pushy.

Back at the corner of the room when the innkeeper brought the clay cups out, Rooster stared. There was not a single drop of beer to be found anywhere. What the hell? Sure the tea was good, but it didn't fill the gut with fire.

He was about to interrogate the keeper of the inn when he heard,"Hey? You there! Yes you, northerner."

A young and unkempt man—the fairest shade he'd seen since the Jewelport—was holding up a bottle of wine and spoke in perfect Patina, "Looking for this beauty? Care to share the bottle?"

His name was Antonius. A Teridian—a south imperial taking refuge in Kahil on the way to the Glittering Wall. A vagabond-soul and a warrior by trade, an artist by instinct. Younger by him by a whole decade and free from any bitterness of regret. There was something virile about that. Antonius yearned for adventure and soft women.

The wine was rich and it was dark. The whole room began to glow and its shadows softened.

Another bottle was produced from the ether and was promptly uncorked as Antonius poured, "My friend, when you are free to wander I must insist you visit the Fountainhead of Araphos. You will be overcome with beauty. There are carvings that would make your mother weep. Even open her legs up!"

"Does yours know her son is a knucklehead?"

"Perhaps," Antonius hiccupped, "I did not leave my home in such high regard."

"Ah. Where do you journey to now?"

"Only the most ancient of cities. Where was stone laid upon stone before man had taken his first breath and fell to its first ruin while our ancestors were but savages digging up roots and hiding in caves. I speak of the jagged edge of civilization itself, Rooster. The realm of Nefara is where I travel to."

"What is this place? What makes it so special?"

"I'm surprised this is not where you are heading towards as well. It's the perfect place for a man to reinvent himself. To find a new calling."

A thief-infested backwater trading outpost? If you were barely old enough to call yourself a man and had no prospects, perhaps. Gray hairs and even a scrap of wisdom would tell otherwise.

But he could see the Teridian still looked at the world with fresh eyes untainted by pessimism. Almost enviable, the naiveté.

"My friend, listen to me. Past the Wall there are things that your northern mind cannot comprehend. The world beyond it is not merely ancient and vast—the gods still breathe there and their hands are seen. Beasts and monsters are as abundant as man. Devils that horde troves of gold that make you richer than any emperor. I can see in your eyes you do not believe me, but ask any that would answer you and the answers will be the same."

"We have plenty of asshole wizards back in the north. You don't need to convince me of anything."

Antonius pointed a finger right at his soul, "As do I, but they are like mere shadows to the magic that lies in that desert, my friend. Nefara and the realm it inhabits have never been conquered. It never will be. The Medeans claim it but they are afraid of their claim to the Ptahira River. Ah, there are stories...Rooster I have heard of a city even older than Nefara that lies at its footsteps, a place called Nemset. The Shah's grandfather sent an army of twenty thousand inside and they never returned! I must see this place and paint it on a woman's chest. Tell me that does not pique your curiosity?"

It did. As did all treasure tales. Always grand and mythological. Never real. Or greatly exaggerated when inspected up close.

Stories were like dreams and dreams were like fire. To believe in them was to breathe wind into the storied coals and build their existence up from nothing. Without the breath of belief, they vanished like all embers.

"I didn't come to the desert for buried gold and supposed gods Antonius."

"No, but you said you were exiled."

"I never said that."

The Teridian shrugged, "You didn't need to. Why else

would a man flee so far from home? And an old one at that. You could be my father."

"Watch it. This old dog can move fast."

It was just then that across the room, in the fuzziness of the wine's attack on his focus, he caught sight of a figure in the midst of the room. A desert rider swathed entirely in orange wrappings to his neck, an ornate saddle over his shoulder. He was a gharib with unkempt hair and strange markings tattoed on his face, an eagle perched atop his arm. As if the stare burned a mark on his shoulder, the man turned to face him. Eagle cry. A dizzying force took his knees.

There was something so familiar about this stranger.

Rooster fell back in his chair trying to see where he went.

"I told you the wine was strong granddad," Antonius laughed.

"Shemsari," he breathed.

"What about them?"

The sun-robed rider was gone, as was his eagle. The very same eagle that had pursued them across Akala-Juradh.

"Shaitan," he whispered to himself.

Logic be damned; Nereel was right. There was something in this land that was strange. Something that lay underneath the surface of the air, that seemed almost spiritual.

"As much as I'd like to chat more I need to sleep. The ice-traders will be leaving early. Safe winds. Perhaps we will meet again granddad," Antonius stood up and bowed.

"Thanks for the wine. Be sure it's not at the other end of my sword," Rooster pretended to nap.

A subconscious creak of the eye; the rider and his eagle were indeed gone. A hallucination seemed fitting but they seemed so real. So tangible.

The smell of chai floated by—ah well. Darwish would sure be pleased by his tardiness. His own tray of cinnamon tea had grown cold. Rooster dumped it and plucked a pair of cups from a passed-out merchant.

The short walk to the cauldron was enlightening. This den was full of varied faces. So many were here to mingle, yet so few left their alcoves and their own cushions. And all serving their own masters, their own interests.

Darwish barely paid him any attention besides grabbing the cups and talking in that brutish tongue with another hillman.

They chatted in simple, curt phrases, taking chai pauses before continuing for another hour. When it was finished the other hillman simply took off into the crowd without formality.

"You make a poor servant gharib. I have cold tea."

"Could have been colder. Who was that man?"

"Our contact. You should have been here to write."

"I don't speak the tongue, how could I have?"

A dark glare, "A mouse finds no food in his warren."

Typical verbal hogwash. Could these people speak in anything other than idioms?

The hour was late and the den was clearing out. White smoke puttered from new logs added to the ashes.

Rooster's stomach reminded him of his neglecting it, and so he made to fill his bowl from the communal cauldron. Maybe there was enough left to scrape from the bottom. A strong grip on his wrist held him back.

"Do not taste it," warned Darwish, "It has been tainted."

"By who?"

A nod to an alcove where a handful of strangers remained, seemingly occupied by a game of chance.

"Tell me if they follow gharib," the little warlord said as he slipped through the door ahead of him.

Out in the dark cold. An orange bar stretched into the white blanket of the street. Rooster trudged out into the cost, shivered, and hesitated after a handful of steps. There was but a moment where the orange-red light was blocked by darkness—by silhouettes. It could have been his imagination.

It wasn't.

"Darwish!"

Shadows leapt from snowy corners. The little man was quicker than he looked—a form was already flailing with blood flashing the pale curtain of snow. Darwish sidestepped, hefting his own dueling dagger and scimitar.

A second assassin came for him, wrapped head to toe in anonymity. Lifting something atop his palm and bringing it to his mouth; some kind of vial? Strange smoke puffed out and would have struck the Rooster's face—a cold draught blew the smoke sideways into the face of another man. Screams from behind a cloth mask and the eerie sound of sizzling flesh. The smell lingered and turned the stomach.

The fool assassin tried another pouch but Rooster already lowered his shoulder and drove a stern tackle, pinning the man with sheer force to the ground. There was the briefest of struggles while the warlord dispatched the remaining assassin to a gurgling end.

Bloody footprints ruined the sheet of snow.

Darwish calmly asked the subdued man who he worked for. The assassin reeked of a strange chemical odor and said nothing.

"We take him to Souzon for questioning. Bind his hands."

Rooster would have too. But in the time it took him to find a rope, the assassin had bit down on a tooth that ruptured into another kind of poison. Like his other partner, the man screamed in relief and agony as his mouth and insides were burned away.

Goddamn.

The only thing found on their bodies was a scrap parchment with a crude charcoal depiction of not Darwish, but the hillman spy. So they hadn't been the target but the opportunity.

Little comfort that was.

They left Kahil that night.

الحديد أرض

Qaryat al Hadid

The Rooster may have been illiterate to the tongues of nomads and savages but he knew enough about the motivations of men and the fires that burned in their hearts—Darwish was riding faster and harder than he'd ever seen him. They drove their horses to near death and only just at the brink of freezing to death. Nor did they wait for any Duskhounds to rendezvous either.

Whatever it was the hillman had told him, the assassins had only expedited it.

Darwish drove them like a phantom rode on their very tail.

"You must have been a great nuisance to your enemies in the north," Souzon was saying as they rested, grinding away with his mortar and pestle, "I can see it in your eyes; always plotting, always two moves ahead."

"Not plotting and not great enough. Or else I wouldn't be here."

The surgeon insisted the Rooster required additional medicine but even the warlord must have seen through the lie.

The sky remained constant gray and blue. Winter was fully settling in the high reaches of the rock country. Permafrost was starting to settle into the gravel—it smelled like iron, rock, and frozen dirt. Kahil was a distant memory in the frostbitten clouds now.

A fire was slowly taking shape and they two huddled around it. Hissing as the surgeon introduced a ceramic bowl of ice with the compound he had created. A tea perhaps but it wasn't chai.

"Was there anything else of the attackers you noticed? Even little details? Anything at all?"

Unfortunately not. It wasn't for lack of the memory's

clarity. It was just too dark and the assassins too innocuous.

"No."

Souzon looked at Darwish, who was tending to his horse, "That drawing had to be a red herring. He was the one they were after. No one would put professionals up to cut up a mere hillman spy. The toxin you described to me is worth more than our horses alone."

"Who would want to kill Darwish?"

But even as the words flew from his lips, the Rooster remembered.

"I see that look in your eyes again."

"Hassan. His lieutenant. I saw him riding off and meeting with a Medean lord in secret a week ago."

The ceramic dish bubbled and was removed from the fire, exuding a pungent scent, "Darwish and him are like brothers. Hassan would never do such a thing. Not even if he wanted to kill him. Poison isn't in his capacity."

Gut instinct cut through the emotional cloud produced by the surgeon. There was something there. But Rooster knew he couldn't press the matter.

Bury the detail but leave the mental shovel at the ready.

Darwish returned from the horses and was greeted with that steaming brew from Souzon before he could sit, "I will not drink it now."

"Horse shit. You'll drink it now. Your spirits will need it."

With great reluctance, the bearded man downed the stuff and doubled over.

Rooster asked, "What is it?"

"Medicine. Speaking of which, you're going to need fresh bandages."

The little warlord looked worse for wear. On the edge of vomiting, it looked like.

"I thought you said Nereel's disease couldn't be cured."

Souzon was pulling out a freshly boiled silk wrap from a pot, "It can't. Darwish suffers from being too popular in this area. It's a pre-emptive measure."

"Which is?"

"The good news is you'll heal completely. It's already scarring nicely," Souzon set the bowl down, "We can't take any chances with poisoners about. This will fortify him for the days to come."

A jarring yelp interrupted them.

Across the fire Darwish went entirely rigid, his spine arched like a crescent moon as he stood on the tips of his toes, chin jutting towards the sky. Electrified or possessed. The little warlord hovered there and fell back into a squat.

Was the cure worse than the disease, Rooster wondered.

Just before they descended from the domain of raptors and eagles, there was a brief window of sunlight. Beams of warmth pierced the cloudy veil and illuminated the trespasses of the deep mountains.

And that's when he saw it.

Like an illusion at first, stretching as far as the eye could see. Grey clouds parted—a trick of the light like white fire that sparkled in heart-stopping brilliance. And that's when the Rooster realized the shadow that stood over the peaks of the mountain reach was not a stormcloud; it was a wall. A wall that looked to be made out of a continent-sized opal, rounded at its top that had to stretch up thousands of feet into the very heavens and endless miles across. Kaleidoscopic fire swirled inside its opaque surface—it looked as if it moved.

No matter how he blinked, it did not vanish from his sight.

"Doesn't it take the breath away?"

Rooster felt small—not insignificant but entranced. Like seeing the fullness of the stars and the celestials above and being filled with a raw wonder.

"What made that?"

"Gods? Whoever came before them?" Souzon shrugged.

Darwish turned back to face them, "Bahram knows."

Bahram, the supposed creator who dwelt in the sun.

Bahram who knew the souls of men. Bahram the eternal light that beat back the eternal darkness. The god of the late Nereel, rest the little man's soul.

"And what lies beyond it?"

He asked a question he already knew the answer to, the dumb question just sort of tumbled out of his mouth. A great desert realm unspoiled by time. Nefara and Nemset and a place that no gharib—at least a pale one such as him, had ever laid eyes on. A fairytale—no different than the myths of forgotten palaces that lay hidden in shadowy woods—told by his contemporaries in the north to explain alchemy or scare children.

Rooster was too old to start believing in a different world than the one he'd lived in. One where he'd fallen in love and had children, went to bloody war and had everything he cared about burn. There was a strange comfort in that. He'd never had a superstitious hair and didn't feel like growing one soon. Maybe it was the cynicism, but even if there were strange things there beyond the wall...well it would all have an explanation.

"Beyond it is a place even a sakshat would find their match," Darwish said, then threw his head back and let loose a full-bellied laugh.

Gods were fool's playthings but Rooster could not tear his eyes away from the Glittering Wall, not even until the steep switchbacks into the granite cliffs blocked them utterly from sight.

Still no sign of the Duskhounds.

Maybe they'd moved on to greener pastures.

Dark greys and blues became a land of copper, taupe, and umber. The narrow and treacherous road spat them onto what looked like a dried riverbed in a steep canyon. It was well-traveled. They found their first caravan—the first people they'd seen since Kahil, bringing a team of oxen loaded down with timber. Darwish exchanged a purse with the caravan-master and soon they were riding alongside as hired swords.

"Ayubin Ishkibil is wary of hillmen," Souzon said, "Madinat al Hadid is a prize to many; foreign tribes, Dawali, and now the Medeans live in disharmony. He who controls the Iron Fort controls the bridge to the Wall. The only other way to get through the Glittering Wall is to go around it—those are treacherous seas."

"Quiet. We look like spies," Darwish hushed them, "Play your role and you won't be hung."

The road became a ramp and the ramp wound like an elevated stair with a sheer cliff plummeting to a valley. And in that valley were high mountain pastures bordering a once-sparkling reservoir, now frozen over with a layer of ice. Great trails of fog rose from the thousands of cattle that were wintered there. Overlooking it all in perhaps the most dramatic of baileys to a motte, was what the miracle of steel must have looked like to the smith who accidentally invented it—the most fortified city Rooster had ever seen, hewn right out of the canyon walls. Madinat al Hadid stood proudly on its sheer pedestal, overlooking both the farms and a crevasse that led right up to the toothy mountain walls.

"Damn," he said.

No way this place had ever changed hands. Even with the gates open, all a lord would have to do is stack bodies shoulder to shoulder. The only siege that would succeed would be by the gods-damned sky.

Patrols went both ways on the ramp, numbering in the dozens. But in the span it took them to run into the first group, Darwish had already doffed a completely new personality. A sash across both eyes instead of two and a walking cane; a classic.

"You must be a popular commodity here."

Souzon grimaced, "In the dungeons."

"How did you escape?"

The little warlord gave him the silent treatment, dismounting and walking ahead.

"Eighteen months. Most men didn't last more than three in there. He described it to me only once as a 'blackness that wouldn't wash off'," Souzon explained, "It was shortly after that we met, Darwish and I."

"Ah."

"Ivory Queen left him and the rest of her Dawali headsman to rot. Their reward for having done her dirtiest, blackest sins."

Loyalty was expensive, betrayal was cheap.

Rooster knew a thing or two about that. Even the thought was a bleak reminder for him to bury ugly memories—what good they would do for him now.

They waltzed right up to its bloody rust-iron granite walls.

Guards didn't so much as blink at the sight of Darwish, they even threw a coin at him in mock pity. Blind geezer he played well, scooped the coin with trembling hands and thanked them. The bastard even kissed the air. He was overdoing it.

"Should have been an actor," Rooster complimented when they were safe inside.

"If I cut your tongue out, you can still be my historian," the little man replied.

Touché.

The Iron City was not at all like the Jewelport. Nothing like the other towns since he stepped foot on this continent—this was storied, cryptic, and bafflingly foreign. From the very moment he stepped into its stony folds and gazed upon a four-story tall tablet carved as a relief into a crimson granite block. Holding the tablet up were statues of brutish, alien-looking warriors carved with a master hand, each uplifting swords like crescents.

Even the text looked like the script of otherworldly beings with its harsh blade-like slashes that moved vertically. What kind of people would create such a stirring, violent kind of alphabet?

"Exegesis of Zrerneq Zo. One of the first Medean Viziers. There are similar carvings in all the High Medean cities," it was just him and Souzon now. Darwish was off finding the other Duskhounds who should have arrived days ago. The surgeon wouldn't shut up about finding an apothecary, "You haven't been to one yet, have you?"

"No, this is my first."

Rooster touched the stone and his fingers felt the grain. Almost metallic. It bothered him and he didn't know why—the tablet itself. He was struck by wonder but knew nothing about its meaning. It must have been too apparent in his face.

"They didn't tell you in the Jewelport did they?"

"What?"

"That you wouldn't get far, not knowing the language."

"No," and that was only half the truth.

Goddamn it Nereel, is more like what he wanted to say. Dying far too early a death.

One thing that wasn't foreign was the signs of mustering. The tang of fresh steel and oil smelled strong. There wasn't a smith in the city that wasn't banging on his anvil or the steam from his cooling barrels. Rooster hadn't seen this many swords since his first foray into war. And not the one bouncing off the hips of mailed guards either. Rough-looking sellswords and swords for hire that were clustering near smoke dens and gambling halls, lounging near caravan inns and just strolling the street in gangs. They didn't look Medean and they didn't look bored either.

"Tell me something Guillame."

"Eh," the man was eyeing some kind of street food.

"What kind of work would a mercenary be taking here in the Iron City?"

"Nothing north this time of year. They winter somewhere south until the sands begin to scorch."

Yet there were hundreds here. The math simply didn't add up. Not when one accounted for the amount of weapons and mail that they were having sharpened and mended. That was damn expensive upkeep for not having silver flowing in. He knew the numbers. Back home, for a score of men at arms to be kitted out would take raising the rents and gouging peasants for a whole year.

"Then there's a border war somewhere."

"Not that I know of," Souzon replied absently.

"Darwish mentioned bandit princes that were sacking caravans to the south."

"If they're cutting up merchants, I haven't heard of it. Not since last summer."

As the search for the herbal shop continued, the Iron City showed more of her belly; gangs of lepers being herded in chains to wagons, cattle slaughtered and butchered before children, incense-burning priests who brayed about end times, and all the signs of urban chaos.

But one constant was the number of hungry-eyed swordsmen that seemed to be around every corner. There had to be two to three for every garrisoned guard.

"More wolves in the pen than sheepdogs," he commented dryly as they stopped near one such den, hitching their horses.

Rooster even noticed some gharibs among the swords-for-hire. They were watching guards shuffle up and down the streets, then suddenly turned to look back at him as if they had supernatural spooks. The group stood and got lost down an alley quickly.

That couldn't be right.

"Come now, I can smell clove and frankincense. We're close," Souzon paid the tacking boy and began walking down the same alley, totally oblivious.

The last place Rooster wanted to go right now.

Especially without so much to defend himself as a fucking butter knife.

Where was Darwish by now? Why had they come here to this city? There was too much ambiguity here, too many questions on the intentions of his captor.

No choice but to follow. With intestinal linearity, the poorly lit alley brought them down a twisty and steep staircase that fed them into a fairly busy square.

Souzon went off babbling about not being able to source the right ingredients and a shortage from the southern herbalists or some other junk. He disappeared under the curtain of a shop that firmly shut its door.

Now what? Rooster was alone for the first time since being captured.

Time seemed to still.

In the cold blue of the winter's afternoon, he was lost in the sea of stone and bodies. He felt like a lone sapling in a field in a blizzard. All of these words and without a hope of understanding them.

An impulsive thought hit him; he didn't belong here.

Freedom was right here, singing to him. Screaming his name to turn north and follow the Souzon's warning. No one would be the wiser if he went back, grabbed his horse from the boarding house, and left this town before the sun went down. Darwish would be unlikely to pursue.

But where would he go? And what would he do? Go anywhere but here, the shadowy voice of his other self said. Escape this godforsaken place now that you've survived. Go to the Fountainhead of Araphos that boy Antonius told you of, or where you can speak the language. Find a new woman and a new life.

What was stopping him from cutting loose?

Rooster watched the open plaza and let the possibility wash over him.

He'd die here.

It was sound logic.

He surveyed the cold, hostile plaza.

A familiar shape swooped above it and perched atop the cornice of a tower. The eagle of the warlock. The shaitan. Pointing its beak and locking its dark gaze on him.

"You again. What do you want?"

It ruffled its feathers and flapped its wings nondescriptly.

"What if I shot you out of the sky eh?"

The shaitan looked away, down to the square.

Rooster followed its gaze and realized he saw something else familiar; a banner fluttered in the wind bearing a red diamond atop a yellow field, pierced by a black halberd.

"Ayubin Suhrab, you're far from home," he noticed that the mailed horsemen were speaking with the local guard.

Looked like a pleasant conversation.

Without any other metric to judge from, this detachment from a distant territory had to have ridden as hard as the Duskhounds and braved early snows to be here. Must have been a damned important conversation too. And yet they seemed to have no urgency to go anywhere, from a bystander's perspective.

Too many coincidences here in the Iron City.

Rooster was beginning to feel like he was at the wrong place, wrong time.

Bells rung crisp notes followed by the call to prayer signaled the end of the day. The haunting melody of the holy incantation brayed off the cold walls. The sun was nearly gone and the light had been a flat blue for some time already. The riders of Ayubin Suhrab were disappearing into a den.

But the eagle remained to fix him with its penetrating glare.

"There you are, bastard. Need you to help me carry these," Souzon had emerged with hefty sacks, "You going dumb? Hey, wood for ears. Come over and make yourself useful."

Being a stranger stuck in a strange land was unavoidable now. Being ignorant to who lived in it was not. While Rooster helped Souzon break down components to brew in the alembic later, he juiced the surgeon for a cultural lesson.

The Medean Caliphate was more empire than kingdom and its throne was carried on the backs of a hundred thousand. They had a taste for order and civilization and had largely got it figured out. Pretty good, considering they'd been barbarians less than half a millennia ago. Like all functional empires, the castes were rather straightforward if not painfully terse.

At the top were the Mutarib—the elite blood with pearl

necklaces and soft beds. There was not an emir or shah or caliph who hadn't originated from their incestual line. The amount of sibling-fucking would put a backwater polygamist to shame. They were the 'respectables' which comprised of clerics, scholars, merchants, and every bureaucrat imaginable.

Then came the Ashab; proud as crows, loud as thunder, perched just low enough to feel insulted. the city-born folk. Smiths, fishmongers, scribes, and everything that required labor. They paid taxes, raised sons, buried them. They carred the empire on their backs and got spit on for walking too slow. Sometimes on the rare occasion an Ashab would climb the ladder to the Mutarib.

Beneath that the Dhimmi—foreign slaves, jannisaries, beggars and the tolerated unclean. Human rats in the eyes of every shah. Every few decades, someone remembered they exist when a disaster would sweep the empire and consume half of them. The other half would be used as the mortar and bones to rebuild. To be born Dhimmi necessitated a transgression from an ancestor. It was also a sentence to live out in mortal hell.

One of the more interesting aspects was their religion. Rather the lack thereof.

The Medeans called it Ilm al-Sirr, the Governance of the Progenies. It was a faith without a god to answer prayers. No saints wept blood. No angels fell. Just dust, smoke, and the long ache of knowing too much. They didn't worship—they studied. The universe was a puzzle box sealed for a prophet with the right key.

Ludicrous as it was, Rooster understood it in his way.

They believed the soul was a spark—something accidental, barely real, but capable of refinement. Like ore into steel. Like lead into gold. Life was the crucible, and pain was the fire. Die too soon and you came back cruder. Die ready, and maybe—just maybe—you'd ascend. Not to heaven, but to *understanding*. A promise rousing enough that even Dhimmi crawled out to the towers at dawn and dusk to join in the wailing to the heavens.

The next morning, Rooster did, observing the horde of the delusional. Wafting in the cool air was the steam of some kind of smoked something; burnt earth dressed in perfume. Bitter smoke, cardamom, a hint of something ancient and patient.

He went back to Souzon's quarters and found himself amused; that Medeans didn't fit a god into their picture of heaven.

If gods were real, they wouldn't care who prayed or who ruled—too vast, too old, too far gone to bother. The castes would be ants to them, the scholars dust. But if one did notice them, it'd probably be out of boredom. And it'd be petty—petty enough to knock over the whole anthill just to hear them scream.

The little warlord didn't approve of the preliminary scribblings. Looking over his shoulder every so often with a disappointed look.

"This must be legible. I wish Souzon to have this transcribed."

"Has anyone ever told you that you whine like an old woman?"

Darwish flinched. Quill and ink weren't cheap in the Iron City. But it wasn't Rooster's investment either.

Rooster took a break and sipped the chai. The stuff here was different, with a robust flavor that made Nereel's remind him of flavored mud.

Under the shadows of the bell tower and away from prying eyes, they waited with their tea.

"Who are we meeting anyway? I should know that at least, if you're having me write it all down."

Darwish leveled him with his one good eye. Funny how the man could do that. There was so much force, so much will in that little ochre orb.

"I wonder why you care so much?"

"Some might wonder back why you're so secretive about all of this."

"Kaleech! Write and stop pestering old Darwish!"

He was breaking through. This was the equivalent of the old man getting the shakes. He was nervous alright—the kneejerk annoyance was exactly that.

Rooster couldn't contain his smile, "I'm a bastard alright."

"How did you know this word?"

"Nereel."

Darwish began to curse the dead man, wishing a thousand ailments on his soul and that it would be sucked into hell before it got to heaven. So much for avoiding speaking ill of the dead.

They were almost at the stage of kicking rocks when their contact arrived. A hillman who emerged from the cold gray stone like he was born from it. Scary how the little hairy men in their pajama pants and big beards could dance like cats from shadow to shadow—even in broad daylight they were almost invisible.

Rooster couldn't imagine what kind of havoc they could wreak at night.

A finger jabbed in his direction—the hillman contact wasn't happy about his presence. An argument from Darwish probably explaining why there was a third. They began to banter back and forth, baring verbal teeth.

Like monkeys in turbans.

Rooster was getting bored and looking for meaning in the clouds when there was a, "Gharib! Are you listening? Write this all down."

"Repeat please."

"I should strike your ear gharib. Masood has said that he has ridden eleven days hard in the saddle to deliver this message in the land of flat spirits."

"Masood needs a bath. What else?"

Darwish conferred for another few minutes, "He thanked Ghazparaba for the healthy birth of a child to his third wife, Surzai. He has praised the blue fire of the bush that is Ghazparaba and that he will slaughter a goat in the presence of the next bush fire to honor our lord."

Unbelievable. That little exchange had been more than

ten minutes. What an utter waste of breath and paper.

"Did you write this all down?"

"Down to the color of the goat, Darwish. Will I be describing how it will bleat in a holy way as he cuts its throat?"

Sarcasm and brevity were lost on these people.

Darwish sat back on his haunches, frowning, then translated all, "Masood has said this; as he was instructed to watch all comings and goings, on the eve of the Shura al Nefara he witnessed twenty-three riders departing from the Vizier's Court of the White Kasbah. It was a night without a moon, which is an ill portent. They bore no marks or banners and were clothed as mudaawi-mujzum—the traveling healers. The riders rode no merchant horses but the prized stallions of the Qumari."

"What does it mean?"

Darwish sniffed at the interruption, "No Ayubin, Emir, or Vizier may obtain a Qumari stallion without it being gifted to him by the Shah himself. They are the finest horses in these lands. No one would ride them unless they were in the service of the White Dove."

"What's Shura al Nefara?"

"The old city is now under the rule of Medea. By the auspice of the White Dove."

"I thought it was ruled by warlords?"

"Stop asking me questions gharib and write as I say."

Masood rapidly fired off in their hilltongue and Darwish listened.

"Pay attention; Masood followed the mudaawi-mujzum. Up the Thieves Road. He almost was caught at Senusret's Wards. The riders were ambushed by the palwogntira. The assassins. Only nine survived the encounter and the rest were taken. Masood found them again on the Plain of Salt, where they lost three more. They made it to the mountains where their tracks disappeared."

The conversation wasn't over yet and it gave Rooster time to let his aching wrist rest.

The little warlord frowned, "You will also write this

down; Masood would guess that the riders will make it to the Madinat al Hadid by the third day since his arrival. He is most proficient a rider in the mountains and possesses knowledge of secret passes. He wore his horse down to relay this information to me, Darwish, as his duty to the Shah."

"And what are the riders doing? Why are we spying on them?"

This whole business had more holes in it than the sandals he came here with.

Darwish paused and scried him—like the devil could read his thoughts.

Rooster gave him the same treatment, "What game are you playing at old man?"

Winds howled at Hanjara Gap; the crevasse between the Iron City and the mountain passage to the Glittering Wall. Those who braved the simple bridge that spanned the treacherous crevasse were assaulted by gales that seemed to strike from every side.

Midday sun lit everything orange and umber.

Midday ruffled Rooster's imaginary feathers.

Midday was when lazy men acted and when mistakes were made. Dawn and dusk were for the bold and the ambitious. Nothing ever good happened at midday.

He begrudgingly spurred the horse forward behind Darwish, beside Souzon. He tried complaining about it to the latter but the gharib surgeon was too obsessed with the geology—his nose firmly wedged into the rocks.

Bad time to be distracted.

The directive had been intentionally obtuse; sneak out of the Iron City and meet with friendly Medeans. Duskhounds were scattered amongst the canyon recesses with their horses hidden, told to stay low and wait for a signal. The remaining leadership posing as a group of travelers fixing a broken wagon. Not that there were passersby to deceive anyway.

Goosebumps ran down Rooster's arms and back the

entire ride there.

Just a hunch but something wasn't right.

One could taste the funk in the air.

Horse-noise ahead; Hassan crossed over from his cohort of Medeans. The man stared daggers over at Rooster under that heavy brow and beak of a nose.

"Ah, so here is our old prisoner, a shabbah in the flesh! Surviving snows that slayed three of our riders and their horses. I did not believe the rumor that the gharib lived," Hassan smiled a smile that did not reach the eyes.

No longer a warlord but a caravan master distraught over the broken yoke of his wagon, Darwish kept his voice level and quiet. Speaking in Patina for Rooster's clear benefit, "Are we all set lieutenant? Our Medean friends?"

A gloved hand dismissed, "Yes of course."

"Any word from the scouts?"

A nod to the canyon, "They spotted the riders less than an hour into the canyon. They are close."

"They should ride quicker—we'll get paid faster!"

That got a laugh from the other disguised Duskhounds, aimlessly strolling about the wagon.

Darwish nodded, "Your friends. Who do they ride for?"

"Ayubin el-Ifazal."

Rooster couldn't control his frown and blurted, "You mean Ayubin Suhrab?"

That got Hassan to jerk in the saddle. Genuine shock crossed like a shadow over his face. Inhaled softly.

"Why would you say that, gharib?"

"I saw them garrisoned in the Iron City."

Now they changed languages, speaking among each other. Thinking he didn't understand them. But there were some words he recognized from Nereel's teachings, such as 'spy'.

"You are mistaken gharib, but this is to be expected. You are a stranger to these lands," Hassan assured him, switching back in the Patina.

But it was a lie.

A dirty, wretched lie.

"Once the messengers are within arrow range, we'll take them and question them," Hassan quickly shifted the conversation, addressing Darwish.

"Good."

The lieutenant looked over at Rooster one more time and departed for his comrades. Whom immediately conferred, and looked over in his direction.

There was that bad feeling again.

"Darwish, I need to speak with you."

"Silence gharib. I'm not in the mood to talk. After."

"It's about Lieutenant Hassan."

The one-eyed hillman grew cold, "You made yourself a fool, by speaking things you don't know. It reflects on me poorly. You and Guillame will stay back and observe. This has to be done with surgical precision, gharib. I can't have you mucking it up."

Souzon was pulled into the present, sniffed at the order, and maybe thought better than to argue.

It wasn't good enough for the Rooster. He couldn't prove it but instinct was the best thing next to a pair of sharp eyes—his had never done him dirty.

Darwish drew his curved sword, hiding it under the cloth blanket. A precaution that seemed too symbolic.

"Clear out, both of you. I won't ask again."

Time wasn't an ally here.

Rooster knew he had to do something quick. An old trick came to mind. Reaching in his pack he found rope. It would have to do. And carefully flung it in front of Souzon's horse when no one was watching.

"Shit, shit, shit," the surgeon cried as his horse reared and bucked, then bolted forward.

Everyone froze.

The grey mare bucked, threw her head, and fled right towards the Medeans and Hassan—perfect. Exactly what he wanted.

"That's right Souzon, go ahead and pull up prematurely," Rooster kicked the stirrups and started his own horse over to the panicking one across the canyon.

Stupid show as it was, everyone bought it. Even Hassan and the others blocked the panicking horse as he arrived. Souzon was able to calm the beast down after a minute or two.

"This is why I hate beasts," the surgeon declared, "Dumb things."

The breeze shifted.

And there Rooster was, almost within touching distance of the Medean riders when he smelled it; metallic and acrid. Faint as it was, the potent stench of a chemical he couldn't put a name to.

Wait that was it; the assassins in Kahil.

It was the same smell.

Rooster's gut flipped end over end.

One of the riders cocked his head and stared at him from beneath the mailed khud. Ever so subtle and ever so flippant. They had to know that he knew.

If he said anything now, his throat would be cut.

"Gharib, take the Souzon back to a safe place," Hassan commanded.

Rooster did intend to do that. Except that he was taken out of the moment when he saw his old sword—the great two-handed thing— strapped to the lieutenant's saddle. All that remained of his family's legacy was now some trophy for this silver-tongued backstabbing big-nosed bastard.

Didn't sit right with him. Not a bit.

A suicidal charge was all it would take to restore that legacy. Maybe he would make it to the crevasse before they cut him down, sword still in hand.

The daydream ended when he noticed Hassan was looking at him, "But first, I meant to ask gharib. What did you call her? Your family's sword?"

Fucker wanted the satisfaction—pour salt in the wound.

Wit would have to do until Rooster was able to find a better weapon.

"She's someone's family sword, not mine. Found it in a shop in the Jewelport. All yours lieutenant."

A smile turned into a scowl, "Go."

As they were riding away, Rooster muttered, "Yeah, chew on that you big-nosed cocksucker."

Eagle scream. That big gold-brown bird wheeled above them. The shaitan wasn't going to miss out on the action.

Souzon got close when they fell back to a trot, "You little shitstain. You did that on purpose, didn't you?"

"Riddle me this Guillame. Why would those Medeans have the same chemicals as the assassins that came for Darwish in Kahil?"

A pause, "You're sure?"

"Dead sure."

Souzon looked worried, "I hope you're wrong Rooster. Who has Hassan got involved with?"

"I'm the last guy on this continent to ask that."

They were in the middle of the canyon and still a few hundred paces away from the group hiding behind the cliffs when echoes of beating hooves rang from ahead. Followed by riders moving at breakneck speeds. Riders in pearl-white.

"The mudaawi-mujzum," Souzon spoke blackly, "Only devilspawn would pretend to be healers."

The riders aimed right at them, and to the bridge at their back. Ignoring the broken down wagon and Darwish who tried to wave them down.

Another possibility struck Rooster all too late.

That eagle cried from above.

"Damn it Souzon. It's a trap. Go get Darwish!"

Hooves beat a frantic tattoo on the stone. Hassan and the Medeans began to ride out to catch the riders in white. Three to one. Those clothed in the pearl-colored robes craned their necks and must have shat themselves. They spurred their mounts and drove harder and faster.

Rooster spurred his horse and drove the beast into a sprinting gallop right at the wagon.

"Gharib! Stay back I said!"

"I swear on the blood of my children—"

Murder had already begun.

Screams of horses hitting horses. Wood and steel hitting flesh. Dust kicked up a whirlwind from the canyon's artery, obscuring the clash from view. A white form toppled from a horse into a lethal crumple on the hard ground.

Death was in the air.

A single rider broke from the confusion; white cloak and hood stained with blood and sand. He rode right for Darwish and Rooster. An elderly face framed by a salt-and-pepper beard was trying to form a sentence. Mouth opening. Then toppled abruptly, an arrow protruding from his spine.

The surgeon was off his horse and got to the fallen man, pulling the arrow free. A broadhead glistened with blood. And something else.

"Poison," Souzon stated, holding it up aloft.

The smell was undeniable.

Darwish asked the man a series of questions rapid-fire. Some were answered. Over a few seconds, they became less coherent and consistent. Then slumped.

Souzon confirmed, "He's dead."

Rooster was watching ahead.

Hassan and his assassin friends were cutting down every last rider in white. Duskhounds were running down from the hills, some on horse and most on foot. The confusion was rampant. A disguised assassin wheeled on his mount and struck down a Duskhound hillman, driving a spear into his shoulder and gutting him like a boar. Slings and arrows began to fly from both sides.

Butchery began in the heat of confusion.

Horns blew from the Iron City of sentries sounding the alarm.

The Medean lieutenant and his squad were forming in a line to ride down the Duskhounds. No quarter was to be given, it became evident. The hillmen began to panic.

"Darwish," Rooster urged, "Bring your men back."

But the warlord was speechless.

"Move you bastard!"

Hassan called out an order and his men charged—

raising their blades against their own. Blood sprayed into the sand. Duskhounds who hadn't the sense or reaction to move were cut down by those who they thought as brothers. The rest scattered and leapt on their horses, pursued by Medean-guised assassins.

No time for permission—Rooster ripped the spear from the warlord's loose grip and drove his horse towards the group. Right towards their leader—towards Hassan.

Big-nose idiot tried to steer away but that spear impaled the neck of his horse. Both went down in a gory heap. Rooster jumped towards the saddle but got kicked by a hoof instead.

Goddamn that hurt.

Wind knocked out of him, Rooster scrambled on his knees and Hassan was doing the same. Only the other man was able to draw the two-handed sword from the sheath on the saddle. And smiled, noticing that Rooster was without a weapon.

"I should have fed you to the sands," the traitor said and swung.

Hassan should have stuck with the weapon he was accustomed to. The man stepped in too shallow and made too wide an arc. The northern-style two-handed sword could lop the legs off a horse in the hands of a master. It was not balanced like one of the rider's curved swords.

Hassan missed wildly.

And angrily attempted again, but this time overhead. Rooster sidestepped and winced as the edge blunted on the rock floor. The lieutenant made a wild bet with a decapitating arc. This time Rooster threw himself at the man's legs, feeling the air shave his neck.

He toppled the mailed man and tasted blood as Hassan's gauntlet struck his jaw. Hassan was on his back, trying to reach for his belt-dagger while strangling him with his other hand. Animal instinct had Rooster reaching for something—his fingers found a rock. A weapon was a weapon. He crushed the man's temple with it, stunning Hassan.

Rooster grabbed his sword and stood, aware vaguely of the fight going around him now.

It was ugly.

Duskhound slayed Duskhound. Hillmen of Darwish were gored by Hassan's Medeans. The conflict was entering bloody throes, its participants unhorsed or in the process. Uncivilized barbarism was unleashed upon one another as hillmen were tied by nooses to their own horses ' tails, strangled as their horses were sent into frightened charges. Others were pushed off by the dozen into the crevasse by Medean horsemen, the sickening sounds of their bodies bouncing off the rocks below.

And then there was Darwish screaming a bloody rage with a sword and buckler, riding into the thick of it with suicidal impart. The one-eyed warlord was a fury of steel that avenged every one of his slain countrymen tenfold. He took a spear to his side and merely snarled like a tiger, taking the head of his attacker with a clean swipe.

There was no sign of Souzon or his horse. Hopefully the man escaped. Rooster prayed to every god that he didn't believe in that the surgeon did.

More horns; from the Iron City horsemen were assembling in a hasty formation. Within minutes they'd be on top of the carnage and find the body of the white riders. With their previous most-wanted headsman Darwish fighting over the corpse. There'd be no escape from that. Rooster knew he'd be lumped into whatever mess they'd gotten into.

The eagle cried above, wheeling once and then headed opposite. Towards the mountains. Towards the Glittering Wall. His gaze followed and into that shadow of a canyon door.

"Is that your sign, shaitan?"

Below, Hassan was stirring. Not quite dead yet. Coughing blood. Smug bastard.

Rooster hefted the sword, feeling the familiar weight of the pommel. While his strength wasn't what it was before being captured, there was enough to bring the blade to bear.

"I lied to you lieutenant. This was my family's sword. Once. My uncle's, who earned it by birthright. I gutted him with it, then his sons, then scoured his entire lands with it to ruin."

Awakener, the sword's name, fell swift. It was a clean cut—Hassan's head rolled away with a gout of blood. Sand darkened below.

"Thank you for returning her to me," Rooster said, then got to his horse.

He entered the fray and cut down three Medeans before they realized the threat. There weren't many Duskhounds left—only those loyal to Hassan. They put up a fight but Rooster was fresh and had the bigger sword. Awakener flashed and gave them a taste of what northern steel did to mail and hauberk. Three more Medeans fell like trees in a forest before they—along with the remaining Duskhounds—fled back to the bridge.

What was left was a butchery. More a massacre than a battlefield. Even Rooster's iron resolve was softened by the sight. Most of these men did not die well or honorably.

"Where's Souzon?"

Darwish was wild-eyed and coated in blood, "I did not see him gharib. Among the dead."

So there was indeed a chance he escaped.

Rooster's heart willed that he did—the surgeon had been nothing but a friend to him, no matter how aloof.

"Gharib...Rooster...they were messengers. The White Dove was slain in Nefara. An assassin. The peace is over. All over the realm. It's war."

Something had broken psychologically in the man. His voice was shaking. His one eye stared off into the abyss of his past sins, rising from the grave like an unwanted corpse. In a total state of shock.

Dangling from his hand was something. A white-gold medallion on a chain, bearing a sheaf of wheat and an olive branch crossed. Thing looked princely.

"What is that?"

"Token of the Qumari. Those in service to the Shah."

Rooster took it from him and the hillman barely noticed. Slipped it over his neck. Might come in handy, if even to pawn.

"Hassan...he knew. Somehow he knew."

Sun was falling and started to cast its long gloomy shadows across this mountainous wasteland, stained with grisly abandon. Soon it would be crawling with Medeans looking for a name to blame.

"Darwish we need to leave. I won't rot in a dungeon."

"Hassan betrayed me, didn't he," Darwish's voice croaked, "He was a brother to me gharib. Why did he do it? Why did he want war?"

Nothing could be said to satisfy such a question.

The eagle gave its last warning, shrieking as it sailed to the peaks and disappeared over the toothy horizon.

Moral dilemmas could wait after survival. And with a day like today, Rooster even thought that was a tall order.

"Can we pass through the Glittering Wall? Do you know the way through?"

Darwish made a slow, subconscious nod.

"Take us there."

Back home—whatever that place was to him now—Rooster remembered the day he saw his father's fields afire. It was dawn. Cattle with their hides blazing were running every way, acres of wheat were consumed by twenty-foot flames, and thatch roofs joined the blaze. It constrained him with an icy amazement—almost respect for his uncle and his villainous tenacity. He'd never forget the feeling he had striding across the cold flagstones into the armory, swinging onto his horse in full kit, riding like a demon up to his uncle's berg atop the hill.

Like lightning for blood in his veins.

No magic or even woman could replicate such a moment in time. It wasn't adrenaline but sheer force—like a god wielding Rooster like a puppet, channeling its power right into his limbs.

Escaping into the mountain canyons with the Medeans hot on their trail inspired such a feeling. Not even as Darwish fell asleep in the saddle and the horses wore down to a weary trot. Rooster was wide awake as they rode out in darkness. Only when it was midnight and their steeds refused to take another step did they rest, and it was brief.

Rooster felt alive in the freezing darkness with but a shadowed moon to guide them. There were moments in those few nights where he believed the eagle perched beside them—some strange guardian angel or demon. When he would awake, there would be feathers strewn across the rocky floor.

Darwish was little help and a mute companion. Whatever grief and anger the man was dealing with consumed him utterly. The first night during firewatch, Rooster heard him howling into the wind. As they rode for days on end the one-eyed man grew more feeble and there was less spring in his step. It was like Darwish was losing the will to live.

It wasn't like they had much to live on. They had perhaps enough water for a few days more and the rations in their packs would stretch for half that.

Survival slowly became the last thing on Rooster's mind.

They were heading towards somewhere that by all accounts and northern scholars would argue could not—should not, exist. That fact alone kept Rooster on his feet and eyes glued to the road ahead. Animating him with a fervor he could not explain.

And then on the sixth day since the massacre, they made it.

Up close and in person the opal surface of the Glittering Wall was more than a spectacle—it was divinity. Glimmering more intensely the longer Rooster stared at it. The mountains simply ended right up against it, creating a small gap of maybe twenty paces between it and the natural rock formations. A belt of sand formed a moat. They stopped in it.

But there were no gaps visible in the Wall. Not even a hairline crack. The road to it simply ended.

Rooster turned to Darwish, "Where now?"

The warlord sat surly in his saddle, staring blankly ahead.

"Come on man. You said you knew the way. How can we pass through the wall here?"

Again silence.

"Goddamn helpful you are," Rooster grunted and started to explore.

He spent hours searching the surrounding area and saw the sun hit its zenith before panic started to set in. The Wall was seamless. If there was any way through this thing, it had to be with some raggedy old wizard.

Always look to the sky for your answers, he recalled an old proverb.

Dark shapes wheeled, not far away. Carrion.

They circled dead horsemen. Their corpses so fresh the blood was still cooling. Strange riders slain and abandoned on the mad rush to reach the Iron City. Assassins or White Dove's men, it didn't matter. Each rider had at least a few days of food and water—for man and horse. Rooster gladly plundered their corpses.

Who knew how far they'd be without either.

Who knew where they were heading.

It seemed perspicacious to relieve one of the riders of his guise; heavy robes and wrappings of amber and red-bronze. Even a turban. Ambiguous enough. Winter was cold enough in these mountains and the last thing he'd want to broadcast was his pale skin, which was already taking on more tan than it ever had.

If he'd a look in a mirror, the only thing that would give him away now as a foreigner was the sword—too big a thing to pass for a desert-dweller.

Like he'd stepped in the skin of someone else.

Perhaps he had.

Decades prior he would have killed to be free of

responsibility—of his fief, his wife, his title. Freedom was such a fickle thing then.

Why was it now that he had it completely and without reservation that it stilled his breath and made him look backward?

Could a man be born anew in such circumstances?

Perhaps.

Rooster closed his eyes and felt the hilt of Awakener to teleport himself back to the present.

There was no turning back now.

And so they two ventured forward into the slit of the Wall and towards the darkness clove within the rock.

المتوحشين جبال
The Crownlands

Those little smudges could have been mistaken on the cliffs, the jagged rims that loomed hundreds of feet above. Could have been bushes hit with a breeze. Or a shadow's blur of a beast.

If you were a damn fool.

Rooster watched them carefully, noting their patterns of movement and pacing. Too human.

"They're watching us," he said, trying to warm himself up with his hands. Cold camps weren't necessary to hide their trail—there was just simply nothing to burn out in this godforsaken place.

Darwish said as much as the rocks.

The man had retreated into himself. Words no longer seemed to matter, food left uneaten. Darwish was withering away.

Worst case of survivor's guilt he'd ever seen.

Rooster unrolled the small tarp and selected his arrows. He had only a few left. Of the least warped shafts he picked to stuff in his riding bag. It felt like heresy. There were antelope and sheep in these badlands—he'd seen them. Wasting any arrows could mean they'd starve sooner.

And yet the dots were becoming more frequent in their haunts.

The further they pressed into this rocky wasteland—of red castles, mud canyons, and bone-colored mesas—the greater sense Rooster felt they were being watched. They were incurring on the lands of something elder and prideful.

He felt the urge to send a message.

So he did; loosing an arrow from the horse bow. It sailed true into the cliffs and clattered right above the heads of the watchers.

The smudges disappeared.

Rooster sighed and lowered the bow.

How many more days in this gods-forsaken place he could last he didn't know. Water was running low and their horses would be going lame soon. The nights were sleepless and the exhaustion only compounded. And that was without their creeps, their watchers.

Even his shaitan eagle had deserted them.

Frost layered thickly on the desert rock in the morning. White upon tan and red mountainous teeth, like the bloodied mouth of a wolf frozen to death. It was the worst weather in the worst kind of place—the deadliest of combinations. One wrong step and even a sure-footed horse could snap its leg.

This was not a land for men. The Akala Juradh seemed like bountiful fields by comparison.

If there was a road it was long swept away by sand. No matter their elevation or perch, it looked like impenetrable canyon wilderness as far as the eye could see.

"Where do we go from here?" Rooster asked and knew he'd get no answer.

Darwish may as well have been dead—sitting on that saddle, staring blankly ahead. Whatever process the man was going through, it needed to conclude fast.

Anywhere with ice would provide water. The problem was starting a fire. This land was utterly barren of anything to start a fire, let alone trees.

A thought came to mind.

Whoever was watching them from the cliffs had access to water. Readily available within a twenty-mile range.

So he did as the natives did, horse-hide skins around each shoulder, ascended the rocky heights looking for his arrow. Didn't take long to find the shattered shaft. There wasn't much of a trail to go off of—whoever was watching left little trace. Except a few small scuff marks from riding boots, which led him down a boulder scramble and a gravel slide that deposited him behind the mesas.

The temperature back here was far colder than where the sunlight barely graced. In the shadows his breath fog lingered thick and almost hung in the dark blue light.

Under the shadow of mountains, he spied something; a frozen mirror wedged into the cold sand. Water. A desert mere. It was dead silent on the descent to its banks, which showed more signs of activity. A chunk of ice had been pried free to give access to the fresh waters below.

Rooster squatted and began to fill the skins quickly.

Hairs of his neck rose.

There was nothing—no rocks tumbling from the slides and ledges around. No shadows or movement.

But he damn felt it.

His sheathed sword lay a few paces away, next to the filled skins. It felt like a mile away.

He stopped filling and looked around; still nothing.

Just cold shadows. Then a scrape of claws, scratching echoes. An inward growl that reverberated some fifty feet above his head. Yellow bulbs that flashed then were gone when his eyes returned to the spot.

Goosebumps went berserk.

"My horse is thirsty," he suddenly blurted, feeling the urge to speak aloud. "My companion and I are simple travelers and do not wish to incur any wrath. Nor harm."

A whistle—something flew from the dim light of the draws. An arrow that lodged itself a few paces from his head into the ice of the frozen pool. It quivered in poetic irony.

Rooster held his breath.

No more arrows came.

Quickly he filled the remaining skins and stood up, turning to the hillside and scanned it. Nothing.

That arrow said it all.

The watchers could have easily killed him there—they chose not to.

Be they headsman or bandits but the Duskhounds picked their mounts well.

Their horses were proving more resilient to the harsh climate and pace than any northern breed Rooster had encountered. His own, a witchwood bay and of fair temperament, was proving to be the best he'd ever had.

He named the thing Nereel. It just seemed fitting given the horse had been the only reason the little man got to Souzon. He even got a rise out of Darwish whenever he called the horse by name, sometimes a questioning grunt.

At first glance, Rooster thought his eyes were playing tricks on him. It was common for riders to start seeing clouds fly away suddenly and minor hallucinations to unravel the bored mind.

This wasn't the case.

Fortresses began to appear everywhere, wedged between canyon walls and even like monasteries against the backdrop of snowy mountains. They were scattered in the dozens in these highlands—abandoned to time and occupied only with the howling wind. They seemed so out of place with nothing but wasteland around them.

What purpose did they serve in the middle of nowhere, guarding nothing?

They paused to water their horses at the crossroads of a ledge. To turn right they would walk the narrow stairs into the darkened mouth of one such fort. It lingered and yearned to be approached, that granite face of antiquity.

May as well, since time was wasting.

He ascended the narrow stairway. It couldn't have fit more than three horses abreast. No hoofprints or sign of the watchers but then again, they likely had a back entrance. At the end of the stone passage was an archway—a yawning mouth before the fortress.

Rooster halted.

He came face to face with a mummified skull, wisps of hair flowing in the wind. Impaled on a spike decorated with fetishes of bone, horse-hair and beads. It was one of many guarding the archway. What was odd was the flesh; a charcoal-gray, almost blackened. Unless his eyes played tricks on him, it was drier than sand itself.

A hoarse whisper like wind escaping a tunnel came from somewhere.

"Do not enter," the raspy voice of Darwish sent his flesh jumping from its skin.

The little warlord stood behind, jaw set.

"Even for you sakshat. Inside is a fate worse than death. You will be condemned for eternity."

"What is it?"

Darwish seemed to read his mind, "You won't find the living here gharib. These are bastions for the banished."

Like nails on slate, that hoarse whisper emanated somewhere nearby.

Even Darwish quaked, shaking his head, making signs.

These people gave into so much superstition here. Their entire lives governed by forces unseen, curses and blessings doled out equally to penitent and blasphemous. The north had no such idolatries—alchemy and science had killed their gods long ago. Rooster didn't see himself as a skeptic but rather a product of his environment. He didn't deny the existence of monsters. They simply didn't fit into his worldview.

What couldn't be killed with the explosive fire of engineer-magicians could be slain with steel. Had there been gods and monsters back in the north, man had simply overcome both. Why else would civilization exist and spread its ugly perpetuity?

Still, he did not enter.

There was something about this place that sent his mind to dark places. Something sinister.

Back to their horses and the hard road ahead.

Before they moved their horses up to a canter, Darwish had reined back, watching over his shoulder at the fortress. The little man didn't take his eyes off it, as if it were a thing that could creep back on them. Odd.

It was long behind them when the next bit of words trailed out of the hillman's mouth.

"They used to be the pride of the Crownlands.

Muffassal al Asab. Fist of the Shemsari. Used to be."

Ah. So that's where they were.

"Nereel said the Shemsari were nomadic and held no lands."

"Urustad spoke true; they are."

"And yet you said this was theirs? These Crownlands?"

Darwish grunted, "It was. Until they angered Bahram and the dead were sent to take their lands from them. Now they roam without end. This is why the Shemsari cannot sleep beneath anything but the open sky. Now gharib, let us keep our pace and be free of this land and its black curse."

No more silent observers. Only the cold wind and their mounts kept them company.

If Bahram existed, then He was hiding somewhere deep in that untamed wilderness of rock and painted desert.

The shadow of His regret cast long over the vacant and desolate land.

Rooster didn't see anything move past the humps of orange. Been watching so long his eyes were beginning to play tricks on him. Those damned dunes just kept going on and on. Darwish insisted they were still in the Crownlands but this terrain told a different story.

How the hell did anything live out there?

"Anything?" the hillman asked, out of sight.

"Nothing."

They came upon the ruin of a caravan and waited for the raiders to circle back. That was hours ago. So far the only company they'd been blessed with were vultures and strange spotted dogs with blackened muzzles. Both were fighting over the flesh of the bodies—their blood still drying.

Didn't look like anyone was left to tell the tale.

"Don't linger," Darwish met him on the saddle of the dune and laid his bow out. "They'll be back."

"Yeah," Rooster didn't feel like arguing with the little warlord. Hard enough to squeeze words out of him these days.

He slid down the steep dune on the other side and entered the camp.

The birds scattered with flesh still in their beaks. The spotted dogs, however, snarled. There were a good eight of them. Damned mean-looking with those black eyes and bat ears. An arrow burred into the flank of one and it sent the pack scattering with yips. Darwish strung another arrow and waited.

Rooster investigated.

Whoever the caravan masters were, they'd chosen the wrong place to shack up. Hadn't put up much of a fight either. Corpses strewn about the wagon train had been cut to pieces. They were a few shades lighter than nut-brown and wore barely rags. And each branded on the neck with a crook symbol.

Slaves. Emaciated ones too. But there was no master to be seen anywhere. Nor the beasts that drew the wagon.

They'd been transporting timber. Nearly all of the cargo intact.

He recovered a few good arrows from the engagement. Flocked with dark vulture feathers, set with wide-slashing heads of a crude iron and fixed on a jungle wood shaft. Not the kind that could make a dent in armor. Barely lethal.

Rooster stepped out to the sand to observe; these raiders had to have been on horseback. Scattered hoofprints in frenzied, short-breadth paces that skittered wildly—like lines of ants bending and encircling on the earth.

The worst detail of all; not a drop of water anywhere.

He ran back up and relayed the bad news, "They can't be far. We can sneak up and grab their water."

Darwish looked pained, thumbing the grip of his bow in somber contemplation, "You say this as it would be simple. These are more hyenas than man. We would be lucky not to be spotted by them crossing the waste."

"And what about the water? How will our horses make it?"

The hillman looked at them, "We drive them until they no longer can be driven. Then we move on foot."

"You mad bastard. We'll die."

"We die stealing from sāreq! I would not cross swords with the raiders of Edis, not even with all of my Duskhounds behind me," Darwish grew animated and voice no-nonsense, "You are a gharib. The bandits of your land are opportunists. Here they live to plunder and rape the sands. It is their religion and these roads of travelers, their temple."

Riveting speech as it was, didn't solve their water problem.

And Darwish was wrestling with that.

Sometimes there was just no good choice left.

"Night's going to fall soon. We have an hour or two of daylight to track them."

Darwish just shook his head.

"Listen up. We're both in this hellhole because you let your best man stab you in the back. I'm not going to make light of it but you gave us no choice, going over the Wall. We need water and if that means crossing swords with some nasty characters, so be it. Rather die that way anyway."

Of course the hillman didn't want to hear that. No one wanted to be told they were a gullible fool. Still it needed to be said.

Surprisingly, the hillman surrendered, "Bahram knows it. And my redemption. If there's to be any."

The yakking stopped there and they made use of the little sunlight left.

The sāreq were bold and did not bother to obscure their tracks or hide their numbers. Rooster counted five sets, though there could have been two more. Carefully they retraced the assault on the caravan camp to an outcropping of sandstone—higher than the dunes, a perfect location to spy on prey.

Even more foolhardy; the raiders had built a fire, projecting their location to everyone for miles to see.

Which meant they weren't used to competition, or

being snuck upon.

Flames illuminated the pit encircled by a dune wall and its inhabitants. Rooster counted five horses, tethered to measly stakes. Their masters far away on rugs beside the growing bonfire. Throwing some kind of strange celebration, dancing on the colorful carpets, and hoisting their swords in the air.

"Your fabled deadly raiders," he scoffed back at the hillman, "Go cut the horses free and I'll start the negotiation."

"Weeks ago you were my kul. Now you speak like my captain."

"If the Duskhounds are no more, I can't be a slave anymore, can I?"

Darwish scowled and slipped into shadow.

Rooster swaggered into camp.

Best chance he had was to surprise the bastards. They had range on him with bows and this was their home turf.

A drunk man could hit back hard and win the day.

The revelry was reaching its zenith. They were small men all dressed in black. Each bore an arsenal enough to arm a small outfit. They were smoking from a deep-bottomed pipe that exuded a pungent scent, burning some local leaf.

They had stuck some strange skinny fellow like a pig to be roasted above the fire. He was blathering nonsense. The flames would be reaching him soon.

Horses whinnied as their reins were cut. They scattered out across the sands; his cue.

Rooster rushed them.

He was almost halfway to the rugs before they realized he wasn't one of them. The desert garb must have been convincing enough at a distance. The raiders jabbered in a bizarre tongue, kicking over their smoke-pot in the confusion and boiling water took one out of commission before the fight started.

The first raider chose daggers against Awakener. Poor choice. The sword tasted blood and went on to kiss the steel of the curved tulwars the next drew, the others lances. They were nimble. But they weren't good. One overextended and lost the hand holding his shield, followed by his head.

A lance almost skewered him—Rooster ducked and cleaved the thing in two, dispatching the last flanker. For whatever maddening reason the raiders had chosen melee.

Perhaps they were too proud to deny his challenge.

The last that was left standing cursed at him in a strange tongue. Not Medean. Barking and edging closer with that short sword.

He just stepped back and let the man enter his killing range.

Awakener sung and did not let up until it was over.

Rooster almost felt sorry for them—it was as if the raiders had never had a swordfight with anyone who was armed or knew what they were doing. They were clearly young. In the light, they appeared fair-skinned and their eyes an orange-gold. Like northerners. But those eyes...

What the hell? Who were these sareq?

He cut down the spit and freed the lanky fellow, who began to roll on the ground to cool off. And got a closer look and immediately regretted it. The spared was a twig of a man who was hairless head to toe and tattooed with a solid blue-black ink besides white dots that constellated on his back. He wore nothing but a loin cloth and stunk of smoke.

The skinny blue-black man did not look grateful but rather displeased.

"You're welcome," he said in Patina.

A dark hand shot towards the fire and some funny little stomp-dance followed.

Rooster didn't get it and didn't quite care to. Kicking sand into the fire to staunch it, he began to pilfer what he could in the dim light. There were a few casks of water, wine, and some kind of spiced jerky. Dog meat probably. Not to mention a heavy purse filled with the local silver.

The little-blue black man howled, trying and failing to rekindle the fire by kicking over coals.

"One got away," Darwish was hissing, running in from the dark slopes of the dunes, "I tried to pursue on horse but he was too fast. I told you we were doomed!"

"Can you understand what Skinny over here is raving on about?"

The hillman frowned, sizing up the blue-black fellow, "He is angered that you have denied his master the gift of ashes. He keeps saying She. You broke a ritual of some kind."

Skinny Blue-Black turned back to them, cupping a white-hot coal in his hands. Painlessly. He shook it as if it were a bad egg and threw it on the sand. Unbelievably the man's hand was completely unharmed.

"Skinny's a magician?"

Darwish said, "In the Ghazwala we call them chārakh. Spirits live in his skin and work his hands."

Skinny was doing something to the smoke to make it curl up out of the coal, coaxing it out like a snake from a pot. It definitely looked sorcerous.

No way—no more curses. Rooster had enough for a lifetime these last few weeks.

He stomped out the coal with his boot.

Skinny wigged out. He puttered and rolled around in the sand. The skinny magician went back to the fire, producing another hot coal. And shoved it into the mouth of one of the raider corpses. It shook violently and smoke flew from its ears and nose, eyes opened and were of a glassy black.

The pit within the dunes was filled with thaumaturgy. The stars above dimmed and the ones on Skinny's back glowed. His very blue-black skin pulsed as if it were waves of the ocean.

Desert-speak that was soft and yet dominated. It took Rooster to realize it was a woman speaking from the corpse's mouth—one of dusky authority. A projection.

It ended abruptly as Skinny fell to his haunches. The sorcery must have been too much. Wasn't exactly a great wizard.

"What was that about?"

Darwish laughed from his belly, "Oh it is good gharib. You made more than one enemy tonight! Your Skinny is a servant of Nafsi, the Mother of Shadow. A powerful djinn. He'd been indebted to the caravan master who the sāreq slayed before we got here. If he was to burn and become ash he would have become one of Nafsi's immortal servants."

Rooster couldn't believe this horseshit.

"You broke his small death ritual and now he cannot become Her ash. He says he will haunt you now and make you pity your existence."

"Oh, he wanted to go to his master? I can arrange that. Step out of the way."

The hillman grabbed his arm, "Do not gharib. The djinn are like gods here. You must never harm their heralds unless it is warranted by another god."

Another patch of sand and rock, another god to piss off.

Rooster sighed and shoved the sword back into the sheath.

They rode and did not stop. Across what had now become a plain of scattered belts of dunes and rocky footing. Low rising hills that rolled into oblivion. It grew and expanded until the entire horizon was filled with a great sandy nothing.

Strangely it was peaceful.

Skinny rode on a stolen pony. He blended in with the surroundings so well it looked at times that his steed was ridden by an angry ghost.

Darwish led with quiet intent.

On the fourth afternoon since the raid on the camp, they noticed the column of dust riding hard behind them. Perhaps a half to a day's ride on their tail.

"Sāreq," was all the hillman said, throwing himself back in the saddle.

"The devils come for vengeance. I told you as much."

"Can we outrun them?"

"No."

"If we leave Skinny behind will they stop?"

Darwish looked back, patting the flank of his horse, "Why do you ask when you already know the answer? Do you enjoy forcing me to speak?"

Even exceptional horses had their limits. The hillman had claimed the desert breed could withstand tremendous strain and distance before they'd break. But that was with ample feed and plentiful water—they had none.

Rooster could just look at Nereel and could sense the horse's weariness.

They couldn't ride their mounts like this much longer.

"How far until we reach Nefara?"

"Do you see this? The shimmer? This is the Ptahira River. We follow it west and we find Nefara. But we will not make it this far."

Rooster spotted it; that distant wide serpent of a river was lower than them by a few hundred feet, moving slowly into what looked like hints of green before slipping out of view—blocked by scattered, hump-shaped mountains. Tiny dots crawled on them with white triangles; ships. Monstrous mother of a waterway.

"What are those small mountains?"

"Three Gates. They guard the sunken kingdom of Nemset."

At the mention, Skinny laughed inanely, wriggling his tattooed fingers.

"Why can't we slip into these?"

"A worse place than any you've ever seen. I would sooner return to the Muffassal al Asab and make it my home."

Rooster was tired of these warnings and trepidations.

Ever since they'd fled the Iron City and made it south of the Wall he'd felt as if his mental state was unraveling—no, it had happened long before then. Perhaps since his unburial. Out of body almost at all times, barely clinging to physical reality. Constantly feeling as if he was trapped in a daydream.

Was he going insane? Was it the lack of water?

Everyone had their limit. A threshold of sanity that could only take so much before mental sundering. It didn't take war or death. Sometimes it could be the mundane events of life, piled on like a mountain that could eventually tip a resolute mind. What little reservations he had left were quickly dissolving the further into this land they went.

Rooster knew he'd never be going back home—it no longer existed.

He found himself staring at the patterns of grains of the bronze-colored sand, mesmerized by their uniformity. Waves that could be compared to the sea, sparkling crimson and gold. An invisible finger traced the lines as he fell into a trance.

"Gharib?"

He ignored Darwish and continued to stare at the sands.

There was no explanation for how such a simple thing could exist by some accident or happenstance. The work of a god maybe.

Just maybe.

Was it just him or was that the shadow of a bird on the ground?

An eagle cry drove him to stare up at the sun. There was a shadow there for just a blink, crossing over the solar glare.

"There's the shaitan to guide us."

"What gharib nonsense is this?"

Rooster blinked and it was gone.

Darwish looked bewildered but Skinny was a different story—man damn near bowed in his direction. There was a sudden deference shown. It didn't need explanation—it just made Rooster feel less crazy.

Or more, if he thought about it too much.

"Gah. We may as well give up now if we keep wasting our breath at this place," Darwish said.

"Take us to Three Gates."

"I told you gharib..."

But Rooster was leaving them in the dust.

To the eye of a raptor, Three Gates would have looked like three boulders arranged to form a flat pyramid. To the eye of a man on the ground Three Gates was a monument valley of dark reds and browns, lone mountains forming an unnatural canyon. More importantly were the statue-reliefs carved hundreds of feet into the sides of the rock walls. Depicting men with bestial heads clutching wicked looking tools—seemingly flawless statues. Guarding the entrance into the dark recesses of the valley.

Beyond that, shadows the size of mountains lurked there.

Skinny was whispering to his arm conversationally, the lunatic.

Hoofbeats—the cacophony of their pursuers. Sure enough, the dark riders of the sands were hot on their heels, riding their horses at a full gallop. They'd overtake them within the hour.

"Will they follow us into the Gates?"

Darwish cursed, "Aie, only if they wish a death as cruel as ours."

"Let's test that."

They rode hard under the merciless gaze of those stone guardians. Into the monument valley that lay half in sun, half in darkness. As if it were in perfect and unnatural contrast. Rooster could barely make out a deeper blackness in the center of the rock beyond; a portal of kinds. A tunnel perhaps.

The horsemen in black were still approaching. Unfazed by the lair of the gods. Their blurs growing larger by the moment. An arrow from them buried itself into the sand, barely missing their horses by a hand.

Darwish took them into the shaded side with his breath audibly held, "They still pursue! They do not know Nemset!"

And so they had no choice but to flee into the tunnel. Swimming into that inky nothing that seemed to have no end. It was a place of total despair that had the horses getting cranky, stomping their hooves in protest.

Until Skinny conjured something that repelled the darkness and replaced it with a gray ambient light. Cradling a sphere of light between his spidery fingers.

Even with that lantern there was no discernible heading, only that the walls bled pitch-black in that tunnel.

They wandered until behind a torch like a flare went up by their pursuers. Joined by several others. Shouts of glee, as they must have seen the silhouettes backlit by the grey light.

"Come on," Rooster urged the others, riding in the opposite direction.

This throat in the mountain seemed endless.

There had to be an exit.

As they delved the air grew moist and cloying—smelling of wet decay, the corpses of gardens buried by a flood. And something worse. Raw stench of a battlefield and opened stomachs. It grew in such intensity Rooster felt his eyes water and insides began to flip end over end.

Something else; a susurration came down the tunnels.

"Do you hear that?"

At first it sounded like wind.

A gust blew softly, tossing the manes of the horses and tugging at their clothes.

No—it was like the quiet death whispers of thousands, filling the walls of stone. Gaining steadily as it approached. As if the voices themselves were growing more terrified, wailing their last breath louder and louder.

The horses began to freak and buck their riders.

Darwish was almost thrown off his, "We turn back and face the riders and leave!"

Only one problem; Rooster could no longer see the torchlight of their pursuers. Must have been blown out.

Doom was filling the entire tunnel.

Over to the right and cradling the grey light, Skinny was not muttering nonsense to himself. The funny tattooed sorcerer was remarkably calm, watching the darkness. If he was swayed by the nightmares ahead, he did not show it.

Maybe his god had a way through.

It was a gamble—this tunnel would be their doom. Rooster felt it in his gut.

What was there left to do now but double down on the spiritual fantasies of these people?

"Listen Darwish. Tell Skinny here I'm sakshat and I need passage through this place. Tell him that in return I swear I'll make sure he can go to his Shadow Woman in ashes! Damn it, don't look at me like that. Tell him!"

The hillman wasted no breath to translate.

Skinny turned sideways to eyeball Rooster.

"He says he needs proof that you're sakshat."

That wind was getting closer.

Rooster pulled the robes aside, showing the scarring over his heart—the gnarled flesh had yet to turn white. The gray light made it look even worse, "Happy?"

What had seemed like deference before became devotion.

The tattooed man said a few words in his tongue and began to make a mad ritual, tapping his glowing grey egg of a lantern and then frantically tapping into it. The egg wobbled and began to spit out smoke.

Whispers of the wind became deafening howls of nightmare.

Smoke trickled opposite of the wind. It somehow maintained the same glow of the lantern as it formed the ambiguous shape of a woman. She raised a smoky appendage which formed a hand—she began to walk deeper into the blackness.

"He says Nafsi accepts your deal."

The spell arrived propitiously.

Black wind and a thousand screams hit them like a wall—yet broke upon the smoky woman like an avalanche cleaved by a boulder. Tendrils of sheer darkness flowed harmlessly around the gray light to continue down the tunnel.

The riders behind them were not so lucky.

Rooster could hear their and their horse's screams echo in his skull.

Invisible ice water froze his spine solid.

It took them what felt like hours to pass through the tunnel. Moonlight at its end dissipated the smoke-woman. Skinny began to drag ass. Then disappeared when they weren't watching.

"Where did he go?"

Darwish looked over his shoulder, "I do not care gharib. He guided us. But we should be glad to be parted from him."

Whatever the tattooed sorcerer had done, he'd led them into an ancient courtyard that was an intersection of kinds. A great building loomed ahead with edifices not dissimilar from the guardians of Three Gates, complete with a pillared archway. Its keystone formed by two great carved hands holding a feather between their fingers—one of flesh, one skeletal.

A layer of mist lingered and its source lay to the left; dark verdant carpets covered what appeared to be streets. A marsh that consumed stone. Visible even in the night was the great canopy of moss and devilish trees that had overtaken civilization.

But on the right was a stairway down of hewn rock, emerging onto a dry sandy belt. Spitting them out only the gods knew where. It was an easy choice.

They went right but Rooster did not forget the feeling in that courtyard.

Never had he felt the presence of so many things—the air heavy with spirit. Crushing the consciousness with a mysterious feeling that he could only describe as being underwater. For all his denial of divinity, there was a presence there in that courtyard that was inescapable and sentient. As if the very walls were watching his entrance and escape.

The hillman had been right—this was no place for men.

Mercifully they passed through a corner of that sunken hell and back into the desert.

Civilization at last greeted them with the warmth of one hundred thousand candles.

Like a celebration cake rose up from the dune sea, layers of light glowed under the sparkling night sky. A metropolis in the sand—erected in the middle of a jagged nowhere, built upon the delta of that great and winding river. An old city consumed by a younger one, housing the souls of hundreds of thousands within orange-tan walls. No realm in the north could boast such a mass of humanity.

They had made it to Nefara.

دلتا

Nefara

For the first time in a long time, Rooster didn't feel like there was a target on his back. So when he heard the colloquial term for his white skin called across the tables of the bazaar, he jerked out a knife from his belt.

False alarm. A Teridian behind him rose to greet a dancer woman who took him by the hand into the afternoon sun.

The knife went back into the belt.

He took a deep breath. Had to stop being so jumpy. Wasn't healthy for the soul.

In the Sword Row, there were dozens upon dozens of gharibs. Professionals, wanderers, and deadbeat northerners who all whored themselves out to the Caravan Court. Else there were hundreds of sellswords gathered as hired lancers or attached to the free companies, drinking or enjoying the many pleasures the city offered. Gharibs were treated like princes here.

Nefara was more empire than any city Rooster had seen—dozens of ethnicities and subcultures collided between her walls. It was hard to tell who belonged and who refused to leave the desert garden. Medean banners of the White Dove dangled from Medean architecture; brightly colored domes, octagonal buildings, steeply pointed arches, and painted stucco of intricate geometry. But these were additions—beneath was the hint of something far older. Bones of sandstone and ancient brick peeked out from the eroding veneer. Statues of long-limbed men with beastly heads had their faces shorn off by later conquerors. Obelisks that had long had their hieroglyphics chiseled off.

Whatever once was did not seem to mind the incursion of Medeans. Either that or it had been put to the conqueror's sword and no one seemed to care about what was left behind.

All interesting details he was trying to drink away with wine. Which was plentiful and cheap. As was the flatbread served with glistening chunks of goat and olives.

Everyone else's problems were their business—not his.

He had a fat purse, a horse, and a roof over his head.

Existence was treating him well for once. Albeit a lonely one.

The moment they crossed the towering archway into the city, Darwish faded into his own shadow. There wasn't a cask or bottle that he couldn't find the bottom of. It was as if Darwish had simply lost the will to exist. Becoming more vagrant than warlord. Pissing himself to sleep.

It was too sad to participate in the sorrow. Rooster began to excuse himself earlier and earlier. He'd wake up to find the haggard wreck of a man passed out on the dirt outside his tent.

And one night Darwish simply never came back.

No man needed no purpose. For those who rode in the saddle and fought, it was a blight to have nowhere to be or go. It became a cancer that ate away at the soul.

Deep down Rooster was afraid of what he saw in Darwish, because he knew that comfort was a masquerade—soon it would be him slumming it out, dying by the bottle. Repeating the miserable past.

Fear of one's inability to overcome dejection and face down the rest of his years in helplessness. A fate that one could easily argue was worse than the sword.

Birds the shade of every precious gem filled the misty air of the Ptahira. Blood-red flamingos, cerulean warblers, ghost doves, and golden herons took flight on the delta. It was their paradise and Nefara was merely witness to it.

Rooster walked the long stretch of greenery that ran the length of the wharf and felt the cool air wash over him. The river was abuzz with more than just birds.

Small galleys with tall white sails wove around sluggish moving barques, rowed by slaves whose chains clinked as they oared. Thin reed-based fishing boats maneuvered around them, hauling up strange fish in their nets. The docks were a constant state of chaos where slave crews and merchants fought for space to unload or take off.

Perhaps that was his solution; take passage on a vessel.

He'd seen a group of gharibs do so already. There was talk of piracy on Sword Row. The pay must have been good enough to protect the merchants.

Banditry was a booming trade in this patch of lush desert. Every direction by land or water had some flavor of highwayman. The need for sellswords was a bottomless cup. The drunk captains of the free companies swore up and down that the Ivory Queen was disguising detachments of her troops as river pirates. It wasn't the craziest rumor in this town Rooster heard.

He stopped and looked out across the dense foliage.

There was talk of a place that didn't have a bandit problem.

Where the birds didn't even flock to.

On the south and east end of the delta where the water stagnated was a constant layer of thick fog that never seemed to wither—even in sunlight. An impregnable shadow of ruins choked by an oppressive swamp of cypress and overgrown palms. By even this angle, the fallen city of Nemset was large enough that it could devour Nefara with ease.

"It's not enough gharib," the shipmaster said, pushing his coins back, "We take a hundred crescents now."

"You'll take fifty and I'll get you your other fifty after."

Someone should have told the man he should smile less, "Do you take us for fools gharib?"

Rooster pushed what was left of his purse back across.

What other choice did he have but to lie?

"Trust goes both ways. What if you take my silver and run?"

"I have a ship, you don't."

"Just take it, damn it. If you're a thief then you just got

richer for nothing."

Calling someone a thief in Nefara had consequences, as it turned out. The shipmaster reeled and cursed blackly, smacking the purse aside, "Fuck you, white dog. You would accuse me, Waleed, of dishonest things like I'm some *dhimmi*?"

"My mistake," he tried to back off.

"Yes it is and now you'll have your tongue cut out. Try calling someone a fucking thief."

Mailed guardsmen were already on their way, sensing disruption at the docks. They looked bored and irritated. Bad combination. The shipmaster began to speak to them in rapid Medean.

Rooster figured honey over vinegar would work, "I meant no offense."

Neither spoke Patina but their irritation was growing into something resentful—their gazes towards him anything but pleasant. They blocked off his exit and started to close in.

"Ha, I told you stupid gharib, you should not have called Waleed a thief."

Rooster had nothing but river to his back. Nowhere to run.

He could think of nothing else and reached inside his robes. And felt the cool metal of the medallion he'd taken from the messenger; the Token of the Qumari. What the hell, it might prove something.

He produced it and slapped it on the table.

The guards looked at it curiously.

Waleed the shipmaster did too.

"You see this? I got this from your Shah. Gifted to me for my actions of bravery. I'm not just any white dog."

With any luck, they'd at least half buy his bald-faced lie.

Instead they picked up the medallion, look him up and down with great scrutiny, then immediately marched off. The shipmaster looked disappointed.

Great, now his only bartering chip was spent.

"Thanks for nothing, black teeth," he swiped his purse

back from the table.

"Gharib. You there."

Rooster didn't feel like lifting his gaze to address the men who surrounded his table. So he toasted them with his clay chalice, "To what do I owe the fine guardsmen of Nefara this honor?"

The lead one, a sergeant by the tabs on his sash, looked as humored as a rock, "You are the gharib who is known as the Rooster, who traveled with the Dawali headsman?"

Alcohol talked, brain took a back seat, "You got the wrong guy. I go by Cock now."

The white-gold medallion of the Qumari was dangled inches from his face, "My men tell me you tried to give them this at the docks earlier today."

Well shit.

Rooster waited for the red-sashed guards to seize him any minute. But the moment never came.

Instead, a scroll of papyrus was placed before him on the table.

"A message from the Qadi al Tughur Ashur of Nefara, His Wisdom and Opulence of the Third Progeny," the sergeant's Patina was rough but his mood was rougher. "Read it."

On the scroll was a gold wax seal bearing the mark of a succulent plant over an eye. Rooster broke it and read. Surprisingly written in a language he did actually understand. A summons, directing him to meet at a plaza at the border of the Sword Row and Haraf Kalat in one hour. The meeting would take place on an elevated and shaded pavilion above the plaza. That was it. No other direction or information.

"What is this about?"

"Your problem, gharib," a hand swept away from the tables, "Now you will accompany us."

"It says here I'm to arrive in an hour."

The sergeant smiled thinly, "The Qadi was clear that you were to be escorted to this meeting. We are here to ensure that."

Meaning that the letter was merely window dressing—a façade of freedom. This wasn't an optional meeting.

"Cover my tab then, will you?"

One of the younger guards angrily drew his switch but was held back by the sergeant. A shouting match and the brash young guard was hauled away.

"Do not test my patience anymore, dog."

Rooster made sure to take the jug with him.

Verdant green was carefully manicured around a glassy turquoise pond. The plaza was more walled garden than it was a thoroughfare. Music strummed and birds sang.

"Come, sit, drink. I pray my friends at the guard have not spoiled your afternoon," the man in the turban said, waving off Sergeant Serious and the others.

Here was a bureaucrat if Rooster had ever seen one; folds of violet and crimson robes that exuded wealth, rings bearing sapphires and emeralds, a mustache curled and adorned with gold. The Qadi radiated wealth but he was no fat old miser—no he was far younger than Rooster would have assumed.

The Qadi pushed a bowl of syrup-infused dates and candied nuts over, "Eat! Please eat. After what I spent on this it would be a tragedy to let it go to the dogs."

Rooster did, lounging on the cushions. The stupor of wine had yet to wear off. He felt invincible.

"Do you know who I am?"

"A dignitary?"

"The office of the Vizier of the Caliphate governs the old city of Nefara, as does every Vizier of every territory of the Third Progeny and his Excellence, Our Shah the White Dove. As Qadi of the Borders, I am secretary to the Vizier himself. It is my role and station to enforce the will of the White Dove and administer His holy law to all of his Empire."

The man in the turban paused to sip his tea, then, "The law of a dead man."

Rooster blinked.

Felt his blood freeze solid.

"What do you mean?"

"I am no spring goat northerner. I know as well as you that the Shah perished at the hands of assassins. Here, during the festival barely a week ago."

A quick look over his shoulders to see if the guards had snuck up on them. Shouldn't have left his sword with them, damn it.

"My servants spoke to a certain Dawali headsman. Your traveling companion, who was serving as an informant for the Shah. Unfortunately, these were his last words before he passed."

Rooster held a silent prayer for the deceased warlord.

A pity. Darwish, like Nereel, had been his only friend in this land. It was a tragedy that it ended like this for the old man. Perhaps it was for the best he did not live longer to endure his failures.

Hopefully some peace in the grave as well.

"What of Darwish?"

"He spoke that you encountered messengers who were delivering the news through the Qaryat al Hadid. You carried the medallion of a messenger, one of the Qumari."

It was time to go, "If you know..."

No one crept up on them on the patio. The guard had not left their station to ambush him.

"Please. You're not in any danger northerner. Your name is Rooster? What is your real name?"

"No one's business."

He still had the long knife of the bandits tucked away under the folds of his robes. Just in case.

"Well, it doesn't matter. That's the name you go by. To my friends, I am Tariq Ashur."

"Sure. What do your enemies call you?"

A faint and hollow laugh, "*Agha-Wasakh*. It's a false honorific. Means Dirt Lord. I did not come to power by the privilege of my caste Rooster. Mine is as low as they come."

A dhimmi lord? How was that possible?

"If you know Medeans, then you know they hate me for

this."

"Do you hate them for it?"

Tariq seemed taken aback, blinking twice then recovered, "Yes. Does my honesty assure you?"

It did to an extent.

Rooster decided he'd hear out the rest of what the magistrate had to say. Whether it was all bullshit or not. The reactions of the Qadi had been genuine—whether or not the man could weave a lie in any other context. Tariq was toying with the tea cup, waiting.

"You have my attention, Qadi."

"Good. News of the White Dove's death has not yet spread through the land. Partially due to the messengers being slain. In any case, when news finally circulates that the White Dove perished all the bowels of hell will unearth. Blame will be laid upon the agents of the Ivory Queen—benefitting a future boy king who lusts for prestige through war. And he will have one; a most bloody one."

"Why am I here then? What use am I to you?"

"Everything. Answer me this. What is something gold can't buy?"

"The ability to be left alone."

That earned a smile from Tariq, "Aha. Now I am getting to know you northerner. But you're mistaken; it's loyalty. True and untarnished. A familial kind that cannot be bought nor sold."

"Mmm. How long did you prepare this speech for me?"

The bureaucrat clicked his tongue against the roof of his mouth, then stood. Strolled over to the perforated stone screen that overlooked the plaza. No one below could look in but they could them—like a one way mirror.

A people who valued the ability to spy on each other and keep secrets, these Medeans.

"Do you want to know the problem about Nefara? It's not that this place is a den of snakes—a city of thieves. No, it's much worse than that. This city is infested with a hundred different loyalties. We suffer a tribalism of the worst kind. To earn one is to betray another. Even the

Vizier's office is run by gangsters."

"Such is the nature of men and civilization."

"I'm an outsider to Nefara, like you. I came here with a dream to build the next great city upon the bones of the last. These factions—these clans who all claim ownership of this sand—they'll sooner tear it down this place, brick by brick."

"Maybe it's their right."

"Spoken like a street prophet. But neither of us will prevail now with the shakeup in the north. The Ivory Queen wasn't born yesterday—she'll seize the opportunity to hit the Medeans before the boy can sit on his throne and declare jihad. We're that opportunity. Nefara sits on the crossroads both by land and water. We're vulnerable."

"Sounds like you've got a real problem on your hands."

"On the contrary, I consider this a bounty from the heavens."

"Go on."

Tariq studied his rings, "Under the rule of the White Dove the merchant lords of the Shalmanisar have waxed in prosperity. Too much. Their rule is as strong as the Caliphate with bottomless coffers. Negotiating charters that exploit Medean law while forcing our dependence on the flow of goods. Slaves, cotton, wheat—name it. They own it."

"So replace the shrewd bastards."

"Tell a serpent to devour its head."

Rooster wasn't shocked. The free flow of gold never liberated a town. Merchants were the tapeworm of industry.

"The Shah was devoted to the idea of growth for the sake of it. His proclamations seemed reverent and wise to His Emirs and Ayubin. But we are a frontier. We suffer a different reality than the safe green lands of the Caliphate beyond the Wall."

"Isolated?"

"Worse; auspicious. Nefara is a gateway to the past and a treasure to the future. Whoever controls her controls the sunken realm of Nemset."

"I doubt it. I've been there."

Tariq's jaw shut and his eyes lifted, "What you saw was barely a glimpse. Trust me when I say that the Medeans do not know what they control."

That ruin in the swamp?

Definitely more superstitious horseshit.

"Now for my bounty; the war. Our bitch in the West is clever as she is beautiful. In the last decade, she's broken and swept up every corsair lord and pirate captain of the Jewel Coast into her kingdom. With promises of betrothal, she's domesticated them. Made them puppets. With the White Dove gone, it's all but a certainty she'll do the same to the Shalmanisar and every free company on the Sword Row."

"Hence your speech on loyalty."

Then the Qadi hit him with something he did not expect, "I need you to start hitting their caravans as a servant for the Ivory Queen."

"The Shalmanisar? You want me to play pretend bandit?"

"Play? No. I want you to *be* one."

"What about the trade from your city? Wouldn't it be threatened if the caravans stop going west?"

Spinning to pluck a handful of grapes, the man in the turban said, "I surely hope so."

What the hell?

Rooster tried to play out the reasoning and couldn't make heads or tails of it. He sat there confused and must have hidden it poorly.

"One cannot prevent chaos but he can certainly steer it how he sees fit."

"What does the Qadi of the Border stand to benefit by weakening the trade to the city?"

The bureaucrat waved his hand like there was a fly, "Absolutely nothing."

Now this was making less sense. One of Rooster's pet peeves was obfuscation. Especially from the mouth of a politician. Oozing hubris for the sake of it.

He was beginning to dislike this conversation, "Get to the point."

"Do not become annoyed with me my northern friend, I'm not trying to trick you. Let me be more plain. If I simply wanted a brute with a sword to be a force of terror on the South Road, I'd have already done so. Or swayed one of the bandit princes to take a chest of my gold and do the same. What both of those lack is *substance*."

"This is hardly plain talk."

"My servants told me you were the thrall to Darwish and his Duskhounds and yet you're now his historian. That you have a scar over your heart and you were once a lord before you crossed the sea. That sword you carry has a name and you wield it well. Is this all true?"

Rooster shrugged.

"Do you know what that is? A story. Substance. Something no other sword for hire or bandit can claim to."

"Now hold on..."

"You're an enigma to them. They don't know your ways. They won't know how to deal with the infamous northerner known as *The Rooster*."

If only he could strangle that drunk one-eyed Dawali right now.

So that's what he was to these Medeans; a steel-wielding spectacle. May as well have joined in with the mad loons that traveled from town to town with fire-eaters and jugglers.

"Not what I came down here for. I don't want infamy. I'm no one's pet swordsman."

One of those well-shaped eyebrows lifted, "Nor do I have use for one. What I require is a hatchet man. With a name."

"And your idea of a reward?"

"Do you have to ask? Name anything. Treasures, women, land."

Rooster sat back.

There had to be a catch somewhere hidden in the

deal—always was. Nothing was ever too good to be true. A juicy and low-hanging fruit wasn't ignored by birds for no reason.

"I need to know what your aim is."

"Here I thought you were a sharper man, Rooster. Can't you see?"

No. Speaking wasn't how he solved problems. Too many pieces that were scattered and adrift in the cosmos of Rooster's brain—it wasn't conducive.

Sweeping the table of the plates of delicacies, he began to place fruit and nuts into a little map. It was crude and childish. But it was the visual aid that he needed.

"This is you," a single red grape was placed in the center, followed by several others, "The Vizier. The Medeans. Here in Nefara. Those up there beyond the Wall."

Olives became the Ivory Queen. Nuts for the Shalmanisar and the Merchant Lords. Then a little wooden skewer for himself.

Tariq folded his arms and studied the process.

"Let's say I become your storied bandit," he said, knocking aside nuts that made a line towards the olives, "And your trade weakens. Then?"

The other man moved his grape up and away from the rest, then placed more where the nuts had been knocked over, "The Medeans are forced to respond. The Ivory Queen does the same and sends sellswords of her own."

Olives and grapes intertwined. Then Tariq stabbed the large grape in the center with his wood skewer, "The office of the Vizier is threatened internally."

"You want his role?"

"No. The Medeans will never let a wasakh rule overtly."

"So what?"

Tariq broke skewers to add to his, "Skirmishes on the South Road mount. Your raids intensify and your outfit grows in size. Even to rival the bandit princes."

A grape was placed amid the skewers, "The Vizier offers a formal Letter of Marque to The Rooster. Winning him to their side. Word of this is carefully dispersed into the Shalmanisar."

"Ah. A defector."

"Exactly Rooster, exactly. A defector who then is established as head of a new office under me; Sanjak of The Road, Enforcer for the Border. Indirectly monitoring and overseeing the merchant lords. For their safety."

"How provincial."

"Not for long."

A sweep of the hand and grapes as well as olives began to war to the left, while nuts began to start a new path on the imagined river. Going both ways.

"War drives the Shalmanisar to trade by water rather than by land. Opening doors that were never thought imaginable. Our goods find their way to the Glasslands of Saramish. Gold no longer fattens the pockets of merchants but enriches Nefara. We become the envy of all our neighbors. Even the Ivory Queen."

"And the gold?"

In a half second, Tariq's eyes flashed something. Gold fire around his pupils. Maybe a reflection from one of his rings—the sun's glare was piercing even the perforated wall.

"We build what few even dream of."

Honesty resounded in those words.

But the Rooster was still wary. Little peculiar details lingered in his mind. How the Qadi referred to the White Dove as 'the' instead of 'our'. Or how calculated the man had been at his every rejection or counter. As if he'd known how the conversation would play out to the last syllable.

This turban-wearing bureaucrat could not be underestimated.

And yet.

Out the diamond holes in the perforated window, Rooster joined Tariq and stared off at the cityscape. At the fan palms that swayed, long-legged and beaked white birds who flew, and the orange-gold of the desert sun. He imagined floating over the domes and flat-topped roofs into that herald of heat and light. Even in the shade, he felt frozen in the hypnotic haze of the sun and foreign sights.

This hadn't been his idea of a retirement. Or his past enemy's of exile.

Did he want to end up penniless and desperate in his final days? An end without purpose or legacy? Rooster lingered on the grim prospect of becoming like Darwish.

"Well, my friend? What do you say?"

"What is it exactly you want me to do?"

Despite the scroll emblazoned with the seal of the Vizier of Nefara that said he was supposed to be there, Rooster felt like an imposter entering the White Kasbah. Even as the side gates of the fortress palace opened and he was beckoned inside. The feeling that every set of eyes upon him saw right through the veneer of the mercenary captain—strolling in with that swagger—and waited for him to slip up.

But the moment never came.

Not until at least, the prison warden stepped out into the sunlight. Flanked by equally bored-looking guards who dwarfed him in comparison.

The White Kasbah was massive as it was curious. A great and domed thing with all the accoutrements of a sandstone castle, yet its eastern gate that Rooster passed by was filled with nobles. It was storied but not decrepit. There were obvious additions to the construction with its outer baileys and fighting platforms, turrets and yet the main building—and particularly the prison gate—had to have dated back a hundred plus years.

But the scoring and scarring on the sandy walls couldn't have been older than a few years. The burn marks hadn't completely washed away.

Whoever controlled the Kasbah had paid for it with blood.

The warden wasn't a Medean but some other type of unruly-haired brooding-lipped desert dweller. Sallow compared to the others.

"Yes?" the man shaded his eyes.

"Good day to you. I'm here on a warrant from the office of the Qadi al Tughur to collect prisoners."

"It's never a good day when I have to do somebody else's work. The Qadi of what? The border?"

Rooster handed him the first scroll.

The warden called for a reader, who read it and pointed out the marks of legitimacy. It became worrying the longer the group studied the scroll.

"Who are you?"

"I am Rooster, Captain of the Birds of Prey. It says it right there in the document."

Warden wasn't having it, "Yes that's on the document. But I've never heard of your company."

"We're a new outfit. Formed up out of the remains of the Duskhounds. You've heard of them?"

"Sure..."

The warden wasn't looking at the other scrolls—he was sizing up Rooster. The visual dressing down didn't take more than a moment but even the other guards became nervous.

"Last I heard the Duskhounds didn't have a gharib in their ranks. What rank did you hold last?"

"First Sergeant."

"Didn't know that Dawali let white dogs boss his tribesmen around," the tone was anything but conversational.

Hadn't Tariq assured him this was going to be a breeze? Did the Qadi title really mean anything?

Didn't matter—he needed to work these guys and make them believe him.

Rooster leaned harder into the idea of the cocky mercenary, thumbing his belt, "Old Darwish recruited me out of the Jewelport. I understood he had a fatwa against him by the other hill tribes. You know what those are, right?"

"Don't lecture me on my culture gharib," the warden hissed.

A distant cousin to the hill tribes, perhaps? Getting

someone angry enough to get sloppy was a start.

"Well if you're asking, the Duskhounds got disbanded. Old Darwish had a mutiny," Rooster thought quickly, out of desperation, "By his fellow Dawali. It was a bloodbath. Turns out there was a bounty too. Happened in the Brushlands, just outside Kahil."

Close enough to the truth. He hoped it shone in his eyes.

Warden whispered something to his guards, and they whispered back.

"Disheartening news. I had a cell reserved for their captain, if he ever crossed my path," the warden grinned a smile only a mother could love, "And now you're a dog to this Qadi of whatever. Just what business do you have here, white dog?"

Doing a bit of peacocking, Rooster unrolled the remaining scrolls without doing them the courtesy of handing them over. It sure pissed off the warden. They squabbled and squawked about someone named Musha and just who this Qadi of Tughur thought he was.

Eventually there was a compromise.

The guards took him down the stairway. Under the belly of the Kasbah was a torchlit hell. The ceilings were unnaturally tall and the exposed bones of the structure indicated there was serious thought chiseled into the complex. Great archways that led to nowhere, ten men high.

"Must keep a lot of prisoners down here eh?"

Warden snorted, "With what to feed them?"

Sounds of picks breaking rocks. A cacophony of labor. The glow they approached was dust-clotted. They approached a wall of scaffolds. On, under, and around it were the prisoners—their long chains attached to poles. Hundreds of them chewing at what looked like a great archway that had long been walled off.

"We would hang them but the Shah wants everything that was built over."

"Built over?"

The warden laughed dryly, "Listen to this *ahbil*. So you

want your prisoners to fight yes? Oszan and Bedir, fetch our guest the little *chelbs*."

Both guards joined him in chortling. They returned later with a small gang of four.

Rooster knew he'd been screwed the moment they returned to the sunlight and got a good look at his recruits. Only one of the prisoners looked fair—a prime specimen, a dark-skinned brute that towered over everyone. Then an emaciated weasel of a man who could have blown over by a light breeze. The last two were but boys. All caked in dust.

"I have orders to recruit twelve," Rooster spun on the warden, "You owe me ten more."

"These are four. Your math is bad, white dog."

"You gave me one and a half. Those boys can't be a day older than fifteen."

The guard named Bedir started to unchain the prisoners by their ankles. When he got to the boys, he barely unchained one before the kid struck him with a kick to the shins and began to wrestle him to the ground. Guards began to jeer from the battlements until Oszan pummeled the kid into submission. It happened again when the other one was unchained.

Wily little bastards. The kids were goddamn feral. If backbreaking prison labor wore them down at all, neither showed it.

Both guards came back bruised—their egos even more so. Above the onlookers clapped and whistled.

"You see gharib, they are fighters," the warden clapped him on the back, "You don't need twelve with these devils. I would not unchain their hands, however."

He growled and it wasn't playing a part anymore, "This wasn't the deal."

"The sincerest of apologies but I have much to do. Take it up with your Qadi. Or visit the slaver's market in the Caravan Court."

Those great doors of the White Kasbah closed but Rooster could hear the bastards laughing underground.

Big black was called Gamba. From someplace that the Medeans didn't have a word for or just simply didn't care to know. Strong as an ox with the temperament of a mouse. Even as they went looking for provisions at the Silverway bazaars the big black man would jump at every loud noise. A muscled coward was still just a coward.

Great.

If weasel-man would have proved a useful charge he'd never know—the moment Rooster turned his head, the lanky character disappeared. Perhaps he should have been grateful it happened before they got in a bad spot.

And then there were the boys.

Rooster almost lost it when he noticed their absence. A bad day was turning for the worst.

Someone tugged on his cloak, a merchant of low status with a caterpillar for a unibrow, "Gharib you must control your slaves! If you wish, I have reed switches that produce the most painful welts. You will thank me later."

Turns out the boys were using the public fountain as their personal bath and making a spectacle. Jeering at guards and merchants alike.

Rooster snuck up and hauled both back out of the water, throwing them against the wall.

"Listen up shitheads. I'm your god now. If you're not..."

Words disappeared from his vocabulary. It wasn't obvious from behind but now that he got a good look at the two—sans dirt and grime—he was shocked beyond words.

At first, he mistook them for gharibs.

Both were suntanned but distinctly white-skinned. Freckled across the nose and on their shoulders. Their hair orange-gold and kept back in braided mohawks. And their eyes were the most profound; an amber color, like an eagle's.

And they were identical twins.

Rooster fell back a pace.

He'd seen men with eyes like this before—the bandits he and Darwish had taken out; the sareq.

One of them made a deft movement to attack him—his

clone grabbed him and shoved him back against the wall. Whispering in a tongue that sounded almost like Medean.

"A silver crescent and I'll give you a switch for each of them," the merchant called, grinning ear to ear, "A grand deal!"

"I've had enough deals for a day."

"Ah. Your choice gharib! Do not underestimate a Shemsari slave! They break harder than a horse."

"What did you say?"

Caterpillar-brow shook his head, "Whoever sold you them did not tell you? The nomads aren't worth the bargain! I always say a good Nebetian is worth a hundred Shemsari."

Rooster turned back to the boys—to the yellow stares that could have belonged to beasts.

So these were them; the infamous Shemsari.

Which made him realize he'd fought and slain several of them.

Well, he'd be a donkey's uncle.

The one who had held his brother back inexplicably bowed deeply and said, "*Kadhib, walamaut yantahi*."

His twin spit at the Rooster's boots and bared his teeth.

From across the fountain, caterpillar-brow cried out, "Sleep with one eye open gharib! For they will surely cut your throat and steal your horse if you let them. Blessings of the White Dove and his Grace upon you this day!"

الجنوب طريق
The South Road

A spire of dust swirled above the depthless desert ahead, its origin concealed beneath a series of hills. Conjured by travelers or by wind dervishes—it was impossible to tell.

"Hey, either of you knuckleheads have a spare eagle to go scout that out for me?"

His joke washed over the Shemsari teens like grains of sand. It did however earn him a black look from the angry one. From now on he'd call him Angry. The subject of controlling raptors was a sore one—apparently the gift has passed over the boys. Or so the first twin had said before sealing his jaw shut. The one he called Reasonable.

Helpful bunch, his 'bandits'.

Rooster descended from his perch on the rocky shelf, approaching the caravan master and his wife. Both stood like limestone statues, hands on hips, "Well I think we'll be safe."

Param sighed in relief while Dhima wasn't satisfied, "Why did we waste an hour to hear this, Master of Swords?"

"Your welfare is my job. I had to assess a threat. It proved to be big fat nothing. You're welcome."

Dhima narrowed her eyes. The woman had a sixth sense to divine fresh bullshit from a pile of old manure. She wasn't half as dumb as her worm of a husband.

"This is the third time we've stopped our wagons for this," she wheeled on him, "You hired an idiot Param!"

"Come now please Dhima, listen to him. Even just his presence will deter the dogs of the road. We will be glad of it when our melons sell at Tyhri. You will see."

"Fool-bastard," she flew off.

Rooster gave his fakest of encouraging smiles and went back to Nereel.

The bitch was right to doubt him. There was no threat ahead. Not at least to them.

As for the Shalmanisar wagon train that traveled back to Nefara with minimal guard, Rooster couldn't say the same. Any day now they'd see the green flags of the Sabean-run merchant guild on the horizon. All pretenses would go out the door and it'd be showtime.

Until then, they'd keep playing charter-guard and pretend like melons and their portly vendors were their top priority.

While the wagon was made ready to head out, he held out handfuls of oats to Nereel. The bay-colored horse was poking his head towards the back of the canvas, whinnying. The beast finally decided the oats were edible and munched.

"Picky aren't we," Rooster muttered.

Couldn't recall a horse back home that would turn its nose at good oats.

Out of the corner of his eye, he saw the Shemsari twins staring at Nereel. Talking conspiratorially.

"Got big plans to steal my horse? Eh?"

Angry made another one of his obscure threats, spitting in the sand. Must have meant a lot in Shemsari because his brother winced every time he lobbed a wad.

"Oi. You two."

They both stared.

Rooster took a step forward towards them. Brave or foolish, neither twin budged a hair. He took another.

Rooster took his last step so he stood right before them, "Do you see this? Go on."

Both of them looked at the hilt of the long knife of the sāreq.

"If you think I'm easy pickings, I took this off one of your dead cousins. Three of them came after me and the fourth ran for the hills. Don't think I won't cut your throats if you try anything—Mean Old Rooster doesn't play games."

Angry twitched. He was big mad alright. Maybe enough to try something stupid.

The boy spit this time, aiming for Rooster's face.

Unknown to Rooster there might have been a good reason for the vitriol. He'd been young and angry once. Wanted to burn the whole world down a few times over nothing. In some ways, he did—his little corner of farms and forests. Took him four decades to figure out that the youthful bonfire in his heart just burned up everything that mattered.

Now all he had was ashes and regret.

These Shemsari boys had potential but it was wasted without discipline.

Rooster snatched up the chains that united both boys by their manacles. And then before Angry could try his sweeping leg trick, he used the distraction to put his boot on the top of the boy's right foot. Just enough pressure to cause bruising.

Angry seethed through the pain. Brave. But stupid.

Rooster pressed harder, "I can take this off at any time. I'm choosing not to. You don't deserve your freedom. Get that through your thick fucking skull, kid."

Reasonable brother said something in their tongue to Angry, who said nothing.

Pressing harder on the boy's foot caused an involuntary yelp from Angry.

"Got it? Do we need more pain lessons?"

Had to hand it to Angry. Any more pressure and Rooster knew the foot would break.

In rough Patina, Reasonable begged, "Yes *sayidi* he understands. He is just a coconut-skull. Bahram knows."

"Lucky for you that you got a good brother," he grunted to Angry.

Enough lesson for one day now.

Rooster lifted his foot, "Excellent. I'm thrilled we understand one another."

Using the stick when a carrot was preferable was poor form generally. But in this instance it was worth the trade-off. Even if they didn't talk, the Shemsari did in fact understand him.

If there was any chance he could use them in a fight, it would have to start with a clear line of communication.

Meanwhile, the black giant was catching a dirt nap on a dune. Snoring like an ox. Rooster didn't bother keeping him chained. While a coward, he was practically docile. The only threat Gamba posed was to a bowl of syrupy dates.

He went over and kicked the man's back, "Come now, Gamba. Let's not waste our client's time eh? We have precious melons to protect."

The road between Nefara and distant Tyhri was forced to hug the Ptahira—nothing but the hoof-beaten path and orange-tan oblivion in all directions. It was a low desert that occupied stray bushes and the occasional patch of boulders. A land that proved altogether a punishing existence. Save the river.

What could live in this land except devils, the Rooster didn't know. Even devils might have passed this place up if they needed something to feed on.

It was warm for winter but not unbearably so. He couldn't imagine what kind of madness existed in the brains of merchants who would dare this hellish road in the scorching heat of summer.

Over the course of days they saw nothing but lonely wind dervishes and hazy mirages. On a crude map by the Qadi he marked about halfway between the cities. The same landscape as ever, though distant bony ridges of blood-red mesas were emerging at their right.

Tariq said that horsemen could make the journey inside a week. Wagon trains and caravans in two.

They hit the seventh day and saw nothing on the horizon.

Sun came up and went down.

Where the hell were the Shalmanisar?

A canine yip, followed by a puff of sand as the beast slunk out of sight.

A taunting gesture.

Those black-maw spotted dogs were back. They'd been haunting the caravan at a distance for a few hours now.

"The hyenas will devour my camels. Quick! Shoot them with a bow, Master of Swords!"

Rooster eyed the skinny dogs.

Clever things kept to the other side of the dunes. Impossible angle to hit. They'd seen more than a few arrows in their lifetime he reckoned. Probably learned to follow the caravans since they were pups—waiting for a camel to stray off or a horse to break a leg.

"Shoot! Shoot now!"

Rooster sighed and unstrung the bow across his knees, "Would be a waste of good arrows. We'll put a watch out tonight when we sleep."

Param touched the beads at his neck, "No no. It is Daalshayvan who hunts us. We did not lay tribute for Wralaapur before we undertook this journey. The god of hunger is angry."

"Not my problem."

"It is now *gaurvas*! Your fate is united with ours."

Not likely.

He grunted, "If we're lucky this Daalshayvan will fatten himself on your wife and leave us alone."

Param turned the color of ice, lips quivering in anger. Crossing into the land of unholy shock as well. What was there to offend anyway? Dhima was many things but pretty or well-behaved weren't either of them.

The hyenas got bold and clustered up on a ridge ahead. Calling out their challenges to any other packs nearby; this was their hunt. Social creatures.

Gods aside, there was a legitimate reason to fear the beasts of this desert. The land whittled them as sharp as an arrowhead. Smart and desperate—a bad combination as any.

"Naming a soul marks one for Daalshayvan to eat. This is not good Rooster. Now I must trick Daalshayvan into forgetting her name!"

"Ah loosen up man. It was just a joke."

Sun slipped beyond their reach and left the land in darkness. They'd set up a camp long before the last rays on the highest point around—a flat-topped hill that provided a decent overwatch. Rooster had them face the wagons outward as a makeshift wall, camels to fill the gaps, and themselves in the center. Circling the wagons worked better against bowmen but it would provide defense against the opportunistic jaws of the hyenas. At least break up their packs if they swarmed.

Granted there wasn't a god among them anyway.

Next Rooster had them start a fire. Without any wood for miles, they improvised; camel-pies. The slaves of the merchants held their noses as they collected the dried out disc-shaped droppings and began to pound them with rocks. It stunk but it provided the light and smoke they needed. Killing the flies off that hung around the camels was a bonus.

With a bucket for a stool, Rooster sat and whittled the staves he'd brought with him.

"What are you doing," Dhima demanded across the fire.

"What does it look like I'm doing," he replied, tossing the first spear next to him.

The merchant's wife wrapped her shawl tighter and lifted her chin, "Wood cannot slay Daalshayvan you fool. The Hungry God will wait until we sleep and then take the unrighteous first. That will be you. By your insides, you'll be dragged across the desert until your soul is eaten."

"Lovely."

Rooster nicked his finger finishing up on the second spear. He sucked his forefinger and then held out the sharpened stave towards Gamba, "Here you go."

But the big black man wouldn't accept it, shaking his head.

"Come on now. Just take the stick."

It wasn't any use—the man just simply wouldn't carry it. Even with the spear forced in his hand. Brute dropped it every time. Rooster sighed.

That darkness around them was getting oppressive. A

faint whisper of howls and yips echoed off the dunes. Or maybe that was his imagination.

The Shemsari boys sat furthest from the fire, staring at the spears.

Rooster took both and leaned them against the wagon. Thought to offer them to the merchants but realized it was folly. Instinct told him these people were pacifists.

So instead he drew out Awakener across his knees, a vial of oil, and the whetstone he'd gotten from Nefara. And began to work the blade. The camp filled with the sound of steel sharpening.

That and the merchants breaking out their meals of pickled vegetables and odorous fruits mixed with rice. They ate and chattered amongst themselves.

Working his blade was an old ritual—it brought him great comfort.

Reminding him of days past and simpler times.

"So," Param had wandered over like a lost puppy, "This weapon you have slain many beasts with?"

"If you mean men? Yes."

The merchant frowned, "Vorshthu does not warrant this. A man should never be treated like the beast of the field unless he has committed great blasphemy."

"Those men did."

"They blasphemed the gods?"

"Sure did. Just one."

Param edged closer, "Yes? What was this great one's name?"

"Awakener; God of Cutting Men in Half."

"I have not heard of this god."

Rooster finished polishing the surface of the great blade. Bastard swords they called them halfway across the world. On account, they were held by dishonorable sellswords—for the most part. The perfect weapon for a man who couldn't afford a horse or a nice set of kit but could storm a keep with confidence.

"Hope that you never do," he tried to say with a straight face.

"Could you provide a demonstration? Of your weapon?"

Sorry little Param, probably trying to keep away from his wife for a bit longer. Almost deserving of pity.

"Why not? You ever been in a sword fight Param?"

"Never," the man looked elated, bouncing on his heels.

Perhaps they were pacifists only by tradition.

Rooster didn't bother to unsheathe Awakener. A wrong move and the tubby merchant would be meeting his beloved Vorshthu sooner than he would have liked. Wouldn't do to spill innocent blood on their first voyage anyhow.

Unless they were a Shalmanisar guard that tried to play the hero.

All while they danced in the firelight, he noticed the Shemsari boys doing something on the edge of the hill that faced the river. Kneeling in the sand, drawing something with their fingers.

He was distracted enough Param slipped and hit him in the ribs with the stave, "Ha! I struck a fatal blow to the Master of Swords! I'm learning."

"You're a real killer now. Hey, let's take a breather."

Param noticed his current focus, "Don't bother with your slaves. The shyvan are practicing their witchcraft."

"What do you mean?"

The tubby man wiped the sweat from his brow, "It is a false religion Master of Swords. One that claims their god needs no idols or tribute—ha! A thousand lifetimes of the worm will teach them to think twice about ignoring Vorshthu and his Grace."

"What god is that?"

Param uttered it like it was hot soup on his tongue, "Bahram, of the Sun."

If this was the notorious Bahram, Rooster wanted firsthand observation.

The man babbled, "Vorsthu will not be pleased that you are choosing the sun pagan!"

"I'll take my chances."

He walked up to them and saw the icon in the sand. It

was a perfect circle the size of a shield, comprised of concentric lines of text in a tongue he didn't understand. The image itself was hypnotic despite him being ignorant to the meaning. Perhaps a trick of the light but it did not seem to have an end or a beginning.

The Shemsari boys froze when his shadow entered the circle.

"What is it? What does it mean?"

Reasonable turned to him, "You darken the Lord's way."

"How so?"

The boy was not unkind in his demand, "Your shadow gharib. Stand back."

Wise-ass calling him white. Like the pot calling the kettle black.

He did however, follow the instruction, "Happy? What is it?"

In a matter of fact tone, Reasonable said, "J'awed."

"Which is?"

"The Pathway."

"The pathway to what?"

No one had ever asked that apparently, since both boys looked at one another.

"It is just this. The Pathway. Shown to us by Bahram."

"Tell me something, whatever your name is. Does your Bahram ever take the form of an eagle? Does he ever get bored up there on his sun throne and decide to pester mere mortals like us? Take holy shits on our heads?"

Reasonable took a moment, "Our father thought so."

"Yeah? Where is he now?"

"Dead," the boy's teeth clenched and Angry beside him balled his fists up.

Judging by their reactions this had to be a recent development.

"Did he die well?"

To Rooster's shock, it was not Reasonable who spoke up but his brother, "No. He was slain by the bastard flame-eater Kizzuran. *Saya-mutu.*"

Every syllable harsh and every tooth gnashed. It wasn't anger but a raw pain that could be felt even from afar. The boys' radiated it like a volcanic glow.

Poor bastards.

Deep down, the Rooster had an inclination of the feeling. Even if he never admitted it aloud. A weakness maybe—not being honest with one's own heart. At least he knew his shortcomings.

Rooster turned to both and dipped his head, "Well…I'm sorry to hear that. Truly."

They turned their backs on him.

What was he playing at? These weren't his sons. Was that how he was starting to feel? He almost felt disgusted with himself.

He looked at the icon of the J'awed one last time.

"Fuck it," time to call it a night.

Afar on a dune, a hyena laughed.

Trust was a mistake. Trust lead to treachery. And on this night that treachery took the form of heavily-wrought manacles that were cutting off the circulation on the Rooster's wrists as he startled himself from slumber.

Still fuzzy from lack of sleep, he blinked up at them and the chains that attached him to the wagon wheel. How did those get there? Why was it dark still out?

It all dawned on him.

There was an empty fan of sand where the boys had been. They even bothered to unmake the J'awed icon. Sand art kicked to oblivion.

"Sons of bitches," he kicked out and started to raise hell, "Param, wake up. Get up, you fat lump."

The merchant came with a lamp, "Master of Swords! Oho! You've tied yourself for the Daalshayvan. Have you decided to sacrifice yourself for the bounty of our journey?"

"No, you idiot. Those desert rats did this. There's a key on my neck…"

Except it wasn't. The boys had taken that too. And the horse, along with all the provisions he'd kept in the saddlebags.

Rooster knew what they were up to.

What else would young and brash boys do? Who knew the identity of their father's killer and had easy access to a horse?

Noise woke up Gamba. Man shone like polished onyx in the moonlight. He could have disappeared in the shadows when he blinked until he smiled.

"Have you any steel picks? Or metal tools?"

Param shook his head.

Back behind the wife was fretting—not about Rooster's predicament of course, but whether the Shemsari had stolen their precious cargo. Shrill and tyrannical, she had her slaves tear the wagons apart while interrogating each one to find out who was responsible for their escape. Down to having them drop their damned loincloths.

"Anything. Does your wife have hairpins? Those could do."

The merchant went to Dhima like he was on his way to the gallows. She was currently pulling the hair of a female slave, shrieking into the poor girl's ear.

Rooster felt himself being lifted up and turned.

Gamba groaned wordlessly—the man was pulling on the spoke of the wagon wheel. Muscles rippled and strained. Jungle wood began to bend...the wheel broke. Gamba beamed proudly, holding the shattered remains of the wooden hub.

Well, that was great. While he was free, the Rooster still had manacles and a chain between them, "Shit. That helps though. Thanks Gamba."

Gamba's mouth was open and now he knew why the man didn't talk; there was a stump where his tongue should have been.

Rooster started to look for a trail of hoof prints. They'd lead to the river. Without another freshwater source besides the Ptahira, the boys would be forced to hug it all the way east.

Nothing but day's old three-clawed dog prints. Unless

Shemsari had some clever trick to cover up horse tracks, they weren't using the river.

"Where did you go, little bastards?" Rooster found his way back to camp.

A grunt from the other side of the wagons—Gamba was waving him down, pointing at the sand. Drawing something. No way. The missing hoofprints were heading in the entirely wrong direction.

"North? What the hell is to the north?"

Tariq had warned him; The Sunscar Wastes laid northward. A brutal badlands borne from hell. Devoid of any water. If the boys were heading there, it was to their doom.

"Stay here with the merchants Gamba. I'll be back by sundown tomorrow."

Param and Dhima were quarreling. They didn't even notice when he woke a pair of the hump-backed camels and led them away from the fire and the bickering. Some of the slaves did and began to snicker. He made the sign of slashing his own throat. They didn't stop. So he made the sign of breaking chains. That shut them up. Morally, Rooster didn't mind.

These Sabean melon merchants were as sharp as rocks. Outwitting them was a testament to willpower. If these slaves lacked that, there was nothing Rooster could do to save them.

The desert did not favor the weak.

Mounting a camel was like trying to vault over a high fence made of fur—he failed and landed on his butt. The camel snorted and stomped its hoof. Took him more times than he would have admitted to finally swing his weight onto the beast.

He clenched up. How did anybody ride these things barebacked that wasn't a woman?

Just like a horse, right?

Rooster started to spur the thing with his boots when a giant shadow trotted up behind. Gamba, waterskins slung over his shoulder and clutching the spears and bow in one hand, grabbed the reins of the other camel.

"You're too big to ride, big man."

Gamba just started to jog and tow the beast. With legs like that, his stride was the envy of any pony.

Dawn came heavy with its lidless gaze, turning everything crimson in its wake. The shallow sea of orange dunes washed up against jetties of near-black mountains that emerged like dark scars upon the land. Petrified forests of thorny brush and warped cacti that jumped up like green-blue geysers, the strange oblong plants sprung up from the ether.

A land that rain had not graced for centuries.

The Sunscar Waste was hell embodied.

Wind began to pick up and toss sheets of hot sand in the air to tear at the flesh of the living.

Rooster clamped his eyes shut. The headwrap the sellswords favored in Nefara protected his mouth but did nothing to keep the grit out of his eyes.

Gamba was impassive. Sand and sun drowned him and yet he remained unaffected.

They followed the trail and there was no sign of the boys.

Soon they'd have to dismount and walk—Nereel might have been of the desert stock, but no horse could ride forever. Not even with teenagers on his saddle.

For a land that was supposed to be barren, there were a disturbing amount of bones in this place. And broken caravans. As the sun rose higher in the sky, there were signs of the hyena and something else. Prints identical to the desert dogs, only far larger. And unless he was hallucinating they seemed to be spaced apart like the gait of a man's.

A hellish wind blew from the tops of those arid mountains, peeling sand away from their black bones. The speed of the winds here was measurable.

He did not have a prayer that they'd find the boys and his horse intact. Not in a place like this.

More sand came and he screwed his eyes shut.

A sound carried in that gale—animalistic. Barking followed by a strange shriek-like laugh. Underscored by a deeper and darker sound. Almost like a man's.

It came from the ridge ahead.

Rooster's skin crawled while Gamba came to a dead halt, "What's it, big man?"

Irrational fear overtook the big black mute. He dropped the spears and began to backpedal.

Rooster wheeled his camel back and blocked Gamba from leaving, "If you're going to run, leave me the beast. Those boys won't make it back on foot."

Gamba twisted his head back in the direction of the strange sounds and whimpered.

"Come on you big lump. Give me those," he pulled the reins away, "Either you get left behind or you come with."

Another howl on the wind and Gamba made the smart move. He reached his plate-sized palm up and scrunched those sausages for fingers to gesture he wanted the reins back.

"Smart man."

Fate had a funny sense of humor today it seemed.

He drove the camel around the cornice of a small dark mountain and found Nereel, kneeling under the shade of a sandstone shelf that had been cleaved in two by time. The horse recognized him and tossed his mane. It was munching on some oats.

"Traitor," he muttered.

No Shemsari boys anywhere to be seen.

Were they really this stupid, thinking he wouldn't follow them? It seemed so.

Taking the horse and leaving the two knuckleheads to their fate would have been fitting. And cruel. Unnecessarily so. The Duskhounds could have done the same to him back with the cannibals and their cookpots. Instead, they gave him freedom.

And the hard fact was that he couldn't take the

Shalminsar caravans alone.

Rooster sighed, "Look at me Gamba. Going soft."

The big black man ambled over and began to stroke Nereel's flank. Knew what he was doing enough to calm the horse down. Could have had a stint as a stableboy.

"Stay here and watch the beasts. I'll be right back."

This time Gamba obeyed.

Maybe it was time to get himself a squire and he had the perfect candidate. Once he dealt with the matter at hand.

Jackal laughs echoed off the rock walls.

Rooster followed them.

Petrified reefs of igneous rock weaved themselves into slot canyons and hollow kettles—giant natural rooms with sunlight peering in from the tops. Folds of black and gray rock crafted by erratic creators.

Two pairs of sandal prints led deeper into the sandstone maze.

With the naked blade held out to the side, Rooster kept his eyes ahead and flickered down only to see where they led. A gap in the canyon opened wide to steep dune banks.

Where he found the Shemsari boys pressed flat like snakes on their bellies. Watching something ahead that he couldn't see.

But he could hear it.

Hyena packs were calling out to one another—had to be close. They snickered and laughed until that other thing spoke. Chatter died instantly when that booming and guttural wobble of near-sentience garbled. A hackle-raising sound.

Rooster was and had been a military man. He knew when something was being commanded. There was no mistaking the vocal deference given to deep calls. It was marshaling the beasts. Yet it sounded so similar to them.

Unsettling.

He took a position just behind them and cat-called, "Pst-pst. Enjoying an afternoon of pastries and chai are we?"

Both Shemsari boys jumped out of their skin.

Despite being identical twins he could already tell them apart by their resting faces. Reasonable's brows flew to the sky while Angry's furrowed.

"I wouldn't try that if I were you," he noted the wood spear starting to hover out of the corner of his eye in Angry's grip, "I'm fast for an old dog. Good trick back there, tying me up though. Real clever."

Reasonable said something in their native tongue. The spear tip fell back from Angry's hand.

"While I have your attention, I have my horse back and two camels for us to ride back on. Let's make this smooth, shall we? Drop your spears down to me and we're going to walk back all quiet like."

"*Ayreh feek*," Angry said colorfully.

"Listen shit-stain. You keep up the attitude and you can walk barefoot back to camp. I'm feeling merciful today."

Reasonable was about to say something but craned his head, whispering again.

Even Angry turned.

Rooster hated being the last one to find out. He decided both boys weren't a threat on account of his big sword and their sticks. He climbed the hill to see.

Nothing.

Just an empty valley of orange-red sand, dominated by a lonely anthill. A big one, pocketed with holes. Lines in the earth raked their way up to it. But there was nothing inside it, nor anything that moved in the lowland between the mountains. It looked like all the other ones before.

"Impressive. You should have hugged the river. Would have dodged me maybe. Instead you two clowns came up here—and for what?"

His voice carried off into the valley.

Instantly Rooster recognized something was off—there wasn't any more jackal sound.

Both Shemsari boys were going pale.

"We were going to hunt the *insan dhaybi*," Reasonable muttered, his eyes fixed on the scene ahead, "It is the

J'awed."

"What do you mean?"

"We cannot slay Kizzuran without first becoming a man."

Rooster snorted, "And your holy text tells you that?"

"Yes. We must initiate by taking the blood of a beast."

"Well, you can kiss the J'awed goodbye for the next little while. I didn't pull you two out of that dungeon so you could go on a hunting expedition."

Angry spun to face him, "You are a loud ogre and now the insan dhaybi is warned of us!"

Rooster had half a mind to strike the kid across the face. For spite.

Something caught his eye—out there at the great anthill. A shape that walked towards them on two feet. Like a man. But it drew close and disquieted that notion. It had the face and body of a hyena with the limbs of a great and dark man, bristling with black hair. Finger bones that clattered from a necklace about its neck, along with human ears and other appendage trophies.

It opened that black maw and out poured that guttural, demonic laugh.

A werehyena. A monster in the flesh. A malign and literal devil.

Rooster stiffened and felt his legs go numb.

From behind it poured a score of hyenas from the anthill. A den of kinds. The drag marks that dug into the earth up to its shadowy confines made sense now.

Sinister laughing rang in his skull—like the werehyena could penetrate his consciousness and sink its teeth into his skull.

When he came to, the boys were both trying to pull him down from the sandy bank. Screaming at him in their language. All fuzzy, Rooster could barely comply.

Next thing he knew they were running back through the slot canyons where they came. All around them were the sounds of the hyenas laughing their hellish laughs. Like they were nipping at their heels.

Rooster knew he was rattled—no different than the first battle he'd endured. Reality was warping before his very eyes. He knew what monsters in a book looked like but to see one in person was jarring.

Only instinct kept him from dropping the sword.

"Sayidi! Behind you!"

Rooster blindly swung and felt impact. A hyena faster than the rest had tried to take a bite out of him. Awakener had struck true. The savannah dog had been cut nearly in two, its blood sprayed the rock like paint on a canvas.

That shook him right out of the daze.

"Get back to the camels," he yelled back at the boys, "Run you whoresons."

They did and found their way back to Gamba and the beasts. The big black man responded quickly and tossed the Shemsari boys both onto a camel. He grabbed the reins of Nereel and began to run out, leading the camel.

Rooster didn't know how he did it the first time, but he was up on the camel and riding like an expert.

"Hyah!"

Familiar terrain was passing them by in the early afternoon light. The camels did well in a gallop, but they were no horses. Nereel was keeping up steady but panting. Poor thing was spent. Riding day and night could maim even a good horse. Those Shemsari boys would get the whip if they did any damage to him.

Rooster didn't dare look behind just yet.

They were out of the canyon but the sounds of the pack were getting closer.

Hyenas were gaining on them. And their devilish master.

What he wouldn't give right now for a good lance and fresh horse.

The Shemsari boys were calling out in their native tongue. But what was more interesting was how they rode the camel—each was cross-legged and balanced perfectly, one facing forward and behind. Angry took up the rear, leveling out a spear.

"Wait," Rooster shouted at him, "Until they're close enough you can smell them."

The first pack appeared and aimed for Gamba.

"Here they come!"

Angry threw prematurely and the spear landed harmlessly in the sand. The hyena yipped and bit at the black man's calf—barely missing.

Rooster ripped the reins sideways and managed to lean down and snag the fallen spear—it was upright, thank whatever desert god was beaming down on them.

He kicked his camel forward and speared down at the nearest wild dog. It wasn't a clean shot but the beast panicked and rolled into the sand. He tossed it back to Angry and thrust Awakener down on the hyena that hunted Gamba. This time the steel dip drove right into the wild dog's shoulder and hit flesh—it shrieked and flopped over.

Both boys cheered.

But there were more to come.

Rooster looked back over his shoulder and saw a horde that swept up with gray-black muzzles and spotted hides. Hundreds of teeth and snapping jaws. And gaining amongst the beasts was something out of legend—the werehyena.

Outrunning was the only hope of survival now.

He'd take any kind of divine intervention. If he had the tongue to pray to a god that would listen.

The wind was kicking up and whipping them good as they ran, buffeting the camels.

The boys shouted and pointed towards the sky.

Rooster followed their fingers; some kind of hawk or eagle descended. Logic dictated that it couldn't have been his bird. Hundreds of miles separated from where they'd last saw each other.

It wheeled above their mad dash, gales tugging at its red-gold feathers. The beaked visitor cried out to the group.

"*Abi*," one of the boys cried out.

Another eagle cry and the bird suddenly lifted out of there as swift as it came. The boys were shouting at it, begging for it to stay.

Rooster suddenly saw why.

"Devil's fiery crotch."

To their left, the entire sky was going brown. A wall of what looked like boiling sand picked up by a whirlwind had suddenly appeared. Each moment it was growing in size and length to cover the entire horizon. Approaching them with unholy speed.

"What is it?"

"Sandstorm," Reasonable shouted to him, "Fury of the djinn! We must find shelter sayidi!"

"No chance. We have to lose these dogs!"

The Shemsari boy bowed his head towards him, "As Bahram wills."

"Whatever!"

Seconds before they would get hit by this storm from the gods.

Rooster took his chance, bringing the camel to a halt. He brought his bow to the ready, drawing the best arrow he had. Keeping both eyes open as he'd learned once on the long bow. He waited for the big ugly head of the werehyena to pop up before he loosed.

The arrow burred as it snapped through the air.

Before the quivering string could come to a stop, the sandstorm devoured the light.

In mad darkness they fought to survive. Animals screamed, overtaken by their nature. A monster howled, insatiable and insane. Steel and wood and teeth all sundered by the neverending storm of sand.

Dunes pulled apart and were thrown into the wind like the gods were giant children and this was their box of sand. Creation itself was being torn apart and churned into a maelstrom.

A break came in the shape of a vortex—the eye of the storm.

In the single wide beam of light, the melee revealed itself. Pieces of living and dead strewn revealed in the light.

Bones snapped and trampled.

Fear was rank in the air.

A knot of hyenas seethed, living and dead. Among them their twisted master, brandishing a spear made of a sharpened femur. An arrow embedded in its shoulder. Blood dripped from the werehyena's maw. It leapt like a nightmare and disemboweled the camel the Shemsari rode on. It would have done the same to the boys.

Gamba roared and threw himself at it, fists like mallets. Grabbing the monster's fur in handfuls and nearly snapping its spine. In a blur, he fell into a cloud of blood as claws shredded his chest.

Just enough time for one of the Shemsari boys to throw his spear.

If it landed true, only the sandstorm knew.

The back end of the storm hit them like a wagon.

Rooster howled and lost himself in the rage.

Nothing was left to bury in the aftermath. So much earth had been displaced, it'd been a miracle no one had been buried alive. Guilt made Rooster think that Gamba wasn't breathing by the time the sandstorm had passed and covered his dark body in the sand.

He almost believed himself.

Cruel how this world took and took. He'd grown rather fond of the black giant and his gentle nature. Taken too soon. The list of his fallen companions was growing too quickly.

"Goodbye Gamba. And thank you."

He swung the big sword down and the head of the beast rolled free with a wet thud. For a big ugly werehyena, it sure didn't take any silver or special magic stick to kill it.

Rooster was glad that most of its corpse was still buried in sand. Looking at the beast too closely gave him the shivers. If something like this could exist in this world, it made the imagination wander to dark places.

The head was adorned in fetishes of bone and teeth. A feature far too human to ignore. Rooster lifted it anyway.

Walked it over to the boys and dropped it at their feet.

"Congratulations, you're both men now. Or so says your J'awed. Thanks to you, we're down a good one too. Being a man means being accountable for your actions."

Both gave a long look at the oozing head of the monster.

And then back at him.

Angry mumbled something under his breath.

"What was that?"

Reasonable chimed in for him, "Jhabari says he is sorry. That he stole your horse. That he got your friend killed."

"So shithead has a name. And yours?"

"Jhamon. But it is I who would take the blame for my brother, sayidi. I know better than to let him be so reckless. We are ever grateful for you rescuing us from that place. If either of us are to be punished, let it be me sayidi."

Rooster threw his sword point-down into the sand and kneaded the bridge of his nose. He began to pace. He needed clear air. Not this dusty crap that crammed the sinuses.

"Jhamon?"

"Yes, sayidi?"

"Stop calling me that. You can call me Rooster."

The boy nodded.

"Secondly, he's your brother. He's a raging idiot but he's still your brother. And you have to look after him. Don't ever apologize for that."

Jhabari glared but winced as Jhamon punched him in the ribs.

"Next...do you have that key to my cuffs?"

"We threw it into the river," Jhabari laughed like one of the jackals, speaking in fluent Medean.

"You think that's funny? You're on shodding duty the next month. I heard your bunch likes horses so you'll be perfect for the job."

Before he could get another word in, their feathered friend cried from above. Back now that the threat of the sandstorm was gone. The eagle soared overhead.

Both boys cried up at it. That same word.

"I don't get it. What's your deal with the bird?"

Jhamon fixed him with those gold eyes, "It's not just a bird Rooster. It is Hazair!"

"Who?"

"Our father's eagle, whom he shared eyes and heart with. Bahram knows! It has to be him. See how his wing was once broken and compensates with his right? And he swims at an angle for missing a tailfeather. It is Hazair, watching over us!"

The Shemsari eagle known as Hazair did not just swoop over them. It dove down and deftly perched on the hilt of Awakener. Cockily gazing over and puffing its chest out.

Not at the boys but at him.

Well goddamn. There could be no mistaking it.

The eagle dipped its beak and tapped the hilt of the sword.

Both boys fell to their knees and Jhamon's voice shook, "Rooster, he knows you. Why?"

Jhabari hissed, "How?"

Because it wasn't just any eagle. Hazair was the same eagle that had followed him all these months. Witnessing his journey southward. Hazair was his oldest companion. In a weird way, his oldest friend now.

"Hello shaitan."

The second wagon smashed into the back of the first, rolled end over end, and came to a dusty conclusion—chaos perfected. Wheels were still rolling and an olive-green cloth fluttered down to the earth.

It only took one guard to lose an arm for the rest to get the message. Halberds and swords hit the sand in swift surrender. They were collected and dumped into a trench dug the night prior.

In a matter of three minutes, the Shamanisar caravan was taken without bloodshed.

Jhamon and Jhabari circled about like hounds, spears

held low and ready.

When Rooster cracked the back doors of the armored wagon he was shocked to find a tiny Sabean woman in its confines. Cradling a crossbow that was nearly her size. She pulled the trigger. A bolt flew forth.

If it wasn't for a lucky stumble, he might have had a forehead decoration in the shape of a feathered bolt. What wasn't was the fact that the finely dressed woman was dead when he chanced another look inside.

Poison, not unlike the stuff he'd encountered north of the Wall.

Bolts of silk toppled from the cargo. Worth ten times their weight in gold. They loaded up as much as they could on fresh horses and made their hasty escape. Not without leaving them with a name of who was responsible, of course.

Tariq's intelligence was dead right; they were caught with their pants down.

But all that—for a few armfuls of silk? The cargo felt more like an afterthought than the intended trade.

And the Sabean woman, her final moments in sheer terror froze on her waxy face. If she had guarded something then it went with her to the grave.

"Twenty-one to each of you. Spend it wisely," Rooster tossed each of the Shemsari their cut.

For a working man, the silver was half a year's worth in wages.

A calm breeze stirred their makeshift camp—spread between the thick bark of the palms that clustered on the banks of the Ptahira. Long-winged flies like emeralds were flitting in their final stage of life across the slow-churning waters. Nereel and the new horses they'd plundered drank from the river without a care in the world.

Rooster added the silk bolts to the hoard pile. Almost too fat to haul back to Nefara in one go. Not bad for a group of amateurs.

He slid off the hyena coat he'd worn and tossed it into

the saddlebags. He made the boys do the same. They'd be identified too quickly. Disguises would have to be worn on the road at all times now. Hopefully, their horses were anonymous enough to go unnoticed.

"Once I can secure us a fence, the silk will go towards the horses and equipment first. Then split up the rest."

Jhamon looked at his brother, then set the silk bag down on the sand, "It is generous Rooster. But I cannot accept. Neither can my brother."

"Shut up," Jhabari squirmed from his brother's grasp, "Don't ruin this for me."

"You know as well as I that we cannot take his gift."

Soon both silk bags were tossed back his way. The brasher brother stormed off in a huff. Kicking over the tower of silks on his way out.

Rooster snorted, "If it's guilt from before, forget it. You both earned this. It's an equal share."

"Do not be offended Rooster. But J'awed would prevent us. Our shame would be too great to receive such a gift while we already owe you our life," Jhamon explained.

"Makes no damn sense."

"To give a gift is to a great honor as it is to receive—it is law. Freedom is the greatest of all gifts Rooster. By rescuing myself and Jhabari we can only hope to give you our lives."

"Horse shit. He was going to slit my throat that night and take Nereel."

Jhamon looked over at his brother, "Jhabari does not see the J'awed as I do, it is true. But I have to. Father would not have wanted us to stray from the Pathway."

Sun was hitting that point of no return, scouring the land with dark red and orange. The silhouette of the Shemsari boy could be seen, stomping up the dunes and kicking up fountains of sand.

"He follows his own winds. But as you said wisely, I have to look out for him."

Rooster knew a hardhead when he saw one. Jhabari would be a tough nut to crack.

"Who is this Kizzuran?"

A curse in their tongue first, then, "*Thubān*. He is The Flametongue of the Floodplains. A prince of bandits. He is more dishonorable than a dog."

"Is he dangerous?"

Jhamon rubbed his knuckles, "He is Rooster. I fear my brother will be slain by Kizzuran, trying to avenge our father."

"We won't let him then, eh?"

Rooster saw genuine worry in the boy's face.

He reached out towards Jhamon and the boy recoiled out of habit. But didn't shy away when Rooster pinched his shoulder. Broad but skinny—a hint of lean muscle.

Being that age felt like a lifetime ago that he couldn't relate to.

What he did remember was when life felt like an insurmountable hill. The future a horizon he couldn't see.

"Listen, kid. Follow my lead and keep your brother in line. The rest will fall into place. Can't promise you shit won't happen but I won't make you betray your J'awed. We stay busy and we keep Jhabari away from this Kizzuran. Got it?"

Jhamon nodded, "Yes."

Rooster had a hunch that this Flametongue would be a problem later on. Luckily they had enough survival and politics and riches to act as a buffer. At least for the moment, anyhow.

Just as the sun was departing the mortal plane, the Shemsari boy knelt, took out an arrow, and began to drag it through the sand. Drawing out the familiar shape of the stylized text in the infinite circle of the J'awed.

This time Rooster watched intently. Silently.

Jhamon's timing was profound—almost sorcerous. Scratching the final letter of the holy icon right as the light died.

"Good. We don't worry about anything. We're the Birds of Prey. We're bad bandits now."

التجارة ميدان
Nomarch's Plaza

Bored, there was nothing for Rooster to stare at but the harsh-flowered hedges—bougainvillea that overtook the length of the walled gardens. Up close they hid thorns in their midst. Bees of a blood-red and shining carapace were attending the giant carpet of flowers, delicately avoiding the thorns. A servant had not been so delicate and left a few droplets of blood behind.

Details, details.

When the spice trader in the ivory headband and turquoise gown approached, it took a moment for Rooster to realize it was Tariq in disguise.

"If it isn't my old friend...?"

"Duqarat," said the bureaucrat falsely, taking him by the arm, "We have much to discuss."

Along the sandstone garden colonnades, they walked.

"I must say I'm impressed. I stopped into the Silkwell this morning and heard nothing but fear-mongering merchants. You've been busy."

"Our debut might have been too successful then. That much talk means triple the guard."

"While I would normally agree my friend, this is the Shalmanisar. They wrote the book on subtlety," they paused near a man-made pond decorated with lilies bearing flowers, letting nobles pass them by. Tariq watched their backs, "My spies already report they're devising a new stratagem. One that would conceal their identity from other caravans."

"Why go through the effort?"

Tariq smiled, "They're terrified."

Rooster thought to mention the woman with the crossbow but held his tongue back. Better to perseverate on that. This world he'd jumped headfirst into was one that operated on double meanings and false intentions.

"Now you're going to explain what they're terrified of. But I'm wondering if you have a field of silkworms you've hidden somewhere in the city."

"Ha. I suspect you never think any closer than the third step in your head Rooster."

"Oh I'm a gambler, I just hide it under a mask of someone who pretends to plot."

Tariq plucked a glass of wine from a servant who arrived without beckoning, "As am I. My confidence investing in you, however, has doubled. Not to kick a camel's corpse but my feelings about this moment of opportunity have only grown stronger since your debut."

"Maybe lay off the wine a little bit there."

The bureaucrat chuckled, "Indeed. But there's been a recent development. One that will hasten the arrival of our hour of history. The merchant lords are already acting upon it."

"What is that?"

"A magician never reveals his secrets. Come."

Up a stairway hewn of ivory stone they went and the garden walk became a stroll across a covered bridge that spanned one of the city's many canals. Flat-bottom barges and thin cigar-shaped boats moved to tunnels and landings beneath the surface of Nefara. Lamplight from boats that disappeared into oily darkness. Green-blue water washing up on sandstone edifices that dove deep.

An entire amphibious layer of structures lay below their feet that Rooster would have never suspected existed.

"They say an entire city exists below this one," Tariq said, "Palaces and temples that were buried under an age of sandstorms."

"Who says?"

"The Ishtari," at his confused look, the bureaucrat tapped the inside of his nose, "Long lost cousins of your young Shemsari companions. This was their kingdom once. Or so goes the myth. If one can believe their veracity."

"I've heard stranger things here."

"Yes well everyone here has a beggar's story to sell."

The bridge led them to a brass door. A stone turret with a narrow, cylindrical stairway that Tariq took them up. Back in the sunlight, they walked to a balcony that saw over the entire Ptahira Delta. A forest of green tropical foliage stood at their waist or below their feet. The turret was as high as those of the White Kasbah.

Tariq leaned on the ornate brass fence.

Show and tell time.

What the bureaucrat led him to see was the procession at the docks below. A kingly one. One hundred guards lined to either side of the quay, their halberds pointed to the sky. A color guard of the Ayubin marched solemnly through them, carrying a great banner over their heads; sea foam green bearing the image of a white dove. They rolled it like a great rug and fed it into an unmanned ship.

And then it was lit on fire.

On the docks, in the reeds, and even standing in the river, thousands of Nefarans gathered and watched the burning ship crawl down the delta. Their chatter was a low hum of confusion and anxiousness.

It was unclear whether they knew its meaning.

Who would blame them?

These people had been a sovereign one until recently—only months ago. They didn't have a dog in this political fight. Which king or lord died was irrelevant to their daily chores and the mundane droll of their lives. Whoever sat on the big cushions in the palace didn't change the fact that wheat needed to be shorn from the earth and cattle needed herding.

At the docks a great fat man in the garb of a guard captain was making a fuss, yelling at his Medean subordinates. When it resolved, there were dozens of cages brought out and shaken. White doves burst out and ascended into the smoky sky.

"And so the days of peace have ended. The Ivory Queen has already placed an embargo on all Nefaran goods. For days now the White Kasbah has heard a never-ending list of demands from the Caravan Court."

"More importantly, tidings of a moot have already reached my ears. Ayubin Khandaq has been called up to the Hijr al Nar. The boy king is moving quicker than I anticipated. He's gathering every ayubin, emir, and sultan in the realm to meet him at Hijraqalat."

It was evident that Tariq was irked and did not hide it well.

"Is this advantageous?"

"It's unprecedented," the man downed the wine cup and tossed the glass down the stone. It shattered and sent a cat into a sprint below, "No Shah has done this in over three hundred years. Since the forming of the Medean realm."

"What can we expect?"

"The Shalmanisar will not accept this embargo. They'll try to sway the Ivory Queen to see differently. They'll be impulsive and they'll get sloppy. They may even act on the Vizier. Put the screws on him. Musha is little more than a bridge-ogre with a badge of authority, he'll want to build up the guard so he can extort more."

Rooster didn't know all the ins and outs of Medean politics but he barely knew the lay of the land. And when a bureaucrat was trying pull his strings too quickly.

"If you want your bandit-puppet to move quicker, he's going to need more men," he began to negotiate, "I need twenty. And not prisoners either. I want hard fighting men with pedigrees. War horses for each one and a full kit."

Tariq raised a brow, "Men and horses cost a hefty purse. Funds like that go missing from the Vizier's coffers and there'll be questions."

"Don't forget that bandits don't often take risks."

"Judging by the talk about your raids I heard this morning, you may not have to draw your sword next time."

Without a contract and barely a handshake agreement, this wasn't going to work for Rooster. Especially given the increasingly volatile geopolitical situation. If the Qadi was replaced tomorrow, what guarantee would he have to not face the hangman's noose the next time he stepped foot in Nefara? None.

A puff of white feathers above as some predatory bird snatched a dove out of the air.

"Flattery might work on a belly dancer in your court Tariq—not on me. I want reassurance if I'm going to keep being your monkey. Levies with spears being the first."

"A monkey with his paws in my purse."

"So raise the tax on caravans moving across the border. Just a coin or two to not boil anyone over. Tariffs on the Ivory Queen. You'll find the money."

A shaped eyebrow raised, "Devious of you, Rooster. I forget you were once a fief lord."

If that's what others wanted to think, he wouldn't correct them. No one had to know how poorly his lordship had been—how little time he spent managing his lands. Learning how the bread was made, so to speak.

Being a lord and staying a lord were two very different things.

Tariq reached into his robes and handed him a badge wrought of pale gold, "Since you're robbing me anyhow. To anyone besides the Ivory Queen and her Immortals, you'll be an authentic mercenary on Her orders. Through and through. You didn't lose that letter of marque already?"

"No, I'm a somewhat competent monkey."

"Excellent. Now our true work begins."

"You mean mine?"

Tariq waved his hand, dismissive.

Coy as it was, there was some serious truth to the inequality of risk here.

Together they returned to the bridge but this time to the bazaar just inside the wharf. Gulls made a nuisance and were swatted by merchants under their colored awnings. Some of the wooden boxes of fruits were looking rather picked-through. Hanging from a hook was an enormous reptile—the length of a horse and nearly as wide, covered in armored scales—dangling from a butcher's hook. Pink meat was being stripped off its thick legs. Down another street was the long-lost cousin of Param, selling spoonfuls of brain from what looked like a bug.

If there was a limit to what these people would eat, Rooster didn't want to know.

His appetite all but vanished.

They stepped into a sunlit plaza and breathed fresh air. Tables were being placed out for the open-air drinking halls. Sizzling goat and some kind of yam brought back that hunger if even a hair.

"I'll see what I can do. Your demands are not insignificant. In the meantime, I do believe you might need help. A friend from your past crossed my path."

Rooster followed Tariq's hand as they stepped onto the rugs inside the wide sandstone tavern. Long-bearded men sat against the wall, smoking from long pipes. Girls with beaded braids and golden veils danced like river reeds.

But most importantly the familiar unruly head of a Terid imperial man.

"Antonius?"

A turn of the head, then a wide grin, "Well if it isn't granddad?"

"I'll let you two get to it. Look for my missive in the morning," Tariq didn't leave before pressing a heavy sack into his hand.

Rooster took a peek inside and clicked his teeth in annoyance. And regret for how he talked to the bureaucrat.

The damned bag was full of opals.

Blue smoke rose from the pipe Antonius clenched between his teeth as he cast the throw-stick into the center of the sand pit. It sunk with the raptor face-down. A successful throw. He used a feathered rod to push his mouse counter diagonally.

The last player did his but the stick flopped with the tail end to the sky. A failed throw. The Sabean cursed his gods blackly, rubbing his forehead vigorously.

The round ended and the mechanical board shifted a

single rotation counterclockwise. The hidden wheel moved the head of a cobra across a constantly moving track that extended the body of the onyx snake while simultaneously eliminating spaces for the mice to move to.

Rooster cursed—his mouse got snatched up by the open maw of the cobra. So did the Sabean's.

Opals were swiped from his pool into the center.

Another betting round began. Down to the last three players. A pile of treasures had been slowly building in the sand.

"The board is ingenious you see. Really. It's all made out of stone. Not a single piece of metal. Supposedly the game's been around for ages. Ishtari developed it to settle disputes, eh."

"Uh-huh. You going to throw down?"

Antonius was acting strange. Whatever he was smoking was doing numbers on his reactions. Eyes almost went cross-eyed. He tossed far too many coins and opals into the sand.

Boy was he going to have a bad morning tomorrow.

"The technique is all in the wrist."

With another deft flip, his red and gold stick once again sunk head-first into the sand pit. Knocking over a pile of pearl earrings in the process. Rooster noticed a pair of fingers try to pinch them off the pile before anyone noticed—the Sabean who had just lost his counter. He got close.

A lamplighter—a mere boy—rang a little bell hanging off his neck.

All gambling and noise stopped.

"Unhand me, you mad bastards. Bastards," the Sabean shrieked as some rough-looking attendants hauled him up. He was sobbing and begging in Sabeish.

"What happens to him?"

"No one steals in The Dens and gets away with it."

A bloody board like the ones used to chop vegetables was wheeled out into the center of the room. Except it had iron manacles screwed into its edge with grooves shaped for hands. And by the dark staining, it had seen plenty of use.

The Sabean tried to run but the attendants fit his hands and locked them in place, none too gently.

Antonius muttered, "And they make it public too. I think I'm going to be sick."

A third attendant came out. A woman by her curves. Save her face and body were completely concealed by a dark wrap. She held a cleaver in her hands.

It swung down and the Sabean's screams filled the gambling hall walls.

Steel met flesh. Harsh justice was dealt. The now-fingerless thief was hauled away with bloody stumps to show for his crime. The attendants dumped the Sabean into the street like a sack of rotten vegetables.

"Hell of a show," Rooster said.

Antonius wiped his mouth, "Like I said friend, they don't mess around with thieves around here."

A light tug on his sleeve. That lamplight boy gave him the spook, haunting right over his shoulder.

"More wine sir," the kid talked like a damned adult but he didn't even look ten summers old.

"Sure."

Childhoods weren't much of a thing down here in the desert, Rooster was starting to figure out. Life started early and cruel. And there weren't many old folks around, so it didn't last long either.

He felt a pang of sympathy for the kid, so he slid him an opal when his cup came back refilled, "Here. Don't show this to your master."

A gracious bow of the head and the lamplighter went to attend another table.

By a stroke of miraculous luck, the two other players both lost their throws. The round ended with the cobra eating their mice counters.

"Wajiit," Antonius cried out the name of the game, "I won!"

The attendant grinned, showing gold between his

stumps, "Congratulations gharib! Don't forget your prize. Please come again."

Nefara did have a mystique at night, the geometric sandy metropolis turned a dark satin blue under the moon creating a cool palette. A picturesque painting. With the occasional hazy orange lamp to give the illusion of safety. It was a maze to navigate without a map in daylight alone.

They were lost.

An hour of walking of what looked like the same flat-topped roofs and sandstone walls littered with vines and colorful graffiti.

Rooster hauled Antonius over his shoulder with the bag of winnings in the other. They must have cut a comical figure to any pickpocket. Wouldn't have needed a knife to hold them up at this point.

When the frustration was too much, he dumped the Teridian man onto the street as gently as he could, "Come on now. Get up."

Antonius was out like a light. Whatever he'd smoked was some genuine stuff. Eyes rolled back in his head, the man whispered absolute gibberish.

Rooster slapped him hard enough to leave a red mark. Nothing. No reaction.

"Goddamn fool."

A child's voice broke the silence, rebounding from the shadows, "He won't wake up. Even if you dunk him in the coldest water. The smoke is poison. Only time can defeat the blue lotus dream."

Rooster wheeled around and saw nobody.

Goosebumps made his arm hairs raise.

Nothing so much as crawled in his periphery.

"Who said that? Show yourself."

A tinkling laugh that grated his nerves, "Tell us something. Who do you serve, gharib?"

He took a few steps back, into the orange glow. Back against the wall. And drew out the long knife.

"Who asks?"

"No one."

"I find that hard to believe."

A wisp of something may have shifted to his left, across an alley.

"Doubt at your peril gharib. Nefara is home to all kinds of shadows."

"I don't like riddles."

"We do," the child laughed, "But this isn't one of them. Which shadow do you serve, gharib?"

Rooster was shaky. Something just crawled wrong about the kid's voice.

"If you want my friend's loot, you can have it."

"We're not interested in petty baubles," that tiny voice fell to a growl, "Answer us."

"I will...if you show yourself."

Little footsteps pattered away suddenly.

No more demands came from the darkness.

Rooster found a sudden vigor and started to haul Antonius up again. They made it to a great archway where the Medean guards were dozing off. Drugged maybe. Under the bug-riddled lamp that illuminated the sandy path was a small shadow.

It was the lamplighter kid from before.

"Hello," he looked up towards Rooster.

Who put the two and two together—the kid's voice was the one from the shadows.

"We have done as you asked. Now, who do you serve gharib?"

If there was any doubt that they weren't alone, the slight inhale followed by a rustle of cloth to his right wiped that all away. There were more than a few that clung to the darkest of shadows around the archway, waiting for his next move.

The lamplighter kid cocked his head to the side, "We don't need torture to find out the truth."

Rooster didn't doubt that if they were capable of this level of trickery, "I serve no one."

"False. We know you have dealings with the Qadi al

Tughur. This Tariq Ashur."

"An arrangement, yes. He's not my master."

"Have you signed a contract with him in blood?"

What the hell did that mean?

"No."

The lamplighter boy blinked and then demanded, "Come forward into the light. You can leave your friend there."

Seeing that he had little choice, outnumbered, Rooster did. He towered over the kid.

If it was an illusion, then he was being duped by the greatest wizard of all time.

The boy snatched his much-larger palm and began to inspect it, "Hmm. And the other? Hmmm. Well. Well indeed. You speak truly."

"Yeah and now you owe me answers."

If the boy feared him at this proximity, there was no sign, "That is not up to you gharib. How well do you know the Qadi—The Dirt Lord?"

"Not very."

"And what of his intentions?"

He shrugged, "Aspirational."

"Be wary gharib. The Qadi is being watched by many—some he is unaware of. The Dirt Lord is feared more than loved."

"Why are you doing this?"

The lamplighter raised the pale opal to the light, "In the thief traditions of Nefara, you have shown your hand as a friendly one. A small act is nevertheless remembered forever. We warn you as a courtesy. For we too are watching the Dirt Lord. Closely."

Rooster felt dumb a dozen minutes later after the lamplighter kid and his shadows dropped him off at the familiar intersection. He'd entirely missed the underlying message hidden in the kid's strange warning.

They weren't just being friendly—they wanted an inside man.

Do a favor to someone in Nefara and they'd want ten

more.

Who wasn't a crook or beggar in this town?

It was morning, the sun was young and Rooster had work to do.

In the small and private courtyard, he stood under a striped tent in the shade and watched his future warband loiter in the sun. They chattered and dawdled as the rich aroma of coffee filled the sandstone walls. A little wizened man tended to the making of the dark drink on a large rug in the shade. This was what the Qadi said Medean lords did and so that was what he would do.

Outsider or not, there was an image he would have to curate.

Dark liquid was poured into clay cups and handed to him and Antonius both. The young Teridian was irritable more than hungover.

"What's on your mind?"

Antonius spoke in Patina, "These are not good men that your friend has found us. Rapers and common thugs maybe. Do you want a translation of what they're saying because it's not pretty."

Waste of time. Rooster didn't need to be told what he already knew. His Medean was getting better. What he did was their potential.

"Line them up and get their names. Then have them divide into two columns with those sticks."

Calling the levies a rabble was an undeserved compliment—many spat in the sand and outright ignored Antonius until he shouted a hellstorm in the courtyard. Took triple the time it should have to get them to follow any instructions. Almost every levy was Medean, except a brace of nut-skinned athletes.

Gamba's long lost and skinny cousins—they might prove promising if they were even a quarter as loyal.

"I can tell you that every other one is called Khalid or Abir or Hassan."

"That makes things easy."

"Most of them tried to join the guard under Musha. The blacks understand me but don't seem to speak Medean. I'm not sure if they've ever held a spear," Antonius shook his head.

"We'll name them ourselves if we have to."

A clatter of sticks and then laughs. The Medean levies weren't taking the exercise seriously. A few were looking over to the tent, making crude gestures.

Not at him but behind him.

Rooster turned back to the rug where Jhamon and Jhabari both sat cross-legged. They were relaxed and impassive but the tension could be cut with a knife. Each like a little warlord in their hyena skins and nomad wraps.

Most of the races of Nefara got along or at least pretended to with the Medeans. Except for the Shemsari. He couldn't figure it out. They weren't treated like gharibs at all—the Medeans treated them with a virulent prejudice that bordered on genocidal.

What could these nomads have done to account for such animosity?

"Antonius, seize that man there and bring him here."

The loudest and most brash of the Medeans walked over to stand before the tent.

"Ask him his name."

The Medean bowed and spoke with unmistakable sarcasm, "Kasim, Ayubin."

"Have him stand back there. Jhabari, come here."

The boy blinked and stood slowly. The Shemsari walked slowly like a cat that expected to be swatted at any minute. Not fearful but anticipatory and distrustful.

Rooster had him and Kasim stand across from each other and tossed a mock spear at each of their feet.

"Good. Tell them to now try to kill each other with their spears. Gut shots only. Any man who strikes the other in the head will get a lashing."

Kasim laughed something in Medean that Rooster thought sounded like 'white skin dogs' and then a few more sentences that couldn't have been pleasant.

"Go ahead Jhabari," but the command fell flat on the kid.

Kasim spat at the boy again—that did the trick.

Copper hair and tan skin became a blur with the stave striking like a snake's head. The mock spear hit Kasim in the nose. He fell back a few paces and grabbed his face. The Medean turned to Antonius and unloaded on the Tarid.

"He's not happy. He wants you to lash the boy for breaking the rules. He said he will not tolerate the disrespect."

"Jhabari, hit this man again."

The Shemsari turned his head and narrowed his eyes. Then surprisingly he did so. This time Kasim tried to step sideways and bat the mock spear away—it hit his ankle first then his collarbone. The Medean fell flat on the sand, rolled then began to rush at Jhabari. And was hit subsequently everywhere that Jhabari could reach with fast jabs, backpedaling deftly out of the Medean's reach.

Out of the corner of his eye, he noticed the dark-skinned men watching the fight intently. Eyes flickering between each movement.

Kasim finally dropped his mock spear.

The other Medeans roared in protest. They didn't like seeing their countryman being humiliated by a boy. They began to mob over towards Jhabari for revenge.

Too bad.

Rooster drew Awakener—the sound of the great blade unsheathing stilled their advance across the courtyard.

"You want me to lash him Kasim? Why should I? Jhabari listens and obeys and you," Rooster spoke in Medean, turned to stand over Kasim, "Are an insubordinate cur. You want to cry unfair? Go cry to Musha and ask to be part of his guard where they kick piles of sand and rob peasants all day."

He stood up and stabbed the sword in the sand, "My outfit, my rules. Any man who has a problem with my authority as a gharib or Sergeant Antonius here can walk right through that archway."

None of the Medeans budged.

"Every one of you stands to make an equal share of the loot we find out on the road. That's including myself, Jhamon, and Jhabari. Anyone got a problem with that either?"

Kasim did.

Arrogant shithead jumped to his feet and began to lambast the Shemsari boys with every curse known to man. There wasn't any translation needed. Rooster heard enough.

"Sergeant Antonius, have those four over there escort this vagrant out of my courtyard."

The four black men needed little instruction. They manhandled Kasim and had him sprawling out the archway in seconds.

"Good. This is my only warning. Do what Kasim just did on the road and I'll have you hung as a deserter from the back of my horse. Have them line up on the wall again."

This time there was a little more skip in each of the Medean's step. They were learning. Slowly.

"More coffee," the little wizened man had refilled his cup without his asking.

Unlike chai, this stuff was much more potent. It tasted like wood but it packed a punch that gave him jitters.

No wonder the Medean lords drank this before battle.

"Good. Keep that brewing. This is going to be a long day."

When they left the walls of Nefara for their second time, Rooster counted their number as twenty seven. A strange number that portended neither good or bad luck. Tariq's promise of horses never came and so they also had only three horses and a camel. Neither Shemsari boy was an officer but the Medean recruits must have thought so and it created even more tension that was unnecessary.

But they were the charge of young Antonius now—it was time for the Teridian to prove his mettle and rise to the occasion.

Hopefully, he wasn't just hot air and wasted potential.

Because their names were unpronounceable Rooster designated the black men as Buzzard, Goshawk, Heron, and Ostrich. It just seemed fitting. They were the only recruits who acted as though they wanted to be there. All of them showed great potential.

Rooster didn't care what they were or what tribe they were from. If they fought well and if they were loyal, they'd earn their place. And if they were anything like Gamba, they'd be worth ten Medeans each.

The Birds of Prey sallied out onto the road.

To any capable warband they might cross they'd look like an easy target. To a well-guarded caravan, they might look like a threat. To Rooster, they were a ragtag bunch whose only unifying purpose was the promise of easy fortune.

Only time would tell if the anvil of the road and the hammer of battle would forge them. Or shatter them.

العواء تلال

Waddun-Sida

A sandal absently stepped on a potsherd and almost gave them away. The crunch echoed off the walls. Like a branch cracking in a dead forest.

From his vantage—a mere crack in the wall of the ruin—Rooster could barely make out the silhouettes of the guards tending to the coals.

Had they heard anything, it would have been too late to know.

"Fuck's sake," he hissed low as that idiot shifted and repeated the crunching sound, "Whoever that is doing that better stop or I'll strangle him."

Some chatter in that strange Sabean dialect. A dark shape moved against the primitive dawn's light. Footsteps approached.

Rooster held his breath. Somewhere behind him, a bowstring tightened, ever so slightly.

Footsteps stopped.

A Sabean called from the camp that nestled between the ruins sandwiched inside the canyon walls. Very close to them now, the shadow yelled back in that slippery, choppy tongue. Enough for Rooster to count how many missing teeth he had beneath that wispy mustache.

Water trickled onto the stone and a foul smell arose; the guard was pissing on the wall.

Rooster closed his eyes and breathed relief.

Another Sabean call from the camp—the second on firewatch went to do the same, abandoning the coals.

Big mistake.

The hiding Birds of Prey drew out from the ruins and rushed the firewatch before they could croak. Then swiftly collapsed on the sleeping Sabeans who outnumbered them three to one.

What could have been a botched raid turned around at the very last moment as a dull light began to fill the valley.

Rooster let himself fall onto the ledge of a pitched wagon. Exhaustion set its claws in him. Funny how he used to be able to stay up all night and battle it out at dawn until the following dusk. But that was just youth, he reckoned.

If they kept this kind of success up, he wouldn't have to play bandit for much longer.

He surveyed the remains of the Shalmanisar camp. Almost felt pity. The canyon must have provided them a false sense of security when they ought to have pressed on another few hours. Out in the open desert, they might have stood a chance.

Four weeks, five caravans. Not bad at all. Besides the lack of a pool to recruit from, the twenty or so of his warband were wreaking havoc on the Shalmanisar. Punching well above their belt.

Back in Nefara, those merchant lords were probably pissing themselves.

He wiped Awakener clean and watched as Antonius approached. The Teridian seemed on edge.

"Good work kid. Where do we stand?"

"A few casualties on our side. I think they'll recover."

With odds like they had, it was almost a miracle they didn't have more.

"That's not all is it?"

Antonius scratched at what was starting to be a beard, "We rounded up the remaining prisoners. Score or so. One of them wants to speak with you. Claims that they're an important member of something called the Qorchi."

"Prisoners are going to be a problem."

Judging by Antonius' face, he'd already figured that out too.

A few survivors could fan the flames of the infamous white bandit in the turban and hyena skin. But leaving enough enemies alive was a dangerous game. Too many to corroborate numbers and faces lessened their chance of anonymity in Nefara. Sooner or later, the Shalmanisar would get lucky and find out where they were before Tariq's plan could come to fruition.

"Let's have a look at them."

They were huddled up in a pile, hands tied. All in their funny little cream robes that left their chests naked. One of them was a woman who wore vestments embedded with lapis lazuli—clearly their leader.

Too many Sabeans and not enough gharibs. Which means they were loyal to more than coin.

"Get her up and have the rest start digging graves. Then we'll cut their throats."

Antonius gave the order and the Sabeans began to protest and beg. The leader said something in Medean, waving her bound wrists at the rest of the sitting group.

"She says she wishes you to stay your hand until you hear what she has to say."

But Rooster didn't much care. There were no morals in this. This was bandit business. Nothing this woman could say would sway him.

"Take her and put her by the wagons, I'll talk to her in a moment."

A Medean with a spear hauled her up, grinning wolfishly. His other hand gripped her delicate arm. Nothing was left to the imagination.

Rape rarely led to fruitful interrogation.

Rooster knew his men were a notch above savages and had needs. A fine line he'd have to draw to keep their morale high without indulging them.

"Tell that whoreson that I'll have his prick on a necklace if he touches her. I need her unspoiled and untarnished."

Antonius growled the order and that smile faded. Lapis Lazuli was dragged out of sight by her guards and servants.

"Keep an eye on him sergeant."

"No problem boss man. Hassan, where are my shovels?"

Rooster found Jhamon and Jhabari looting and pillaging. They weren't shy about picking through corpses, kicking aside limbs to scavenge what they could. Both found their quarry; small bows with deep curves in their bellies and their limbs to the tips. They looked ecstatic.

Regular little vultures. Whoever dad had been, he'd brought them up on battlefields.

Whereas the Medeans and blacks stood to the side, wary of the dead.

"You two. Go back to the river and bring back the animals. We need to start moving these goods to the cache. This is our last run before we head back so make sure the animals are well fed."

Jhabari sniffed and garbled in Shemsari and Jhamon shoved him aside but turned back, "The bodies. We must burn them, not bury them Rooster."

"Why?"

"Bahram's light leaves them. Soon those with dead and gray flesh will come to feast on them."

The walking dead could wait their damn turn for all he cared.

Rooster spun around to the rest of the outfit. Maybe one of them would know what that meant. Some days he felt like he needed a lexicon that could translate all this supernatural gobbledygook desert horseshit.

Boom. A deafening explosion rocked the canyon. One of the wagons was rendered into a million shards of wood that flew outward in all directions, followed by a plume of flame. A hot shockwave buffeted everyone gathered in the middle of the ruins and sent most on their asses.

Dull ringing filled Rooster's ears, "Antonius. What the hell just happened? Antonius?"

The young man was holding the side of his head, pitching sideways as he ran, "Gods I can't hear out my right ear."

A bonfire was raging in the litter of wagons. A form flew from it and ran in a dead sprint to the end of the canyon. Human-like. Shooting something from its hands at Rooster—a hand-sized ball of flame. He barely had the instinct to duck behind a ruined pillar. Sandstone turned as hot as an oven and his arm hairs were singed.

The form pressed on, throwing a series of flares his way that all splashed harmlessly on the stone. By the lithe movement and shape, he realized it was the Sabean woman—her body licking with red and orange blazes, hair a streaming inferno.

A sorceress.

She cried out in that eastern tongue and shot something into the sky—another flare, this one a brilliant white stream of light. A firework exploded above the low mountains of the canyon.

"Someone shoot that bitch," Rooster ordered.

Goshawk drew back and put an arrow between her flaming collarbone. The she-witch went down in a heap of ashes. A fine shot. Whatever she had done had the Sabean prisoners in an uproar.

It was a damn shame that no one could figure out what they were saying.

Many of the warband were still reeling and coming to. The ones who hadn't been impaled by flying wood or the flame. Rooster counted three slain. A fourth who was still breathing but was losing blood fast.

The prisoners got the worst of it. Only a few of them remained not in pieces or turned to molten slag.

Antonius staggered around like a drunk, "She was a witch?"

Up in the sky was still that burning glow she'd thrown up. It shone nearly as bright as the sun.

"Yeah. We got tricked. You alright?"

The Teridian nodded, still holding his ear.

"Round up the wounded and have them ready to be brought back to the river. Have the living dispose of these prisoners. I don't want any more surprises."

"What of the dead? Do you think we should burn them like the boys said?"

"The hell if I know," Rooster said, "I'll be right back."

He started off towards the end of the short canyon where the boys would be coming back with their mounts.

One of them was already fast approaching, probably Jhamon to find out what the commotion had been.

Good kid Jhamon.

Rooster wiped ash and sweat from his eyes—it getting too bright out to see properly. He started to wave the Shemsari down.

"Where's your brother? I need those mounts over here to move the wounded."

The kid on the horse came to a stop.

Which was when Rooster got a clear look at the rider. Trick of the light. It wasn't Jhamon—it was a faceless man with a turbaned and pointed helm with a faceplate. Dressed in the loose-fitting robes and kit of a light cavalryman. Who immediately wheeled his horse to face back westward and took off in a cloud of dust.

The woman casting the orb in the sky made a whole lot more sense; it was a goddamn beacon.

The real Shemsari boys were coming up not even a breath later, Jhamon asking, "What's happening?"

"We just bit onto the bait and now we're going to get rolled like a carpet."

Jhebari scowled at the cloud of dust, "And him?"

"A scout. Don't just sit there. Go get him before he rats us out. Go. Get!"

While they rode off after the scout like bitches in heat, Rooster saddled up on Nereel and rode the bay horse back into the ruins. Passed over the ashes of the witch-woman—no doubt who was laughing up from hell right now at them. He spat down for good measure.

Antonius was like a chicken with his head cut off—command pulled in every direction. Triage, prisoner management, looting, and corralling the unruly Medean levies.

All four of the black men were guarding the dozen or so Sabeans prisoners, watching Rooster ride up with solemn statuesque gazes.

"Sergeant Antonius."

A strained, "Yes, Rooster."

"Find out which of these dogs is the most senior ranking and knows what's what."

A Sabean stood defiantly. Bastard glanced up at the orb and grinned. He knew. And that made Rooster's decision even easier.

He threw a length of coiled rope down, "Go ahead and have Heron tie this around his neck. A self-closing knot if you would."

Antonius was puzzled but carried out the order and soon the Sabean wore a noose.

"Tell this man," he tied his end to the horn of the saddle, real tight, "That I need to know who is riding to their aid. Who is going to come try to stick us with pointy swords? Ask him."

Translation. Nothing back. Rooster figured.

And acted. With a press in the stirrups, Nereel leapt forward a few paces. It was enough to cinch down the knot and drag the Sabean man off his feet. The prisoner choked on his defiance and flailed his legs.

"Tell him I appreciate his honorable silence. Tell him for that, I'll have my horse drag him until his head is separated from his body."

Another drive of the stirrups and soon Nereel was riding at a canter. The rope went taut. The Sabean man wheezed as the breath was sucked from his chest and his neck strained by the horse's strength.

Rooster had the horse stop long enough for the prisoner to catch his breath.

Give a little hope and take it away. Even hardened soldiers broke eventually. And these servants weren't hardened.

"Sergeant Antonius, would you kindly tell this gentleman that I'll start tying his limbs to the rock walls to test out my ropes? I wonder what will be pulled off first; his legs or his head?"

The Teridian gulped, going whiter than chalk.

Poor kid didn't have the intestinal fortitude for torture—nothing to be ashamed of. Wasn't in his wheelhouse. Probably imagined that war was supposed to be honorable and clean always.

But Rooster needed answers and the Shalmanisar wouldn't give them so freely.

"Sergeant. Tell him."

It was translated to the Sabean, whose face was going purple and the knot on his neck was blackening. The man weighed his options silently then said coughed out a few words.

"No more, he says. He'll talk."

"If he wants his life he'll spill his guts here and now."

"He's gathering his breath damn it!"

Rooster leaped down from his horse, pushed aside the Teridian, and put his boot on the Sabean's throat. Gently. But enough pressure to put stars in the eyes.

If that scout made it back to his destination, there was a slim chance they'd be alive to tell the tale.

"Sergeant?"

Antonius relayed the statement and the Sabean began to blurt tearfully.

"He says that we're all dead men. The Ivory Queen sent a detachment of her heavy cataphracts to safeguard the passage of the Qorchi Dynasty and all Shalmanisar into her lands. And that these elite horsemen are led by someone called an Immortal. So we're good as dead eh? I think he pissed himself."

It was a good hour before the Shemsari returned and corroborated the story. And even better—details.

One hundred heavily armored troop and twenty light outriders were waiting at the bend of the road below the canyon. The scout had been one of a half dozen. What more; a character among described as demonic in some wicked armor. This supposed Immortal basked in an unnatural glow even from afar.

So likely protected by magic too, to boot. Fantastic.

Neither boy managed to nab the scout, unfortunately. They said they got their good look and hightailed it back as fast and safe as possible.

Rooster paced about.

Nineteen against one hundred and twenty. Not favorable odds. Especially not when their foe were armored, mounted, and seasoned.

No way the Birds of Prey made it back to Nefara without being slaughtered. Especially not buggered down with their stash of pilfered goods they'd collected and hidden away near the river. Going back empty-handed wasn't an option.

There had to be another solution here.

Rooster walked.

The rest of the Sabeans had been tossed into shallow graves. Buzzards hadn't even picked up on the scent of the dead yet. He kicked around the scene and felt himself lost in the glassy eyes of the dead. A shame they'd be food for scavengers and not given a proper burial.

Not burned eh?

What if…?

Rooster found himself sifting through the scorched sand from the wagon. Smearing it on his arm. Poured a bit of his water skin on it and turned it into mud. Now it coated with a graying kind of ooze. That once dried, would look rather flaky and deathly.

A devious idea started to form in his head. It was mad. It was uncalled for. But it just might work.

"Hey Jhamon. Tell me again about these so-called graythirsters. What exactly do the dead men look like?"

A storm of hooves foreshadowed the arrival. Elite horsemen soon filled the narrow neck of the canyon—a wall of steel and horseflesh. The boys had reported accurately. At least a hundred lances danced in the air along with a new banner; black as night, a pearl-white crown emblazoned with a crescent moon flipped sideways and upside-down below.

These weren't levies on mules either. Back up north, they would have been called knights. Mail-clad and mean, such a force could accomplish what an army could but in a quarter of the time and suffer little consequence.

Force like that didn't just pop up out of thin air at random.

Vultures had arrived a little before they did—ugly things descended like the reaper in dark cloaks, picking at flesh. There were a dozen and more wheeling to join in the feast.

Slowly and methodically, the cataphracts began to scour the ruins and the remains of the caravan. It wouldn't take them long to find the mad tracks leading away and into the eastern desert. A scout did and reported it. Notably, in Medean.

Rooster held his breath. Every fiber in his body screamed to run as the horsemen approached their hidey-hole.

He ground his teeth and closed his eyes, "Jhamon. Does Bahram listen to your prayers?"

"My father said so if one followed the J'awed," the boy spoke from the shadows in the little nook.

He, the Shemsari, and the black men were cramped into a crouch where the redrock met the ruins. As were the horses and camel, cloth wrapped around their mouths to shut them up.

This whole plan banked on the scouts finding the tracks—not looking at them too closely. Anyone with half a brain would realize the tracks leading in and out of the canyon on the eastern end were made by the same four animals and at the same time.

"Then I need you to pray like you mean it. We're going to need all the divine help we can."

Jhabari snarled, "A gharib thinks Bahram listens to him? Your blood isn't one bound to Bahram, fool!"

"You're right wiseass, he won't listen to me. That's why you're going to your knees and beg Bahram for us. Go on."

An irked sound followed by them folding up, foreheads dug into the sand, chanting rapidly and softly.

Atop a sable stallion, Rooster spotted the figure called the Immortal. Decked out head to toe in ornamental armor that looked way too old—polished silver steel with grotesque faces in the pauldrons and joint pieces to match the one covering the Immortal's own. The helmet was an ugly thing with tall horns that curled back and a ridge shaped like a sea-serpent frill.

There indeed was a dull glow that emanated from the figure, where the air grew fuzzy and distorted.

Scouts were milling about and inspecting the tracks too closely.

Waiting became uncomfortable—like the urge to crack one's knuckles but only dull pain came from trying.

A raspy howl flew from the north.

Finally.

The vultures suddenly took to the skies in a panic. They cackled wretchedly and left with abandon. The Immortal shouted something. A raspy and brassy voice that sounded wholly unnatural and yet soothed. The command in Medean sounded convincing—was it sorcerous?

Cataphracts froze all at once. Mail clinked like a thousand tacks hitting a tile floor.

Silhouettes appeared atop the plateaus of the canyon. Dark-gray forms that shambled and lurched into view. The cataphracts were cursing in Medean as their horses began to paw the ground and grow nervous.

Graythirsters.

Another ungodly howl from the walking dead as they gathered at the rim, looking down upon the horsemen and raised their desiccated limbs.

The Immortal raised a short and decorative spear and belted out an order. Then rode off.

Trumpets blared and the canyon shook once more. The host of cataphracts hastily followed their leader—departing out the eastern-facing canyon. Dust filled the air in their wake. The horsemen grew more distant, following tracks that would go nowhere.

Both Shemsari lifted their heads.

The coast was clear and Rooster drew them out of hiding. They gathered at the ruins. He waited impatiently for the graythirsters to climb down from their position.

"Damn good thing they don't have eagles," he muttered.

If they did they would have spotted fifteen naked Medeans caked head to toe in an ashy mud-paste. Who all fell into a jog, laughing all the way.

Antonius grinned ear-to-ear, "Back in the Terid we say that a donkey calls the rooster a stubborn asshole. Not today eh? Your plan worked!"

"Not for long."

"Nonsense. They'll be halfway to Nefara before they figure out we pulled their tail like an ass on Idaemis Day!"

Rooster feared differently.

He turned to the copper-haired Shemsari, who were saddling their horses—which were more like thick animal skins secured with braided strips under the horse's belly. Not big on comfort, the nomads.

"What do you two think?"

Soberly Jhabari noted, "The raptor always circles back."

"They will not be deceived for long Rooster," Jhamon added.

"If you were them, what would you do? Once you knew you were had?"

"Circle back, retrace my steps, and look for fresh droppings."

"And you Jhabari?"

The boy sniffed at his brother's suggestion, "Waste of time. My enemy would predict this and may try to catch me by surprise. I would let him think I am a fool while I find high ground to watch for his dust cloud."

Both were sound advice. And not mutually exclusive either. Which put their situation into perspective—far grimmer.

"With a force of a hundred and more with plenty of scouts, both can be true. What then?"

"I have my scouts look for the easiest path of escape. One with water and plenty of places to hide a horse or scatter a party."

Jhamon bit down on whatever he was about to say, "Yes, I have to agree with him. My enemy will become easy to predict."

Wisdom from the mouth of babes.

Rooster found himself in total agreement.

Tactics and strategy were just the extensions of thought anticipating behavior. Something that it took him an entire lifetime to understand—yet these boys mastered it before manhood.

He could only imagine what a horde of fully mature Shemsari could do to the fat earls of the north.

Scary thought.

"They'll wait for us at the Ptahira. Where the bends make it sluggish and slow enough to ford by barge."

Gold eyes glinted confirmation.

Jhamon had his bow out across the knees, "I don't know what we should do Rooster, except run."

There wasn't any shame in running. Not when it saved your skin another day.

A shadow crossed his vision on the rocks. A winged shape glided darkly against the bone-white sandstone. It might have been Hazair. Or a nameless vulture. Too high up to tell. It went up and over the cliffs—northward.

What wasn't a mystery was where it was heading; the sandblasted waste of dark rock and deep defiles where the gods did not even walk. That damned Sunscar Waste.

Rooster wanted to laugh at the irony.

But it seemed the only logical choice. Hide out in the wastes for a day or two, head back to the river, and then carry whatever they could back to Nefara. And hopefully, the Ivory Queen's men would be none the wiser.

He gave the order.

He was wrong.

Tufts of harsh grass sprouted from the scarred plain. It gave the impression that beneath the sand was the skin of a bristling abomination lying dormant—they were treading across its boundless flesh without assent.

This was no escape.

Dust clouds of the horsemen were ever just out of reach but never left their sight. The cataphracts had chased them into the Sunscar—pushed them deeper into the waste like a guard spearing a prisoner's back. They were simply waiting Rooster and his men out.

To die and shrivel in the sun; that was their kismet now.

After days Rooster realized the eagle had led them astray. Felt the fool, thinking some benevolent divinity was watching his back. He watched the morale evaporate as the water in their skins was spent.

"How can they call this winter?" Antonius looked like he stopped bothering to wipe the sweat off.

"Because they're sadists," Rooster croaked, licking his lips without moisture to wet them.

"Ah."

"Now I know why your friend spends a small fortune on ice," the Teridian smiled like a simpleton, "The Qadi."

"Mm."

"Chilled wine eh? To think."

"Yeah."

"Frost worth more than its weight in gold. It's absurd. Chunks of it just hacked off a mountain top and tossed in barrels."

Humor was the only tool left in his bag. No more ploys or clever tricks. Laugh into the face of death.

Rooster felt his mind wander as his eyes did the same. Hard to keep his attention under the duress of the sun.

He saw shapes flicker in the warped heat. The desert folk called them mirages. Some claimed you could see your fate in them.

Like that would help him now.

No, that was something moving towards their makeshift camp. Maybe a man. Too early to tell.

"...lucky lady, whoever he gifted it to. Never got her face but gods she had long legs. Thought about disguising myself as one of her servants and climbing up into her chambers."

"What did you say?" Rooster thought he heard wrong.

"The woman of my dreams? The devilish waif I'm going to plow like a field?"

"No the other part. About the ice."

In their little shelter against the hill, Antonius kicked his heel into the sand, annoyed, "Wasting my breath trying to talk to old wood ears here."

"You never shut up. Repeat what you said about the Qadi."

A scratch of the chin, "That your rich friend had us ferry in ice from Kahil and gave it all away? Mad bastard, that one."

"Where to?"

"My dream woman's palace. Haven't you listened? She likes them rich because she hasn't met me yet."

"Why?"

"How should I know? He's trying to buy his way between her legs!" The man was daydreaming, voice going hazy, "Didn't see much of her with that veil though. Damn shame they hide their women behind potato sacks here."

Rooster couldn't make heads or tails of it. But something didn't add quite up. Maybe it was nothing.

"What could you see of her?"

Antonous had to think, "Skin like ivory and she had these nails. Looked like emeralds."

“Hold that thought. It's one of our scouts.”

The shape emerging from the mirage was the dark man named Heron. His skin was like wet obsidian but the man looked unfazed by the strain. Prime marathon runners, these four. Rooster would trade all twenty Medeans for even just another handful of these lean black men.

They spoke in a strange tapping language—beating their chests and gesturing in complicated signs—but they compromised with fairly legible drawings. Heron did not scrawl into the dirt.

"Sergeant. What does that mean?"

"He saw nothing."

Rooster licked his teeth but had to accept the truth, "How many miles did he cover?"

Some translation and a small picture was drawn, "Until great hills I think."

A good few dozen miles. Not bad for a scout on foot in half a day. Unfortunately, not good tidings either.

The dark man shuffled back on the other side of the hill to wait for his three companions to return.

North bore nothing. Three more cardinal directions until the hard decisions would come.

"Rooster," Antonius warned as a group of Medean levies approached around the hill.

They began to bark and demand with hoarse voices. Rooster realized his Medean was improving—half of what they said he was understanding.

To call them insubordinate would have been charitable. Their demands verged on mutiny. They made it clear that it was written in the heavens they would die here—their solution was to go to the river. A comment was made about Shemsari devils and their backwards ways cursed the entire party. Kasim was even mentioned in passing.

Rooster recalled how back when Darwish had understood everything he said in Patina and feigned ignorance. Time to take a page out of the hillman's book. Playing dumb among those who he couldn't determine were friend or foe would be useful in the desert. Could even save his life.

If they ever made it of this hell.

Back to the levies—culling these men from the pack and reminding the others of the chain of command would be justice. It would also lead directly to mutiny without any shadow of doubt.

"Sergeant Antonius, please translate."

The Teridian did and it was redundant. But it served one purpose.

"Boss?"

"They're your men. You deal with it."

The young man faltered, "But you're their captain! They're speaking of taking up arms against us Rooster."

"Wisen up Antonius. If I carry out the punishment, it undermines your authority as my right hand. They need to respect you. And also fear your wrath."

Speaking of which, he turned over to the Shemsari. Jhabari's silent judgment was bearing down on him. The kid was white-hot pissed off and didn't hide it.

"What's your brother's problem Jhamon?"

They met in the middle of the groups, "He says you have upset Bahram."

"Hence why we're in this predicament."

"I am worried Rooster. I have never seen him like this."

"Enough that he'll try something?"

Jhamon's jaw set. The Shemsari teen looked twenty years older, staring off into nowhere. He was turning out to be one to think carefully and operate without the cloud of emotion. Good traits in a leader. One day he would be.

"I'll watch him carefully Rooster."

"Answer me this and be truthful. Do you think I've made a mistake? Do you think it was the eagle showing us to come here?"

Jhamon delayed before he answered, "I do not believe Bahram is angry with you. I think Bahram sent you to us."

"Why?"

"I ask the J'awed this every night."

Rooster didn't know what to make of that but it was an honest answer.

His attention was drawn to the shouting. The situation with the levies was getting hairy. Antonius and Heron were surrounded by a dozen angry Medeans. Could prove to get uglier and quick. The hired help was getting less and less helpful.

A cruel and pragmatic general would send these men to the slaughter to cover the escape of his trusted soldiers. Buffer and draw out the enemy as a bait and switch. A win-win if he ever knew one.

Perhaps it was time to get cruel.

Rooster drew out Awakener from the saddle and Nereel neighed deep.

"I suppose you want to tell me off for my poor leadership too? Is that it old friend? Be glad that I have camels to eat first before you."

Nereel chattered at something behind him.

At first he thought the horse was warning him of a jackal. Another silhouette appeared in the mirage. But it was Ostrich, returning from the south. The dark man fell to the sand and began to madly scribble in the sand, drawing.

Judgment was postponed—even the Medean levies were distracted.

"Translate Sergeant Antonius."

"It's the river Rooster. Ostrich says there are hundreds of soldiers gathering."

Rooster didn't get it, "The Ivory Queen's? There's only a hundred of them or so."

"No, he's not drawing horses. They're someone else's and they're doing something. Trying to cross the Ptahira to land on our side."

"Did he say where they arrived from?"

Antonius asked and Ostrich nodded, digging another furrow that was unmistakably east to west.

"Nefara. They were spotted by the Ivory Queen's scouts not long ago."

Jhamon and Jhabari were sent out to look for the dust cloud. They came back not even a full minute later. Sure enough; the Ivory Queen's cataphracts were going south to the river.

A cheer went out among the men—their pursuers had found a bigger fish to fry.

But Rooster had other plans.

"Sergeant Antonius, have the men ready to move as soon as possible."

"What's the move?"

"We're going to the river."

"But they'll be snagged up in that battle. They'll be too distracted to pursue us."

All perfectly reasonable assumptions. And a gamble.

They needed water and sooner or later would have to go to the Ptahira. With horses to block off the narrow and steep banks of the river, the cataphracts could easily prevent a force three times their number from fording.

And the last thing the Ivory Queen's men would expect would be a flanking assault from the wastes. Twenty or so men coming out from nowhere could turn the tide in the chaos of a battle.

It was risky. It was going to cost them. It was unexpected—his style.

"Forced march Sergeant Antonius. The hunted are going off to hunt."

By the time they descended to the river banks, the Ptahira was already boiling over with blood. Arrows hissed death across the wide waters. Steel on steel filled the open desert with its vicious battle cry.

Rooster counted eleven barges, not including those sunk or listing off without masters. Two hundred men give or take were trying to make a landing. And half that were blocking off the way.

"Blind fools. Should just keep moving downriver to land."

The Birds of Prey were lying there flat against the ridge just above the carnage and hadn't been spotted.

The decision weighed heavily as that afternoon sun.

He'd sit forever there, waiting for the perfect moment to strike.

"The enemy of a good move is the pursuit of a perfect one," he grunted the adage.

"What was that Rooster?"

He ignored Antonius and started drawing lines against the hill they laid on. What they needed was a clean break. But mounted men could turn fast. He spied for the uneven terrain between him and the cataphracts and got his answer.

It was time.

Quickly and quietly, the levies with spears were sent to squat low in the belly between low dunes. Goshawk, Ostrich, Vulture, and Heron would remain as a backline with bows and javelins.

"Alright Sergeant. This is your day. I'm going to lead them to you. If it goes south or we pull too many, get back to those four and get on a camel."

Antonius rapped his shield, "I'm not going anywhere, eh. You can count on me."

Rooster was worried he'd say that.

"Just spear them like you chase women."

He swung onto Nereel and rode to the Shemsari boys, "Alright you devil-pair. Nothing showy. But I need you to piss these guys off."

Jhamon was firm, but Jhabari—whatever it was about the kid was worsening. Had a shadow under that brow. Didn't blink once. Just stared hard. Like murder.

"Fine. On me."

He drove Nereel to a gallop, kicking up sand as they fast approached the river. Riding as close as he dared to the backs of the cataphracts—where the flies that buzzed around their horses flew into his face.

This close up he could see blood and bodies floating in the water.

"Oi," he shouted as loud as humanly possible, "You shiny turds. I'm the bandit king who's about to buttfuck you."

That sure got their attention.

A fist of faceless horsemen wheeled around with pikes raised, immediately moving to retaliate. Rooster found his gut clench when he got a closer look at how very armored they were. Barding hung from their horses and each sported thick-wrought mail.

Bandit-killers.

Far too many of them were poised to chase; a good wall, a dozen.

Rooster spurred Nereel into a gallop and almost fell off like a damn amateur. The heavy cavalry had closed a good chunk of the gap between them, preparing to spit him like a boar. He tried to steer Nereel at an angle to shear the sand and only slowed them more.

By the time they crossed the road and into the dunes Rooster could almost feel their pikes brushing Nereel's tail. He didn't dare to look over his shoulder. The cataphracts were too close.

From his periphery, a blur broke the haze and whistled behind him—an arrow.

A rider closest to him suddenly jerked and catapulted over the neck of his horse. A vulture-feathered shaft had buried itself in his neck.

Out of nowhere, the Shemsari boys flew in from the flanks, riding parallel to the chase. Jhamon strung and loosed another arrow in quick succession. The boy wheeled his horse and banked safely out of an errant pike before it could catch him. Jhabari on his left side doing the same. Pairs of cataphracts broke to catch them but couldn't get close enough to spear them. They disappeared behind the hills of sand.

"Holy hell," Rooster cursed.

Now he knew why Shemsari were so feared.

Jhabari did something he'd never seen before—the suntanned kid jumped up deftly, crouched on his heels to stand low, spun to fire off several arrows, fell back onto the carpet saddle, and guided the horse away by jerking the braided mane—and did it all in a breath. And his shots weren't reckless either. By the time Rooster mounted the crest of the dune, only seven cataphracts remained to charge after him.

Gods and gods-damn.

Shemsari were devil archers on horseback.

He was so distracted by the spectacle he flew over the dune and almost ran the Medean levies over—ripping away at the last second. Nereel almost fell sideways into the pit of spears.

The cataphracts fell like flies to honey.

Spears thrust up at unarmored spots in their horses between the barding. The horsemen who dodged the spears were pelted by enfilading fire from the four black men. All that heavy armor did nothing to help them escape the pit of death.

Blood rained. It made the river look like a fair fight. Horse and man were gored as they stood.

Antonius roared a premature triumph below.

Rooster rode up to Jhamon, "New plan. You and your brother will strafe the backs of the rest of the horsemen while we drive a wedge and create a landing. Don't engage, just skirmish."

"Ai-yee," the Shemsari boys replied in a war shriek.

The devils rode off.

"Form up a column," he picked up a pike from a fallen cataphract and brought Nereel to a canter, "Birds of Prey. On me."

Again he rode for the Ptahira—this time with twenty men on his heels. They must have looked a sight to any of the Ivory Queen's men, appearing where their comrades had vanished into the desert.

Except the heavy cavalry weren't looking his way.

A barge had landed since and Nefaran soldiers were starting to form a beachhead of bristling spears and shields. Cataphracts were trying to push them back into the water, harrying the front line. More and more men were lining the banks of the beach—a premature shield-wall was gathering. As many wounded and dying lay as standing.

Rooster leaned back towards Antonius, "You see that line in front of the first barge? Spread the men out and spear the bastards from behind."

The good old hammer and anvil. Favored move of every veteran northern field marshal. Technically the hammer was supposed to be horsemen but traditions be damned.

It just might work.

"Aye! We'll prick them good," the Teridian called orders and led the charge.

The Birds of Prey crossed the road at a sprint. Antonius looked like a hoplite statue of his imperial ancestry—round shield and lance in either hand, ordering as he raised both. Suddenly bandits became infantrymen who drove spears right into the backs of the horsemen. Javelins and arrows flew over their heads from Goshawk and his brothers. The missiles hit true and the spears struck mail. Cataphracts tried to turn but had little room to maneuver. They tried to swing their sabers and pikes down and were rewarded with punishment—the first five fell without inflicting a single blow.

Nefarans on the beach began to swarm like a nest of hornets. Shoulder to shoulder they pushed into the horsemen with their stingers and the air grew nasty with hissing missiles. More made land from the barges and added to the ranks. Their captains called and pockets of their men streamed through gaps of the cataphracts—driving wedges to aid the Birds of Prey. Angry cries for the former White Dove began to drown out the sound of braying horses.

The tide was turning.

Rooster knew it when the pinned cavalry began to break ranks and ceded the ground they were losing.

The Shemsari caught his eye—riding towards him, their bows firing like mad. The cataphracts were in tow, a few of them with bows of their own.

"Keep pressing them," he shouted down and jerked Nereel to the left.

With a lance in hand, he rode head-on towards the boys. They were about to get swamped by cataphracts fleeing the river and heading to the road. One Shemsari boy peeled away and brought half of them into the desert—Jhabari.

"Jhamon," Rooster cried out in warning.

The kid ducked and a sword missed his neck by a hair. A cataphract drove his armored horse into the boy's. And seized the reins from the kid. Saber flashed and caught the sunlight.

Rooster leaned hard in his saddle and raised the lance.

Seconds hung like an executioner's blade.

Jhamon toppled in a dust cloud—it looked like a spray of blood too.

Like he was in a tourney back in the north, Rooster charged down the cataphract. Levering the lance so the steel tip lifted at the precise moment of impact. The horseman tried to raise his saber—catching the lance in his belly. Wood splintered and the man was sent flying back onto his spine into the dirt. Dead.

Jhamon was lying in a pile when he rode up.

"Get up boy," he yelled to hopefully stir him.

Something was riding up on them fast—another rider. It was Jhabari. Pressed against the saddle and riding low. Alone and driving his painted horse at a full gallop.

Not at the cataphracts.

Right at Rooster.

An arrow cracked past and buried itself in the sand. Narrow miss. The Shemsari boy was shrieking his primal cry, stringing another arrow. Shining point aimed at Nereel.

Of course.

Little fucker had been planning this all day. Without Jhamon to keep him in check, this was how the kid was going to repay him.

Mutiny.

The boy missed him again and thundered past. Jhabari banked his horse to make another pass.

"Come on then," Rooster growled and leapt down to rip the steel shield from the fallen cataphract, "You want to join your dad huh?"

The Shemsari rode in and shot before he could mount Nereel. The arrow glanced off the shield, shaft tumbled wildly off into nowhere. Jhabari wasn't slowing and made another failed shot before circling back again.

But at this rate, Rooster wouldn't be able to get on the horse without getting an arrow in the back. So he ran to Nereel and slapped the horse's ass.

Jhabari was too focused on his marksmanship to see the horse come barreling at his. The horses collided into flailing limbs and the boy got tossed into the sand.

Rooster ran to close the gap. He held the shield out in one hand and had Awakener in the other.

Another arrow tried to bury in the shield but flew off.

"You're a fool boy," he said.

Jhabari spat towards him, "Demon! Bahram witnesses me slay you now."

The boy was clever—dropping to a squat and shooting for Rooster's knees. Who predicted the Shemsari would do so and let the shield drop before he charged in. Two hundred-plus pounds hit Jhabari like a wagon. Bow flew uselessly to the sand.

Rooster tossed the shield aside and hefted Awakener as the Shemsari boy scrambled to his feet, drawing one of those long knives.

"Make your prayers then boy. You picked the wrong fight here."

Fearless—he had to hand it to Jhabari. The kid didn't waste time begging or showing any weakness. He struck swiftly and slashed the air where Rooster had been.

It was a damn shame he had to be put down like a dog.

Rooster parried the strike of the dagger and swung back. Jhabari howled as the great blade struck his arm and drank his blood. Dropping the knife, the boy grabbed his arm to staunch the bleeding.

And there Rooster was, Awakener raised over his head. Like an executioner. But this had to happen—mutiny had to be treated in kind.

The blade fell.

When the eagle flew in out of nowhere, its claws glanced at the blade to knock it aside.

Hazair.

Jhabari cheered at first but the sound died in his throat—the eagle flapped to a landing. On Rooster's shoulder.

Primitive fear froze him. Like a mouse in a field. That razor beak mere inches from his face. Lidless golden eyes—like the twins. The damn thing was heavy. He suddenly realized the pain in his shoulder was the claws, burying into the muscle. Slowly. Methodically.

"Kill him Hazair," the boy cried, "Do it for father!"

But the eagle didn't heed him.

Just stood there and stared into Rooster's eyes.

Like hypnosis into golden-orange pools.

"How can this be? He's gharib!? You obey me Hazair!

Obey me you stupid bird!"

Sand softly crunched from footsteps behind.

Rooster dared to look back, fearing the eagle would gouge his eyes at any moment. It was Jhamon. Tears streaked down his dirtied face. The boy fell to his brother's side and pointed out.

Towards nothing.

Just another mirage.

Jhamon choked up, "No Jhabari. It's him. It's father. He's with us."

Rooster swore he did see something. A shimmering silhouette. A phantasm of the man he saw back in Kahil.

For the first time in his life, he felt embarrassed to be godless. To have had no faith in anything beyond the steel he could swing. That if there were forces beyond, their songs fell deaf on his ears.

Because the Shemsari were shaken to their bones.

Rooster envied their awe.

"He's going away," Jhabari said in disbelief, "He's leaving us."

Jhamon shook his head, "No brother. He's with Bahram. And Bahram watches us."

The eagle chirped and dug its claws in deeper.

Rooster dropped Awakener—muscles involuntarily made a spasm.

"He's a pretender brother. A demon. The J'awed says we must slay them," Jhabari snarled up at Rooster.

Three sets of golden eyes upon him.

Judging him.

What they failed to see was what Rooster did—the silhouette. For behind it and around it the sun was perfectly falling behind it as it set. And formed a ring of ethereal gold.

The eagle squawked as if it knew his thoughts.

Rooster began to walk into that sunlight, mindless.

That shadow in the sun—it *was* real.

"Bahram?"

Jhamon got to his knees and bowed his head. Jhabari was slower but followed suit.

Rooster did not bow. He did not think to.

The silhouette had become an eclipse and the solar halo around it more intense. The figure beckoned forth to walk into the sun.

"Why?"

The eagle made a sound like it was laughing, chirping deep in its feathered throat. Extending both wings to flap slowly, rhythmically. By some spell, their beat started to make a drumming in his head. Gaining louder and faster with every beat.

The figure in the sun raised an uplifted palm.

Before melting away with the falling sun.

مدمرة متاهة

The Maze

Few ladies of the courts could match the gaudy opulence of the Vizier of Nefara—let alone any duke or earl Rooster had ever met. This fop wore an entire treasury in jewels and silks on him. And wore far too much makeup, to boot.

To his credit, Vizier Jahan Al Azraq was a great listener and wanted to do nothing with his day besides beg for stories of adventure. The man saw little outside his palace walls. Or had anything to do with the actual function of the city. Not a surprise there.

Tariq stepped in at times to offer his council and explain political scruples. The Vizier dismissed him like a fly. Their relationship seemed one-sided.

To an outsider, maybe.

The other attendants listened just as well but for other reasons Rooster distrusted. Captain of the Guard Musha and his late brother Khandaq had been the warlords who ruled Nefara before its annexation. The fat hungry vulture sat idly and acted bored. Poorly disguising his interest whenever Rooster was asked to explain his strategy.

The Medeans should not have left him in charge of anything in this city. That was a massive oversight. Warlords never became meek and civilized. An analogy of milk and cows and their cost came to mind.

Lastly at their conference was a very comely Sabean woman who smiled like a doting wife to Rooster. Who had perfectly manicured nails of emerald green and skin like smooth ivory; the Qorchi heiress of the Shalmanisar.

He stiffened at her presence.

Tariq didn't seem to notice. He seemed thrilled that the heiress had been dragged into court to answer for the crimes.

Wine and candied fruit were brought in by the wagon to accommodate the strange meeting.

Vizier al Azraq laughed like a madman, lounged like a whore, and ate like a beggar. Rooster recounted everything they'd faced on the road and when he was done, the Vizier clapped like a fool—a servant came with a scroll.

It was read aloud.

Nefara owed the vagabond known as Rooster a great debt. To the tune of ten thousand silver crescents or a hundred golden leopards, a small estate in the farmlands to the west and a title. Sanjak of the Road, Enforcer of the Borders. Just as Tariq had promised.

Musha pretended to be unhappy. The Shalmanisar heiress was stoic. Tariq was flush with satisfaction.

Which made Rooster apprehensive.

But turning down the Shah's appointed governor was downright inane. It was a lot of money. Enough to set him up good for years.

Rooster bowed deeply and accepted graciously.

Like the devil incarnate, Tariq waited for him on the immaculate tiles of the palace. There was not a single piece of pottery that did not fit into the intricate pattern of painted flowers and shapes. Even the curved ceilings weren't safe from the bold orange and red paint. There were still scaffolds in place where calligraphers carefully worked.

An eyebrow climbed up, "I see my courtier failed to dress you appropriately for the occasion."

"No, he was persistent alright. I'm just more stubborn. Besides, isn't that overkill?"

"The Vizier is quite sensitive to the aesthetic. You're lucky he wasn't offended."

A servant appeared from thin air with a vial on a cushion, offering it his way.

"Poison?"

Tariq sniffed, "Perfume. You smell of horse still."

Rooster took it and sprayed. He knew he looked rugged enough. Better to insult the eyes alone without the nose.

They walked into the archway, "I'm sorry. I thought your Vizier wanted to meet Rooster the Bandit Lord, not Rooster the Opulent Poof."

"Our Vizier is a depraved man. If I wanted to woo him, I'd have a prostitute waltzing in here with a cock ring."

"Charming."

Tariq seemed enthusiastic despite everything, "No matter. You made an impression out there. One that won't soon be forgotten."

Before they entered the last great room and the silver-paneled double doors to the outside, Rooster grabbed the bureaucrat by the wrist and hauled him up to a pillar.

It was a perfect place in the shadows to get some answers.

"Just a moment of your time Qadi. Just when were you going to tell me the Shalmanisar were in league with the Ivory Queen *before* I met you."

Tariq was unreadable, "It's punishment by maiming to touch an officer of the Vizier. Even for a lord."

"This is me being friendly. I don't like tricks Tariq."

"I understand your anger, I do—"

Rooster didn't see any guards nearby, so he grabbed the man's hand in his and began to squeeze. Almost enough to break it.

"For someone who talked about loyalty, I'm surprised you don't know it works both ways, *friend*."

The bureaucrat dropped this voice to a whisper, "Please forgive me. I sent the detachment as soon as I heard from my spies in Tyhri."

He began to squeeze harder.

"You knew that it wasn't just guards we'd be facing."

"And I knew you were capable as any of defeating them," Tariq glanced at the doors, "Things have transpired since your last stay here. I will tell you when we are done with this meeting. But the blame lies on me I know. Whatever I can do to earn your forgiveness, name it."

"Breaking your hand would be a start."

"And it would be just, but the guards patrolling these corridors will have your head."

Rooster let go and stepped back, "I'll decide my price later."

The bureaucrat adjusted his robes and brushed them as if they had dirt, "Indeed. In any case, you are a rich man now. I have delivered everything that was promised."

True.

Many would have ignored the details and taken the blood money without question.

"One more thing, Qadi."

Rubbing the sore fingers, "With you, it's always more than one."

"You had a deal with that woman in there? The Shalmanisar?"

Tariq did not react, "What do you mean?"

"You know her, don't you?"

"It's my business to know everyone who operates in Nefara."

Rooster chose to be blunt, "No history with her?"

"She's not my type, fortunately. Or else I might be corrupted."

"No reason, just a hunch."

It could have been an innocent lie to cover up muddy waters. But Rooster didn't notice any sparks flying between the two. If anything, they'd acted quite cool in each other's presence.

Tariq leaned in, grabbing his arm and patting his hand with the other, "Nothing to worry about now. You whipped the Ivory Queen like a beaten bitch. The Shalmanisar won't be a problem any longer. Enjoy your spoils, my friend. You've earned them."

"I will. And just maybe I'll join you for some chilled wine eh? From all that ice you had brought."

Playing his hand was worth the momentary horror that crossed Tariq's face. Rooster revealing he knew he was being lied to was impulsive maybe. But it did prove something.

Not everyone was some mindless pawn in the Dirt Lord's game.

And that had to have gotten his goat.

Feathered cushions, wine, and roasted lamb beat the hell out of starving to death in the desert.

Wealth; oh how it was missed.

Rooster kicked back his boots and leaned into the cushions. Gladiators below his private box were beating the piss out of each other. An errant tooth now and again. The Scorpion Pit was just the place for a fat bandit cat to spend his days—a sellsword's paradise. Wine, women, and someone else was fighting in the arena built in the center of the den.

Antonius was more interested in the dolled-up pieces of meat that lounged in a box across from theirs, "What about those?"

"You're better off dumping your silver off in a river."

"Miserable old turd you are eh. They're looking at me!"

Rooster chortled, "Because they know they can swindle you."

The girls across were playing their tricks, flipping their hair and batting their lashes. The kind of moves that drove a young man mad.

"Oho, see!"

"If you were on the street they wouldn't take a second look."

"Spoken like a shriveled old goat," Antonius snickered,

leaning to throw a date at one of the women. It bounced off one of their servant's glistening chests and they giggled, "Women adore me and I adore them. Hang me."

"The only thing they adore is your purse."

Bold creatures they were, the girls walked over to their box. Antonius whistled as they strutted right up to bodyguards—Musha's men, assigned to guard the Sanjak at all times.

Rooster suspected they were likely spies more than anything. But to dismiss them would anger the Vizier.

"Ladies, welcome," Antonius laid out on the rug, patting the cushions nearby.

Nefarans were all brunettes with a particular olive sheen and eyes like great dark opals. Similar to Medeans in many ways. Someone had told Rooster they were cousins in a way. But everyone in the desert was some byproduct of interbreeding. Except for the Shemsari.

One with a thousand braids adorned with topaz and silver clasps found her way onto his knee, her Patina enriched with a husky accent, "Hello."

"Sorry sweetheart but I can't afford you."

She laughed like a bell and patted his arm, "Funny gharib. I'm not for sale. Tell me a story of your home."

Bad memories floated their way up—the wine didn't help.

Rooster forced a smile, "None are pleasant I'm afraid."

"Seduce me with one gharib."

"I can't."

The Nefaran girl sighed and drank from his cup, "Do not worry. Your wife will not know."

"My wife's dead," Rooster replied without thinking.

Whatever romantic air had lingered between them was sucked out of the room. Those dark eyes accented by makeup went blank. The poor girl was young, used to men of baser instincts.

His psychological shield protecting him from his past had slid down. Just enough for someone to see inside—that ugly monstrous mass harbored under the flesh. Rooster didn't blame her for the reaction.

A wise man told him that a man could change but he was like a tree, one that grew far and wide but could never rid himself of his roots—no matter their evil and gnarled nature.

The Nefaran girl almost fell off his knee.

"I think," he offered to lift her, "You will find another man to warm his bed this evening."

She didn't even look at him, just fled.

The rest of the box were too captivated with feeding Antonius grapes and oiling his chest. Caught up in youth and in the moment.

He said to no one that listened, "I'm going to get some fresh air."

Every city had its miserable side. Dereliction was impossible to avoid. It was only natural to push everything into a slum—ram as much of the filth and social decay into one place.

Unless you were Nefara.

Rooster stepped outside into the cool air. A moon waxed half-full. There was almost as much activity here as there was in the daytime.

He turned and felt his jaw fall to the sand. A turbaned cyclops appeared for a moment and then vanished in the crowd.

"Darwish?"

Rooster began to pursue. Heart thumped in relief. The dead walked again.

Sandstone corner after the next, soon they were passing out of the radius of lamp-glow. Rooster had assumed the center of Nefara to be a hill—since no light came from it at night. He watched Darwish melt into the darkness of that place and realized he'd been dead wrong.

The vast middle of the city was unlit. A district bigger than all the others combined.

A stray cat crooned, padding up to rub against his leg.

"You going to protect me, little mouser?"

It purred dumbly. But it was a maniac and it fled to the

light to chase a flying roach.

The truth was Rooster did feel nervous.

But Darwish was a friend in need.

Into the darkness, he plunged. The air was cooler in here. There were windows into places and doors that looked hollow. No guards or stalls or even old men at stoops. This was not the same city he had just left.

Warped shadows played out across the dim sandstone. Some bodies moved here, skulking and wandering aimlessly. They may as well have been dead—they barely mumbled.

A gauntlet of dilapidated squares and avenues were paraded with beggars. And worse. Rooster stepped onto a body that didn't move. Flies buzzed angrily as he disrupted their feast. Peals of ghoulish, mindless laughter echoed off the walls. Somebody reached to grab his cloak—a spidery hand.

A face emerged into the moonlight attached to the hand. An emaciated child. Skin taut like a skull. Eyes shrunken and hollow. Stumps for teeth.

It smiled. There was no light of intelligence in its eyes.

Rooster outstretched a hand and the kid continued to smile as it retreated into that dark nothing.

Goosebumps rippled across his flesh.

He drew his knife and continued where last he saw the turbaned shape. But it had abandoned this hell.

"Darwish," he dared call out.

Stagnant wind and unfriendly attention were all that replied.

Rooster did not like anything about this. Something screamed in his head to panic and flee.

He sniffed a thing in that stagnant air. Smoke tinged the nose. That burned leaf, the strange drug that Antonius had in that den. Overwhelmingly prevalent in this place. Every street reeked of it. That and unwashed filth.

If he didn't know any better, Rooster would have figured the place was consumed by this stuff. He was beginning to feel woozy as if being here was enough to affect his senses. A second-hand effect.

Fear had him scramble for fresh air. And found something else.

A new smell came and sobered him immediately; metallic and acrid. The assassins from Kahil and the Iron City. Faint as it was, the ammonia-laced copper was too distinct to ignore.

Rooster began to follow it like a bloodhound. Careless as it might have been. Caution could go to the wind.

He had no idea how—losing it a few times and almost giving up—but the trail did take him down a new path. This district seemed to get even sparser with bodies the deeper he went. Mazelike. The scent grew stronger until it filled his nostrils.

Rooster expected to round the corner and find one of the dark-clad assassins nose to nose.

Nobody. Just a well—long abandoned and boarded up—with a public yard. Decades ago maybe it was a place where Nefarans gathered and chattered. Layers of dust-coated rags from disintegrated clotheslines and rusted pots home to scorpions and mice.

The smell had suddenly vanished.

Rooster felt horrified—that his imagination had led him here. But then it returned and banished any thought of madness, albeit coming at a slow trickle like the tendril of a campfire.

Ammonia-laced copper came back even stronger.

Quickly scoping out the houses and the boarded well brought up nothing. There were no tracks in or out of this place that he could see either.

Wherever the source of it emanated was beyond his abilities.

However, a distant glow like a torchbug shone for a brief moment ahead—there was a crack in a wall. A district that bordered this dark one. He climbed through it and found himself back in the land of the living. Coated in dust and exhaustion.

Rooster turned back to remember the place.

Just in case.

Darwish was a survivor—he held out hope the hillman was still in there, fighting for his sanity. A faint hope.

"Shields up. Spears ready. Advance. Steady. Retreat. Line—rotate. Not like that. Without tripping like fuck-ups. Repeat," Antonius was going hoarse.

There was a certain point where drilling became an act of futility.

This was such a time.

Rooster called for a break from the pavilion of the villa—his villa. Still hadn't gotten used to that. Everything in the compound was his. The novelty hadn't rubbed off yet. He wasn't in good humor so there was a distinct possibility that would happen soon.

Men milled like it was their profession by the time he got out into the yard. Shattered tile in the dirt hinted that the villa had once served a more elegant purpose. But like all old things well beyond their fruitful years, the villa was learning new tricks.

"Sergeant Antonius, a word."

"Yes, Rooster?"

"Captain Rooster," he wanted to hit the Teridian upside the head.

Antonius winced—finally figuring out what he'd done wrong.

"We'll talk over it later. I need your perspective on something. Assemble the pieces and I'll find the cracks."

He walked them back to the elevated pavilion to watch.

Twenty or so had now grown to fifty. Mostly Medeans. Four black men had become twelve—the Pta-Ophi they called themselves. Goshawk seemed an unofficial leader and they gravitated towards his direction, superseded by Antonius. They were being tutored in Patina and learning it quickly. Meanwhile the Shemsari boys were doing what they did best; chasing chickens and servants on horseback.

"What are our setbacks now?"

"Coordination. Communication. The usual problems. But..."

"Spill it."

Antonius folded his arms, "Musha's men."

"What do you think of them?"

"They're professionals. Soldiers raised from birth. They take to commands well."

"Too well?"

Antonius nodded, frowning.

"I noticed that too. Acting very un-Medean I noticed in the yard."

"Grew up skirmishing these guys my whole life until our Terid made peace with the White Dove. I know them. It's not in their nature to treat us equally."

Old prejudices died harder than any other societal appurtenance. They were often the backbone to geopolitical nature, Rooster understood. Especially in this land. Under empire where many cultures clashed, a dominant one would always seek to reprimand the rest, to yoke them; Medean in this case.

"As if they've been ordered to play nice."

"My thoughts exactly, eh captain."

"One wonders why."

"I don't," Antonius muttered.

Rooster patted the man on the shoulder, "I'd be worried if you did. We aren't fools but the Medeans think we are. Musha didn't gift us anything but a contingency."

Either the man had no nerves or was arrogant enough to think they wouldn't notice. It was pointless to dwell on it. The men couldn't stay. Yet they couldn't be dismissed outright—the Vizier would have a fit, Musha would send more of his loyal men, and they'd be back to square one.

Antonius rubbed his chin, "I had a thought."

"Spill it then."

"Elect one of them as an officer and invent a need for them on the road. Send them on a patrol to nowhere."

Bold plan.

Rooster didn't dare show how proud he was of Antonius—not yet at least, "I like it. You're catching on. Go on and do it."

Antonius did, running back out to the yard, barking for everyone to fall in line.

No use in celebrating. One fire put out always meant ten more were just about to light up.

A Nefaran servant had come from the yard, bowing, "Ayubin. A messenger at the gate for you. Says he's come from the Qadi Tariq's office."

As he went down the stairs and across the yard shaded by even rows of palms and giant blue succulents, Rooster recollected their last conversation. It had been over a month since then. Spring was in near full bloom. He was beginning to think the bureaucrat had forgotten him.

The man before him was crooked in posture and tall yet, bearing an everpresent and subtle sneer, "Lord Rooster. Your presence is requested at the bathhouses with Qadi Tariq."

"When?"

"Now. You'll follow me."

Some cheek, this guy.

"And if I'm preoccupied?"

"Whatever it is you're accomplishing here," the man's eyes tracked the movements in the yard and smirked so slightly, "Can surely wait. The Qadi cannot be kept waiting."

"That important is it?"

Pure venom back, "I wouldn't be here to summon you now if it wasn't, would I?"

Rooster swallowed his anger. He hated this beck-and-call business. He wasn't anyone's hound to call on.

"Go on then you vulture. And hey, you're important, right? Enough that you'd be missed if I hacked that ugly head off your shoulders?"

Steam infused with eucalyptus and rose oil cloyed the air. The private bathhouse even boasted gold leaves for faucets and polished ivory for decorative embellishments.

Almost relaxing enough to banish reservations.

"Nazsif says you threatened to behead him," Tariq lounged in the waters, pausing to sip from a chalice, "Please, join me, friend."

"I did. He annoys me."

"Servants will at first. Until they prove terribly useful. You'll grow accustomed to it, with time."

The waters were soothing, Infused with some kind of serum that coated the skin and opened the pores. Rooster basked in the calmness of it, closing his eyes. When he cracked them open, Tariq was staring at the wound at his chest.

"Does it ever pain you?"

"Sometimes," he grunted, looking for a servant who could bring him a chalice of his own.

Tariq's gaze was sharp, "Did the blade strike your heart?"

"Nicked it. Or that's what the healer told me."

A drink then, "I heard a story once. A long time ago. Down in the wastes beyond the river, there was a tribe that would kidnap travelers and cut their hearts out of their chests. With a blade of black stone, said to come from the belly of a mountain. Still beating."

"Every village has a ghost story like that. Keeps peasants in line."

"Yes, I suppose, but this one was different. They said the victims would still be breathing, screaming even, for days. Scavengers didn't dare approach them. Because the tribe used the living hearts and souls of djinn to attract their god, who could only feast on the primordial spirits. The god rewarded them with powers that allowed them to walk among mortals for eternity."

"What were they called?"

"Djinn-eaters. Devnawe."

"Hmph."

A silver tray of fresh wine and dates arrived for each of them.

Rooster didn't care much for old wife tales or nightmare stories to spook children.

He picked a plump date, "I'm pretty sure it was my purse and sword the man wanted, not my soul."

"You'll forgive me, I get sidetracked when I'm trying to

avoid more present conflicts. My mind is not where it should be. I need your counsel."

"Mine?"

"There are few others I can trust now. The situation has altered. Enough that things in Nefara are about to change in ways even I can't predict."

There was sincerity there enough to scare Rooster if just a hair.

The bureaucrat had rarely shown much candor.

"I'm all ears."

"A moment, if you will. Nazsif?"

The servant flew in like a damn ghoul, "Yes, master?"

"Make sure there are no prying ears or eyes."

A bow, then it was done. Nazsif returned in a matter of a minute, affirming this. For a bony crank, he moved fast.

"No one can disturb us. Not even the Vizier. Go now," Tariq leaned back and rubbed his mouth, deep in thought.

Rooster was anxious, "What is it?"

"Chaos in the capital. Read those."

There was a collection of scrolls aside from the pool. Bearing royal seals, all broken. Rooster began to pore through as terse he could. His Medean was still rough.

"What's the *Tahatama*t?"

"The Gathering of the Thirteen Lords. The head of every province accounted for, locked in a sealed court with the new Shah. Or in our case..."

Rooster continued to read. Until his eyes grew heavy. He felt as if he'd read something wrong and went back.

"His eminence Caliph Jahwar ibn Anwar ibn Abar Ayadin? What a stupid fucking name. Why doesn't it just say Shah?"

"Because the Boy King has declared jihad against the Ivory Queen and named himself Caliph."

"Sounds like we expected that."

Tariq nodded to the scrolls, "Read the next one there."

Rooster did. What he scanned made him double-take and it took a conscious effort to continue and not blurt out. None of this could be repeated if it was true.

Tariq's solemn face all but confirmed it.

"Shit."

"Yes, my thoughts exactly."

"But...why?"

"Is there ever a reason why men do what they do when it comes to the great game of power? No, Rooster I'm afraid I'm as much at a loss as you. Some men have no reason besides they feel spurned from birth. They want to start fires for the sake of it," Tariq drained an entire chalice and started on another.

Rooster did likewise.

He'd heard of kings who isolated their noblemen by hasty proclamations when sitting on the throne for the first time. But in all his life, never one who declared half the lords in his kingdom as traitors and rebels. Certainly not when said king had to muster armies to march a thousand miles away.

"What we do know is that Sultan Sulman Mastoor is the most powerful lord in the Caliphate besides the Boy King. His and ten other lord's heads will roll.

"And?"

"Civil war is all but inevitable now. But the Boy King won't be in the capital to witness his first failure."

"Elaborate."

Another scroll appeared from behind Tariq, "The Caliph left the Sunstones ten days ago. He didn't just declare jihad to sit in his fortress and wait for the Ivory Queen to make the first move."

Rooster was almost afraid to read this one.

It was worse than the last.

The Boy King called out his banners. A force of ten thousand mamluks, cataphracts, levies, and janissaries had been seen massing as he moved south to the Qaryat al Hadid. Black smoke over the Iron City—it was under siege by hillmen and tribal forces of the Ivory Queen. The bridge spanning the gorge had been destroyed ahead of his advance. The last report read that the Boy King and his rapidly expanding army were moving east towards a place unfamiliar that would give them passage through the Wall; Sha Ghishum.

"He's coming to Nefara," Rooster thought aloud.

"It's not an army. It's a force of reckoning. An apocalypse," Tariq's voice wavered, "There has not been such a force in these lands for centuries. Maybe millennia."

"How many can he amass?"

"My eyes say they count thirty thousand now. But there are still legions from Sipahis and cohorts from Ghulam that will be joining him. And...the Confederated Tribes of the Shemsari. If they see the Boy King succeeding."

Thirty thousand was a hurricane of steel. A quantity like that was more than just a quality all its own—there wasn't a city in the north that wouldn't tremble at the prospect. No wall could withstand that.

"Where will he go?"

"First here, to establish a foothold. Then Tyhri to pluck the prized pearl. If the Ivory Queen doesn't beat him to it."

"Would she meet him openly?"

Tariq rifled through a few more reports, "Unlikely. Her efforts now are concentrated on proxy armies battling it out on the Caliphate's western borders. When she finds out he's left the capital, she may not have time to respond."

Gravity weighed on Rooster's shoulders.

Nefara had tall walls. But not tall enough and not a garrison big enough to repel the likes of the Ivory Queen. If her cavalry were any hint at her might.

"How long will it take him?"

"Who can say in the desert? Three weeks? Three months? It cannot be predicted. Summer is coming. He must make it to the city or his men will die in the dunes."

"And the Queen to sally out from Tyhri?"

Tariq shook his head, "You saw firsthand if just a taste. Her advanced parties could be sieging our walls within the week. The entire brunt of her forces within two."

The news would travel fast. If they knew, then the Ivory Queen did too. And based on the rumors of her, she was already moving pieces across the board.

"How recent is your information?"

"This report came to me this morning. Three hours ago."

Rooster set the goblet down, "I have but thirty-some men, counting those I can rely on not to stab me in the back. Even if you gave me a thousand to train, we couldn't be ready to repel whatever she can throw at us."

The likelihood that Nefara was about to get put to the sword and torch was certain. Not something they could hope to prevent. Or want to be in the middle of.

Across from him, Tariq was working up something, maybe preparing to reveal more information.

"Unless you have something hidden up your sleeve?"

"I just might, my friend. Your eyes on this have been counsel alone."

"My advice? Don't tell Musha. Not until you get a handle on what can be done."

The bureaucrat was the first to ascend from the pool, "Keep practicing with your men. I might be able to pull some strings in the Sword Row and call in a few favors. With what our future holds, we can use all the loyalty we can get."

"How forthright of you."

In a separate antechamber filled with a dull amber glow, there was a washbasin and silk rags. Tariq began to dry himself and it appeared spiderweb cracks were stitching across his flesh. In the light and up close, Rooster saw it was scarring. From the neck down, thousands of tiny cuts.

For all the tortures and botched alchemies in all his life he'd never seen anything like it.

Tariq noticed, "Even for all your anger, you know that I have always been honest in my dealings with you."

"How did you get that?"

The bureaucrat looked down at his arms as if they belonged to someone else, "My upbringing was harsh and cruel. As a child, I used to envy slaves for their luxurious life—compared to mine."

"Where was this?"

"A place far beyond the delta. I left the moment I could. There was a trader I met who spoke of an ancient and miraculous city, built on the banks of the river. That is how I found Nefara."

"How many have you told that story?"

Tariq answered, "No one."

"And yet the masses call you the Dirt Lord."

Rooster toweled off and began to dress in his new lordly get-up. But Tariq did not. The bureaucrat was staring into the depths of the washbasin, contemplative.

"Yes, they do. They call me many things because they have judged me accordingly. Based on what they see."

"You disagree with them?"

A faint chuckle, "Why should I? They see what I want them to see—I control the reflection in the mirror."

Rooster did not care to be intellectual at the moment. He was thinking about more present matters. Horses, steel, manpower, and all things a lord had to consider when war was upon him. The topic just seemed to be more rant than discussion now.

"If that's your style I suppose."

Tariq made a derisive sound, "For a moment consider what power is."

"I don't need to worry about controlling puppets. I have soldiers to field, remember?"

"Who must both love and fear you. Just as the delegates of the Vizier and every soul in this city must do for me also. Our battlefields may be different but one thing unites us—the image of our own making. Strategy, influence, these are both necessary but what is of greater import is how we are seen by our friends," the man said, dabbing his face with the rag, "And our enemies."

Rooster left the bathhouse. A promise of summer's infernal heat blew over the delta and hit the streets.

Oh, the winds of change were coming—and they were hot as hell.

For once Tariq overdelivered on his promise instead of

his standard mediocrity. The favor took the form of four able-bodied and seasoned warriors—so they claimed. Gharibs who were deep with the loan sharks and bargained their service over debtors' prison or worse.

Good things happened in fours, Rooster speculated. He was awed by his own supersition—the desert was starting to rub off on him.

They went by Rafe, Lancer, Big Mug, and Diedegris who others called Carver. They already came sufficiently armed, mounted, and a black smudged past. It wasn't discussed but Rooster suspected the loan amounted to Rafe's failed attempt at a sellsword company. Judging by their starved looks, this was their shot at redemption.

Yet for all their hunger the white mercenaries were more interested in fortune. And renown.

Behind the walls of his compound, Rooster had them swear an oath of fealty to the standard the Shemsari boys had erected in the courtyard. It might have been the shaft of a cataphract's lance and a piece of one, lashed together with horse-hair rope. Or just any old stick. A simple orange-red banner that had been torn from who knew where. And speared at the top was the skull of the werehyena, scoured of all flesh. It was a menacing thing enough that the servants begged for it to be taken down. They claimed devil's hands made it.

But Rooster liked it too damn much.

For good measure he had every one of the Birds of Prey cut his palm and leave a bloody print on the wood while swearing a similar oath. No reason, it just felt right.

When all was done they looked to him. His print joined theirs.

The Ayubin had conventions to their standards—they were principled men. But he wasn't a lord in the eyes of any Medean. Why pretend to be one?

So declared the grotesque banner of his warband.

"I didn't know it could rain here," Rooster commented.

Cinching down the leather loops to adjust the mailed harness, the armorer grunted from below, "A portent of the heavens gharib. One must always pay attention to signs disguised as gifts."

"You people get a miracle and you think it's a trick," a strong tug tightened his waist and almost doubled him over, "Hey you said the guy who wore this before me was the same size."

"He was a great fat man with wide shoulders gharib. I swear on my life."

But the armorer did loosen the adjustment. When all was done the harness fit like a glove. Steel plates a finger length long and wide were nailed to a treated leather shell that covered all the vitals—the armorer said it was crocodile. It was the best Rooster could buy.

Rooster tapped a spot where there was a missing plate, "What about this?"

"A small problem but not for you."

"You said the sellsword who owned this died in his sleep."

The armorer punched the spot and smiled, "Yes yes. He drank too much. But this, even an arrow would only graze your hip gharib. Just use a shield."

"I need both my hands. Big sword."

The armorer shook his head in amusement, "Incredible. So I will recover this armor again!"

"You wish, gravedigger. So what is this going to cost me?"

"A thousand crescents. A price you can't beat. You could not remake this for that."

There were a few minutes of haggling that went nowhere. The armorer was a miserly old nut. By the time Rooster walked back out from the stoop into the humid air and gray skies, his whole purse was left behind.

Under the enchantment of the rain, Nefara exuded a chthonic air. The old city released a sweet earthy tone merged with wet stone. An entirely new side of the place that Rooster had not seen.

He walked the wet sand and avoided puddles. Feeling that he might have spent far too much and would regret it later. A few drinks would rationalize the purchase.

Two shadows waited for him—Jhamon and Jhabari.

"Come on you two."

Nothing like a late morning stupor to watch the rain.

Rooster stepped under an awning where an establishment served wine from cups chained to the pillars. A man brushed him—a musician who sat on a rug and produced an oud. Immediately he began to play a tune that filled the room with mystique.

The Shemsari refused to enter, clinging to their cloaks like soaked street cats. Shivering.

He called to them, "You miserable bastards going to dry off or what?"

Jhamon's teeth chattered, "It is J'awed. We cannot stand under a stone roof."

"Bullshit. Does the J'awed also tell you to get the plague by exposure?"

Stubborn mules they were, they just found a pillar to warm up against.

"Wild are the hearts of Bahram's sons," sang the man with the oud, folding in a new rhythm.

"Nice tune. Can't pay you for it though."

Fingers plucked a soft yet melancholic song on the bent neck of the instrument. The player with the skull cap and beard was good. Good enough to play for kings.

"Sorry."

The man's voice fell, "Your silver isn't what we seek...Rooster. Only your ear and your steady hand."

“Come again?”

He hadn’t misheard, the player said, “Did you think we forgot you, servant of Tariq?”

For a moment Rooster didn’t piece it together. Then it did; the same strumming in the gambling den, the tall shadow that hung by the lamplighter kid.

Not these creeps again.

With a hand on the hilt of Awakener, “You again. Bold of you to come at me in daylight.”

No one in the drinking hall had noticed them. Perhaps

they wouldn't. It was slow and only the regular drunkards were afoot.

The man continued to strum, "I come only as a messenger."

"I doubt it."

"It is true Rooster. We must meet with you. An urgent matter has arisen that involves your master."

"Stop calling him that and I'll think about not cutting your stupid lute in half."

"We don't aim to offend you. But what our tongues hold onto is sensitive and it is dire."

"And?"

The player nodded, "Down the street on your right is a passage. It leads to a square where the dye-makers usually work. The second house on the left will have a lamp glowing in the window. You will know it by our hidden mark above the door."

"What happens if I don't want to meet?"

"Nothing. Except that you will not have a hand in stopping what is to come."

Rooster hated being kept out of the loop just as much as he hated being spied on.

He paid for the wine, drank from the public cup, and threw it so it swung to hit the musician. It barely missed. From behind the bar, the proprietor began to bark and stomp.

"Thanks for the entertainment," he said, walking back out to the rain.

"Where to now Rooster," Jhamon came up on his right.

"Go back to the villa."

"Why," Jhabari, the ever suspicious.

"It's nothing I can't handle."

Rooster supposed they were capable enough. He'd never admit the soft spot he'd developed for the kids. Or how it scared him to think of something happening to them.

He'd just play it off like they were his inferiors.

The problem was that they were Shemsari.

Goddamn Shemsari.

"Whatever it is, we will follow you," Jhamon insisted.

Rooster went to the alleyway and paused, gathering his thoughts, "First sign that something's off, you two go back to the villa and get Antonius with the others. Got it?"

Both just looked at each other.

"Got it? I want to hear it from you Jhabari."

"Yes Rooster," the boy practically hissed.

"Good."

Rain bled the dye-maker steps a palette of every color, combining into a rainbow river. The great vats usually full of powdered dyes were brimming with water. By the time they waded through it, the stuff turned into a gray sludge.

Nothing about these shadowy folks he trusted. Not worth a grain of salt. So when they got to the house with the lamp glowing in the open hole for a window, he made sure to unloop the handle to the bastard sword. Before he pushed the door—slightly ajar—inward, he looked up for the hidden sign.

A desiccated hand of a corpse had been nailed to the lintel.

"Listen and watch," he told the boys before leaving them.

Inside was cold and dark beside the single lamp.

The deep hiss of Awakener being drawn filled the void.

A child's voice, "You will not need your blade here Rooster."

"I respectfully disagree."

"It is poor form to enter one's house in such a way."

"While I commend your discretion, how you stalk and harass me won't have me dropping my sword anytime soon. Try anything and you'll have another hand to nail to the wall."

There was disagreement amongst the shadows with multiple sets of voices.

Another lamp was lit, held by a boy. He was not much older than the Shemsari. Just another poor Nefaran. He had oil stains on his smock and wore a sash.

The boy illuminated more of the vacant house, sitting

down at the table, and beckoned, "Please sit."

"Give me a good reason to."

"Because while you think us as devious, my friends and I are quite civilized."

"Yeah? Rats live in cities and are mistaken for house mice all the time."

The boy looked to the blade, "Illusion is our shield and secrets are our sword. We do what we must to survive. No different than you have, living among us desert-dwellers."

Rooster tried his best to scrutinize the kid. He wanted to detect that he was lying. No chance. Unless his usual bloodhound senses were screwed up from all the rain, there was something honest there.

In the eyes especially.

He laid down the bastard sword so the handle was readily accessible, and sat.

"Since our last meeting we've tried to reach you but it has not been so easy. Without being detected, of course," the boy responded to his expression, "Until today, it wasn't worth the risk."

"I've got a question; who the hell are you?"

"My name is Amir."

"Who am I dealing with here? Who do *you* serve, eh?"

Amir twitched involuntarily, "No one. We are united by a common purpose."

"Horseshit. Stop jerking my chain."

Onto the table, the boy produced a pale opal—the very same that Rooster had given them. It had gone unspent then.

"We are the Dead Hand. We serve no king."

"And I should believe you, Amir?"

"In your position, I would not. But what I'm about to say might change your mind."

"I'm all ears."

Another item was put on the table and pushed his way. A bright blue flower. The petals were delicate and almost glass-like.

"You don't know its name but you know it by its effect.

This is the cerulean lotus. Also known as the crystal dream. Your Teridian friend partook of it back in that den when we met last."

"What about it?"

"What if I told you the Shalmanisar were in secret negotiations with the Ivory Queen—desperately attempting to prevent the cerulean lotus from finding its way into Tyhri, as it has Nefara?"

"And I should care?"

Amir rolled the stem with his forefinger, "You should. With the Qadi you have all but ensured that the cerulean lotus can reach every corner of the desert, unimpeded. That Tyhri will suffer the same plague, as the lotus cannibalizes the mind and destroys the will of its victim."

"But what is worse is *who* you have empowered by your exploits. A group far more powerful than the Shalmanisar—a cartel hidden in this city that even we have had difficulty detecting. Who have already cut the throats of anyone they couldn't bribe or kidnap."

"Why are you telling me this?"

"Because Rooster; this cartel has now targeted your Dirt Lord. We've been following their agents for days now, haunting his private residence. They must have detected us and slipped back into the shadows. But we have reason to believe they'll emerge and make a move."

Rooster didn't know what to think. Everything resonated. Tariq's hubris had no bounds. The bureaucrat played politics like some did card games. It was inevitable he was going to step on someone's toes. And pay for it dearly.

"What do they want from him, this cartel?"

"Based on what we have discerned, they'll try to kill him. Publicly. And slander his name as a meddler and war profiteer."

"Why not go to him directly?"

Amir narrowed his eyes, "Do you seriously think that the guard hasn't already been paid off to look the other way?"

"Fair point."

"These gangsters are dangerous Rooster. They call themselves the Scorched Serpent Society. From what we have learned they came from the East, as master poisoners for a wicked king. They brought their cerulean lotus with them and now half of Nefara is under its spell. With Tariq dead, they'll have no one to fear from reproach."

"Except you."

"We are but humble thieves and graverobbers. If anyone can stop them, it's your Dirt Lord."

It seemed poetic—the Shalmanisar knocked down a peg and an even bigger threat took their place. No rest for the wicked, Rooster supposed.

"You said today it was urgent. What are they planning?"

"Not them. Tariq. There's been a rumor circulating the dens of someone who claims to have been with the White Dove at the moment of his death. A musician and known poet, Idris. The servants of the Dirt Lord have made contact with him. They'll meet today at Qeyoub Plaza, just after the afternoon prayer."

Qeyoub Plaza wasn't insignificant; it was overshadowed by the White Kasbah. A very public meeting. There'd be hundreds of eyes watching. Last place that anyone would conduct shady business.

"You think these Serpents will strike then?"

"Either Idris is working for them or he's authentic. Which bodes poorly for anyone who was involved in the White Dove's death."

"Wasn't the Ivory Queen behind it?"

Seldom did the Rooster feel dumb or inadequate.

Somehow Amir accomplished both by giving him a piercing look, "Do you think so?"

When he thought about it seriously? No. Considering the events leading up to the Qaryat al Hadid; Darwish and his hillmen working with the Medeans, the assassins who worked tirelessly to keep the news of the Dove's death under wraps, it all screamed conspiracy.

One that he was not clever enough to figure out.

Suddenly he felt his feet grow cold and his breath short. And it wasn't from the weather.

"How do I fit into this?"

"Get to Tariq. Accompany him. Protect him."

"Yeah. And what will you do?"

Amir got up from the table and lifted the lamp, "Watching. With any luck, we will find out where these Serpents are coming from. If they do strike."

"I don't like games, Amir. I don't like getting played. I'm the worst kind of enemy to make if you're pulling a fast one on me."

The boy reached out a hand to shake, "I don't doubt it Rooster."

He took it.

Awakener was lifted and thrust back into his belt—naked steel exposed. Then he made for the door.

"We may have our tricks but we wouldn't cross blades with you."

"It's not me that you have to worry about. I've got Shemsari devils watching my back. Slay this old boar and you've got some nasty piglets that are going to run you down."

Rooster swore that when he crossed from the verdant cloister of greenspace into the archway that fed into Qeyoub Plaza, Tariq lost all color in his face. Like he saw a ghost from his past. Then quickly recovered composure.

"My friend, what a pleasant and convenient surprise."

For the first time since they met, the bureaucrat was dressed down. Trading his silks and slippers for rough wool robes and sandals. The dead giveaway was the way Tariq walked and stood. Otherwise, he passed for a peasant.

"Shut up. I know why you're here. The informant."

A blink that must have encompassed a calculated thought, "However did you find out?"

"I have my sources, as do you."

"Very well Rooster. I underestimated you. But how did you find me in my guise?"

A nod towards the ropey shadow that lurked in the

green. The shape was indistinguishable. Then Nazsif stepped out into the light, irked. Especially at Jhamon and Jhabari, who padded right behind him.

"Who else do you have guarding you?"

"No one. This was meant to be a private affair," Tariq adjusted his clothes, smoothing them, "But I see now that you've stuck your beak into mine."

"On account of your protection."

Just then came the droning from the towers of the White Kasbah. A melodic voice rebounded off the walls, echoed by others that projected into all the districts of Nefara. The afternoon prayer called for the Third Progeny and its ruling son, Caliph Jahwar ibn Anwar ibn Abar Ayadin. The plaza ahead became abuzz with those standing to face the tower, bowing their heads.

On cue, Tariq began to walk through the archway, "I don't need your protection, thank you."

"I'd beg to differ. Slow down, damn you."

"Information is my trade, war is yours. Forgive me my northern friend, but let us speak on another day."

"You're being hunted. Even as we speak. By some cartel called the Scorched Serpents. Wait."

They were a quarter way across the packed sand of the plaza. Rain had all but let up. The storm had been broken through by small beams of light. Giving credence to the believers who gathered between the sandstone walls to cry praise up at the white domed building.

Tariq almost skidded to a halt, "How did you hear of this?"

"I can tell you about it later. But I can almost assure you that you're walking in a trap."

"*Who* told you?"

"Does it matter? There's a high likelihood they'll strike here, in front of everyone," Rooster grabbed the man's arm to pull him away, "Let me find this informant and question him. Or bring him before you."

"I'm afraid it's too late for that."

He followed the other's gaze to the tables that were set

out in the middle of the plaza. Surrounding a weathered statue of a bull hewn out of deep orange stone. Its craftsmanship screamed old kingdom. With his back against the square block, a flutist was playing atop a tall wicker basket.

Bodies began to fill up between them to join in the afternoon prayer. Hundreds of them. An entire city block.

Tariq began to push through them.

Rooster didn't like this.

Too many unknowns. Too many people they couldn't inspect. Too little time to sway Tariq.

He squeezed through to follow the bureaucrat's dust.

Medeans and Nefarans alike filled the air with chants. The prayer had long vowels and soft consonants with songbird-like harmony. If Rooster wasn't here to prevent an assassination, he might have enjoyed it.

All the sounds and bodies did was promote chaos.

Out of the corner of his eye, Jhamon and Jhabari both were spreading out in the crowd at his wings.

Tariq waited for him in the last group of chanters before the flutist, "Please, if you will. Keep your mouth shut for the next few moments. Unless you see something."

Rooster nodded but his head was on a swivel. Looking for anything out of place. An exercise in futility. If anything came at them, it could be easily hidden in the masses.

They made it to the bull statue and the flutist sitting on the basket.

There were long hieroglyphs scratched in lines wrapped around the statue—over five men in height. Thing had to have been carved here on the spot. If it had a meaning it was long lost.

Tariq had stopped just before the flutist, "Idris? You are the one they call Idris?"

But the musician was bowed in prayer.

The sheer noise of people chanting was enough to mask their conversation, even if it was yelled.

"Idris?"

Tariq grabbed the flute player. Who toppled sideways

from the basket. Painted wooden flute rolling away into the sand. Idris was a she, as it turned out. Obvious only because half of her face was still intact, frozen in horror. The other had been melted by acid, leaving the visage of a screaming skeleton behind.

A note had been nailed to the corpse's chest, but Rooster couldn't read it.

Because something sailed out of nowhere and struck him in the chest. Hard. The impact knocked him on his ass. Something smacked into the bull statue and landed by his eye; a long feathered dart, its iron tip coated with a liquid.

Rooster looked down and saw darts that had punched through his cloak and robes.

Shit.

Jhamon's voice rose above the din, "Rooster!"

Shapes were flying through the crowds—masked men in peasant's garb. They had blowguns stuffed into their belts and veils over their mouths. A dozen of them at least. They made it to the statue and Tariq.

The bureaucrat raised a hand, beginning to shout but the masked men had him over their shoulder and gagged before he could make a coherent noise. Like a sack of potatoes, they began to haul him away—towards the opposite end of the plaza.

Same ammonia and copper smell—his assassins.

The Serpents.

Rooster ripped his robes aside—all of the darts had hit the steel plates. But he had no time to leap up.

One of the assassins hung back to finish the job. Lifting a blowgun to his mouth. Too close a shot to miss. Then the dark-clad man suddenly fell back—a knife hilt sprouted from his chest. Landing only a few feet away from Rooster, coughing blood.

From the crowd, a servant who'd been carrying a tray of olives was bristling with throwing knives. Amir in the clothes of a Kasbah eunuch.

"Behind you," he shouted and pointed.

More assassins. Another dozen appeared from thin air,

rushing the statue. With long knives and curved sabers.

Rooster rolled in the sand and was able to bring Awakener up in the nick of time—a saber arced and barely missed his eye. The others would be on him to overwhelm in moments. The assassin before him was good—pantherish in his movements. He was forced to duel.

Steel on steel they danced in the square.

A step back on his heels invited the assassin to overexpose. Rooster drove the pommel of Awakener into the veiled man's face, took a wide step, and cleaved the man from shoulder to hip. Crimson sprayed the bull statue.

Four more assassins came simultaneously. One fell forward, another grew a throwing knife in his groin, and the other speared by a javelin.

Jhamon and Jhabari had arrived, along with Amir.

The last distracted assassin was easy to cut down.

Past the statue, Rooster watched helplessly as Tariq was getting further away. In a matter of seconds, the kidnapped man was taken behind the tightly packed buildings in an alleyway. The reality of the situation was settling in.

The assassins were still coming—like termites from rotten wood. They began to flank and surround the Shemsari boys. A pang of fear had Rooster begin to try aiding them.

From the crowd behind him, figures were running into the fray. Innocuous citizens. They produced daggers and fighting sticks of their own and clashed with the assassins. Both were falling like flies, splashing gore on the sand.

An assassin tried to cut off Rooster from Jhamon. With the bastard sword, he harried the veiled man to his knees and then split his temple in two. He didn't know how he did it—paternal instinct maybe.

Eagle cry alerted him above—Hazair was swooping down from the gray skies. Again the bird flew down a mere arms-length above the tops of their heads.

Trying to warn them.

Rooster followed its flight path; a wall of red cloth and

steel. Guards were running out from the direction of the Kasbah with shields and spears ready. Led by officers on horseback who marshaled them in a wide formation.

He wanted to cheer but it died in his throat.

Among the melee Amir was blood-stained, "Flee Rooster! It's a trap. They've come for you."

"How do you know?"

"Do you trust me?"

The end of the conversation came when an assassin hit Rooster in the back. The blunt force nearly knocked him over but the steel harness did its job. He wheeled and blindly swung the sword where it would decapitate.

The assassin didn't have time to bring his sword to bear. Like a melon, a head rolled onto the sand.

In the confusion of the melee, he spied one of the officers on horseback riding down one of the thieves. Flaying the back of a vagrant boy no older than nine. Hooves stomping the boy's lifeless back and head.

"Jhabari, Jamon," he shouted in the fray, "Where are you damn it?"

They were cut up but intact. Both were splashed with blood. A fever had taken over their eyes. The feral nomad had taken over.

"We're getting the fuck out of here. Find you a horse."

"Rooster!"

Hoofbeats closed in. That same Medean officer was gunning right for them, charging across the open square. Lance aimed right at Rooster's chest.

Any notion that the guards were confused about who he was got banished.

The horse was closing in and he had nothing to defend against it.

Jhamon shouted in Shemsari, to which Jhabari began to run at him. In a move the former interlocked his fingers and took a knee— his brother leapt deftly onto the hands and sprung himself onto the officer. Jhabari cut the man's throat mid-air and kicked him off his horse, then put his arm down to let Jhamon swing on up. All in a breath.

Damn and double damn.

Rooster grabbed his spear and hurled it at the next officer who tried the same. And missed by a lot. But the boys rode up and managed to rip him out of the saddle all the same.

By the time Rooster was up on the guard's horse, the massacre had begun. Assassins and thieves alike were piling up around the bull statue. A score or more dead. Red was everywhere—blood and guards filing into the square.

All to capture Tariq.

The betrayal hadn't yet set in.

People were screaming in the plaza, running amok. They had no idea what was happening. Their little minds were consumed by the bloodbath. To them, this must have been a scene of sheer horror.

Rooster forced himself to swallow the anger.

Had this been the plan all along—him and Tariq, sacrificial lambs for the slaughter? The fat bastard Musha and his guards in on the take the entire time? Perhaps the Vizier had known even. How deep did the rot of Nefara's politics go?

Out of the corner of his eye was Amir. A gauntlet of anonymous thieves fighting off guards, shoving daggers under mail coats, being gored by spears. They were being forced to retreat—to scatter along with the fleeing citizens. To abandon their dead and fight another day. He saw the Nefaran open his mouth to shout something but it was lost in the clash.

Time to go.

He spurred the gray horse on, towards the nearest archway.

"Pray to your god that the gate is still open," he shouted to the boys.

A group of guards made a grave error and tried to stop them under the archway. They were too green to know where and how to hold their spears. Poor bastards realized it too late.

Rooster dug the spurs in hard and yanked the bit on his

horse.

And plowed right through them.

The game was lost.

All of their political plots had been but a blind mouse bearding a great serpent in its cave. A great evil had been rotting away the bones of this city for some time and waiting for an opportune moment to sink its fangs into the unwary.

And Rooster had been lured right into it.

From the flat hilltops rising out from the arms of rock that swung above Nefara, he and his band watched the fire consume the villa. A bonfire that spat a black column into the sky as flame licked stone, reaching twenty feet with orange-red tendrils. The glow was intensifying.

Guardsmen walked like little ants around the perimeter, hurling torches into the courtyard. Soon their shortlived headquarters would be a blackened ruin.

It didn't matter if it was redundant. It was a symbolic victory.

Rooster turned in the saddle to face the dread that all leaders came to, sooner or later. Twenty or so faces looked at him—a mix of emotions. Doubt, anger, anticipation, anxiety. Waiting to see if he would damn them further—if he would drag them down another rung of hell.

So far none had deserted. That could easily change.

Good old rock-steady Antonius was the first to croak, "What's the move captain?"

"I don't know," he replied in earnest.

"We'll get the bastards, we'll get Tariq. Then the Vizier will pay us good and fat eh?"

This was the hard part—Rooster scratched his beard. Chasing after the Serpents in their turf, without the protection of the Qadi or the Vizier and hunted by the guard? It was suicide. No matter the reward. Just like Amir had said; this had been a plot long in waiting.

What was going on in his head must have shown on his face, Rafe was frowning, "Captain knows we'd be gutted the moment we walked back in there."

"Yes."

"But Tariq is our proprietor. He held our treasury in his office,"

Antonius argued, "Our entire war chest!"

"Wisen up boy. They'll put your chest of silver just inside the gate so they can noose you good," Rafe cackled.

"That's sergeant to you or I'll have you lashed!"

Tensions were getting out of control. It could have stopped a knife blade. The divide in the group was far too great and Rooster knew without the promise of payment, nothing could bridge that.

"He's right Antonius. Going back to Nefara is a death sentence."

Optimism faded from the sergeant's face, "I got a girl there now."

"Forget her loverboy," Rafe cooed.

Antonius shot him a black look but chose to take the high road.

Down on the dirt, the Ophi were grim but stood firm. Goshawk wandered over to Rooster, "We are with you captain. Wherever you go. Our spears are free and they are yours."

Loyalty wasn't the issue he was concerned over.

Each man had with him a few sacks lashed to his saddlebags and they had a few camels to carry them. Supplies to last them a week, maybe just outside that. Then the situation would get ugly. Horses needed to be fed and watered, men likewise. Even for twenty, that was a tall bill. They couldn't go to Tyhri—the Ivory Queen would happily mount his head on a pike. And that was a generous assumption that they'd even reach the enemy's walls, notwithstanding what they might find on the South Road.

Staying wasn't an option either. Hazarding to linger around Nefara any longer would be as much a death sentence as going into the desert. If the Serpents were competent they'd have spies everywhere.

Between a rock and a hard place.

Rooster almost respected the sheer evil of his foe, but

he was too stricken by the reality of their situation.

Jhamon rode up beside him. Toting that great ugly standard. Noticeably, the boys had begun stitching something on the orange-red canvas in white silk. It hadn't yet taken a form.

"I saw Hazair earlier. He was flying north and east," the boy said.

"Forgive me Jhamon but I'm not in the mood."

"It's a sign. He's telling us where to go."

From his other flank, Jhabari sidled up, "What are you saying, brother?"

"If we have nowhere else to stay and must flee...we can always go to uncle."

Bonfires lit in the eyes of Jhabari, "Ai-ai! Why didn't you suggest this earlier?"

"Because it is not for us to decide! J'awed says we must follow where Rooster goes."

Brotherly cursing in Shemsari followed.

Rooster turned to Jhamon to regard him. The boy was nervous. Fidgeting. Whatever prompted him hadn't been for any old reason. The suggestion came out of desperation.

"Who is uncle?"

"He is known! He is Azim Altaruk! He can protect us," Jhabari grew excited.

Where had he heard that name before? Like an imp dancing on the end of his tongue, it leapt off the pink thing. Racking his head did nothing to jog the memory.

"He used to ride with our father," Jhamon added.

"*Will* he protect us?"

The Shemsari boy failed to answer, chewing on one.

"Does he have the means to?"

To that, Jhabari laughed like a jackal, "Just wait until you see gharib!"

Rooster did not know what to make of any of it, but there was a clear difference of opinion. The problem was that opinions were about as worthless as dirt. They didn't have the luxury to indulge in disagreement right now.

"Jhamon."

The boy perked up, "Yes Rooster?"

"I'll leave it to you. If you think it's our best bet."

They spent a considerable time on that hilltop while Jhamon deliberated. Off in the shadows he and Jhabari held a hushed argument. It took enough time that the men grew bored enough to sit and catch a dust nap.

When Rooster felt his eyes growing heavy, Jhamon returned with soft footfalls in the sand, "We will be the safest with uncle. But we must tread carefully."

"If that is what you think."

Jhamon nodded, serious as a statue, "It is."

The decision might be their doom. Fate watched them like a raptor above and knew what would happen next.

Midnight winds flew across the dunes and tugged at their banner. Gusts that passed through the werehyena's maw like a ghostly howl.

"You two lead us then," Rooster spurred Nereel into a trot and rode across the hilltop, "Shows over gentlemen. Birds of Prey, mount up!"

part II.

اللصوص طريق
Thieves Road

Imagination wanders as the feet shuffle and clouds race away from one's unreliable vision. Mind and eye become discombobulated, in the desert. Every crest of orange sand the hump of a beast or the peeking cornice of a buried temple.

In this land, it was presumptuous to assume the perfectly bare skies would offer such a relief like clouds.

Well, at least the daydreams staved off madness.

"What do you see," Rooster demanded the Ophi man who they called Quail.

The black man shaded his eyes.

The elevation was limited and their vision poor. The track that caravans used to take was too low, cutting across the bellies of dunes and clay reefs. They'd be long spotted before any alarm could get raised. Such had been their journey—a belly-like crawl up this joke of a road for days.

It was pointless to ask the other Ophi questions—their former masters hadn't thought it wise to teach them a language beyond their native one. Goshawk was the exception because he'd been a free man working on the docks long before he joined in.

Quail conferred with Goshawk, who then beckoned for them to join him, "He says there is a leopard that has been following us at a distance. A large one. Perhaps female."

"Where?"

A finger pointed out a tiny black dot on the orange-tan horizon that could have been anything.

"How the hell did he see that?"

Goshawk sounded proud, "Quail is a good scout. He sees what others can't."

It was intriguing but entirely useless information.

"I'll keep it in mind."

Down on the road the rest of the troop waited impatiently. Sans the Shemsari boys. They were sent ahead as advance scouts and trackers both. The road was getting more difficult to follow as the days went by. Without regular use, the desert was simply reclaiming it back into the wilderness.

Eventually one could assume it would all be swallowed back by the sandy tide.

"Anything we should worry about captain?" Rafe asked, ever cavalier.

"Not unless you're a fresh carcass. We move out in five."

There came a natural grumbling. They were weary. It hadn't been an easy stretch since their last rest. But it was a matter of survival.

"Cheer up lads. We've got girls and agave liquor waiting for us ahead," the man called Big Mug jostled his fellow mercenaries. Man wanted to be friends with everyone. It was a weakness but it was saving morale.

The last two did nothing to inspire camaraderie but like all weak links, they'd have uses elsewhere. Lancer who was as chatty as a boulder and the sociopath that others called Carver. It didn't seem like a pleasant nickname. Supposedly it had nothing to do with his carved-up face—he looked like a walking cadaver.

"Say captain, can I speak candidly with you," Rafe approached.

"If it's not life-threatening, you need to go to the sergeant."

The blonde man looked back, "Forgive me captain but that's our problem. Me and the boys were talking about that."

"Tread lightly Rafe."

"Nothing against the kid, he's just young. He won't talk to us. Spends more time with those darkies, you catch my drift?"

Rooster rounded on the man, "Yes I hear you. Antonius has proven on more than one occasion to be an exceptional leader, hence his rank."

"It's just that we don't know if he'll have our back."

Rooster set his jaw.

While Rafe was pushing the boundaries he was also a shrewd sellsword with scars to prove it. Antonius was intimidated and wasn't handling it well, rank or not. By popular vote, the former would soon overtake the latter.

There were natural hierarchies amongst men that labels could never hope to defeat. Pin a field marshal's badge on an idiot and sooner or later, everyone would begin to conspire against him. With all this fresh blood in the warband, there would be an organic reorganization of the pack.

"I appreciate you bringing this to my attention Rafe," he couldn't play favorites, not at a time like this.

If the Birds of Prey were to survive, it would have to be of the fittest. Even in rank.

While the men began to ride out, he found Antonius bringing up the rear. Lost in thought. Looking like a lost and scruffy mutt.

"We need a chat, you and I."

"Yeah captain," there was a defeated sway in that tone.

"You're letting up on your grip. Hardnose swordsmen like that? They smell weakness like cats can milk. They'll start pushing you out and take your place."

The Teridian said nothing, just rode in silence.

Wasn't like him at all.

"You hear me?"

"I hear you Rooster. I'm just not in a good headspace, that's all."

"Rafe's going to take your job if you don't start acting sergeant."

"Maybe he should," Antonius muttered something else.

"Come again?"

But the man changed subjects on him, "We had it good there for a bit in Nefara. Those days were some of the best I've ever had. Then this all had to happen."

"It was an illusion, Antonius. We got duped and our

hands stuck in the scorpion trap. The only reason we're not dangling from a rope is because our enemy overstepped. And we got lucky."

"This is lucky?"

Rooster chewed his lip and fought the urge to yell, "You haven't seen unfortunate yet. If you could have seen what I did in the north...you'd be talking differently."

Wisdom came with age, sometimes.

The old watched the young repeat their mistakes and thus the ugly cycle of pain renewed.

Camp was set up on a high shelf overlooking the day's previous ride. It was a stretch that was unfathomably similar to the last.

Jhamon drew out in the sand. Something the kid did that resonated with Rooster was his habit of visualization. It made everything far easier.

Lines for the Thieves Road, waves for dunes, and circles for points of interest. Simple and efficient. By the map drawn it appeared they were making good time. Within the next few days they would make it to their uncle.

"That's good work. We'll have water to spare then. Let's move onto Shemsari."

The boy sighed but began to draw the letters out in the sand.

"What's the matter?"

"You learn slowly. Like ox."

Bit by bit, Rooster was making progress. The Shemsari language was difficult. He had no reference point. It was like a puzzle with ends to each edge that fit into multiple meanings.

The map was erased and replaced by a glyph.

"*Wódri*," the boy stated, "Water. But it also means spirit. It can carry things."

Half the night later they finished another four glyphs in the great circle that was the J'awed. The thing still seemed too antediluvian and impenetrable to understand. Rooster's brain was aching—it was time to break.

From his pack he tossed Jhamon a strip of lamb jerky.

Making sure none of the other men saw it. The rationing now was down to tough bread and date preserves.

"So. How many Shemsari are there?"

"Many," the boy replied after chewing, "Or so my father said."

"Many is not a number."

Jhamon stared off at the darkened dunes, "Many is thousands. There are over a hundred clans who haven't confederated."

"Confederated by whom?"

"Back during the last war between the Medeans, their chief invited every known clan to break bread and form an alliance against the Ivory Queen. A few did. The rest did not trust the Medeans and their stone forts."

"Why?"

Jhamon smiled wryly, "Our history was not so good with them. My father said the Medeans feared the sound of our war cries and hid within their walls."

"You think the Caliph will call on the Confederation again?"

"If he is not a moron. Many of our strongest clans dwell between the Sunscar and Tyhri."

"How many warriors do you estimate?"

"A thousand and five hundred."

"And how many Shemsari warriors aren't confederated?"

Jhamon had to think, "Nobody knows. But my father said it could be ten thousand."

Rooster whistled. A society of horsemen even half as capable of these two devils would displace an army triple its size. They wouldn't do much damage to city walls but they would be like a whirlwind of death on the open plain.

"Why are there so many clans?"

"Few chiefs can agree on even small things Rooster. Like all men."

"But they have to know their strength. They aren't stupid. The Medeans are if they haven't outright laid you to waste yet."

Rooster continued with his questioning.

The true divide between the clans was a matter of religiosity—the J'awed itself. Every Shemsari had its own shaman who divined answers for the chief to lead his own people with. And those shamans all had their own tunnel-vision version of what the J'awed was supposed to fulfill; a prophecy, a code of law, or a hidden combination. Bahram might have been sunlight to guide them, but the Shemsari were blinded by zeal.

Besides the physical manifestation of the god paying them a visit, the Shemsari clans seemed content to scrape a living out in the sand. They made a fine art of it too, all things considered. But it was a half-life.

One of the last things Jhamon spoke of before heading off to sleep was the old war—The Blooded Plain. Bits and pieces remained. In those days the Medeans were fording the Glittering Wall and established forts. Every time they sallied out, they were shredded by Shemsari raids. Anyone with a spyglass from afar could have predicted who would have won.

When all seemed lost, the Medeans got lucky and happened on a clan gathering. They decimated the leadership of the biggest and baddest Shemsari. The war ended not out of any treaty or show of force—the horse nomads simply scattered. Without any way to maintain lines of communication, the clans went into hiding. Self-preservation. Some had never come out. Jhamon and Jhabari's father claimed to have met warlocks of the wild clans while controlling his eagle—those deep in the Sunscar.

Much to sleep on.

Fists of redrock began to stud the landscape. Bronze and amber mesas emerged from the wind-scoured horizon. The road topped a skirt of dunes that fed into a great basin with a promise of an incline via a stony stair onto the vast plateau above. The basin was more like a dry channel of a long-dead riverbed.

This was looking familiar.

The land that Darwish called the Crownlands they'd barely skimmed.

Without a map, there was no certainty but what he felt in his gut.

Into the basin, they delved and were met with tall yucca plants that sprouted from clefts of rock. The men began to pick their fruits. Big Mug claimed he could make a fermented mash from them.

When suddenly thunder began to drum up from the earth.

The Ophi fell into crouches, jerking their heads every which way.

The other men simply frowned and looked up from their harvest.

Blue skies and not a single chance of a storm. And yet the thunder that tolled was like the rush of an earthquake from the heavens.

"What is it captain," Big Mug was asking.

"The hell if I should know. Ask the locals."

Except Jhamon and Jhabari hadn't returned from their reconnaissance over the stair.

The thunder ran its course a few moments later.

Rooster would have sworn it sounded like the beat of a thousand hooves. But they were in the middle of a waste, fifty good miles from any semblance of a merchant road.

Unless it was an army of ghostly horsemen, it had to be the earth.

He didn't like how long the boys were taking but if there was a danger, they would have come back. Chalk it up to their laziness. They were still boys after all.

"We press on."

The ascent proved a challenge that he underestimated. Men and mounts grew winded in the direct sunlight and began to falter. It took them half the day to slog up the switchbacks to overlook the basin. The plateau of rock simmered in the early afternoon sun.

It would have been cruel to push them further after the climb. Rooster called for an extended rest where they could set up canopies.

"Antonius, get that Ophi over here."

The sergeant, Goshawk, and Quail trotted over.

"Going to take a look over that rise there and see what the next leg looks like," he was determined to make the best of the energy they had left.

They walked to the rocky outcrop and peeked over.

Racing dust flew into their faces and obscured them at first.

Staring back at them were giants. Orange-red behemoths carved out of mountains, each two hundred feet in height, with an archway that bridged them. Identical to the edifices of god-headed statues outside of Nemset. They guarded an enormous badlands—humps of silt and sand, which rose to high hills, then shadowed by mountains still pocketed by glaciers. Etched into the wild red land were draws and defiles, steep and treacherous slot canyons winding like serpents into a nest.

The Ophi quibbled in their tongue.

Rooster's heart hammered blood upon that anvil of flesh.

"Antonius, go and grab Rafe."

A sideways glance, then a, "Yes Rooster."

The veteran merc was there in minutes, gave a low whistle, "I'll be damned."

"You know the place?"

"Heard of it. Senesret's Wards. Old kingdom stuff."

"Anything else I should know of?"

The man scratched his chin, "Used to be a coming and going place for groups sneaking through the Wall. A long time ago."

From this distance, the giant statues and their gateway had only wind for company. Their mere presence amidst the brutality of the wilderness was jarring.

"Have the men be ready for anything," the words came out without thought. "We'll make camp alongside the base of those things."

"Sir," Rafe slipped into the role with a wry grin.

"You're still corporal."

"Of course, sir."

Word was passed around the ranks and the men began to trot and ride out towards Senesret's Wards. Slow and steady. Their complaints got lost in the high winds that blew down from the badlands beyond. It wasn't unwarranted.

Rooster, however, was getting paranoid.

Where were the boys?

He began to urge Nereel ahead of the warband. Antonius said something but it was drowned out by the breezes. In no time he outdistanced them, captured by illogical fear.

There were horse tracks dug into the silt and gravel here and there. Looked like more than one. Of those maybe less than a handful were fresh. Rooster followed them where they began to verge from the hard-beaten path that peeked its head above the sandy veil.

He looked across the few dunes that remained between them and the Wards.

There was a blur across that mirage, a dark blob that could have been a horseman or two.

He squinted and shaded his brow for a better look—no good.

Just then the thunder came back. The susurrance this time was barely noticeable.

Rooster kicked Nereel into a trot to meet the mirage head-on.

Out of the corner of his eye, a horseman rode down a dune and almost got thrown off the saddle. A Shemsari wicker saddle to be precise. Jhabari came close to colliding horses, yanking on the bit in the nick of time.

"Where the hell have you been?"

"Looking for uncle. Isn't that what we were supposed to do?"

"I told you to scout and report back every ten miles. Not go off to hike in the sand as you please."

Boy did the kid have a face that screamed to be

slapped, "You asked us to lead you to him and we did. Where is your gratitude gharib?"

"It's coming right after I roll you up in a magic carpet and launch you into the sun, you little brat."

Jhabari blew a raspberry.

Little shit had it coming but that blur was indeed closing in and it looked like Jhamon. With a dark cloud on his tail. Smearing across the heat-warped horizon.

"And what was he doing?"

"Asking if uncle is home."

"Asking *who*?"

All Jhabari did was give him a sideways glance.

Jhamon rode in hot, horse tossing its mane in protest. The Shemsari boys held a small, fast-paced conversation. It was all still gibberish besides an occasional word.

There were only so many days under the sun to learn all these languages.

"What's going on?"

"I don't think we should have come Rooster," Jhamon sounded worried, "We should turn back."

He was going to start to demand answers.

Only there was something more pressing.

That dark storm wasn't a cloud—it was a line of horsemen. Fifty or more. Clothed in all black. Riding at them like demons summoned from the night.

Familiarity hit him like a gut punch. It was the sāreq. Who'd come back for revenge. These fuckers would ride them down like dogs.

"Uncle would never forsake us," Jhabari argued with his brother in Medean for once, "You're a coward."

"We don't know if he still lives Jhabari! And if he does, why didn't he greet us?"

The boys didn't seem bothered by the oncoming horde of horsemen.

"Maybe he doesn't trust we are real and this is one of his games."

"You're blinded Jhabari!"

"I told you we should have rode out here weeks ago!"

Rooster yelled, "*Boys*!"

At their rear and around the hills, the Birds of Prey were rounding the corner. They had no orders but to keep going forward. But soon they faltered and spilled out in a blob of a formation, seeing the horsemen. Even from this distance, he could hear an argument playing out between Rafe and Antonius on a plan.

"Shit."

This was chaos. This was how good men died. And all the while the Shemsari boys were completely oblivious, caught up in their brotherly feud.

Rooster rode out to meet his warband and orchestrate a defensive position. But it was too late.

It wasn't fifty horsemen. It was a hundred and fifty. And this wasn't maneuvering on cataphracts with the element of surprise either. This was them getting caught out in the open with their pants down.

Like a column of smoke warping around a boulder, the riders in black peeled wide on the sand—encompassing the Birds of Prey with ease. Letting loose bloodfreezing screams Rooster recognized as Shemsari war cries. Even as they wore the robes of all-black, the uniform of thieves and murderers. Above their heads, they whirled sabers and hatchets and lances.

The riders finished a complete encirclement and came to a stop.

Then slowly began to close the circle.

The Birds of Prey were regaining their footing. Panic turned to resolve. Ophi began to cluster in the center with Rafe's armored men protecting them, while Antonius rode back and forth. But it was futile.

Rippling waves of amusement came from the riders in black.

Bows were drawn and leveled at everyone in the killing circle.

Jhamon and Jhabari cried out in Shemsari.

A lone rider in black raised an outstretched palm, turning his horse to meet them.

Rooster joined in.

"*Hahk*," Jhamon greeted using the word brother.

The conversation was indecipherable but the dark-clad rider did not break eye contact with Rooster, making more than one motion to him. It wasn't lost on Rooster that Jhabari folded his arms and made no attempt to argue.

"Get me up to speed Jhamon."

"This is Mhiqual. He is wondering why we are insulting him so greatly."

"He doesn't seem insulted."

The boy said, "It is assumed that you and your men are a tribute for uncle. In the J'awed, this is considered a gift. Gifts must be rewarded with something of equal value."

"And what did you tell him?"

"That you're not a gift. And we're not here to war."

Rooster felt like laughing but it would be hollow, "Yeah? How about you tell him to start by lowering their fucking bows and spears."

"I'm afraid they will not Rooster. We are in their territory. It is assumed we are here to fight."

"Jhabari. You go and tell this Mhiqual that we're not here to talk to him, we're here to talk to uncle. Tell him it's either that or I'll duel him in the dirt right now."

It was a gamble. The boy did not look happy translating it. The man in black drew back a full pace, narrowing his eyes. Then said something that got nearly every black rider to laugh. They seemed unimpressed.

Rooster moved Nereel to ride up right next to Mhiqual. Then drew the ivory-handled and horse-hair decorated dagger he'd plundered from the sāreq, months ago. Made sure they all got a good look at it. And threw it down in the sand between them.

That triumphant laughter stopped.

"Tell Mhiqual if he doesn't want me to take his knife like I did the last black riders I came across, he'll do as I say."

Jhabari said it all.

Bows lowered and arrows were put back in bags.

"So?"

"We are to wait until uncle arrives," Jhamon said, coming up close and looking down at the dagger, voice tightening like a bowstring, "I don't think you should have done that."

"What's done is done."

Three hours of kicking sand. The black-clad horsemen were less restless than they—taking shifts to watch while the rest gambled and wasted time. The sun finished its setting and darkness began to blot out the light.

A plume of dust was barely visible as a rider came to deliver some portent. Orders in Shemsari echoed off the sand.

The horsemen began to unfold like unwelcome shadows lingering at the candlelight's edge.

Jhabari was animated while his brother was still tense, "He's coming! I told you fool-brother! Uncle is coming!"

Ground began to shake. That ghost thunder again. Only it built like an avalanche. Loosening grains of sand and displacing small rocks. Growing louder ever still until it sounded as if the mountains would break apart near them.

Rooster saw what caused it.

From the grim horizon, they came like the black wing of a vulture, bristling in steel and carrying torches. Hundreds more riders flying out from the dunes to the south. In the early night it was too hard to tell their true number, but the din of horses was deafening. They condensed into a narrow formation behind one man who cried in the Shemsari fashion, whirling a great scimitar and a shield in the other.

The one hundred and fifty riders who'd been babysitting them half the day joined in the cry, thrusting their sabers to the sky.

Joyous and dark, they clamored for the man like he was their king.

He led that dark tentacle of riders around the circle, making it so large that Rooster could not see dunes past the black-wrapped heads. Torches cast a sinister shadow on already unsightly faces.

Shoulder to shoulder, horse to horse, now there truly was no thought of escape.

That man emerged into the center of the circle, utterly fearless. He regarded the Birds of Prey for only a second before turning to the boys. He almost ran towards them.

"*Nuymāni*," the man opened his arms wide and embraced Jhabari first, clapping each on the shoulders.

There was an unmistakable resemblance. The man could have been their elder brother. Save the graying in his forked beard and temples. He was not that tall of a man but his gait was nothing but swagger.

The three chatted for some time.

"So," in Medean but still thick in accent, "You are the one who rescued my nephews from that death mine in Nefara?"

"I am."

He waltzed over, "Jhabari and Jhamon are like my own sons. I am in your debt...?"

"Rooster."

"Rooster," their uncle chewed the words and his sharp gold eyes flickered over Nereel's saddle. Lingering on the bastard sword. Then he approached with a smile and bowed, "Thank you Rooster. I am Azim Altaruk. If you know who I am, then you know a favor from me is no small thing."

"I don't."

Azim cocked his head and his smile grew even wider, "Ah is this so? You should Rooster. You slayed nine of my men in cold blood."

The air grew real quiet for how many were present. Even the moon feared to show its pale face.

"Is that so?"

"Do you deny it?"

"No."

Azim played with the dagger in the sand, and began to walk behind him, "The survivor said a pale-skinned demon came from nowhere and cut his brothers down with an enormous sword. Like meat to a butcher. That this soulless swordsman rode with the one-eyed hillman Darwish. I did not believe it when I heard it."

Rooster did not find the words to speak.

"I assume the other four riders that were sent after you suffered a similar fate?"

Truth at this point couldn't do any more harm, "They followed us into Nemset. I do not know what happened to them."

"Ah. I see," Azim turned to the boys, "How strange is fate? That the very same demon comes to me, delivering the blood of my blood at my doorstep. What is the phrase in the north? Two birds with the same stone?"

Jhamon looked to say something but Jhabari shoved him.

"What I should do is give you the traitor's death," Azim raised his voice, "Perhaps a skyfeast would be fitting?"

A bloodthirsty roar came from the black riders.

Rooster did not want to know what a skyfeast was. He safely assumed it was tortuous beyond imagination.

"He's protected us uncle! You said it yourself. It would not be J'awed to kill him."

"Shut it, boy. Just like your father. Beating the holy script at every moment. Did he whip you like hounds, his little soldiers?"

"We have our freedom. We owe him our lives."

"Ah of course," Azim turned to Rooster, "Holy law is so pesky, is it not?"

No comment.

The dark-clad man walked over to Jhabari, "My favorite nephew. You've been quiet. What do you think? Give the demon up as a skyfeast?"

Rooster's spirits fell if any had been left. There was no chance he'd live another day. Between him and the kid was no love lost.

Jhabari locked gazes with him—that everpresent sneer on his face.

Above cried an eagle, faintly.

Azim looked up at the gloomy sky, confused.

"Jhabari," Jhamon urged, desperate.

Rooster recognized his fate was not his own anymore. The reins had been taken from him.

He nodded to the boy, "Go on."

A baffling, "No uncle."

Rooster swore he misheard.

"You say *no*? Why?"

"Because Jhamon's right. Father would have let him live."

The laugh that ripped out of Azim was manic, almost insane, "Do you hear that brother? Even from the grave, the White Dervish still casts judgment that overshadows mine. In my kingdom, a ghost has more say than the Bandit Prince's!"

This time, none of the black riders joined in the humor. Their lust for death became cold and quiet.

Azim screamed down at the dirt, "It's my land, not yours Dervish. And I want to kill him."

Rooster said, "I would demand a duel."

"A duel he says," the man danced.

The Bandit Prince's theatrics would put a court jester to shame. In body language and facial expressions equally. Almost spooky how the man jumped from mood to mood with ease. His men laughed both out of fear and awe.

A man who was unpredictable and unreadable was the most dangerous kind.

"I am a madman, not an idiot."

"What if I called you a fool?"

"Then you'd be right. I am a fool, like the crow. The crow laughs as it rips flesh from the bones."

The imitation turned to a bird's as the Bandit Prince lifted his robes as mock wings. Then flapped them, running in a zigzag. The performance earned him jeers from the other riders.

"Who would win I wager? A crow or a cock?"

"Draw your sword and let's find out."

Azim slowed, "I would not duel you, northerner. I'd shoot you with a bow from a safe distance. And besides, I would not risk losing the love of my nephews."

"So what then?"

"I believe that we are at an impasse," the man tugged one of his many golden hoops in his ears, "Indulge my curiosity Rooster. Are you an agent sent by Kizzuran? Sent to spy on me? Sabotage me? Cut my throat?"

"I've never met him."

"Surely? And how can I know if you are truthful? My men call you a demon."

"But you don't believe that."

Azim grinned, "No I don't. It is a difficult life I lead, you see. To be hated by many and loved by few."

Rooster was put in a position where he had no choice but to be open and honest, "My men and I had to flee Nefara. It grew too dangerous to stay."

"The city is wretched. As are the rats who dwell there."

Madmen only took orders from impulse, disguised to be gods. In Rooster's experience anyhow. Who was to say if Azim believed in anything?

If he was to respect anything, it would have to be as mad as he was.

Rooster tested his theory, "Perhaps that's why I've come here."

"Ooh? Do tell."

"I'm looking for allies to take the city. Or put it to the torch."

A dubious, "Why?"

"I know its weaknesses. The Vizier wouldn't be able to stop you—he's barely a puppet. With five hundred men we could storm Nefara's gates and claim the city for ourselves."

"You *are* insane Rooster," the Bandit Prince had another wry grin on his face, "I think I'm beginning to like you. But no, I must turn you down. I would rather be crucified than rule over that stinking pile of rock. No air blows in those walls."

"You have a greater army here than anything Musha could repel."

"Oh, it would not be the first time I have crossed

swords with that corpulent one. But he is not my enemy. Not now."

"Kizzuran?"

For just that moment the trickster veneer died, "Twenty of my oldest friends the Flameblade has cut down. Their father one of them. Now the treacherous flea hides in the swamp—hiding from me. But he can't hide forever."

"Where?"

"Nemset. The toad calls himself the Bandit Prince and his band the Floodplain Raiders. A shadow of Yhizzir's glory. Bah!"

It would be news to the Sword Row. Then again, they also didn't know about the Serpents either. Maybe there was a connection.

If they ever made it back to Nefara.

"My men and I are looking for shelter. Food and water. For a short time."

"I did hear of a group on the South Road making trouble for the caravans, led by a gharib with a sword like yours. If you are the same, we would have you join us."

"Now it is me who must refuse you."

"Careful Rooster. I just began to enjoy your company."

Nothing else came to mind besides what had been lingering there the last few nights. In the J'awed, the act of giving gifts in return for hospitality could not be underestimated.

Rooster began to loosen the bag of opals—the last of his wealth.

But the long dagger of the sareq flashed and nearly struck his hand. The hilt quivered as the blade stuck through the horn of his saddle.

Azim stood there, hand still outstretched from throwing it, "Keep your treasures. Today I am the richest man in the desert. Not just in the hoard of silver and jewels I plunder. There is no greater jewel that a man can possess than to be reunited with his kin. For that gift, you may stay here with my blessing."

In a blink, the Bandit Prince suddenly drew his saber. A

white-blade bearing a damascene pattern set in an onyx hilt. It pricked Rooster's forearm before he could move. Warm blood dribbled down.

As fast as it came out, it was sheathed back in the silk sash belt.

Eyes wide with madness, Azim croaked, "Hah! You bled. How unexpected."

A far cry from a palace, the mountain village erected at the Wards kept out the elements. And the amenities—while leaving much to be desired—were plentiful. For a group of raiders, it was as close to a fortress as they came.

Parapets of wood and catwalks stretched between the statues with modest fortifications built around the base. The wood had to be scavenged from caravans. Word was Azim had set up shop only eight months ago after Yhizzir had been cut down by Jhamon and Jhabari's old man. In that time they'd attracted a sizeable camp of followers, beasts, and slaves to form the beginning of a functional town.

For thieves anyway.

If the dunes were like a sea, Senesret's Wards was an island hideout for Azim's black-clad pirates to enjoy their hard-earned and ill-gotten spoils.

The Birds of Prey enjoyed their rest and settled in. After a while, they began fraternizing with the local populace. They drank cactus liquor, harassed the girls who worked the steppe farms, and got into spats as all soldiers did while on leave.

Jhamon and Jhabari became more distant—their uncle demanded their presence from dawn to dusk. They left with Azim and his horde without any forewarning. No one knew where to or when they'd return.

Without lessons in Shemsari language or culture, nor a campaign to prepare for, Rooster felt like an unused blade in a sheath that gathered dust.

He was growing restless and frustrated.

With nothing better to do, he went down to the only entertainment in town; the gladiator pit.

Nightlife chirped as he strolled the outskirts of the shanty arena and stockades where the prisoners were held. There wasn't any place for the gladiators to train—it wasn't expected for them to last very long.

The black-clad raiders claimed the only gladiators here were those who refused to work or cooperate with their new Prince. Rooster highly doubted that. This blackguard derived too much pleasure from the fights.

Most of the paddocks remained empty.

Those filled were nearly all Sabeans.

Talk about a place called Ziqarum and the roads east were abuzz among the raiders. Caravans who didn't pay Azim a protection were subject to raids.

"Shalmanisar?" he asked a cluster of them, out of curiosity.

Either they didn't understand him or ignored him.

"Qorchi?"

Nothing. A witch among them was counseling them in that insect-like language.

He moved on around the circuit. Smelled like shit over here. A donkey was rotting up against a few cells.

Rooster almost left but was drawn back by, "White demon. Over here."

The speaker was a Shemsari brave. Red tattoos stenciled a band over his eye-sockets and nose as if it were a sash. He was elder to the boys by a handful of years.

"Yes?"

"My friend and I," he jerked his head back to another Shemsari in the cell across, "Need help. We're thirsty. Damn guards passed us by all day."

"What's in it for me," he asked but didn't mean it. The conversation would be enough.

"We will tell you how we have lived through a hundred fights here."

"I'll get you water."

The brave shook his head, "Yucca wine. Or we don't tell our story."

The local liquor here was barely a grade above

dungeon hooch. For the life of him, Rooster could not understand what possessed these people to enjoy the stuff.

Hell, with a barrel full of northern whiskey he could have these desert kings kiss his feet.

"What if Azim sent me?"

The other Shemsari grumbled something and the first said, "We've been the best entertainers to Azim's pit that he's ever had. The least he could do is reward us with spirits."

When Rooster returned with the waterskins filled with the mouth-puckering yucca wine, they drank like the damned. Emptied their skins in a matter of moments. Within was enough alcohol to put them on their asses. Probably enough to knock out a mule.

"Will you be fighting tomorrow?"

"Tonight," the brave burped and stretched.

"You'll barely be able to stand."

A shake of the head, "Ah but we could be sleeping and still live another day."

"I gave you the drink. Don't pass out on me now."

"Shalsem is always good on his word," the brave said, pointing across, "That is Ahffan. Remember our names, demon."

A group of black-clad raiders came down the way, striking the outstretched hands of begging prisoners. They looked more frustrated than entertained.

Shalsem stood and yawned as if he were not going to his death.

The two drunk Shemsari were pitted against a creature Rooster had never seen and wished to never see again. It was orange and black striped like its northern cousin, but a hundred times the size. A hornet the size of a horse with a lance-sized stinger that dripped venom on the sand with a carapace thicker than plate armor.

No way in hell these two would make it past this abomination.

It was clear by the crowd of raiders that they had gotten sick of seeing their cousins survive. Bets were already up on the hornet, ten to one.

Rooster bet on the Shemsari—why the hell not?

The raider who took his opals grinned like a devil, already counting the loss.

The fight was over in minutes and not at all what anyone expected.

Shalsem danced with a shield and a long-hafted spear in the other, prodding at the chained hornet as it drew near. Testing it out. A stinger strike—Ahffan went down hard. The Shemsari brave feinted and caught the stinger in the wooden shield. Twisting the shield so it wrenched the hornet sideways, away from the other. Then began to poke the thing's eyes.

A sound like buzzing hell resounded in the arena.

Shalsem was thrown aside, losing his lance. It looked bad—cut and dry.

The raiders stood pre-emptively, cheering for the hornet.

Then suddenly it shuddered, banked hard into the wooden walls of the arena, and then inexplicably nosedived into the sand. Shalsem roared triumphantly as he rammed his spear home—finding a chink in the bug's armor. Green-black goo flashed onto the sand.

Rooster could not believe it.

"You cheated," he said they were back in their cells, munching down on stale bread.

"Did I not say we would live another day?"

"How?"

By a miracle, Ahffan appeared unharmed. The man snored like a baby.

At the clinking of the heavy purse he'd won, the brave chuckled, "Aie. So you did remember our names. Why do you act so distraught? You are richer now!"

"The yucca hooch, remember?"

"Ok demon," Shalsem nodded with a tinge of shame, "You are more or less correct. And we owe you an answer. Promise me you'll tell no one?"

"My word as lord."

The rotten fruit had gone to the brave's brain. A champion fighter with a trick up his sleeve or not. He was going to spill his guts.

"Ahffan is a witch-man," Shalsem winked, "Bet you've never seen one before."

Rooster hadn't.

As far as he'd been taught, no such thing existed. Unless...

He took a closer look at Ahffan—erect as if awake, fingers twitched erratically, eyes rolling behind eyelids. Only an observer up close would notice all that behind the face tattoos and ram skull piece he wore anyhow.

A lesson from Jhamon. Speaking of his father's gifts, bonding with an eagle at a young age. Dreaming as he stood, controlling the thing. It clicked.

"He's a skinwalker, isn't he? A druid?"

Shalsem stiffened, "How did you...?"

"Does Azim know?"

A perimeter check, then a shake of the head.

Interesting. These clowns had everyone fooled.

"I thought they could only take the spirit with eagles?"

"To a druid from any tribe. Ahffan is not from any clan gharib. He's Ramali."

Rooster racked his brain, came up with nothing, and shrugged.

"An elder clan—perhaps the oldest. They come from the White Wastes. Their blood runs ancient, it is said," the brave said soberly.

There was more to this.

"And you?"

"Medawi."

That one Rooster had heard of—a great and powerful clan to the west. Hugging the boundary of the Ivory Queen's dirt.

"What are you both doing here?"

A patrol of black-clad men lingered but did not notice their conversation. It wouldn't be wise to stay longer, but Rooster was intrigued.

"Doesn't matter gharib. We'll be free soon."

"How so?"

Shalsem gave another wink, "Azim won't be back until dawn. The patrols are minimal. By morning they'll regret ever putting us in here."

A jerk of the head towards Ahffan, "Him?"

"Him. You see we knew this day would come—we watched you arrive."

"The leopard?"

"Uzasi," the brave said, "Is her name. She has already slain four of Azim's men. Tonight her belly will be full after she disposes of the guard."

Below Ahffan made an internal grunt, rocking from side to side. Like he was climbing.

"She is coming."

"Wait. I have something to ask him. Wake him."

"This is not something you do to a skinwalker..."

Rooster had questions and this druid had answers. He was tired of being led along by mystery. For once, he wanted to grab the gods by their tail and make them squeal.

He turned back performatively, eyeing the raiders who were just within earshot, "You'll wake him up or I'll tell them what you're up to."

"You devil dog!"

"Go on. Do it."

Shalsem hissed in the nomad's tongue. A few simple phrases. Affhan startled as he awoke, clutching his chest with a spluttering cough. Upon hearing Rooster's request, he shot fiery daggers with those gold eyes.

"Translate this; I want to know if the soul of a skinwalker can be trapped in the beast it was bonded with, after death."

Shalsem did, listened, then said, "He says no. Not to his awareness. A skinwalker can surpass a normal death if he is lost in the skin-dream for too long, however. And will transform."

Odd but not what Rooster was looking for.

"Ask him what he makes of this then; why would the

eagle of a skinwalker follow a gharib like me across the desert? Over hundreds of miles?"

"Ahffan asks if you have ever been marked by one of our shamans. Perhaps you raped a chieftain's daughter without the proper rites?"

"Not that I'm aware of. Tell him that the eagle was that of the White Dervish, brother to Azim."

That bit got Ahffan to sit upright and stare up at Rooster, then yammered in nomad. Every syllable serious.

"He does not believe you demon. And if he did believe you, then he would say this is possible only with old magic. Such a thing has not happened since before the White Wastes. Before the curse of the Wandering."

"Tell him if he doubts me, go look to the skies now," then Rooster described Hazair.

The Shemsari witch-man fell back down into a trance only briefly. Returning to grip the beams of the cell, as if to snap them. The druid didn't look thrilled as much as terrified.

"By Bahram," the brave started but got cut off as Ahffa rambled.

"What's he saying?"

"The elders of the Ramali sent him away to the outlands to look for a sign. To find a cure for a terrible apocalypse that awaits them. He was not hopeful for the last few months when he was captured. He believed the elders were themselves mistaken," Shalsem translated, glancing over at Rooster, "Not anymore. Ahffan believes that you are a demon who has been visited by Bahram. That you are the sign he's looking for."

"Horseshit."

"Evening captain. Something on your mind?"

Rooster made himself comfortable by the table and kneaded his nose.

Rafe shrugged and tipped his cup, "Three fours. You're on Lancer."

The mercenaries went on gambling and he became a fly on the wall. In that stone tower that reminded him of Kahil, tucked on a plateau with mountain views.

Simpler times then.

Rooster wondered what would have happened had he taken Souzon's advice. Taken that horse up north, taken up a new name, and taken up something other than war.

"He's lying to you Rafe," the field medic said with that face that could scare an old woman into an early grave, "Captain likes his secrets."

"You're just saying things Carver."

"Cause he likes to hear himself talk," Big Mug chortled.

Carver didn't even look under his cup, "When people lie, I know."

Cups rattled and numbers were called out.

"What I want to know is what kind of lie would he be keeping from us?"

From the corner of the room, Antonius appeared, "Shut up. If you know what's good for you."

"Don't talk to me like you've earned it."

Before Antonius could cross the threshold, Carver produced a wicked dagger from under the table and laid it next to his cup. Gave the Teridian a stare that was still trapped on a battlefield.

"Go on boy. You're my sergeant. Try and have me flogged."

The gambling table went cold. No one tried to prevent what was happening. They wanted to see what went down next.

Rooster did too.

Antonius continued to walk, right up to Carver, "Get up. Apologize to Captain Rooster."

Carver glared, "If I don't?"

"We got along just fine without a stitcher before you. We don't need you around."

"Putting bodies back together necessitates a mastery of taking them apart. You're nothing but a slab of meat."

Antonius was sweating, fist clenched.

This could be the snapping point. There was already so much pressure on his shoulders.

He calmly tipped Carver's cup and said, "He's got two ones and a five."

The nerve—nothing but pure guile. Disrespect begotten and repaid. It was nicely done.

Antonius walked back to his seat amongst the Ophi.

"Got some balls on you sergeant. Ruining a man's game like that."

Without missing a beat, "From what I've heard, you don't have any. You were a mamluk, right? Medeans already took your manhood eh?"

If it weren't for Lancer there'd have been blood. The silent man had a grip like iron on Carver, wringing him like a chicken. The field medic writhed like a mad hound.

"I've seen enough," Rooster stood, "Lancer and Rafe. Escort Mister Carver to the yard and have him restrained with rope. Five lashes for disrespect to Sergeant Antonius. That goes to any man here who thinks he can do the same to an officer."

There'd be hell to pay if the insubordination went any further.

Just as much as the whip would earn.

Out in the yard, Carver didn't so much as yelp as the punishment was administered. The man was stone cold. Blood on the flagstones meant nothing, nor pain. When he was pried off the post, he just stared death at Antonius.

Knives in those bulbs.

This was the price Rooster realized he was paying.

This outfit would eat itself out of idleness. They could not survive in the desert wilderness. Neither could they sit around until the Bandit Prince or his men grew tired of their company. A third option he had.

But was it the right one?

A fat vulture sitting upon a pile of carcasses, Azim Altaruk was in a pleasant mood on this day sitting on his throne. Which meant in this case he gathered up some thirty-odd old women to bark their shrill predictions of his fate.

"Ah Rooster, you come to deliver me from boredom."

The crones continued to beleaguer the Bandit Prince, inspecting patterns in dust piles, mashing beetles into mortars, and casted bones on the floor. All were predicting his fortune.

Any sanguine ruler would lose their sanity having to listen to this.

Azim almost had to shout to speak over their chants, "My nephews tell me your old employer—this Qadi of the Border—was taken captive by cutthroats. This is why you left the city. This is true?"

"It is."

"I would never suffer such a fate. I have too many wisewomen to warn me of what's to come," there came that crazed smile, "Soon I will have a hundred seers. And I shall be the wisest of all princes, aha!"

Rooster was the furthest thing from a priest, but he failed to see the logic.

Then again he wasn't a madman.

Azim clicked his teeth in annoyance, "Though I must profess, they have not produced me good augurs of late. I dwell in a desert of ambition, Rooster."

"Greener pastures over the wall, all ripe for the taking."

"A green paradise ruled by a boy. That is where you would advise me?"

"I did not come here to counsel you, Prince."

An invisible hourglass was flipped—the crones had used their time up. Azim started lobbing half-eaten chicken and grapes at them. The women of various priesthoods fled.

From Azim's point of view was a sea of orange and blue. A living picture of his desolate land. The chamber was carved into the mountain beside the statues—pillared and already furnished with braziers. At one point it might have served a ceremonial purpose.

The Bandit Prince jumped down and punted a painted skull as if it were a child's ball, "Useless bitches. I am harassed by a demon sent by my enemy—not you. Slayed six of my men last night. Disemboweled by the thing. Ate two of my finest pitfighters too."

So Shalsem and Ahffan had made their escape then.

Their final words imprinted on him like a sun-sear on the eyes.

Rooster held back a grin, "This is grave news."

"I don't want your sympathy, I summoned you to give me counsel. Tell me what you northerners do with demons."

"We would summon an alchemist to the house, and have them cleanse it with salt and tinctures. For a small sum of coin."

Azim waved his hand, "Yes but what then?"

"Demons are more prevalent here. Different methods might be required."

It wasn't inspired. The night and its activities were affecting everything now. Even his instinct to appease the Prince.

There was simply too much to mull over. He needed empty land to look at and talk to.

"So neutral Rooster. You are a hunted man and your enemy is a coward, using cowardly methods. What do you do?"

"I let him carry on. I watch him carefully. I wait for him to slip up but I don't let him notice. I let him overextend his hand so I may see his face."

"But your men see you weak and helpless—even as bait. They may even consider mutiny."

"One way of looking at it. Another is that you're allowing your closest enemies to out themselves. Cull them along with the cowardly enemy. Two birds with one stone, as you said."

Slow clapping from the stone seat, "Genius. Cunning. Today a crow learns from a chicken."

It occurred to Rooster this was not the actual advice that Azim wished for.

That unpredictability again.

"Nothing I'm saying is new to you."

"Did I not say earlier that men lie, Rooster?"

Was this any different than arguing with a toddler?

Maybe slightly more dangerous.

It was nigh unthinkable to imagine someone like Azim being the right-hand man to anyone. The Bandit Prince had been born to rule—with a scepter of chaos and fear. Old Yhizzir had to have seen the writing on the wall. And perhaps there had been concerns of mutiny between Kizzuran and Azim long before the White Dervish slayed the old bandit king. Wouldn't be bold to assume that the facts had been muddied in the aftermath.

"You're a plotter, aren't you northerner?"

"What makes you assume that?"

Azim wiggled his bejeweled fingers and looked off, "I dreamt last night you conspired to kill me. You were the same now but you had no tongue and no arms. I laughed at you as you dug a pit into the mud. Somehow I fell into it when I wasn't looking. A flaming sword struck me. Then…darkness."

"Believe me, if I wanted to kill you I wouldn't dig a hole."

"My seers warn me about strange dreams. They aren't to be ignored, they say."

"What do you make of it?"

Azim clapped his hands and strode across the chamber, pointing down the open archway to the sky, "Tell me what you see?"

Rooster squinted. At the foot of the steps was a parade. Black-clad raiders were trying to wrangle the ugliest bird he'd ever seen; a gigantic albino ostrich, fitted with the gaudiest saddle of supple cream leather studded with pearls.

Impatiently from behind his shoulder, "It's a gift."

"For who? The Vizier?"

"The Ivory Queen."

"You're joking?"

The silence made Rooster turn—the Bandit Prince had a fire in his eyes, stroking his beard.

"My seers tell me nothing. My dreams tell me I'm to die. So. Instead I will make my own fortune. I'm going to seduce this Ivory Queen and she will make me her king. And you're going to help me."

This was pure and utter madness.

"I don't follow."

"You and your men will go to Tyrhi with my princely gift and present it to the Queen. You'll tell her all about me and how gracious a ruler I am. She'll be flattered beyond words and have no choice but to invite me to her palace."

Rooster wanted to laugh but Azim's face began to twist as soon as the corners of his lips turned, "Ah, I see."

"You have reservations northerner? After all my hospitality? You wouldn't want to repay me in kind?"

Should he speak his mind honestly and lose his head? Or agree to this batshit-insane plan? Rooster began to feel himself sweat.

"How do you know that the Ivory Queen wants a king? From what I have heard she bent pirate lords over her knee. She seems, ah, *sovereign*."

"Don't try to talk me out of this northerner. This plan will work. She's heard of me I'm sure."

"Let me think on it."

"Will you?" a mistrusting hum in the man's throat, "We have another dilemma that must be put to rest."

"And that is?"

Azim was pacing back and forth with enough friction to start a fire. Then barked in Shemsari to the lone raider who stood guard at the open doorway.

Moments later Jhamon and Jhabari shuffled up the stairs. Both were dressed in the black garb of The Bandit. They gravitated to their uncle's side, nervously.

So they'd been recruited. Hadn't that been obvious? Stepping into their father's boots? Now they were at home, among family and kin. Jhamon was disquieted. Reluctant to be there. Like a baby wolf stuck in a cage.

"The blood of my blood," the Bandit Prince said softly, "Do not know what they want to be. I have given them every opportunity to decide. Well, I have grown ill waiting for their answer. Tell me now—both of you!"

Rooster did not want them to choose. The decision had been made in his mind already, once they stepped foot before Senesret's Wards. The bittersweet moment had already come and passed for him days ago.

Rooster straightened himself. What was he playing at anyway? These were another man's children. Whatever selfish creature who longed for another shot of fatherhood had to be buried deep and forgotten. He had Antonius to worry about still.

Azim threw himself into a slouch on his throne, "Go on. I'm listening."

"We must think of the J'awed before we answer," Jhamon said bravely.

"Fuck the J'awed. I'm your uncle. My word is as good as any god's. What has Bahram done for either of you?"

Jhabari was shaking his head, for indeterminable reasons.

This was stupid.

Rooster urged them, "Listen to your uncle boys."

"See, even this gharib you follow agrees."

In such a quiet voice, Jhabari said, "Hazair follows him."

The Bandit Prince scoffed, "You would let a fucking bird decide Jhabari?"

"You tell us you listen only to the spirits uncle. Don't you claim to be guided by their divine hands?"

"Don't lecture me on what governs my actions, brat. I thought you would have been smarter than this—smarter than your fool father," Azim flew into a rage, standing up from his throne.

Rooster blinked.

Uncertain what would happen next.

Jhabari walked up to the step before his uncle's throne and threw down the black turban, "Apologize."

"Ha! Do you think so, little Jhabari? Or what are you going to do?"

The smell of ammonia hit first, then the sound of pissing second.

Rooster didn't know if he was more proud or scared for

the boy.

"Here's my answer uncle," Jhabari said defiantly.

The Bandit Prince boiled like a kettle. He roared and swept aside a brazier, sending hot coals and sparks down the steps. Which started to smoke the piss-soaked turban. The smell was unpleasant.

Jhamon looked at the Rooster, then tossed his turban into the pile, "Goodbye Uncle."

Rooster did not linger for fear of his head leaving his shoulders.

Behind him, the chamber became a tornado—ripped apart by its master.

There was nowhere in Senesret's Wards that was safe from Azim Altaruk's wrath.

At midnight they made their exodus.

A lone black-wrought owl was rustled from its perch, hooting as it soared for a new roost.

The demesne of bandits slept drunkenly as the Birds of Prey rode quietly down the stairs of the village. Fortuitous that the raiders were nullified by their recent victories. It made for the perfect window to leave.

Rooster led from the front. The Shemsari boys right behind him. Though he knew nothing could truly protect them from Azim.

Hoofbeats were muffled—he had the men bind their mount's hoofs and mouths with cloth to muffle them.

So far so good.

They made it to the edge of the statues and those monstrous shadows. Torchlight hinted around the corner. Rooster went first around them. No sentries on this night—they had lucked out. One final crossing and they'd be home free.

Abruptly Jhabari rode off towards the pens by the arena.

"Where is he going?"

Jhamon whispered, "He's trying to anger uncle."

"No way. He's already pissed. Get your shithead brother back here."

Dust kicked and the boy took off.

The problem was that they were in too precarious a spot. If any sentry were to look down from the top of the statues or stumbled through the great archway, they'd see a crowd trying to steal away. And then there'd be serious trouble.

Antonius and Rafe both rode up.

Now both sergeants with their own squads—there was no sense pitting the different men against each other. Eventually, a rift would have occurred anyway. Rooster was just trying to get ahead of the curve.

Rafe and his mercenaries as a heavy cavalry element, Antonius with the light shock infantry. A complete opposite composition to any troops he'd led back in the north. For whatever inane reason, there might have been a method to the madness.

Hopefully the Birds of Prey didn't have to defend a fort anytime soon.

"What's the hold-up sir," the latter pretended not to notice the former.

Antonius sniffed, "Goshawk and his lancers are ready to go scout out a trail. On your word captain."

"Stay put and stay quiet."

Both shut up, avoided eye contact with each other, then fell back.

Perhaps elevating the sellsword with an ego would prove a mistake. Time would tell.

Jhabari and Jhamon returned bearing a gift. That ridiculous albino ostrich complete with its saddle. Thing was honking like it just got born into this world. Trying to wake up the whole town.

"No. Put that thing back."

"Uncle is going to turn red," Jhabari chuckled.

"Do you think that impresses me? This is damn stupid, boy."

The Shemsari kid patted the bird's side, "You won't get far with any chieftains without a gift."

What more were youth than imps sticking pitchforks

into the elderly's eyes?

Rooster couldn't believe he agreed to it, "Fine. Put a bag over its goddamn head. Or it's going to wake up this entire damn village."

Had he ever been this lenient with his own sons? No.

Age; the great blunter to man's sharp instincts.

"Wait, captain. Aren't we going the other way," Rafe asked as they turned into the shadow behind the wards.

"No, sergeant."

Whispers of uncertainty trickled through the Birds of Prey.

They were heading into the mountains.

The leopard made itself easy to find.

Hazair was circling the beast that perched atop a boulder. Its gold and black hide easy to spot in the moonlight. The lithe cat swam towards the hills and away from sight. Ahffan awaited, beckoning forth.

Deeper into that wild country.

المقدس السهب
Shobai Hamada

"All things begin as they end. The sun is the life whose veins fill man. The moon is the death that bears the beyond. No thing can ever taken from another if it is a gift; gifts must always be repaid tenfold. Greed is for traitors and thieves. The fallen on the white death waste, whose sacrifice brought us here was the greatest of all gifts. I am bound by their same creed; I am a wanderer of the seas of sand; I am a voice in the hollow wind; I am the eye of the beast of the air; I cannot dwell under the stone of pretenders; I lose sight of man not witness to sun or moon. All those bound to this law are on the path and I shall not harm them even as I would move mountains. The knowledge of this path is sacred; it must open and close by the king sun door. This is the path—this is J'awed."

The words trickled and fleeted over the sand grains. Ethereal.

The notion that they could not be captured on any parchment by quill seemed less superstition and more lucid.

Rooster felt the most out of place sitting crosslegged with the three Shemsari. They formed a triangle in front of him, the text of the J'awed inscribed in the gap of dirt. All of them younger than him by decades. Which meant nothing because he was an infant in terms of their culture.

Jhamon was translating Shemsari for Ahffan, "We will go over the introduction again."

"Again?"

"He will take you no closer to the clan if you refuse."

"Yeah? Tell this skull-wearing asshole to take a dive off a tall cliff and see if his magic keeps him from turning to paste."

The boy blinked, "Shall I translate that?"

Rooster shook his head and cleared his throat, "Ahem. We arrive at the boundary. I get off my horse. I am unarmed. I take the gift and walk to the big tent—"

"Where is your gaze," Jhamon translated as Ahffan prattled off.

"At the earth. I am not worthy of looking the chieftain in the eyes."

"Good. What do you do next?"

"As I was saying, I'm leading the gift to the chieftain's tent. I bow and wait for the first warrior to inspect me. He might challenge me," Rooster could not remember the next part, "Damn it. Ask him to repeat the next part."

"You ignore the challenge as you might a fly. The chieftain will only meet you if you can withstand the first warrior's insults. Ahffan asks what you do next."

"I present the gift before the tent. I stand there until the chieftain receives it. How long can that take? What's the longest anyone's waited?"

Some translation, "He says some have waited days."

Shit. That would be miserable.

Rooster continued, "When he accepts my gift, I acknowledge the chieftain. I do not introduce myself until he asks. I may have to wait that time as you said. And then if he accepts my gift, I must petition the clan to accept us."

A nod, "Yes."

"That's it then? Easy as pie?"

Jhabari sniffed, "What's pie?"

"Just gharib-nonsense."

Jhamon listened with one ear to Ahffan and him the other, "No Rooster. This will not prove easy."

The Shemsari wizard chattered another few sentences, grew bored, and jumped up from his cross-legged seat.

"What?"

"If you succeed in all of this, then you have now introduced yourself to the clan and the chieftain of the Ramali. This does not guarantee that you won't be slain by the first warrior—you will be the first outsider and non-Shemsari to speak with the chieftain since the splintering,"

Jhamon finished.

The Shobai Hamada.

Now Rooster knew what Darwish was prattling on about. This was the first land the Shemsari conquered and it showed no virtues of domination.

Untold miles of pitiless high desert and badlands raced beneath the shadow of flat-topped mountains. A trackless and unbound terrain. Bristle-cone, leather-leaf, and blood cacti made uninhabitable forests that studded the landscape randomly. There was no soil, only gravel and sand. Arid in summer. Bitter cold in winter. Deadly to navigate incorrectly. Without a guide, they would have been bones already.

They had only plied into its outer reaches and were already hit with an existential sense of smallness. This was not a land fit for any civilization.

The hills were just the beginning. Every valley grew deeper and the passes taller. Plateaus were hard-fought to climb. Ahffan led them on ascents that were barely a man abreast—from atop a horse the gravel paths promised to pitch them off into crevasses at any moment. Barely fit for goats.

Nowhere did they see anybody or anything here.

Not even vultures.

Hazair was their lone watcher, coasting on the thermals.

But Rooster got the sense they were watched.

On the fifth day after entering the Hamada, the Ophi spotted another eagle. So high up it might as well been a cloud. The dark shape lazily crossed the heavens.

Ahffan corrected them, "That is no eagle. It is the rokh, the king of the skies."

The bird shape dropped out of sight and soon returned with something in its clutches. What looked like a rat, was actually a horse. Ascending until it was lost in the heights.

A shiver ran down Rooster's spine.

"Where does it go," Antonius asked, awed.

"The God Wall. He is elder and beyond mating years," responded Ahffan. "There have been skinwalkers who have tried talking to him. And bond with his soul."

Rooster asked Jhamon to translate, "What happened to them?"

"The rokh picked them up and dropped them from the heavens. They died before they hit the ground."

"Clever bird."

The continued journey, the more pressure the land exuded on them. There were undoubtedly traces of primordial ether woven into the tapestry of steep buttes and deep red defiles, sheathed in the juniper and cedar that grew defiantly from bare rock. As if the land itself was flesh and each feature was a scar left cloven into it, unhealed and ever growing.

Only a few more days of eating lean. The wizard swore that they neared sanctuary. Beyond the mountains safeguarded by the Ramali was a gauntlet of salt flats—an anvil of bleak terrain that pushed right up to the mountains that folded into the Glittering Wall.

Rooster did not look over their shoulder even once.

He did not fear the Bandit Prince's wrath.

He feared what was ahead of him, lurking in the storied hills.

Their last camp alone was made on the beaches of a dried out lake. At its epicenter an island featuring a massive mound, topped by a stone totem. There was once a deciduous forest, now fossilized. The warband tried to burn their wood to no avail.

Rooster watched and listened to their complaints from afar. He prepared himself for the isolation ahead. It might be days before he would see them again.

"Just me and you buddy," he fed Nereel absentmindedly, gazing up at the stars.

A night sky painted by the gods. No light pollution here. The black void was drowned in constellations.

He was caught up in the scene and didn't realize

someone approached, "Eh?"

The approacher jolted him, "Captain?"

It was Lancer. The man had a presence like a shadow in the doorway. A brooder.

"Yeah?"

"Mind if I sit here?" even the man's question seemed a sentence too long.

"Go ahead."

Gravel crunched as Lancer leaned against one of the dead trees.

There were no words passed for a long time.

Nereel made a horse grunt and passed out. Making a low rumble of a snore.

Rooster scratched his chin and felt the beard that was starting to go unkempt. Throw a turban on and he might get confused for a Dawali. The thought made him chuckle. That shifted to recalling the last time he spoke to Darwish. Humor soured to reconciliation quickly.

Lancer shifted, looked over, then went back to brooding.

"You seem good at listening. Eh?"

No answer felt like acknowledgment.

Rooster didn't know what came over him but he began to spill his guts, "I've never been a good man. Not in these four, almost five decades of my life. Took me too long to figure it out. I suppose you start rotten and either you fall off the tree or you get eaten by birds eventually. But you know what? Every man is capable of doing evil. There's larceny in the softest heart. I'm not justifying my history—just stating the facts here."

"Good men have their lives made for them. Gods know I've met plenty. They died by the sword as much as they died at ripe old ages. All remembered fondly. Their deeds won't soon be forgotten. And that's what I fear most. Only the worst of bad men are remembered. I lacked the ambition of any villain. My middling deeds won't be recorded or put to paper. Back home? I'm already forgotten."

"Got scared shitless the first time I fought in a battle. It wasn't a real battle either. My uncle burned my father's lands over a tax dispute. I took matters into my own hands. I was seventeen and I had boiling blood. Slayed my first man outside his door—a local boy that I grew up playing in the river with. Younger than me. Wrong place and time. He died slowly and horribly. I don't think I even remembered pushing my uncle into the fire, I was trapped in the horror of my first."

A ghost of a grunt had him pause.

"Slowly I think you just get accustomed to it. I'd get rattled now and again. Our nature I suppose. But it's a dull fear by then. You start to fear your mistakes as you grow long in the tooth. I think my father feared mine more than his own. Never said goodbye to him. For the best, I think. The disappointment was too great for either of us to bear."

"So now I'm here in some godforsaken desert and you know what? I'm terrified. It's not the death. It's that I might have neglected something for so long and I'm at the end realizing how big of a fuck up I've been. That shaman thinks his god is talking to me. Why me? I don't want to talk to *me*, Lancer. Sure as shit don't think any god does. He's got better things to do."

Rooster had to take a moment to breathe and look over. The other man was still staring up at the sky.

"So in many words, I suppose I fear that I'm on the footsteps of a temple I've built out of my hope. And that I'm going to have it crushed tomorrow. I've let myself wonder too deeply and wish too strongly and I'll be shot down. That this has all been a dream and I did die back there in the dirt before all of this began."

The rant died against the gentle repose of the mountain wind.

"All men dream," Lancer said after a drawn-out silence, "But few of them ever have the courage to seek them."

"Explain."

"You have your answer," the big man said, then turned back to the stars.

There was nothing more to say.

Rooster went out for a walk. Wandered up to the mound and the upright slabs that stuck out like a boulder thumb. There were carvings hewn into the rough granite in rings bound by lines—primitive iconography of horses and men in motion. Ancient red chalk pounded color into the carvings with flakes of bronze. The movement resembled a strange wave, the horse and men blending sometimes into a single entity. Strange.

He strolled around the warband and felt a pang of worry about what his absence might cause.

It was too late to turn back now.

The Birds of Prey would adapt without him or they'd implode as the Duskhounds.

He dreamt that he was an egg-shaped boulder overlooking a sea of blinding-white salt. Talons of a great bird scooped him from its nest and took them to staggering heights. He pleaded with the bird—it laughed back with the voice of someone he'd buried a long time ago. And dropped him. The mirror earth thousands of feet below rushed up to meet him.

Rooster woke up with his heart in his lungs, sweat cold on his brow.

The sky was still painted grim as the sun had yet to break it.

Ahffan was squatting beside his bedroll.

"It is time," Jhamon translated.

Rooster walked the path alone. If dragging an ostrich by a lead didn't count. The big ugly thing sure didn't seem to have a brain bouncing around that shriveled pale head.

He walked the two of them on a serpentine belt that dared cut across the steep trunk of the mountains, under the watchful gaze of red castles who rose to the sky. They would suffer no sieges, impregnable blocks of crimson rock that had stood far longer than any kingdom.

Owls and bats darted overhead, ruffled at his

trespasses. They dove into cracks and the organ-fluted cactus that made a thorny forest on the ledges over the trail.

The walk went on for hours longer.

A dim yellow breached the last vestiges of blue dawn, threatening warmth and light.

Rooster took a small break on a fallen chunk of redrock and drank from the waterskin. Letting the bird drink from a puddle he made. Half of it was already gone. The day would prove to be the hottest he'd faced yet.

With thoughts of dehydration, he got up and started to move again.

To dwell any longer his limbs might become too relaxed.

The trail followed a dried streambed that once spilled from the mountains. It widened but the grade grew steeper—enough to almost be a scramble. An intimidating draw formed from spurs of redrock, rippling down from the apex of the mountains—a blood-colored flatiron like a chipped obsidian dagger, stabbing the belly of the heavens.

Which was when the ostrich decided to become a nuisance.

"Not this far in damn it," he yanked.

The bird started to pull back, pecking at him.

Rooster fell to a squat and felt something strain in his right knee. It had been bothering him more and more, he just hid it from the others. The last thing he needed was to develop a limp now.

"You win you gangly bastard."

The ostrich squawked.

Too bad it was a gift. Frying up one of those big legs would have tasted like chicken, he reckoned. Why couldn't the gift be a big bag of silver?

Rooster tried to pull the reins while seated. And got more resistance back. Almost sending him down the draw in a tumble.

The bird tried to peck the hand that held the reins. Without thinking he clocked it in the side of the head—a solid right hook. Suddenly the ostrich became that much more docile.

"Should have thought of that awhile ago," he grunted.

And then started the climb up again.

His right knee started to crank that dull ache about halfway up. It didn't keep him from hiking—it was a portent to a more serious injury.

Rooster pressed through pain.

They made it to the saddle that offered small respite. A ledge provided shade. Succulents and gnarled juniper grew here, somehow. When he'd caught his breath, Rooster walked towards the redrock flatiron. A valley began to grow at the bottom of his eye, shielded in the mountains.

The promised oasis; the Ramali sanctuary. Pools of rare turquoise ran right up to the walls on one side, fed by step-like waterfalls that were fed by a waterfall tumbling from the underside of the flatiron. Vines and moss clung like a cloak of green from the cavernous overhang. The mist from the falls alone almost reached the saddle. And in the pastures and deep red earth below, was a village of tents.

But that's not what Rooster was paying attention to, as he started down the breakneck switchbacks down to the valley floor.

Black smoke choked a plume from below. A mound of something was burning. It smelled something like death. So strong it brought tears to the eyes.

Why did it smell like a battlefield?

He found out why.

Rings had formed around the outer perimeter of the Shemsari camp. Earthen ramparts piled up a good thirty paces from any palm tree and were no taller than a man. Some had been hewn down and rolled up to the base of the ramparts to create tinder. Blackened fronds remained. The smell came from bodies—hundreds of them, stacked like fallen wheat. They were heaped tall enough to create a fortification of flesh.

Even in the warped heat, he saw they had a distinct gray inhuman pallor. Those who had not melted to black skeletons. And swore they still twitched in those flames.

Graythirsters? The smell they created was fouler than any death he'd come across.

Rooster walked the gap between the burning corpses. There were no warriors to greet or challenge his entrance. No Shemsari brave to challenge his right to even bring a gift—let alone stroll into camp.

And yet he did.

Tents of horsehide blew in the light gales. Seemingly empty. There were horses tattooed in red paint that ran through the camp, afraid and without masters. Cookpots were left neglected, the coals beneath them scattered by the hooves. Somewhere a child cried out to its parents—it went on and on without relief. Where were the people?

The air itself tasted of apocalypse. What might have been a serene scene had recently blackened and turned sour.

Rooster continued to saunter through the camp. Dragging his metaphorical gift-horse.

He came upon the first Shemsari in the flesh. An old woman. Dust streaks of tear trails ran down her stoic face but she made no sound. The shriveled face regarded him in restrained wonder. In her hands she clutched a horse-hair dreamcatcher with a bone frame imbedded with turquoise.

More tents, more faces. All either elderly or too young. There was a staggering and frightening lack of adolescents or fighting-age adults. If there were any, they were hiding.

But that wasn't Shemsari—that wasn't J'awed.

At the center of the clan's camp, the flaps of the greatest of the tents had been thrown open, the rug half-spilling into the sun. Where a white hair with tattoos covering nearly every inch of his skin was waiting, cross-legged. Eyes like pale gold. The ceremonial dagger strapped across his chest marked him as the de facto chieftain.

Rooster faltered because the chieftain was making eye contact.

Something no outsider or gharib could *ever* do.

The law was stone; to denigrate the chief like that

would to mark oneself for death.

But the white hair put his palm to his forehead, then flipped his outreached hand to the sky. Then with the same hand over his heart, bowed.

Rooster was at a loss, totally in shock. He bowed back.

Up close he realized the chieftain's cataracts—the man was blind.

"Beyik Alghasan," he said.

The eyes closed and white hair spoke not in Shemsari, not Medean, but in perfect Patina, "Hello stranger. We have been waiting for you."

Without a choice, Rooster listened. First fear, then deference, and eventually pity.

For inexplicable reasons the Beyik Alghasan of the Ramali was fluent in several tongues. The notion these were a primitive and stupid people was quickly put to rest. Sheltered from the outside world? Yes. Blind to the events outside the moat that was the Shobai Hamada? Not even slightly.

With their skinwalkers watching through the eyes of beasts, the Ramali knew of things far beyond the oasis. Up to the Glittering Wall and down even past Nefara. The chieftain mentioned a great army pushing through the mountains east—raw intelligence including troop movements of the Boy King.

But that was quickly diminishing as the skinwalkers were vanishing.

The Ramali were dying.

The blight had come; the graythirsters. Before they hadn't been a direct threat, the chieftain explained. They were a cursed apparition, a scattered and frenzied phenomenon. Until very recently.

Something had awoken them, originating deep within the south. Beyik Alghasan had no explanation, only his skinwalkers said it was black evil from what they could see from their beast eyes. Someone had animated the dead who'd been dormant for centuries. And they didn't stick around to see what doom it wrought.

The walking dead rose from the sands at a place across the salt plain to the north—redoubts that Rooster knew of. He'd almost walked in one, months ago; The Fists of the Shemsari.

The graythirsters were drawn to water, the chieftain explained. Like moths to a flame. The evil creatures quite literally sucked the water from the earth and destroyed the source. All part of their curse. Due to the purity of their oasis—using language Rooster could not wrap his head around—the dead were relentless in their sieges. For months now, hundreds had struck across the salt plain. With every attack, fewer Ramali warriors were left alive to defend the next merciless onslaught.

An enemy who needed no resupply, no rest, and existed with a single purpose, waging a punitive war of attrition?

Rooster knew the end of this story. It wasn't pretty. What he expected next was a plea for help in this mythological fight for good versus evil.

Beyik Alghasan instead veered into the clan's history.

The clan who were called the Water Keepers and the Ramali suffered every indignity. What name had struck fierce respect from every rival tribe had eroded with the wind. It had been a hundred years since any clan had recognized their eldership. Spitting at their name was a precious waste.

White hair Beyik Alghasan looked remorseful, yet accepting of bleak circumstances. A man smiling as he walked towards the hangman's noose.

He said there were no Ramali fit to take his place as elder. Fittingly none of them wanted the job either—knowing it would end in ruin either way. He expressed that he wished a warrior had slit his throat and taken the role by force. But sadly none ardent or bold enough still lived, after the graythirster raids.

So Beyik Alghasan admitted his decision.

He sent Ahffan to find an outsider not to save them—

but to observe and document their demise. To watch helplessly as this garden oasis was destroyed and its guardians obliterated. That was his wish.

Rooster tried to argue.

The chieftain would not hear any protest sallied out against his wishes. They were final. Absolute as stone. If Bahram had wished for the Ramali to live, he would have provided such a way long ago.

That gift that was existence was a fleeting and precious thing, said Beyik Alghasan. While words inscribed in stone were eternal.

Rooster was forced to agree to the bullshit philosophy.

The Birds of Prey were allowed access to the oasis and all the amenities of the Ramali camp. As if they were another clan visiting, barring the typical Shemsari proclivities of wife-taking and intertribal raiding. When the graythirsters came, they would be allowed to take shelter atop the mountains and watch. Write all that they saw. Go back down to camp if there were survivors. For however long it took.

Until eventually—and it would be, without any doubt—the Ramali were destroyed.

And there wasn't a damn thing Rooster could do about it.

Gossamer veils of water misted the underside of the oasis. The turquoise hit with indirect sunlight was the most inviting water Rooster had ever gazed upon. Enchantingly clear.

Hell of a place to bathe in.

The men weren't the only ones who had the idea.

The orange-gold-haired Shemsari brides joined them at a distance, rinsing off in the late morning. They didn't act nervous in front of outsiders. If anything they dared the men to stare.

"Forbidden fruit, eh?" Rafe's eyes had not wandered from their nakedness.

"These aren't your soft-bottom tavern wenches."

No hyperbole needed; the nomads didn't make their women soft. They were lean as a whip, tanned, and even tattooed—albeit the crimson glyphs made snake-like tracks from their buttocks to their nape. Then the red tattoos made their way over the brow, nose, lips, and chin.

Savages; every last man, woman, and child.

Rooster equivocated them to lithe pantheresses—but only in the safety of his mind. He forced himself to appreciate the flora of the cavernous red-rock dome above.

"Do you have to break them in like mustangs, I wonder..."

"Keep wondering."

"Have to imagine they're quite lonely eh? No man to take care of them anymore," Rafe shrugged, feigning innocence, "Someone's got to fill that role."

"I don't think those knives at their belts are for show, but you're always welcome to test that out."

The sellsword gave out a full-bellied laugh, "Why you think we came down here eh captain? Southern girls are fun. They like northern men and our northern cocks."

Some men were dumb as rocks. Some were sharp as razors. Most were impulsive and violent. But all of them suffered the same affliction; woman was a sorceress, her flesh a spell, and her magic turned the most meek man into a witless hound.

The worst dogs of men were those who wandered without abandon, seeking the attention of any woman. They could be dormant and docile for short moments until they got the scent—then all reason was lost.

Sellswords were the worst of those dogs.

Rooster moved on to get dry. The girls had already left to dry out on flat-faced boulders that angled perfectly towards the sun. Their hair glistened like bronze dishes after a summer's rain.

One of the girls flipped onto her belly and stared back at them—not just anyone. A turn of the head and he saw Big Mug. Broad-shouldered, tall, always-grinning, dopey Big Mug. The air between them flickered with a little more than mere lust.

It portended something serious.

Rooster couldn't enable this.

"Oi," he called out to the man.

"Captain," the big man blinked and woke himself up from the dream.

"Everything good?"

"Peachy, captain. Peachy," Big Mug got a playful shove from Lancer.

Nothing about this situation was fair—certainly not to men who'd been marching for weeks and away from the pleasures of civilization. Girls were a welcome distraction but Rooster couldn't afford to let it become any more than that.

At least the Ophi seemed too shy to gaze at the women.

Rooster got curious, trudging over the rocky bottom of the pool, "Goshawk. Where are the Ophi women?"

The black man had a glazed look in his eyes, "They wait for us captain. In the Gudoc."

Gudoc was far east. Grand and storied pastures. Tariq said it was where the Sabeans tried to establish their Shalmanisar before giving up, and moving on west. The pastoral Ophi must have given them a good licking.

"Why didn't you go with them?"

"Women make poor slaves and fighters," the man smiled, "They hide like trees. No one found them."

"But you are free now?"

"After all that and we come home empty-handed," Goshawk, "Our wives will leave us for cattle."

Rooster later realized the man had been joking.

"Keep your damn paws up."

Rafe didn't and got a swift punch to the ribs. The man staggered back and almost fell on his ass. A point to Antonius.

"Again."

Antonius had an unfair advantage. Teridians were natural boxers. He feinted with his lead foot, waited for

Rafe to commit to a jab, swung his back foot in a J-shaped pivot, and countered twice to the head. The blows were softened with gut-laced gloves and wads of grass to protect teeth.

Didn't change the fact that the northern man got whopped good.

Rafe fell on his butt the second time.

"Help him up Antonius," Rooster warned.

Boxing; the cure to an unstable pecking order. The tried and true way to bring any mob of dick-swinging vagabonds together. A trick from a salty old sergeant Rooster had met long ago; you could make the men think it was their idea to hash out grudges and simultaneously force them to breed familiarity. Someone lost a tooth now and again. But it broke bread in ways no other activity could.

Rafe looked at Antonius' outstretched hand, locked gazes, and then got up himself.

The mercenaries dusted his back and gave him a good ribbing.

They sparred in the dirt and between the palms. A few Ramali pretended to be busied with chores—they were watching. More of the Shemsari found an excuse to linger on the ledge overlooking the makeshift field. With hard gold eyes like raptors. Ahffan and his elderly father Ahbdan numbered among them.

Didn't much care for outsiders, this bunch. Yet they tolerated them with distant curiosity.

"Care to join in," Rooster walked over to the ledge where Ahffan lingered, holding up the mitts, "We've got room for more."

"Your Shemsari is very bad still," the wizard sneered.

"Yeah? But I speak it. How many gharibs can do that?"

"A demon can play many tricks."

In the days they'd spent here Rooster had finally learned what the demon comment meant; a white skin that wasn't a Shemsari was considered a trickster spirit. Prescribing all kinds of mischief and chaos that they were capable of. Not dissimilar from the skinwalkers, only that 'demons' were capable of appearing like Shemsari but only in the flesh.

Judgmental bastards, these barbarians.

"For a demon your chieftain sure likes me, eh?"

No comment from Ahffan.

Rooster shrugged and got back to herding hounds. Antonius and Carver were going at it now. The latter being much more versed in boxing than Rafe. They had traded a few good strikes. Harder than playful.

The scarred man started to throw haymakers. Antonius ducked, wove, kept up his guard and withstood the vicious onslaught. The punches got less friendly.

It might have been time to step in. Continued strikes like that would make a man piss blood. Death was also a possibility.

Rooster wanted to let it play out just a little longer.

Carver was sweating profusely. Throwing everything he had at Antonius. The younger man endured it. He was bleeding above his left eye pretty good. Bruised like a tortured fruit. On the backfoot, the Teridian just kept taking it.

Then Carver threw a low blow, catching Antonius just above the knee. Who hobbled back.

"That's enough," Rooster started to step in, "Break it up."

Antonius waited for the scarred man to turn his back before he got him in a chokehold and pinned him to the dirt. It took the whole group to break the two apart, riling up a dust tornado.

"You getting smart on me boy," Carver coughed a lung.

Antonius fired back, "Don't like your own medicine eh?"

"Sleep with those eyes open. Or else."

"Shut it, Carver," Rafe said, "You're out of line."

The scarred man wiped the spit from his mouth and went off walking.

Rooster shook his head. As a unit, they had a long way

to go. Too many hotheads. They could get everyone in trouble if they had to fight.

A damn good thing they were miles away from one.

For the next few hours, he started to mix the groups up more. The Ophi were the quickest to pick up with their long limbs and quick reflexes. Jhamon and Jhabari went off with Antonius and worked on wrestling. Rooster didn't stop them—they three had started to bond more than he expected. He jumped in himself, facing down Lancer and Goshawk. Both were more than capable boxers—giving him a run for his money.

"Let's call it gentlemen," Rooster found himself out of breath and with a bruised rib.

How had afternoon come so quick? They'd gotten lost in the practice.

The Ramali almost looked disappointed the sparring ended.

Maybe there was some hope for them yet.

A young one of them grabbed Ahffan, who came down from the ledge, "Rooster. You'll come with me. Beyik Alghasan wishes your presence."

"Does he now? Can it wait?"

"It cannot," the wizard pretended patience but was a poor actor.

"You're mad at him, aren't you?"

Ahffan kept walking.

"Curling up and dying wasn't what you had in mind for your clan?"

"The chieftain's word is final," Ahffan was almost grinding his teeth.

"Sure it is. Did you tell him about the eagle?"

"The peculiarity with the ad daal is not a priority for the moot."

"Soon your skinwalker friends are going to be ad daal. You're not better than them."

Ahffan stopped, wheeled around, and hissed from below that ram skull helm, "You speak so casually of our clan's extinction. You have no concept of what this does to us. Do you think you are so wise to our ways because you have learned our language, demon?"

Actually yes, yes it did.

They had made it to the big tent.

Rooster jerked his head that way, "Hey. You want to preserve your clan? Go in there and knock off grandpa in there. He's practically begging for it."

Ahffan said something he didn't pick up.

"Not the ambitious type?"

"We see many things demon. Much is changing and coming to pass. The chieftain doesn't listen. He wants to parley with a trickster in his last days."

Rooster patted the man's shoulder sardonically and spoke in Patina, "Ok asshole. I'll be sure to let the old man know."

Beyik Alghasan was insistent that their meetings were private and inside his tent. So he was surprised to find the elderly chieftain atop the albino ostrich, waiting for him. Something about the image and knowing it was meant for the Ivory Queen's rump made it that much more humorous.

"Rooster. You are smiling. Is something amusing that young Ahffan said?"

"No. We're going for a ride?"

"Walk with me. I will ride slowly. We Shemsari can ride even until death, you see. Even if we cannot walk."

Rooster did. The Ramali chieftain took him on what looked like a gametrail. Red earth cleaved between bushes and blue-green agave plants. It hugged the backside of the camp. A natural staircase that climbed the lower spine of the flatiron.

"Did you have any children, Rooster? Back home?"

"A few."

"Did they listen to you? Heed your wisdom?"

"Sometimes."

"And as a lord, were your subjects loyal?"

"Not as much as I would have liked."

The old man glanced back at his camp, "Your men look

to you. They follow you. They would not be here if they didn't believe in you Rooster."

"To a point. If they aren't paid, they'll desert me I'm sure."

"Mmph. You see so little in yourself. You think it's money that keeps them eating your dust."

"Chieftain, most of my men are little more than cutthroats. I've been around their kind all my life. I'm acutely aware of what their motivations are."

"Even murderers believe in something Rooster."

A bowl-shaped depression was scooped out of the base of the mountain that the flatiron jutted from. There, they found the source of the oasis' water. A font bubbled up from a gap in the crimson rock itself—seeping crystal waters passed through bloody teeth.

The Ramali chieftain dismounted, "Hold onto my arm Rooster. Walk me to the water, so I might drink from it."

He did. Beyik Alghasan was frail but stronger than he looked. He could have been ninety.

"Do you see that there? At the bottom? Reach in there."

Rooster did; a glowing chunk of something at the bottom of the font. Like a miniature blue sun. His fingers found ice-cold crystal. He brought it to the surface.

A flawless diamond of the slightest cool blue hue. It felt cold on his palm. The gemstone refracted light and produced a faint rainbow sheen. He'd never beheld such a pure and priceless gem.

"Hold it up to the sun," the chieftain whispered.

"What is it?"

Sky-blue facets covered the sun. At first, Rooster didn't see it; a thin but piercing blue laser visible even in the afternoon light that shone from the depths of the diamond. A dozen similar beams went in different random directions.

"It's name is Ayzaraqaw. The Blue Eye. The most prized possession of the Ramali."

"Magical, isn't it?"

"Old magic. God magic. The Blue Eye came with us across the White Wastes. Whenever it touches water, it makes it pure and drinkable. The lights are not a trick. It will guide you to the nearest pool or well."

"So the Waterkeeper name..."

Beyik Alghasan winked, "A sort of trick. You see now. *This* is our water."

"What happens to it when all of you die?"

That humor faded, "The dead will destroy it. Or bring it to their master."

"You're showing me your ace in the hole chieftain. What if I steal this and pawn it back in Nefara? I could buy a lordship with that."

"Then that is Bahram's will."

"How do you know what your god wants eh?"

Beyik Alghasan stroked his beard, "My ears are open, and my eyes see clear Rooster. I have seen the signs."

The shadow of an eagle cast on the rocks. It was not a portent. A half dozen of them cried out at their kin's return. The flatiron was the roost to many raptors. The desert below was littered with their feathers.

All the same, the elderly man stared up at it.

So did Rooster.

"When we are gone, you will hold onto the Blue Eye. To safe keep for Ahffan until he is given a sign from Bahram," the chieftain glanced at him sideways, "Or you receive one."

Rooster felt exasperation.

Was there nothing he could say to make the old man see reason?

Every culture had its absurdities but this ingrained gravitation towards suicide served no one. With nothing but time, he'd mulled it over. Nothing indicated that other clans would care if their eldest brother fell like a fly. No Medean historian would dare waste ink on pages dedicated to dust-dwelling savages. Their way of life would be preserved as well as melon under the hot sun.

And it was a way of life that Rooster was beginning to appreciate, what little he understood.

The camp below was one of industry despite its proclivities towards violence. Men and women were currently harvesting several antelope that had been caught in the morning. They wasted nothing—even the brains were boiled and used for glue or to treat hide. Ore from the mountains pounded into sand to reinforce crude tools or for their red-copper tattoos. Old and young, it did not matter.

To any outsider, the Shemsari were a dirty and crude people—feather-wearing barbarians squatting in the hills, sleeping with their horses like they were women. Yet what a thousand city-born slaves could craft, a dozen Shemsari could make better in a quarter of the time. They bathed regularly, cleaned their teeth with foraged herbs, and ate diets heavy in cured meats and dairy of their herds, but also nuts and fruits and whatever they could find.

If there were any who deserved to thrive out here in the desert wilderness, it was them.

Through a chimney-like crack in the roof of the cavern, Rooster spied a lone woman at the oasis beneath them, singing to the water. Haunting sound. There was enough sorrow in the melody to make hard men weep. Her song echoed from the cavernous room, reverberating down the canyons into the Shobai Hamada.

"Pretty voice," he commented huskily.

Each note was long and fell like the spray of the waterfalls that rained into the pools. The siren song began to warp into the natural landscape, carried into the breeze.

"She sings to the wild herds to return. Wild horses who lived here before man—before the first kingdoms. They are wise and inconquerable Rooster. They left our pastures before I was born," the old man's eyes were shining, "Something I wish I could have seen before I left this world.

Her song faded into the afternoon sun.

"Perhaps you will if you reconsider my proposal."

Beyik Alghasan took a moment to recover, "The other clans will not come to aid us."

"How do you know? Send one of your skinwalker's eagles to them."

The chieftain began to lead the ostrich down the hill,

"Come now and let us speak of brighter things. Of the past, of rosy memories."

"No. Listen to me, damn you. We sit here while you throw away your clan's lives. Why don't you care?"

"I care greatly Rooster. More than you can ever know."

"Then act."

"Tell me; in my position, what would you do?"

"Send riders to the Bandit Prince. Offer him water and pastures in return for troops. Send your skinwalkers to every clan within a hundred miles. Demand their fealty in exchange for your daughters. Fortify the pass between here and the salt plain. Even the old and young can carry bows. Have them scattered on the hills where they can fire down from afar and be prepared to pull them back to a more fortified position—the pools even."

Beyik Alghasan shook his head as if someone had told him the sun was the moon and sheep were men in disguise.

"From your point of view, this makes sense. But I cannot agree with you."

"Why in Bahram's fucking name not?"

"Precisely who you blaspheme; I was visited by Bahram, the night before the last attack. In a dream. For this reason, I sent Ahffan out to find an outsider with your description."

"Come again?"

"In the dream was a night of fire. Horses ran ablaze. I walked across a valley of skulls that were whispering to me as they smoked black smoke. I saw my tent myself in the flames. I heard the voice of Bahram call my name. And you were there Rooster. On your horse on a hill just beyond it, with the sun at your back. Seeing you brought me an overwhelming sense of peace. I do not know why."

"Why didn't you tell me this earlier?"

The chieftain paused, scanned the horizon, "I was cautious. But last night the dream came a second time. This time I saw the heavens were almost identical to ours. My doom approaches soon—I know it. I will not live to see another moon."

The first breakthrough between cultures came when Rooster noticed his men huddled around the huge fan-like agave. They were bickering with a group of squat Ramali witch-men. It was a friendly beef. The two groups argued like old fishermen and their wives. Rafe and Carver could barely be seen—smoke was curling out from unseeen trenches dug around the base of the agave. The witch-men were using them as labor to dig out the sand.

Whatever they were up to smelled like mischief.

"What's this then," Rooster poked his nose in.

The short witch-man looked up like a black little mandrake root with eyes and a mouth. He quibbled gibberish and went back to his dirty work.

"Hooch," Carver grunted, wiping sweat and smoke grime.

"How the hell you get that from burning up a plant?"

Rafe jerked his head and showed him the blackened pit below. It dug out the base of the agave plant a good man's height, half the width, with palm wood supports to prop up the succulent. Coals were arranged below its shorn roots. It wept a liquid that was collected in a copper basin.

He tried to taste it but a blackened finger swatted it away—a witch-man wagged a warning, "Begone crow! Keep your filthy claws from our nectars. Or you'll spoil it!"

"How long does it take?"

Rafe shrugged, "These gremlins say it takes days. If it grows too hot they have to slough off tar. See here."

Blackened ooze was being piled below one such plant. A dark and viscous resin that reminded Rooster of the boiling pitch he'd seen used in siege cauldrons.

"Sometimes the liquor has to be separated from the resin. They'll use it for torches or whatnot later. Crafty eh?"

The witch-men Rooster recognized as Ahffan's fellow skinwalkers. Maybe the alcohol was to help with the beastly dissociation. Or maybe because they were just lazy little wizards.

Something stung the air and offended the nose, "If it's

like that gut rot yucca wine..."

"Nah this stuff will scorch your eyebrows off."

"It better," Carver muttered, "I'm not busting my ass for watered-down piss."

Barely a week in camp and they were already kneedeep in creating a thriving brewing industry. Rooster shook his head. If only this bunch were so determined at their jobs and not getting drunk.

"You see the others?"

Rafe put his back into the work, "Beats me. All I've seen is dirt and old men today."

A walk around camp found Lancer and Antonius sparring. The Ophi were out hunting with Jhabari and Jhamon, showing them the finer things with javelins. Leaving just one big good-looking lout missing; Big Mug.

Rooster scoured everywhere he could think and saw no signs of him. Odd. Wasn't like the northerner to hide. The man was reliable as they came and always came running.

He almost started to organize a search party when two shapes silhouetted against the ridge of the hillside. A man and a much smaller woman. Both were nude as they'd been born and slick with sweat. They appeared for barely a few breaths before diving back out of view.

Motion caught Rooster's eye; another shape perched on a slab of rock across the hillside. That deep-orange and black spotted leopard. Ahffan's creature. Who must have seen everything.

"Oh shit."

Tonight went against everything Rooster stood for as a captain and commander. There was a time and place for punishment. In his eyes, no evil had been committed. Men and women would always find an excuse to split off and indulge their base natures.

But he was not the arbiter, nor judge in this land.

"This is wrong," Carver snarled almost too quiet to hear, "We can't let them do this. You're just going to stand by Lancer? He's your blood brother."

The big man was impassive, showing no emotion. Maybe the hint of a frown on his chiseled face.

"You're all fucking cowards."

"Watch it cutter," Antonius hissed from down the line.

"Easy for you to say, boy. He's not your friend."

"He knew the rules. We all did."

Rafe jabbed an elbow and whispered something into Carver's ear to shut his trap.

The scarred man was right for once.

It was night, the camp glowed with sinister torchlight, and the Birds of Prey stood idly by as their own was humiliated before exile. They formed a parallel of lines with the Shemsari that ran a gauntlet all the way to the edge of the canyon.

Disarmed by the codes of hospitality shown to them, no matter how frayed.

The punishment for sleeping with an outsider was exile into the waste, that salt plain. A slow death usually followed. It was only by the Beyik Alghasan's mercy that the offender hadn't been castrated, as was one tradition. It was the only mercy tonight.

Big Mug and his new lover were walking down the aisle. Just as nude as they had been before. Walking in shame.

Every Ramali greeted them in line first, spitting at them. The girl held her chin high.

“Brave girl,” Rafe commented.

“They can both be brave as they starve to death,” Carver hissed.

The shamed couple walked slowly until they reached Beyik Alghasan, who was cloaked like moonlight and had his hood drawn over a crown of feathers. The elderly man held a pair of torches in each hand. He did not speak, merely offering the torches out to each of them.

Big Mug and his Ramali girl both walked around the shoulders of the chieftain into the canyon.

Exiled without any process. Where the salt plain lay between the mountains. Where the dead would come from.

If they were not already near.

"Captain," Rafe wandered over, "We let them have their charade. Fine. But we're not letting them get away with this."

"It's not up to us anymore."

Anger flashed on the sellsword's face. He seemed at the edge of bloodlust, "So you're going to let him fucking die? For nothing? Over a girl?"

"What would you have me do?"

The moral quandary played out on his face. All while Jhamon and Jhabari folded their arms, watched with muted disagreement.

Maybe they all took issue. Big Mug was popular. He was a pure and rare gentle soul, albeit a hopeless romantic. It killed Rooster to stand by and let the man be exiled.

There were no more easy choices anymore.

The Birds of Prey stood there amidst the upright torches at the edge of the canyon. The chieftain looked at them with sadness. Then was escorted back up to his tent.

"Captain," now it was Antonius who spoke up. He looked as troubled as anyone else. The torchlight aged him twenty years.

"You too?"

"I don't think you made the wrong decision. But it wasn't the right one either. Big Mug could have been any of us. Eventually, it was going to be."

"We go out there and rescue him and then this has all been for nothing."

Antonius frowned, "I believe you, captain. We aren't here with these barbarians just for any reason. I'll follow you into hell if need be. But just know this doesn't sit right with me."

His comment rippled over the men—even the sellswords.

Letting any good man go to needless death over a tradition they didn't adhere to or care for must have seemed caustic to the others. Rooster knew he must have appeared as a heartless and cruel lord at that moment.

But to give up on the Ramali at this point was unthinkable.

Ahffan and his skinwalkers knew something—their eagles were following Hazair wherever the crippled bird went. At high noon when the birds of prey hunted, the soulbound eagles were busy haunting the White Dervish's old bird. The witch-men gathered in secret and only took breaks to burn their agave plants. Their conferences were guarded by sentries watching for Rooster specifically.

And Beyik Alghasan; something told him he was a trickster. All his life the chieftain had been one. It's how he got the job. Maybe the sentimental old fool act was genuine.

There was a secret hidden on the tongue of the white hair that he wouldn't dare admit.

The burning question became whether the life of Big Mug was worth trading for it.

That next morning Rooster went to the witch-men to root out that secret and find out. Thumbs were coming out of asses and jaws needed to start yapping.

Or else.

The secluded oldsters had set up little tents on the earth shelf bridging the colony of smoking agave plants. It would yield enough liquor to fuel an army. Drunkards. The pile of black ooze tar that had been hauled out by the bucket numbered in the dozens.

"I need answers. What is it that I'm not being told?"

The witch-men skinwalkers sniggered between sips of their premature brew.

Rooster neared them, "We've been here for two weeks. You've taken my blood for your magics. You've been consulting your circles of power. And the Beyik Alghasan is privy to it. I need to know."

"Fool outsider. No respect for your elders," one piped up gravelly.

They thought this was disrespect? He would show them.

A whistle and Jhamon and Jhabari both led horses.

Water skins sloshed from the saddles. The boys began to douse two of the liquor factories.

"Stop stop stop," the witch-men began to squeal like pigs.

"We stop when you start talking."

Steam shot out of their ears and noses. They began to lambast Ahffan for bringing such mischievous demons to camp. Lumping in the two Shemsari ad daal boys. Courtesy to the clanless didn't abide with most Shemsari.

"Boys. Douse them all."

More shrieking.

"A group of wizards like you should be turning us into lizard turds now."

"Insolent imp," the widest one said, who wore what looked like a hideous cloak made of a thousand tarantulas, hairy and ill-sewn, "You've set us back weeks!"

"If you all don't start talking, sand is going to start being kicked into pits."

Ahffan grabbed tarantula skin cloak and they started to grumble amongst themselves. A consensus slowly was found. They two turned back.

Rhuïma turned out to be the name of tarantula skin cloak. He looked like a pear left out in the sun for too long. In a moment he had his mortar and pestle grinding the bits of a blackened feather and Rooster's blood. Packed it all up into the skull of a rat, then lit it aflame.

"What's this horseshit?"

"Divination," Ahffan said.

The witch-men got quiet when Rhuïma took the flaming skull and placed it atop a disk of the liquor. Then lobbed a load of spit into it, whispering something druidic. A strange aroma took. Smoke began to dance atop the surface. They saw something in it, fixating on it. Whispering.

The smoke ended.

"Well?"

Scared faces. Concerned fingers tapping talismans.

Rhuïma flapped his tarantula skin cloak and went away

red-faced.

"How bad is it?"

"Bad," Ahffan sniffed, "If you are Ramali."

"Give me more than that."

"Fate is at best smoke that can be seen. Try to speak its name and grasp it and it slips between your fingers. To utter prophecy is to create another that is hidden in its place."

Maddening.

Rooster wanted to crack their old skulls.

The fact he didn't leave the tent made the skinwalkers antsy.

"That's a stupid analogy. Tell me what you all saw."

"As you wish. We saw your bird eating the heart of our chieftain."

More mysticism. Nothing to work off of.

Bahram laughed at his floundering.

The coals in the pits that were smoking gave the false impression the Birds of Prey were asleep. But there wasn't a bedroll occupied or a shadow left in camp. Even the horses were gone—somehow, they'd silently moved them.

Anger hit first, then acceptance.

They'd gone to save Big Mug.

In their position, Rooster would have done the same.

He saddled up Nereel and went looking for his wayward delinquents.

Nighttime on the salt plain was wicked by the full moon. An eyeball of a colossal god amidst skin of the deepest black, turning the entire ground into a luminescent mirror.

The dust clouds were a dead giveaway. Rooster followed them.

It was spooky how dead quiet this place was.

The valley of the plain was perhaps a fistful of miles between the hooded black mountain ranges, though it widened to the left in a blinding sea of white. Not a bat or a lizard dared to show its face on that seamless horizon.

Ahead a rider approached—Jhamon.

"We didn't know where you went," the boy began.

"Save it. What's the plan?"

The shame was quickly subdued, "We found a trail. We think it's them."

Big Mug and his girl weren't as stupid as they were weak to impulse. They'd decided to cross the plain the night prior. By now they'd have to be in the mountain range next.

The other Birds of Prey said little else.

"Well, let's go get them then."

"And then what," Rafe asked.

"Didn't have a plan for that, did you wiseass? Well, the Ramali won't be letting us come back anytime soon. So we'll need to find a new watering hole. In case you didn't notice, there's not a whole lot of them near."

There was collective grumbling, maybe even self-awareness.

Good; this should be a learning experience.

Jhabari was riding up fast, "Rooster! Come quick."

"There should be a captain in there."

Together they rode ahead. There might have been a mile before they'd hit the mountain range. Rooster made out two figures running towards them, faintly. It was Big Mug and his girl. They were hoofing it like all the imps of hell were nipping at their heels. They threw them on the backs of their horses and brought them to the rest.

Big Mug broke down, as did his girl. They sounded wrecked. On the edge of sanity. Like they knew they were seconds from death. The big man started to babble incoherently.

Rafe was trying to calm him down, "Hold it. Stay steady. Take a breath. Tell it slowly."

"Dead ahead…the dead are ahead. They almost got us. They were right there," Big Mug was wheezing and shaking.

"The dead?"

"The damn graythirsters," at the mention the Shemsari boys went stiff like statues, "That's what he means. You two with me. The rest of you back to camp. Don't take any shit from the Ramali."

Across the white plain, they plied towards the mountains. Which grew gloomier the more they filled their vision. As if the blackness was impenetrable by the ripe moon.

"Rooster," Jhabari said over the drum of hooves, "We cannot fight the graythirsters. They cannot die."

"How did the Ramali do it then?"

Jhamon piped up, "They can be burned. It's the only sure way they can't come back."

His brother said, "We should leave this place."

The plain ended and a crevasse took its place. A massive rift in the earth that would have sent their horses plummeting down a good three hundred feet. The boulder-strewn gash in the earth was half-lit by the moonlight. It continued like an ugly scar into the canyons of the mountain folds.

At first, Rooster thought he heard water. Realizing it was the sound of sand being displaced. By footfalls. The moonshadow was rippling like black water in the crevasse—only the moon hadn't moved at all. A piece of that moving shadow spilled out into the light; a man-like shape of a gray husk with holes for eye sockets and a mouth. Howling inwardly as it threw itself in a mad scramble up the sand.

Hundreds and hundreds of the dead were pouring out from the canyon into the crevasse. Their boiling mass was like mad ants spilling out from the mountain anthill. A menacing sound was building below, like a thousand nails dragging across a gigantic piece of slate.

A goddamn army of them. They'd reach the white plain in mere hours. The oasis? By morning.

They needed to tell the Ramali but what good would it do? The nomads wouldn't move. They'd stand and fight an impossible situation. Every corpse that spilled onto the white plain was another sliver of hope hacked away.

The Shemsari boys were worrying themselves—their

horses were going bugfuck over the drone of the dead.

"We must turn back Rooster," Jhamon shouted.

Rooster knew they had to. But he was beyond any cheap verbal parry.

He found himself staring at the ungodly horde and slipped back into the tactician atop the battlements of his past. Dealing with overwhelming forces, unwinnable sieges, and pitched battles with odds never in his favor.

Twisting to look back to the torchlight of the men on the plain.

Fire...? If only they had some way they could control fire...

He maneuvered Nereel to canter away when genius struck. Grabbed the torch from Jhabari and threw it down the crevasse. Tar fire claimed one of the corpses, then three more as they dogpiled onto it and smothered the flame.

Graythirsters weren't attracted just to water but to heat too.

A harebrained plan started to form.

Quickly he delegated. The boys didn't ask twice. They rode off towards camp to pillage from the Ramali. They surpassed the rest of the warband and continued.

Rooster split from them and grabbed Antonius, "Have everyone ready here to sally out."

"You're a madman. You're not going back out there?"

Rafe demanded, "What do you intend?"

"To do what the chieftain can't."

"Why? Why risk our necks for these people?"

"Invent a reason if you need one. Glory. Honor. Hubris. I have mine."

Lancer was stone-faced, nodding.

Rafe shook his head, "Yeah? Is the chieftain going to gift you some bride? You're in it for Shemsari gash?"

"No. This has been in my dreams."

The sellsword sergeant looked dumbfounded.

Yeah, it sounded stupid when Rooster uttered it aloud.

But he knew it deep down. The spiritual haunts. The weird way the skinwalkers looked at him. The prophetic

Hazair hanging around. What didn't make any practical sense was also his only explanation left.

"If we leave, they go extinct. They have no warriors left. If you want to die a different way, you're free to go back to camp."

Lancer pushed through his comrades, joining Rooster's side. Words out of his mouth wouldn't have sounded right. Just his presence alone was enough.

So did the Ophi, holding their lances and tall bows. Big Mug and Antonius too.

The scarred man gave that thousand-yard stare, then joined them, "Nobody ever called Carver a coward."

Which left but Rafe, who regarded the bone-white plain, "How many are out there?"

"A score for every one of us. Or a hundred. Could be a thousand of them."

The sellsword sounded nonplussed, "Couldn't have dreamed us all getting fat and rich, eh?"

"Who knows?"

Rafe laughed—perhaps at the absurdity of his situation—then joined in, "In hindsight, I think it was a damn fool thing to not take the Bandit Prince's offer. Bet the Ivory Queen had some girls to reward us for swearing to her."

"Didn't take you for a romantic Rafe."

"You have your dreams, I have mine. I want a beautiful woman to cry over me when I die drinking wine from a golden cup."

Jhamon returned and wasn't alone. A gang of Ramali had come. All elderly warriors; stark-haired, sun-leather skin with ancient tattoos, yet all clutching horsebows. War was in their eyes and locked jaws. Even skinwalkers led by Ahffan and Rhuïma joined them. Tarantula skin cloak and witchfire in the latter's eyes.

As well they carried buckets of the black pitch.

"Arrows?"

The elderly father of Ahffan, who was named Ahbdan, laid out blankets where scores of arrows were spread out.

From behind the group was Jhabari, holding something under his vest. He tactfully snuck into the ranks.

Ahffan waved at the spread, "How can this hope to defeat the *ghūl*?"

Rooster wrapped a piece of palm frond around the narrow flint point, dipping the whole thing in the agave tar, and finished by sticking a little frond string off the side. Took him less than ten seconds to demonstrate, leaving the finished arrow propped up on a rock.

Antonius caught on, "I've seen this used to fire boats but not an army."

"That's why you and the Ophi are going to build a bonfire out there. Grab every dead plant you see."

The rest got busy making arrows and balls of pitch layered with grass and dead palm trees. They only had a few hours at best before the dead came.

What looked like a shadow mirage appeared on the white salt. Growing in size and width with every minute.

The defenders on their horses finished whatever prayers they would make. To gods who were asleep. The middle group who were dismounted would stay behind to execute the last part of the plan.

If they succeeded in the first two.

A big if.

Rooster moved Nereel forward, signaling the first group to move out. That being Shemsari boys and the elderly Ramali riders. All carrying small javelins and spears.

"We ready?"

The Shemsari hooted and howled.

The first part of the plan began with them riding out directly at the graythirsters. The horde of the dead looked an ominous sight, marching with the vigor of fresh troops unspoiled by marching. They were at a dead run, packed shoulder to shoulder.

Jhabari took the lead, lifting something hidden by cloth. His painted horse outpaced theirs by a good bowshot.

Like bloodhounds catching a scent, the dead began to

move right for him. A foul wind from their inward breath was pulling sand and salt into their mass.

The boy turned his steed at the last moment and began to pull them towards the destined burn pile. Graythirsters were clumping up into a bloated formation without any discernible shape. While the other riders swung left like they were herding cattle. Only a few straggling dead were distracted enough to pursue them.

Rooster felt his spirits surge—this was it.

"Jhamon, get the second group in position."

The boy did but looked fearfully at Jhabari.

"He's got it handled. Go!"

Dust flew up. Soon dozens of little flares popped up—the second group was lighting their torches and lit the pitch-balls. A candelabra of men who waited on bated breath for Jhabari to pass the burn-pile.

He did, screeching the Shemsari call.

Bows loosed. Slings hurled. Fire lanced across the darkened sky.

The first dead made it over the pile, streaming like gray maggots through the debris. The next ones weren't so lucky. Pitch-soaked timber sparked. An enormous flame reached the sky, unfurling an explosive flower like the immolation of a fire-djinn. Dozens of dead were sent asunder. The rest became fire-carriers, spreading the disease to their kindred. And the dumb dead did not care, running right into the liquid flames.

"Second group," Rooster was riding up, shouting.

Rafe and his men carrying torches started their approach. Riding on the outskirts of the burn, placing the standing torches in the sand. The elderly Ramali would use them to light their fire arrows and start sending shots into the horde. Then the sellswords started their secondary objective; they were carrying skins sloshing of water. They rode dangerously close to the horde, throwing the water onto the tar-fires. Which roared and spread further on the hard-packed salt.

For a breath frozen in time, the moment was theirs.

It began to go to shit when a cluster of graythirsters suddenly smacked into Carver's horse. The man got toppled off and fell. Flames shot chaotically around him. His horse went berserk, stomping on dead men and flames.

"Jhabari," came his brother's scream.

The Shemsari boy was supposed to be leading the dead in a giant circle—a whirlpool of flames that would spread as more fire arrows and water built up the bonfire.

Except a group of dead had somehow bulged out and closed in from the front and behind. Trapping him.

The Ramali riders noticed. They lit their arrows and began to ride to Jhabari's aid, loosing. A few hit their targets but there were too many graythirsters. Piling on like fire ants to swarm over a much larger spider.

Dark possibilities were becoming realities before Rooster's eyes.

They were losing their edge, very quickly.

He had to do something.

The third phase of the Birds of Prey were starting to loose as many fire arrows as they could string. The Ophi were hurling lances too. They fired hopelessly into a neverending horde of undead who were starting to dogpile onto Jhabari's position. The Shemsari boy was barely in his saddle, swerving out of the bodies as best he could.

Rooster rode up next to them so they could hear, "Antonius! Third group. On me. Grab those firepots."

The Teridian grabbed one himself, Goshawk another. Despite it not being the plan, they adapted quickly.

He indicated the places he wanted them set, "When you see my signal, ignite them all. And get the hell out of there."

"What if it doesn't catch them?"

"You fall back to camp. Fill up your water and take to the hills above the flatiron. If you don't see us, you go to Senesret's Wards."

Antonius didn't look happy but he barked out the commands. The third group of unmounted infantry started to push towards the brush pile.

Not before Rooster drew Awakener and dipped it in the

firepot.

And charged in.

The graythirsters fell like wheat before the scythe. They were too busy trying to swarm Jhabari. Out of the corner of his eye, Rooster saw the second group of Rafe and the sellswords dealing with a large body that had split off the main horde. The men were bleeding—as if their flesh was being torn from the air sucked in by the dead. Rafe and his men were being pushed with their backs to the flames. There was nothing Rooster could do.

The bastard sword burst into flames at the first torch he swung it over. The pommel already started to heat up.

Rooster pushed into the ranks of the dead and began to cut down.

A foul wind swept over him—they were sucking in wind and emanating an accursed aura. He felt his soul leaving his throat. A spiritual disemboweling. Any air to breathe was being sucked into their black mouths.

He swung Awakener down in a frenzy, trying to see where Jhabari was. Somewhere trapped there, but there were too many graythirsters between them.

Too many dead had come.

The withered hand of hell reached up. Tearing at his scaled mail, bringing him down to oblivion. To the eternal grave and join the ranks of the cursed. More hands reached up to grab onto him. A ghoulish fossilized face sunken into a black skull summoned his attention.

Rooster could not tear away from the hollow, bone-dry sockets.

A dream like a drop of tar sinking into depthless shadow filled his mind. Forever trapped in the howling torment.

An eagle cry stirred him from doom—waking him in cold sweat.

Rooster exhaled and rammed his sword right into that face and watched it burst apart like paper in a firepit.

Nereel was insane, bucking wildly at the crowd trying to overwhelm him.

And there Jhabari was, half-out of his saddle as the dead were finding purchase on his saddle and side. Sucking the life out of the air. As the boy held out that perfect pale blue diamond—The Blue Eye.

In slow motion, Rooster saw it tumble from his fingers.

A manic creature awoke in his flesh. He somehow threw himself sideways in the saddle and reached with his left hand. Felt the cold gem fall right into his fingers. Suddenly aware that every dead face was focused on him.

"No," Ahbdan the elder cried out, seeing the Blue Eye, "You've doomed us all!"

Every graythirster within sight came rushing in.

The Ramali horseman charged hard, plowing right into the oncoming horde. Clearing a path he shot wildly and fell back to his spears. And got overwhelmed instantly. The white-haired warrior fought like a wild animal even as he was dragged onto the plain. Undead tore him apart.

The sacrificial move gave Rooster just enough time to get to Jhabari.

The boy righted himself and spurred his horse—jumping the beast over the mound of bodies. All he had left were his spears, throwing them at anything that neared Nereel. Impaled dead flailed like crabs, pinned to the sand.

All around them, the pits of hell were brought to the mortal plane.

"We need the standard to signal Antonius," he roared over the drone.

"I've got it Rooster," the boy replied, wheeling his horse.

"Don't you dare drop it."

"I won't."

Rooster kicked Nereel into a mad dash. The walking dead were assembling. He rode right into the open space between them, holding the Blue Eye aloft.

That got their attention.

If the dead could get angry, they showed it. From all corners of his vision they swarmed. A mindless arm of destruction came.

Stilling the blood in his veins.

Rooster looked and saw their standard being waved madly, Jhabari almost standing in the saddle to hoist it up.

Nowhere did he see Antonius and the Ophi. Dread set in. They might have fallen.

All he saw were dead faces of dead men.

Pure fear reigned.

Somewhere in the middle of the chaos, a horse was ablaze. Mane and tail like bonfires. Screaming as it charged blindly through cursed men who did not feel pain.

Another eagle cry.

"Hyah," he heard himself shout.

The wind all around him drained the life from the very air. And yet Nereel galloped with the vigor of twenty horses, knocking back body after body. Somehow they made it through the mass of dead. Where the firepots had fallen, oozing tar onto the salt. The graythirsters were coated in it.

Instinct took over. Rooster stabbed Awakener into the nearest graythirster and let go of the flaming blade. And continued to ride.

Everything became a blur.

The night exploded. Heat wash over him before succumbing to darkness.

With a raging headache Rooster woke up in a tent. The explosion still rung in his ears. Poultices all over his body indicated fresh burns. Everything felt stiff.

When he dared to venture out of camp, it was night still.

How was that possible?

Carver came around and bullied him back into the cot. Explaining that he'd been asleep for a full day.

Their mere existence presaged their victory over the army of the dead. But at what cost?

Rooster asked, almost afraid to learn the answer.

The scarred man had a different air about him. Meditative. Still always on the edge of violence. He pulled up a stool and began to recount.

Many had died. Four of the Ophi had been felled including Vulture and Heron. Goshawk was on death's door. Nearly all the Ramali had been slain, going to the golden pastures of their ancestors. The father of Ahffan, Ahbdan, among them. Three of the skinwalkers too. Finally, there was Rafe.

Against overwhelming odds the sellsword had made a heroic last stand, taking nearly twenty of the dead into the flames with him. Big Mug tried to save him but was dragged off by the others. The body had just been recovered.

Rafe's death hit the hardest. He'd proven a stubborn but good sergeant. The core of the sellsword's morale. No one would easily replace him. Camp would be a quieter place without his humor.

Fading again, feeling the necessity of sleep pull him back in.

Rooster dreamt of his failures.

Barely a few hours went by before he was rudely awakened.

"Beyik Alghasan wishes to see you," Ahffan said.

It was a short and painful limp over to the white hair's tent. Rooster would have asked for a stick if it wouldn't cripple his ego.

As if that could take any more of a beating.

Inside on his well-woven rug the chieftain had prepared hot agave liquor, passing him a cup. The craftsmanship on the horsehair rug was impressive. Soft even, despite the decades of wear.

"Sit my friend. Sit and drink with me."

Rooster did not feel worthy. He did anyway.

"So," the elderly man said, "How do you feel?"

"Like a turd left in a brazier."

"Aha. How you weave words. And yet you are intact. My witch-men say they saw scarring over your heart. It does not seem that you die so easily."

"Unfortunately."

The chieftain sipped, "Look at us; aged men. We cannot help but be touched by time and its wickedness. Until we die we carry our scars—those on the outside and in. Even still I am joyed to see that you are still standing."

Rooster bowed his head, waiting for reprimand.

One that never came.

"You look pained, Rooster. What's troubling you?"

"Do you not know?"

The glint in the old man's eye was nothing short of knavish, "If it's in the Shobai Hamada, there is little that escapes me."

"Then you know how we defeated the dead."

Beyik Alghasan nodded, refilling his cup before his own, "Yes I do. Ahffan recounted it all to me while you were recovering."

"You have my apology then."

"Why?"

"Stealing your clan's most prized possession was a desperate move, I know..."

The bastard had a smile creeping up on the corners of his wrinkled face.

"Please keep going, don't mind me Rooster."

"I'm going to mind damn you. Why do you look so cheery? I almost got your precious waterstone destroyed. I got half your clan killed in the process."

"Yes. Yes, you did."

"And?"

This meeting was getting to Rooster. He felt himself flush in anger. This was the witch-men giving their obscenely mysterious portents all over again.

The old man stood up and clasped his forearms, "You did exactly as I wished you would."

"How...?"

"I watched as you weighed every action. As your man transgressed and was exiled you were still wary to rescue him. This was the stroke of a careful gardener, pruning the ivy that threatens his flowers."

"What of the Blue Eye?"

Beyik Alghasan snorted, "Did you think we would have been able to protect it against hundreds of the dead? Almost a thousand, the witch-men said. Taking it and using it to draw them out? This was always the best plan."

Rooster was bewildered.

His emotions were hardly opaque, making the chieftain almost giggle. The madman.

"*The best plan?* How did you know what I was going to do?"

"You don't think I became the chieftain because I was the right man for the job, do you?" there was that knowing, almost evil eye.

And then a wink.

"You sly son of a bitch."

"Back when I was your age I crushed the Faari and the Heqqari clans by pitting them against each other. To this day, they're still oblivious to how they were nearly ruined. Now...this fire...you taught me something new Rooster. Quite clever of you."

"If you knew what to do that entire time...?"

"Why didn't I take action as chieftain? Why did I let you—an outsider, that many of the clan consider a demon—protect us from destruction?"

"Yes."

The chieftain drank long and deeply, draining and refilling the cup twice.

"Because Rooster, it is simple. If I were to plunder my own clan's treasure, I lose all credibility. By fighting without warriors or a replacement, I look weak. Even if I were to succeed as you did, the cost to my reputation would be devastating. Even J'awed cannot protect me from judgment."

"By stealing the Blue Eye and taking the fight to the ghūl, you show the initiative that none in the clan have. You're an outsider yes. But you understood the Shemsari way at our very root. Something they will vehemently deny, even as our nemesis burns in a great grave," came the admission.

Finally the truth.

A wave of lightheadedness had the Rooster swaying. He felt the urge to sit down.

"Your dreams and prophecies? They were conjurations meant to manipulate me too?"

Beyik Alghasan blanched, drew in a quiet breath, "No. Bahram as my witness."

Rooster fell to a crouch.

The night of the dead was coming back to him in disorganized vignettes. They'd faced horror as stoic as anyone could. He'd seen many battlefields—that was not one of them. Armies were comprised of men with feelings and ambitions.

A disturbing thought occurred; hadn't the chieftain mentioned someone was raising these graythirsters? A necromancer of kinds, unleashing them onto the world?

They had gotten lucky. And that fact rattled Rooster.

"Does your Bahram do anything besides give you dreams? Is he out there somewhere?"

The chieftain's brows furrowed, "Ah. No one has asked that I think for some time. Almost."

"Ah?"

"As you know, Rooster, our history is an oral one. If such an answer existed it is not written in any book. The sins of our ancestors were too severe and there are no words in our language harsh enough to condemn their acts."

Behind the shadowed face and wrinkles was the hint of knowledge.

"You didn't answer me directly."

"Some things cannot be uttered casually upon untrustworthy winds," the chieftain looked to the flap as if it might rip open, "Rooster. I will speak to you now as my friend, and openly."

There wasn't anything else he could do but nod.

"Before you, a rider came to us from the east. An ad daal and a witch-man. You might know him by the White Dervish."

The father of Jhabari and Jhamon!

His knees groaned but he ignored them.

The story was recanted, "He had seen something south, in his eagle-form. Like a great storm of darkness, rolling over the White Wastes. In it were the forms of gods who have been long dead. Some of their bones lie in the sparkling wall to the north—we call it the God Wall. How they were alive I cannot hope to know. And in that darkness was Bahram, speared by a black obelisk. He was alive but trapped for all eternity."

"The White Dervish was struck by something in that storm. He wandered for days in a state of limbo, half-dead and struck by an ominous countenance. This is how my witch-men found him. Since I spoke to him then, I have had dreams."

Which might have been an explanation for the eagle-form. If Rooster had to speculate on things he knew squat about. As a mortal that up to recently, didn't believe in gods.

"How does this involve me?"

The chieftain set down his cup, "In my old age I have no shame admitting where my weaknesses lie. In this case, it is that I never inspired a successor. I tried talking to the White Dervish into it. But he wanted to follow his madman brother. Then got himself killed over nothing."

"Jhamon would make a fine chieftain one day."

"One day is a long time from now," Beyik Alghasan said, then began to push himself up from his cross-legged position, "Help an old man up, would you?"

Shaky himself, Rooster managed to guide the white haired chieftain to a bent-over stance, holding him by his right arm. The old man had his free hand over his chest. Frail, but surprisingly lean and strong for his age.

"A funny thing just occurred to me, outsider. We came from a line of warriors of the old kingdoms. But when we crossed the White Waste, we had mixed with the blood of barbarians who were among the first horsemen. To think we would have never made it without them."

Senile ramblings, Rooster thought.

"Where to?"

The chieftain just smiled, scrutinizing his face, "Forgive me in your own time, Rooster."

He hadn't seen the old man draw the ceremonial dagger from the sheath on his chest. It happened too fast.

Beyik Alghasan plunged the dagger into his own chest.

Grabbing Rooster's other hand and placed it on the pommel.

Time slowed as blood soaked the ivory-white robes of the chieftain.

Rooster was frozen in shock.

"Do what I couldn't, outsider," teeth rattling in pain, the old man grinned at the imaginary face of death, "Ahffan come here."

By the time the skinwalker threw aside the flap, the chieftain was dead.

Sun was setting bloodily.

All of the Shobai Hamada soaked in its death. The high desert entered the last day of spring with foreboding heat. A dominion on the cusp of metamorphosis. Stars were beginning to paint the dimming sky without the light of the moon.

With a bowl of life's nectar, Ahffan began to paint the holy script on the face of a slab of redrock angled towards the sky. It served as their obelisk.

It was the J'awed, but it was longer.

The Ramali had secretly clung to sentences that harbored deeper and ancient meanings. To a people who wrote nothing, the words were their treasure.

A Ramali woman walked down from the flatiron, carrying the Ayzaraqaw in her hands. She was one of the most beautiful women Rooster had ever seen. She knelt and presented the flawless diamond before him.

He accepted it.

She spared him one glance with those golden eyes before departing.

Behind him, Rooster could hear the sounds of Shemsari on their horses, standing up all at once.

Unspoken but undeniable was their disbelief.

They did not accept him as Beyik Alghasan and yet they could not deny him either.

Hundreds of years of tradition dethroned and replaced with a bleak unknown. No outsider had ever become a chieftain. Without being of the blood of the ancestry, the mere idea was taboo. But it was reality for the Ramali now. That scared these people. Their entire world was being walked off a cliff for all they knew.

Rooster himself felt the air flutter and the hot air buzz in anticipation. He was grappling with doubts, too busy to enjoy the moment.

Ahffan turned, knelt, and bowed his head, "Beyik Alghasan. The J'awed."

Rooster cleared his throat.

A great bird landed beside his rug. Hazair. Or perhaps it was the White Dervish in there. The eagle twisted its beak, craning to get a look at him. All too sentiently.

Back to the redrock obelisk.

To the ring that seemed to glow with the sun's final grace.

"All things begin as they end. The sun is the life whose veins fill man. The moon is the death that bears the beyond. No thing can ever taken from another if it is a gift; gifts must always be repaid tenfold. Greed is for traitors and thieves. The fallen on the white death waste, whose sacrifice brought us here was the greatest of all gifts. I am bound by their same creed; I am a wanderer of the seas of sand; I am a voice in the hollow wind; I am the eye of the beast of the air; I cannot dwell under the stone of pretenders; I lose sight of man if not in the witness of sun or moon. All those bound to this law are on the path and I shall not harm them even as I would move mountains. The knowledge of this path is sacred; it must open and close by the king sun door."

The last sentences took longer as they were unfamiliar,

"In my hand, I carry the heart of the water, the soul of creation. My breath for the font of all life. My flesh for the ruin of all mortals. I swear this until the day of elders, as a water-keeper."

"This is the path—this is J'awed."

البدو مخيم
Nomad's Camp

The map laid out on the rock table had to be made out of a single seamless skin of a creature long extinct. It was so old it might have predated steel. The tattooing on it was faded but wasn't completely worthless.

If Rooster's memory served right, the one he'd seen in the Vizier's court was far less proportional. One could suspect less accurate too.

"Was this made by a skinwalker?"

Ahffan wrinkled his face as if it were an insult.

"It looks bird's eye."

"This is a sacred map," the skinwalker declared as if that wasn't already obvious.

"Yeah. What are these indicating?"

Blue glyphs were shown to be water. Red lines of Shemsari runes for migratory paths. Rusty mounds for kurgans and meeting grounds. The almost translucent white waves indicated patterns of summer storms.

If it was believed to be accurate, two hundred years ago when this map was supposedly created the Shemsari had it figured out. Down to the bone.

And like all maps Rooster had seen of the desert south of the Wall, the space beneath Nefara's delta was a giant blank mystery. Except one line in red letters; *Hātfyyad*. Their White Wastes.

At the moment, it was just a highly detailed, topographical relic.

The map would see use later, he was sure. Much use indeed.

He rolled up his provenance.

In total, there were one hundred and thirteen of the Ramali clan left. The vast bulk of them women and children.

Seventeen of the remaining lot belonged to the warrior cult Ahbdan had led. They were wiry and old, but they refused to retire their bows. And lastly, the witch-men of Rhuïma, of which there were six left.

Barring Ahffan the eccentric and bizarre little witch-men had all gone into hiding. No one saw their beasts, so it was safe to assume they were ranging out beyond the borders of the Shobai Hamada in the skin dream. Whatever they were looking for, they deigned to keep it a secret.

At first, it pissed Rooster off. The skinwalkers were valuable eyes that could go where no man could and see things man couldn't dream of. They could talk to other animals in their form and get intelligence otherwise impossible to obtain.

Then it dawned on him later they might be the only ones who approved of his position and had taken the initiative.

Stubborn little shits had motives of their own—he could exploit those later.

Rooster focused on what he could.

He found Jhamon and his horse at the troughs carved out of the oasis pools, "Morning."

"Chieftain," there was too heavy an honorific there.

"It's always just Rooster with you Jhamon."

A nod.

"Go get me the Ramali horse warriors. Bring them back here."

It took half an hour before the old men and Jhamon returned. They did not look surprised to be summoned.

In Shemsari he addressed them, "Who is the First Bow of the Ramali?"

A weathered tribesman croaked, "No one, Beyik Alghasan. Our last chief did not name him."

"And Ahbdan?"

"He was of us. An arrow in the wind of death."

Good. At least Rooster was only breaking tradition and not displacing another. So far the Ramali culture had no tenets about who could become Ramali, so far as they were already Shemsari. As far as he was aware.

How far could he push the letter? He was about to find out.

"I name Jhamon a member of the clan. Furthermore, I am giving him the rank of First Bow of the Ramali. He is the best fighter I have and a more than capable leader. He will lead you and future warriors of the clan, until he is surpassed by another or until I am dead."

The leathery warriors showed no emotion at the declaration.

No one was more surprised than Jhamon.

In his entire life before the desert, Rooster had seen only one natural order reign; that of the strong-willed. Down here some hierarchies and orders hadn't been explained. Without a chieftain to guide him through the wilderness of culture, he would rely on what he knew best. If the Ramali were ever to be a force to be reckoned with—now he was bound to them—it would not be with him parlaying with centuries-old and nonsensical customs.

It would be by ridding themselves of any unpractical tradition.

"Does any man here take issue with this? Speak now."

The old warriors did something unexpected; a few ran back, returned with mortar and pestle. They ground the copper-red powder and began to tattoo the inside of Jhamon's forearms. Leaving script that formed the shape of arrows.

The boy gritted his teeth and endured the pain of the stick-and-poke method. It left a mess of blood.

When they were finished the old warriors grinned, patting his face with the copper-red dust and all called him one word, *"Rhāqib."*

Maybe he misjudged the Ramali. Perhaps they were more practical if given the leeway.

Without being ordered, the riders climbed their horses and began to wail their Shemsari war cries. They took their new First Bow to train out in the pastures.

That solved one of many dilemmas.

Up on the terraced grove, nestled in the palm trees the Birds of Prey were entertaining themselves. They'd found a tangerine-colored scorpion the size of a cat that they had fed the agave liquor. They made a circle around it and dodged its drunken stinger and claws. It had the makings of a game.

A few of the Ramali girls who had been lingering in camp scattered like chastised cats. Metaphorical tails between their legs. Big Mug's was one of them.

Rooster wasn't displeased.

Only that his cadre had nothing to do and busied themselves with boredom.

The road ahead would prove more than just challenging. He was now chieftain to two clans; Ramali and Birds of Prey. Any action currently that favored one neglected the other. Only so much time that he could put out fires and quibble over the day-to-day dealings of either. The reality was no king could rule two kingdoms—not efficiently.

As tragic as the death of Rafe and the Ophi had been, something had changed within the Birds of Prey. They'd all shared in the losses against the graythirsters. It would be a lie to say there wasn't bad blood still. But a fraternal bond had formed overnight. A reforging, like iron heated with flux. To anyone watching from the outside, they were acting like brothers.

Fool he would be not to nurture that.

With time, training, and some honest enemies to fight, they could make a hell of a unit.

He grabbed Goshawk, Antonius, and Lancer. Those he knew were capable of setting aside their prejudices and getting what needed to be done.

First and most importantly he dissolved the hierarchy that had been established before. Then in theme of their name, Rooster named them his Talons. Each was given freedom to pick his own squad and encouraged to train according to their strengths. When able to, they'd recruit anyone into their ranks so long as they swore to the banner.

Then the banner; Jhabari he made their bona fide bannerman. After all, the skull and orange flag was his invention all along—the stitchwork was done, the fierce white talons coated in blood. It was bold. It radiated with notoriety all its own. The Shemsari boy argued that he'd cut down anyone else who wanted to carry it anyhow. Until he was able to beef up his own squad, Antonius volunteered to ride alongside Jhabari.

Two forces. Two claws. Each working in tandem towards a unified purpose.

Now Rooster needed to find out what that would be.

They'd been in the Shobai Hamada for a full cycle of the moon. Locked away in a bubble from the outside world and its ugly affairs.

It was time he found out what was happening out there.

Four riders went in four cardinal directions. Each accompanied an eagle-bound skinwalker. The witch-men didn't like being split up and used like scouts. Too bad. An eagle could travel to Nefara and back with intelligence so fresh it may as well have been a fish netted from the Ptahira that morning.

Anything and everything was of value.

The skinwalkers bickered and moaned and dragged their feet up to the point that fingernails would need pulling. They didn't know just how valuable they were. Before long they'd figure it out and start demanding special treatment. Rooster would sweat out those particulars later.

No one knew how big an ace he had up his sleeve.

By the time the sun set, all four pairs delivered him portents from dunes that were hundreds of miles away. And even given additional orders to observe specifics.

It was likely there weren't magicians up north that could even handle this degree of magic-mirror talk. With the witch-men watching everywhere, they could fight and end wars weeks before they happened.

"You better come quickly," Ahffan rudely awoke him. The night was old but hadn't passed its dark glamor over to morning.

Rooster followed him to the skinwalker tent, half-asleep and short-tempered. It had been one of many long-nighters this week. With the temperatures rising even in the darkness, he had the urge to break off and take a swim in the oasis.

And maybe spy a glance at that pretty Shemsari girl again.

She was the to-be bride of the First Bow before they'd arrived. Her name was still a well-guarded secret. To no one who would ask, she was inspiring a feeling that took him back to much younger days. He feared it wasn't a mutual one—she'd stopped frequenting the pools at the times he tried to catch her attention.

Tonight was not one for distractions.

"I'm here. What's happening," he threw open the tent.

An eagle awaited him, perched on the stone table more dog-like than bird. It appeared to be sleeping.

Rhuïma came in from the other side. The definition of onery. For whatever reason it was the clan's best-kept secret the beast form the wrinkled old skinwalker took. He skittered over to a waterskin and began to drink from it heavily.

"Hey. I need you cogent."

Ahffan soothed, "It's water chieftain. He has been in the skin dream for hours."

"Word from the south? Or west?" Rooster indicated to the eagle.

"No," Rhuïma gasped for air, licking his lips, "I will tell you in the morning."

"You'll tell me now."

A low muttered threat barely audible, "Don't test me demon. Or Clever Rhuïma will turn you into a steaming camel turd."

Rooster wasn't feeling humorous tonight, "Eh? Come again? Louder please."

Unlike all other Shemsari, the skinwalker's eyes were like flint during their stasis in the animal form. Making Rhuïma look more like a crafty arachnid than a human.

He wanted to stuff this cobweb-spinner into a sack and see if he bounced off a cliff.

"Eewwk. I said you speak of the wrong directions. We hear from the north and the east."

Rooster let the lie blow over, "What of them."

"Black smoke beyond the god wall. A great stone *sijn* burns. It is a bitter fight among many tribes," Rhuïma hissed.

Shemsari called cities prisons. Something to do with the curse of the J'awed and their inability to dwell beneath stone roofs.

"Describe the sijn to me."

When the skinwalker did, Rooster nearly jumped, "You speak of the Iron City. Who controls it now?"

"It cannot be said. But there is more. East."

"What of the east?"

"A great *habūd* has been spotted. In the land called the Sunstones."

This wasn't a word he'd heard ever used. Completely unfamiliar. Rooster demanded translation.

Ahffan leaned in, "The wrath of a dying djinn, chieftain. A wrathful storm of sand and wind that covers the sky. It is rare. No Shemsari would dare ride into it."

"How far are the Sunstones?"

"Three weeks as the camels ride. On Shemsari horse, perhaps one and a half."

"So why is this relevant?"

Rhuïma smiled in a sinister kind of way, "This habūd moves in a straight line."

Ahffan made a sound and explained, "Impossible. Such a storm moves like a blind animal, chieftain."

"You're implying something is controlling this sandstorm."

"What are you saying Rhuïma?" Ahffan gestured.

The wrinkled skinwalker scowled and responded in

kind.

"What does it mean?"

"The sandstorm covers a valley. A valley with a road. Djinn has no use for roads."

"No, but an army does."

Both witch-men looked intently at Rooster.

"I need you to get word to our western scouts. Have them move to Tyhri and see what the Ivory Queen is doing. Find out if her troops are readying to march east. And for our eastern skinwalker, is there a way he can move into the habūd? Fly above the storm and enter the eye. Do it quickly."

That eagle was woken and flapped off immediately.

Rhuïma waited until he was out of eyesight before whispering lovingly to the shadows.

Creepy, obnoxious little bastard. It was a shame he was indispensable.

Rooster could not sleep. He paced in his tent. Stomping up a dust cloud on the horsehair rug. Where was a coffee-brewing servant when he needed one? That bitter earthy taste had grown on him. Traditions be damned—the strict Ramali laws of chemical abstinence—he'd start raping and pillaging for a pot of it.

When fatigue began to set in and he longed to sleep, Ahffan came again.

"The eagle is back. You need to hear this."

The report was terse but proved his theory correct.

The great sandstorm wasn't a random act of chaos. It was a ruse of holy magnitude. Concealed within its wide eye was an enormous host of destruction. The eagle-talker could not spend enough time there to count them all. Tens of thousands of shining troops. All carrying hundreds of identical grim banners; a blood-red field, marked by white calligraphy. The flags of the Jihad.

The Boy King had slipped past the wall, virtually undetected. With an army that could have numbered well over fifty thousand.

And he was heading right for Nefara.

For the first time in centuries, the Ramali returned to their nomadic heritage.

The redrock oasis was in utter chaos as man and beast were uprooted. All that could be taken was packed and loaded on horseback—the rest discarded or left for scavengers.

A few of the clan could not leave. They were too frail, too old to ride. They asked to be culled, rather than to be shamed and left behind.

Rooster had a northern solution; he showed how travois could be built by lashed poles and antelope sinew. Drawn by horse, they could carry more than just the elderly but extra supplies and water.

Within a little more than a day, the entirety of the Ramali were ready to move. Alongside them the Birds of Prey, their unwanted and yet willing guardians. Who were almost as disappointed to leave their new residence as the natives.

The next morning they departed the oasis.

Their chieftain carrying the Blue Eye around his neck.

The red dirt trails leading out of the mountainous sanctuary were one of tears. The Ramali were a proud people. They did not wail or beg. They walked in stoic silence while moisture ran rivers down their dusty cheeks. This was home. Some of them believed openly that they would never find such a place like it again.

Rooster swore to them that one day they would return and find it populated with the wild horses that the last chieftain dreamt of.

They swore back they would give him to the eagles and crows as a skyfeast if he didn't.

And he believed them.

The storied copper-haired people donned their sun cloaks and began the long march out of the Shobai Hamada. Becoming nomads once again.

Senesret's Wards welcomed them like ghosts.

It was a very different reception than their first.

A screen of bandits rode out to inspect them, went berserk, then went back to their fortress in the rocks. No one came out after. So they passed right through the gates unmolested and set up camp on the south side, under the faces of the towering statues.

Until evening came.

They were roasting antelope in firepits when the black-cloth maniac strolled right into their camp, kicking over miniature dunes.

"I'm the lord of these lands. This beast here? Mine. You poached it. I could have all of you slain for this violating the law. I just might," Azim Altaruk tore a leg of sizzling meat for himself, waving it like a scimitar, "How about this, hm? If your chieftain does not make himself known, I'll start hanging ten of you by your ankles from the sky bridge."

Jhabari was making his way to the firepit, war in his eyes.

"Ah, nephews. My little rebel nephews. I see you're still doing the chicken lord's dirty work. Where is that bastard anyway? I want a Rooster head. Has anyone seen one?"

Steel was drawn and Azim spun, drawing his own in a flash. It was Jhamon with his long knife. Icy contempt hung in the space between them.

"Ah but what a surprise Jhamon. Drop your sword. Before you force me to become unpleasant."

Behind him, Jhabari had his blades drawn, "You first, uncle."

"You disappoint me, boys. After all the love I've shown you."

The whole camp was beginning to grow hostile. The bandits in black were starting to file in after their leader.

"I demand to speak to the Beyik Alghasan of the Ramali," Azim roared.

Rooster stepped forth from the tent, "You summoned me, Azim? What do I owe the pleasure?"

The Bandit Prince's eyes almost bulged out of their skull, "You?"

"Is there a problem?"

A slow laugh rolled into an insane one, "Well now. How a bird changes its feathers. I suppose I cannot have your head as a decoration now. Yet?"

"My offer to duel always lies on the table, Azim."

The man almost snapped at the missed honorific, looked thoughtful, then rammed his black blade into its sheath, "Never. Not while Kizzuran draws breath. You have me at an impasse...*chieftain*. To what do I owe for your sudden visitation, inviting yourself onto my lands and eating my herds?"

"War. The Boy King rides west."

"Aha, but I already knew this."

"How so?"

"A stranger from Nefara came, a few days after you fled my hospitality. An odd creature who told me all about this jihad from the north," the Bandit Prince twirled his mustache, "Funny. He inquired about you and your chicken soldiers. Said he knew you."

"What's his name? Where is he?"

Azim tore a chunk of antelope, chewing first, "Where else would he be? In my fighting pit. Bleeding and dying at my pleasure."

With Antonius and Lancer as backup in case of trickery, they headed to the slave cages. Far fewer cages were filled this time around. They found the pale, stooping figure bent within one of the last in the row.

How someone could maintain the pallor of snow in this climate of endless sunlight was remarkable. The servant must have only left the darkness of whatever dungeon he called home when his master commanded it.

"Nazsif?"

The servant bowed, ever the soulless vulture, "Rooster."

"What the hell are you doing here?"

"Why else? My master wishes to negotiate terms with this Bandit Prince. And find you."

What? Rooster didn't understand a lick of it.

Antonius stated, "Your master was taken prisoner by thugs. We barely escaped our lives because of it."

"Yes. But much has changed since your departure."

It was hardly an answer. The pale cretin seemed amused by their confusion. He slipped something through the bars—a tiny scroll.

"The Qalid is alive and well. All will be explained there."

Not much got past Antonius. The Teridian might have been deaf in the ears but he was a bloodhound to bullshit. He reached into the bars and rattled the sallow-skinned servant, "I don't buy what you're selling."

"All of it true, my young and unwise friend," Nazsif smiled falsely.

"Someone get me a torch," Rooster broke the seal and read quickly.

It was Tariq's hand all right. Even a master copyist would find difficulty making such a perfect imitation.

If the words could be believed true—and he could not conjure any reason to deny them—the Qadi was more than alive and well. The aristocrat was working tirelessly at his station. Urgently preparing for '*a sandstorm arriving from the east*'. So Tariq had also seen the Boy King's ruse. Albeit there was a puzzling cipher added below; '*a mission for the yard-bird; the river burns, paid for in silver and ivory*'.

At the utterance of it, Nazsif merely cocked his head, "I'm afraid my master did not want me to imbibe certain, delicate details."

"What about the kidnappers? The Serpents?"

"Too many unfriendly eyes between the city and even here. My master did not dare have this fall into the wrong hands."

Mighty convenient, that trifle.

And yet it was like the Qadi to be paranoid.

"His captors let you leave, unmolested, to play the messenger?"

"They are not what you suspect Rooster," Nazsif said.

"I fought them. I killed them. They grabbed your master

like a sack of potatoes."

"When you meet with my master, I assure you that all your doubts will be washed away."

If Tariq wanted a meeting, he'd have it. But it would be somewhere of Rooster's choosing. Where he could have bows in shadows, ready to pincushion these Serpents if they so much as breathed wrong.

"Very well. What now?"

An inward groan, "The Bandit Prince has a better reason than you to work with my master. Grudges to be settled and laid to rest. But he's barking mad. Like a crow who cannot be goaded from his cage no matter how much food you dangle before him."

"Azim Altaruk does what Azim Altaruk wants. You can't convince him of anything unless it was his idea from the beginning."

Nazsif sounded bitter, "Yes, I've become quite aware of that."

There was only one reason why the Bandit Prince would ever leave his fortified nest of rogues, surrounded by a sea of sand. Where he could rest on his laurels of villainry and his immense prosperity.

The traitor; Kizzuran Flameblade.

The Bandit Prince could not tear his eyes away from the albino camel. Rooster found it fitting to have it tacked right outside his tent. In an amusing and underhanded kind of way.

"That's mine," Azim turned back.

"That old thing? I thought it was the Ivory Queen's?"

Eyebrows went frenzied, then fell like hammers, "You *stole* my gift. No one steals from me Rooster. No one."

"Oh? But I didn't steal it. I took it to the Ivory Queen. She didn't like it. Sad really. So I kept it safe for you."

Azim's hand went right for his sword, snarling. The man was quick. And it wasn't any act either.

And then roared in laughter, releasing the handle, "Ah you think you are so clever northerner. So very clever.

Perhaps you are. In any case, I shall seek your head for when you fall in battle. I'd like it to be preserved and animated by one of my witches so you can serve as my table ornament. Or perhaps my advisor."

"Lovely."

The Shemsari did not serve as others might. Which left the two of them to pour their own wine.

From the open flap, Ahffan looked in revulsion then away in shame.

Rooster thought about it and set the cup down with a sigh.

"Is it poison, dear servant," Azim sniggered, filling his another time.

"You rejected the Qadi's offer?"

The cup froze, "What did you say?"

"You heard me, Azim."

"Your master thinks I'm one of your sword-whores for hire. That I have need of his grubby little merchants coins. As if I could not take such coins at my pleasure."

"He wants you to slay your nemesis?"

A dark look crossed the Bandit Prince's face, "I'll fight my wars on my own time. When the stars align. Only a fool would commit to fight his nemesis when the heavens are waning."

Something slipped in the voice.

And Rooster suddenly knew he underestimated Azim.

On the outside and without sugarcoating it, the Bandit Prince truly was insane. But it was only in voice. Hidden well beneath the veneer of an impulsive madman was a cold and calculating tactician. How many of this man's enemies had been distracted by his smoke while missing the flames behind?

"You're afraid of Kizzuran. That's it, isn't it?"

"I fear no one," that voice did not betray fear.

"He has an advantage over you, doesn't he?"

Azim drank and did not speak. So Rooster moved the flagon. Earning a black look.

"Why does the Qadi need Kizzuran taken out?"

A scoff, "My beloved Ivory Queen pays her pirates handsomely in silver. The Flameblade was always one to take money and never ask where it came from. Or why."

"You'll lose face not fighting him."

Azim folded his arms, "Anything but. It was the Flameblade who scurried away to the river first. Hiding in the swamps among the crocodiles and fish. It was *he* who chose to avoid confronting *me*. Why did so many of Yhizzir's men follow me? Because I did not run Rooster. Azim never shirks from his enemies."

"Nevertheless...you knew you would lose."

Azim snatched the flagon out of his hands, snorted, and poured another cup. And grunted.

A thought occurred. Not that it would be prudent or wise. But it resonated like all that had in these past few weeks.

"What if you and I both united to slay him?"

"And just why would you do that, Rooster?"

"Because of the bastard, your nephews have no father. Because there's a big pile of treasure in it for me. But because Bahram would not want us as enemies, but as friends."

Azim leaned back in his chair, studying him, "This thing Rooster. You speak and my brother's voice comes out. He possesses you to haunt me—to remind me of my sins!"

In total truth, if Bahram wanted anything it was lost on Rooster.

He hadn't felt a holy thing. No urges warnings or dreams. Besides the calming feeling when he carved the J'awed out, it seemed like the god had been a figment of his imagination. And with clarity and honesty, that might have been reality.

"Even so...why should I ride with you Rooster?"

"You already have your reason. You just want a justification. If I draw out Kizzuran from his swamps, you can ride him down."

"And you? What does a northerner, a gharib like you stand to gain?"

Rooster corrected, "Not a gharib. A Beyik Alghasan. One who needs reputation."

Azim half-chuckled, half-snorted, "Why would you need reputation?"

Playing all your cards on the table didn't seem shrewd in most situations. Better to play close to the chest and hope everyone else didn't have a clue about what you held down to the last call.

But Rooster had known since leaving the Shobai Hamada he'd need allies. And the Bandit Prince was not one he could bullshit and lead around. Better he shot straight and right for the throat with his intentions.

"How else can I get other Shemsari clans to join me but fear of my name?"

Azim stopped laughing. Eyes widened. Mouth opened slightly ajar.

"My, my Rooster. You're almost as mad as me."

"Almost."

"Why?"

Though some of what he and the old chieftain had spoken of couldn't be uttered to anyone, "Same reason your brother went to the former Beyik Alghasan. Call it a hunch."

"A hunch. Hah!"

"So? Do we have a deal?"

Azim ran his hand on the edge of his night-black blade, holding it out. Rooster did the same with his. They clasped bloody hands. The oath was made.

Dunes were waves to the Ramali, and they crossed their crests as a coastal people would deftly on a canoe. They wove across the golden dune sea with nothing short of mastery. To even the Medeans, the barren sands were hell and had to be crossed only by road.

Not the Shemsari.

They refused to move sluggish upon the manmade roads as a caravan or outsider.

Somehow—maybe instinctually—they charted paths through the desert that seemed more animalistic. And while the beasts of the skinwalkers didn't hurt, there was more to it. Innate. No different than how the stag knew to avoid the scent of man without ever having to be taught it.

Traveling on the shoulders of the days when the sun was at its weakest at dawn and dusk, they held an incredible pace. Their sun cloaks doubled as canopies to shade them while they rested through the body of daylight, using saddles and rugs as comfortable cots. During midday they cajoled and sang to Bahram, giving blessings to the god who gave light to the earth—even if that light was harsh and blistering hot.

The longer Rooster spent time traveling with them, the less he thought himself their leader. Out of deference, they gave him respect. But it was just that—skin deep.

The Ramali followed him as he was their chieftain.

But they made it clear he was not one of *them*.

How could any hope to lead with such contradiction?

Amidst a redoubt of stone and sand, they were slowly waking. It would be dusk in a few hours. Time to move.

Rooster found Jhamon and Jhabari sitting cross-legged on a small rock ledge, overlooking desert. They may as well have been any of the Birds of Prey. The Ramali treated them with the deaf ignorance of any outsider.

He wondered how that felt.

Clanless.

"So," he trudged up the hill, "I need a favor."

Jhabari grunted indifference. Jhamon turned and nodded.

"Change of plans. But I don't want the others to know. We're making a slight detour."

"Where to, Rooster?"

"Not Nefara yet. I need to solidify my position."

Both boys looked at each other, Jhamon asking, "You mean the clan?"

"You've seen it too."

Jhabari was much more willing to answer, if brutally, "What did you think was going to happen? Without any wives?"

"Even if I did take wives, they wouldn't fear me."

Love could build kingdoms. It couldn't win wars.

Rooster needed the Ramali to look to him as something more. Bringing them into a battlefield wouldn't win him their respect. If anything, it would make them brittle. Even break away. What they needed was to see him as a symbol. As something primordial.

A scan across the landscape; the south end of the Crownlands. At some point, it crossed into the Sunscar. They were north of Nefara by a good hundred miles or so.

A deceptively empty place.

Ahffan had spoken of other clans. Dozens of wild ones who wandered the waste. Who were more raiders akin to Azim. Only more zealous. They'd been a greater threat to the Shalmanisar's trade across the eastern desert than anything he could have hoped to achieve working for Tariq.

And as Ahffan would explain to him later, no wild clans had ever fraternized with the Confederated. They were pure as the hot winds that assuaged the raw desert.

Out of his robes he produced the Blue Eye, held it out to Jhabari.

The boy eyed it like it was a cobra, "What are you scheming now, Rooster?"

He showed them how it produced the blue lasers when the diamond was hit by direct sunlight. How it worked like a compass but far stronger. Then relinquished it.

"Ride out to the nearest oasis. Then the next if need be. Until you find wild Shemsari. Tell them the Ramali want a word."

And a word he would get.

The next morning the two returned bearing good news; they'd found one of the wild clans. It was not an insubstantial one either.

They met in the belly between two dunes, presided over by a clan of bushes that rooted right on the saddle.

There were so many of the wild Shemsari they

encompassed the entirety of the Ramali. Perhaps three hundred or more that dotted the crests of the dunes.

It was a not-so-subtle threat. The wild clan saw this as a prostrating move, a peace offering.

How very wrong they were.

Rooter ignored them—throwing down his rug in the middle and sat down. The other chieftain did not.

He chose Medean to speak to Jamon, "Am I doing something wrong?"

"No Rooster. Their Beyik Alghasan is intentionally insulting you."

"Bald bastard. Alright. Bring out the gift."

A Ramali girl came out, carrying in her arms a finely made sun-veil. It had antelopes in bright green and blue stitched across the thick band that was worn across the forehead.

The wild chieftain looked at it and made a performative scoff, throwing it at the sand.

He spoke in Shemsari and did not make eye contact, "What is this demon playing at? Where is the great Beyik Alghasan of the Ramali?"

"You're looking at him."

The other's eyes widened, narrowed, then spoke loud so all his clan could hear, "I am mistaken—it is a djinn with its hand up this demon's ass, controlling its mouth like a puppet. Aha!"

The wild Shemsari laughed like jackals.

Rooster gave them the eye sweep.

This clan—the Faari—might as well have been a totally different race. They had no traditional dress, save their faded sun-veils. Their clothes were just as tattered. Bone piercings wherever they could find flesh, tattoos in abundance. Pieces of strange chitin and bone-encrusted harnesses for armor. They looked feral, even barely human. Among their ranks were extremely tall and hairy Shemsari who could have been mistaken for bears—a full head taller and meaner. The longer Rooster looked at them, the more unsettled he became.

They leered at the Ramali and ignored the Birds of Prey. There was no love lost then. Who knew how long it had been since the two clans interacted.

The Faari chieftain was bald and had raccoon spots tattooed on his eyes. Besides that and the necklace of human teeth, he could have been someone's grandpa.

Who suddenly raised a hand, making a wild howl.

The Faari fell dead silent.

"So djinn, what game are you playing? Nhaijeb has fought many of your kind. I will only barter with you if it is in my favor."

For this to work, Rooster needed this asshole to look worse than him. There was no guarantee that it would—these savages might take his maneuver in a completely different way. They had enough spears to poke the Ramali three times over.

Jhamon looked concerened, "I do not know why you have met these riders Rooster. They will not listen to you. They will try to kill you."

"Try? They definitely will," Jhabari snorted, "He's a fool who thinks everyone bows to him."

"When's the last time you took a walk in my boots boy?"

Jhabari sneered.

Another look around; everybody was on edge.

This wasn't how the clans did things. Uncertainty of what came next clouded the faces of everyone who had come down from the Shobai Hamada. Except maybe Carver—the man could win a staredown with a boulder.

Confusion would eventually shift as the scales tipped.

Right now, they were even. The Faari didn't know that yet.

Rooster changed over to Shemsari, addressing the other chieftain, "Now that I have presented you our gift, I expect the same in return. As is J'awed."

"*As is J'awed,*" the chieftain repeated every word with deliberate agnosticism.

Rooster waited.

The chieftain made a dismissive sort of gesture, halting halfway and smiled something wicked. A large Faari brute returned with a bow. It was shaped from a dark wood, tipped on either end with horn. The middle of the shaft where one would grip was formed from dark grey hyena hide.

The brute held it by the curved limbs, gently setting it on the rug.

"Vizzaeg. Its name. Fitting for a white demon," the bald man clasped his hands, "Now I have given the better gift. What will Nhaijeb receive from this djinn?"

Which now necessitated Rooster to do the same or declare his rival chieftain the superior by gratitude. Gift-giving was a game of cat and mouse.

He wanted to get liquor from his witch-men but the crafty bastards were nowhere to be seen. Though the bushes had rustled a few more times than they should have.

"Will one of you find me Ahffan?" he asked and Jhamon scurried off.

For the next gift, Rooster chose a bolder strategy. One of the unwed Ramali girls. Which gained him ire from just about everyone on their side. She twirled and showed no excitement in her face.

"Another wife to add to my harem," Nhaijeb had her brought over, slapped her on the ass, and bowed sardonically, "Or maybe I should take more of your women. I see few warriors of the Ramali clan. Or are you hiding your soul-bent warriors close, so they might ambush?"

"We are what you see, chieftain."

Skeptical raccoon eyes scanned, "A weak clan does not ride out to my lands. They will be eaten by the dog and the vulture."

"Who said we're weak?"

"Why else would you leave your waters then? Then you must be djinn, tricking these fools to their slaughter."

Noticeably, one of the few Faari allowed to sit next to Nhaijeb twitched. A lean man with a bonfire for a beard and head and eyes bugging out of their skull. It was obvious he disagreed vehemently with the statements made.

Perhaps an ally.

"We've come down for a simple reason. War comes."

"The Faari *are* war," Nhaijeb declared.

"Precisely why I have come. Your clan will fight alongside ours."

Nhaijeb was the atypical tribal war chief. No one told him what to do. How he became chief was probably unpleasant. The aura he exuded was sheer vitriol.

The bald man threw his new wife to the sand like she was a toy, leaping up as if the sand was lava, "Will? Will? You—demon—come tell Nhaijeb this? As if you have *power* over me?"

"I do. Bahram as my witness."

"You silver-tongued bastard son of a goatfucker. The sun god does not heed demons or djinn," Nhaijeb snarled.

So salt in the wound it was, "The Faari will ride to war with me. With or without you."

Just when he was needed, Ahffan came jogging in looking perturbed. The skinwalkers weren't used to being bossed around either. They operated on their pretenses.

A glob of spit landed on the sand a few hairs from splattering Rooster's boots. Nhaijeb then dropped his trousers and threw the entire book of Shemsari insults at him. Lesser men would have drawn swords. But it was mildly amusing to Rooster.

It violated the hospitality of the J'awed.

Even the feral Faari knew that.

By violating hospitality, Nhaijeb had forded the moral waters that could not be turned back from.

"Ahffan?"

"Yeah chieftain," under that ramskull, the skinwalker was sweating.

In Medean, he said to the boys first, relayed to Ahffan after the meeting, "This one dies. Tonight. I don't care how it's done. Just make sure this son of a bitch is dead come morning."

Dawn had not yet come when an excruciating, drawn-out scream awoke the entire valley. More screams. Then silence. No one saw who did it. The Faari were out with torches, tight-lipped as they searched for their chieftain's killer. There was no way any of the Ramali could have snuck into their camp—they may have been bandits but they had a firewatch.

Everyone was accounted for. Save Rhuïma.

Big Mug swore he spotted a cat-sized shadow-thing scuttling away into the void of dunes.

"Chieftain," a head popped in, one of the old Ramali riders, "It's the Faari."

"About time huh."

The procession this time was only three. Fire-hair, flanked by a crooked little skinwalker and one of the great bear Shemsari. They introduced themselves quickly as Yhuuf, Scorchhide, and Bonechewer. They wanted Rooster to come with them. He took Antonius and Jhabari with him as a precaution.

Most of the Faari had left the night prior. The little assassination stunt had cost them dearly. Coals from their campfires still smoking. A fraction remained, gathered in a knot of fifty or so. Including the majority of the big hairy Shemsari. The air among them had changed.

"Nhaijeb was false to question you white demon. The spirits of the desert swell around you. So we will fight for you. But first, you must answer a question," Yhuuf said.

"Yes?"

"You are djinn," it was a statement.

"No," Rooster said, "But I am Beyik Alghasan."

"Of course. Your true identity can never be revealed. The Faari will still follow you to your war," the fire-haired man winked, "Djinn."

And so twenty warriors became seventy. It wasn't a real horde by any stretch. But the Faari were blooded, many of them young and lean. They had no women. They lusted for thrills. Even a dozen of them would make a difference. They were the perfect warriors.

Above it all, they were awed that Nhaijeb had expired. To the Faari braves, it was no random act but that of the vengeful dervishes who rode banshee-like across the sands and created avatars to enact their will. Yhuuf—more priest than warrior—had been ignored by their chieftain for far too many years. This pent-up zealotry had finally been sated.

What really mattered to Rooster was the way the Ramali began to look at him as they turned their heads southward. Overnight was a noticeable shift. It wasn't a total watershed. Some of the skinwalkers were holding out, pretending that he didn't exist. But the rest of the clan had been awed. They invited him to the cookfires or to speak with them so they could show off their daughters to him. They wanted to know if there were more wild-blooded gharibs like him—north of the Wall. Their prayers to Bahram included him by name.

They started to believe in the symbol, not the man.

المدينة الموتى
Nemset

On the surface, Nefara looked the same. Even as they five rode her streets as anonymous, clanless riders. Appearances could be deceiving. Nothing that Nazsif would be taken at face value or with a grain of salt.

The one thing that was worth noting was the beggars. They'd seemed to quintuple over the last few months. As did the dealers of the cerulean lotus. There wasn't a sandy corner of this wretched city that didn't have a drug pimp.

The criminal element walked around in broad daylight.

"Tariq's new friends have been busy," Antonius said in muffled Patina. No one looked past their sun cloaks or turbans.

Even without them, Rooster wouldn't have been recognized.

Pain lanced his cheeks where the tattooist had made the first lines below his eyes. He knew looking in a mirror would have him see a total stranger; a wave-like line of crimson that followed his cheekbones from the bottom of his ears and across his nose, then a dagger shape under his right eye for the Faari. Not to mention the beard. Beyik Alghasans always grew their beards out.

The Shemsari had claimed him; he was theirs now.

For better or for worse.

When they made it deep enough in the city, Lancer and Antonius split off to Sword Row to explore some old connections. Leaving Jhabari, Carver, and Scorchhide with him.

"This place reeks of soft flesh and treasure," the skinwalker cackled beneath his mask.

"We'll be raiding soon."

Scorchhide eyed a pair of Medean women doing laundry in the street, "How soon is soon?"

Meanwhile Jhabari could have been a dog returned back to his former haunt, sniffing the new air, "Do you smell that Rooster?"

"Yeah."

It wasn't their imagination; a smoke lingered above the air of the Maze, flooding into the thoroughfares of Nefara. The heat had a smell of its own as it entered the nose. But even the greenery that decorated all of the ancient city's bones paled in comparison to the sharp, metallic smell that he associated with the assassins.

They found themselves on the street of the dye-makers. Jhabari noticed. They dismounted and crossed up the steps where the colored powder was bagged. There was no sign of occupation at the building where the Dead Hand and Amir had last met him. Cobwebs and dust everywhere. Like the apartment had been abandoned for decades.

"Strange," Rooster commented, looking for any kind of hidden entrances.

Nothing but a scorpion that scuttled away at the lamplight.

"They are cunning. They wouldn't stay in the same place," Jhabari added, looking out the street.

"How do you know?"

"Me and Jhamon. We never stole bread from the same place. The city is too large Rooster. It's a thief and urchin's paradise."

They dropped off the message on the ledge of a fountain that Tariq's pavilion overlooked. The perforated stone wall looked as though a shadow moved behind it, watching them.

Passing by the dens and plazas, Rooster noted that a crowd was gathering near a broken obelisk where a crier was standing on the broken slab. Usually, they hawked flatbreads or declared which decree the Vizier instated that day.

This was different.

A nameless tomb raider had entered a place called the Market Vault. Someplace deep and dark nobody had ever penetrated since the end of the old kingdoms. Full of horror and booby traps. The tomb raiders had brought forth tokens and relics thought lost to all Nefara. Their leader had returned and called himself the Prince of Many Faces.

To his congregation, the crier declared the Vizier's bounty on this Prince, as well as banned any merchant from taking the ancient kingdom coins in payment. Beggars had been finding them scattered around the Dust Quarter. Any information on either was to be brought up to the Vizier or Captain Musha at once.

The crowd pelted the crier with crusty rinds of bread in outrage.

The poor couldn't catch a break. Not even when pieces of gold fell into their lap.

The most dilapidated and abandoned part of Nefara seemed the perfect place to meet. They laid their bows against the stone and arrows pointing down in the sand. If anyone who wasn't them or the desired party turned up, they'd get turned into a porcupine.

Even in the daytime, it was an unnerving place. Dervishes blew through sandstone dwellings no longer fit for humanity. The gusts of wind created ghostly howls that imitated the lives of those who had once called this place home.

A rustling up ahead.

Someone was coming.

A beggar who threw up his hands, "Don't shoot."

"State your name," Jhabari called in Medean.

Tariq pulled off his hood.

"It's him," the bows lowered.

Rooster did his, although the strange Faari bow made a strange noise. He could have sworn it was in his head, a booming laugh part-man, part-hyena.

Was it cursed?

Stuffed away in an alcove where only Rooster could see, Scorchhide twitched, grunted, and shook his head like a drunk—scouting the area from the eyes of his bird above.

The sign meant no one had followed the Qadi here.

Everything about Tariq seemed the same. All except the bejeweled leather sash that covered his right eye. Acting as if he was on routine business, meeting here in the disguise of a pauper.

Jhabari let him into the courtyard and closed the gate.

"An unfortunate accident during my kidnapping I'm afraid. I wasn't tortured, I assure you," the Qadi said blithely as he adjusted the eyepatch, taking a seat on the well. He produced a wine bottle and glasses. When no one else partook he shrugged and drank right from the bottle.

"You have a great deal of explaining to do."

"As do you," Tariq pointed at his face, grinning, "Those tattoos, are they permanent? What do they call you now?"

"The same. Except there's a chieftain at the beginning."

"Well well, Chief Rooster…"

In an hour and a full bottle of wine, Tariq laid it all out bare. The kidnapping was his plan all along, the flute player an actor. The Scorched Serpents had been the willing players to evoke a reaction from both Shalmanisar and spies within the Vizier's office to make themselves known. An entire network of pro-Ivory Queen agents was identified and rolled up within a week. A fight had broken out on the docks between Serpents and said agents, resulting in a pyrrhic victory. Nefara's offices were made secure and Tariq became a public official once more, now turning his focus on the privateers of the Ivory Queen.

Only four of the Ivory Queen's agents remained at large. A pair of saboteurs and smugglers nicknamed Skulk and Sable, then the infamous Kizzuran. The fourth was not named because they had none to give.

Almost every query had a satisfying answer. Tariq answered every one and subjected his limbs for inspection. No swelling from cuffs or abrasions from imprisonment. Carver immediately began to assess the Qadi for any injuries.

Now if Tariq was under a spell? That was a different story altogether.

"He's clean. Besides the eye," the surgeon announced but never touched the sash.

Rooster paced.

Tariq looked relaxed. Almost too much. Then again, he'd always been a bureaucrat with a head too big for his shoulders. In another life, he'd have been a trueblood prince.

"I want a meeting with your partners. Same conditions."

"I can try. They're not keen on being out in the open. Malaki and the Black Nizzar are still highly sought after by the Shalmanisar."

"What do they want? Ultimately?"

Tariq widened his hands, "A chance to fight for their seats back in the Glasslands. The merchants exiled and enslaved all their rivals. If the Serpents could claim their ancestral seats, they would leave this desert at once."

Rooster didn't begrudge the Qadi for teaming up with a powerful ally. But he had his suspicions still.

"It's a big ask, for us to trust these Serpents. We heard about them from other sources. Nasty rumors about being poisoners back home."

"Indubitably. Their reputation is well-crafted to inspire fear. They come from the east, like the Shalmanisar. It's in their nature to, *exaggerate*."

"They also tried to kill us."

Tariq shook his head, "Miscommunication. The Fangs responsible have been dealt with accordingly. The objective was never to let you or your Shemsari friends be harmed."

Jhabari spoke cooly, "They could try again. They were easy to kill."

"All of that is behind us. The Ivory Queen is the real threat now. Once she gets wind of the Boy King's ploy, she'll be a beast backed into a corner. She'll be dangerous."

Rooster agreed but only to a point, "She does not have sixty thousand troops."

Carver's scarred jaw almost dropped, "You said the Caliphate was coming. You didn't say sixty fucking thousand of them."

The cat was out of the sack now. Metaphorically. There weren't even rats in this godforsaken backside of Nefara for them to chew on.

"An unexpected windfall of levies from the Chainfort was waiting for the Caliph at the Sunstones. Yes, sixty thousand. An entire city of steel moves under the cover of a sandstorm," Tariq said to the sellsword, waving over his head, "And yet the Ivory Queen has been industrious in her exile. They say a mountain of treasure lies below her palace from every sovereign city and Teridian port along the coast; the Opaline Vault. She could move a fleet of her pirate Nebetians up the Ptahira and sack Nefara before the Boy King sets foot in these walls."

Carver gave a low whistle.

"But Kizzuran can strike swifter."

Tariq withdrew a shell-encrusted scroll and tossed it to Rooster. A brief read. The contents were a generous offer from the Ivory Queen to the self-proclaimed Bandit Prince, Kizzuran Flameblade. A chest containing a thousand pearls, an estate on the Terraced Gardens of Tyhri, and lordship. All for the Flameblade to aid her in the taking of Nefara.

How many bandit princes could fit into the same desert, he thought in humor. There was a new one every other week it seemed like.

"We intercepted this in the boat of those smugglers I mentioned earlier. Kizzuran got the message anyway. The Floodplain Raiders attacked the docks a week ago. Various points where the canals met the river. We retook the docks almost immediately."

"A probing attack," Rooster said.

"Indeed. Word is the Flameblade himself was seen in Nefara, gathering support in the Sword Row and the Shades."

"He has help on the inside."

The Qadi licked his teeth and grimaced, "Yes. The other agents of the Ivory Queen were easier to uproot. This branch, however, has proven quite the challenge."

"And if we were to take out Kizzuran? What of our reward?"

Tariq smiled, "First, I must admit I did not believe it when I heard from Nazsif you were the clan chieftain of this Ramali."

"Not just them. The Faari too."

A lone eyebrow hiked up the unblemished forehead, "You defied all my expectations, Rooster."

"I aim to be unpredictable."

"The Vizier and my partners have already agreed; if you were to defeat Kizzuran, you can have more gold and horses than your clan can carry."

Gold wasn't the end-all and be-all. There was a sun god now that Rooster had to please. That and almost two hundred alien souls who wouldn't sleep under a stone roof. But unless they were to turn bandit, those two hundred needed to eat, arrows to shoot, and horses to breed. With coin they had maneuverability.

Gold would do for now.

They finished the rest of the meeting out without event. The bureaucrat left quietly and assumed the guise of the beggar on his fade away.

Rooster watched him go.

Until he was sure of Tariq's authenticity, he'd learn how to grow a second pair of eyes on the back of his head.

Later on the road out of the city, they rejoined Antonius and Lancer by the old farms. The weeds and dust were thick. Even the flies were starting to drop from the heat.

"What'd you find out?"

The Teridian pulled down his veil, scratching at where wool scratched his shaven chin, "It's bananas in there. Caravan Court is half-empty. The Shalmanisar stopped taking the roads. There's talk about companies up and leaving if the war comes."

"Anything else?"

More rumors and gossip about this so-called tomb raider Prince. Thieves around town were leaving public trophies of their pillages out in Nomarch's Plaza.

What piqued Rooster's attention were the cults.

Nefara hadn't always been agnostic. The old kingdoms were notably pagan, no matter how many faces of the gods in statues and reliefs the Medeans chiseled off. For centuries they'd been dormant pursued only by the most eclectic pariahs and madmen. A mockery of the pantheon of yore.

Up until very recently.

When the last moon died in the sky, the earth quaked. It had rocked Nefara. A Medean depot was laid to waste and in the debris of dust stood an old kingdom tablet the size of a wall—a shining black thing like volcanic glass. In its facets were hieroglyphs of a language that was no longer spoken or understood by the living.

The black wall was not just an omen but a crisis of faith.

Suddenly bald-headed cultists were everywhere. Sprouting out of the sand like ants, going door to door collecting alms and filling their ranks. They were filling the town squares every day, demanding the Medeans reopen the temples for fear of heavenly reprisal. They had come close to a religious riot gathering in mobs outside the White Kasbah with torches.

Dozens became hundreds became thousands.

If they were north of the wall, such a thing could be chalked up to coincidence.

But Rooster did not believe in those anymore.

They rode to the plateau overlooking the river valley—the nomad's camp where other Shemsari shepherds and drifters called home when it hit him.

Three events had all occurred within days of each other; the Market Vault being plundered, the earthquake and the night the graythirsters attacked.

He went to his tent and suffered a night of sleeplessness.

Nearly all the Talons agreed to take the Qadi's offer;

Jhamon, Jhabari, Lancer, Ahffan, Yhuuf, Scorchhide, and Bonechewer. The Faari wanted to prove themselves. They yearned for fighting. As much as the sellswords wanted coin.

Everyone had their reason to fight.

All except Antonius.

The Teridian knew more about Flameblade than most. Even the Shemsari boys. As well as the sunken city of Nemset where the Floodplain Raiders had fallen back to gather their forces. For fear or wisdom, Antonius tried his damndest to voice rejection of the fight. It failed.

With a motion passed in favor of to attack, the war council broke to ready the troops.

Light dust billowed from the rocky heights, bypassing the nomad's camp. It sent tiny dervishes in all directions past Nefara. The heat was becoming nigh unbearable and induced sweat even as the sun had set. Locals claimed the changing winds from the eastern seas soon would lift as they swelled over the Crownlands—a season of monsoons would be upon them soon. The hottest days they said, would strike at dusk and the land would flood with enough water to fill the Ptahira.

As impossible as it seemed, their conviction was adamant.

In a land so hot and dry, the promise of rain must have felt rapturous.

With Antonius on his left shoulder, Rooster walked through camp. Mostly for the younger man's benefit. He felt it owed to Antonius, to hear his grievances out.

"Just doesn't sit right with me. You don't feel it, do you?"

Rooster grunted, "Feel what?"

"That we're being played like lutes."

Soaring over the camp, Hazair trilled and dove down to snatch a desert rat who had come a little too close to the tents. A flash of talons and a dying squeak came next.

Ironically that was exactly how Rooster felt ever since

he came down from the Wall—he was the rat.

The scary reality was that something or *someone* was holding the dice to his destiny. A force neither malevolent nor its opposite. Bahram? A rogue pagan entity? A wayward djinn? All he could do was take one more step after the last and keep a sharp eye out. Everything else was out of his hands.

"I do. I just don't broadcast that outwardly."

"Why not?"

"Truth is a deadly tool. Use it only sparingly. Especially when dealing with a politician or a prince."

Antonius frowned, looked at the city as if it might give him inspiration, "I don't get it. By letting him dupe us, we could be risking our lives for nothing."

"Never for nothing. You think I would do you all dirty like that? Hang you up like headless cows?"

"No..."

"Ask yourself this; why did I send away all our skinwalkers, besides Scorchhide? Upriver fishing? In the Maze where we met Tariq? On the docks? In the canals?"

They walked through the Faari section. The clans had not melted together as he'd hoped. The wild warriors were tying fetishes of bones and feathers to their hair and jewelry. Sharpening the broad belt knives they carried on their chests.

"The attack is a front."

"Nice. You're close. Azim Altaruk is a day's ride north. He won't budge unless we *do* bring the Floodplain Raiders out of hiding."

Antonius pondered for a little while longer, "The attack is legitimate. But you're not sure about the picture that's been painted. You're leaving eyes to watch your back as you move."

"Bullseye."

"So you don't buy Tariq's story either?"

"It's not that we should believe it, Antonius. I believe he may be coerced into spinning the yarn. The Serpents aren't a direct threat to us. Yet. They're thugs. Thugs don't operate out of pure spite. It's not profitable."

The other man scratched his head, "This is confusing. Everything is upside down."

"Think for a second. The Boy King is coming. War is bad for legitimate business. It's good for the black market. Contraband sneaking into cities demand high premiums."

"Aha. The smugglers."

"Who are just competition. We had it all figured wrong. The Serpents aren't villains—they're just capitalizing on chaos. And the Flameblade is a rogue ace they can't buy out."

"How do we find out how we're getting played? How do we know that we're not the ones getting trapped?"

Easier said than done.

But in Rooster's experience, only by desperation or inexperience did captains go looking for a battle with straight odds. Fair fights were for fools.

If they could sniff something with the skinwalkers, it gave them an in to start fighting back with rumors, speculation, and bad intelligence. They'd start there and work their way back until someone got sloppy and slipped out into the light.

They needed to make the first move.

With any luck, then Azim Altaruk would swoop in and play his part.

Sunset had them at the docks.

Reluctant to leave their horses for water, the Shemsari followed Rooster onto the boats complaining the whole way. If anyone else had asked them, they would have probably gutted the hopeless bastard. The nomads were unsteady even as the water was glasslike in the dark. If not for their bows, they'd have been utterly useless.

With this crew, stealth was their most valuable asset.

On barges that the Qadi had seized from the Shalmanisar, they waited until the deep of night to cross. Like wide bats gliding across the delta. They established a small beachhead on the long, claw-shaped island at the center. Birds of Prey took the lead, arranging brush on the wet sand two men tall to act as blinds to any hostile scout. A little time was spent and a hundred warriors were concealed by all but the birds above.

Before them, the hideous swamp of Nemset boiled quietly in nocturne; ever the eternal green hell.

Bugs were so abundant here you could swallow a handful with every breath. Shapes moved lazily in the water, too reptilian and large for comfort. Black bushes rattled and yawned by the trespasses of apish silhouettes. The fog grew thicker with every paddle of the oar.

If they could work their magic right, it would only be one night in this godforsaken place.

A waterfowl call hooted three times—sign to proceed.

A cluster of Faari warriors led by Goshawk and Antonius climbed into a smaller vessel, paddling furtively off towards the eastern bank. A sellsword back at the Row had drunkenly spilled the Flameblade's secret hideout; a half-flooded dock of the old kingdom tucked away in a lagoon. They'd scout it out, spot sentries, and prepare for the main ambush.

Hours passed with no word or sign.

Disturbance broke the black mirror—the thin canoe-like boat was returning back and not at all stealthily.

It was Goshawk. Blood made his dark skin look shiny in the faint moonlight. The infallible and unkillable warrior. In his hand, he carried the shield of a southern imperial—Antonius', splattered with red.

"What the hell happened?" Rooster hissed.

The Ophi calmed himself down a few breaths, "It looked empty captain. The Faari went in too fast, too deep. The pirates—gah, they closed in from all sides. Antonius went in to save them but they were everywhere. I do not know how I was not taken or killed."

"The gods love you, that's why," Carver grunted, shuffling in to check the man's vitals.

Rooster stopped hearing fewer words, more the pumping of blood into his heart. Mouth clammy. Sweat beading and not from the humidity.

They had Antonius. Dead or alive. Being tortured maybe as they knew it. If he had been gripping a wood stick right now it would have shattered into a hundred splinters.

Antonius, the voice of reason who bravely took the lead despite his vote against this battle.

"Those motherfuckers. How did they know we were coming?"

Someone had to have talked—hadn't they?

Except this plan hadn't even had more than half a day to cook amongst the Talons—a few hours for the rest of the men. It was inconceivable that the Flameblade could have been notified and reacted so swiftly if they did have a rat.

Jhamon and Jhabari looked devastated. Antonius was one of the only gharibs they saw as a brother. They were reliving the horror of their father's death.

Rooster refused the idea, locked it into a mental chest, and kicked it away into the shadows. Not now.

"You saw them grab Antonius? Was there a chance it was accidental?"

Goshawk thought, then shook his head.

Meaning that he was recognized as a valuable hostage or this was premeditated.

Something wasn't adding up.

"The plan now chieftain?" Yhuuf had crawled up, looking expectant.

Only one way to know if they had a rat for sure.

"Prepare to embark and return to Nefara. We need to rethink our strategy," he replied, looking over his shoulder towards Scorchhide, hoping the look wasn't too obvious.

When the rest of the men were filing onto boats, he whispered the rest into the skinwalker's ear.

At first, those shadows on the small craft must have thought they were enlightened wise men among their piratical kind. Cruising upriver with total indifference, lazily beaching their patrol boats to see what their enemy left behind. Walking up to the brush walls laughing all the way.

The brush walls bristled as bows released.

The arrows that fired back reminded them harshly of their lot in life.

Pirate screams filled the swamp air.

Even from the vantage of the docks, Rooster could see them like dark rats scurrying back to their boats. Pelted by arrows from carefully hidden positions behind the brush walls. Bodies floated on the water if they weren't strewn over the beach. Those who did make it and began to paddle out must have thought themselves blessed.

Until eagles swept down and raked them with talons. The pirates had nothing to fight them with. They flailed and Rooster almost felt pity for them. Disturbing splashes erupted around those who went into the water, followed by crocodile hisses.

He whistled low.

The drifting craft were swept up and pulled before they could drift into Nemset.

While all this was going on, a little fishing craft moved right up to their position and a diminutive figure scrambled out. Grumbling about the stink of fish. Rhuïma in the guise of a fisherman stomped his way right over to the stone jetties.

"What'd you see?"

"Notice the little shape there, crawling along the mangroves?"

If Rooster hadn't had it pointed out to him, the little sliver-shape would have eluded him. A dark slender thing bobbed carefully among the marshy roots. Another small craft, piloted by two.

"Your rat," the skinwalker informed with a crooked finger, "Right as the arrows flew, they got on that floating stick. I almost missed him."

"What did he look like?"

Rhuïma blinked at him with beady eyes, "Just like you, demon. An identical twin."

"That's impossible. I've been standing here this entire

time."

"Don't question me. I've told you what I saw. Bahram can curse you impotent for all I care, demon. You were walking down there by the waterfront, cursing up a storm. *He was you.*"

Fog thickened. Oars pushed forward with speed and aggression. And arrows were as thick as flies in the air.

Rooster, who had abandoned the notion of planning, felt the thud as the steel broadhead embedded his shield. He tossed it into the water and grabbed another. Another arrow clipped the wooden disk.

Bastards!

The Floodplain Raiders had barely made it out of their lagoon before the counter-ambush. Now—like the cowards they were—the merchant murderers and jumped-up bandits were plying deeper into the watery folds of Nemset. Perhaps to spring an even larger trap. Gut instinct told Rooster that they'd been punched in the nose hard and were making a tactical retreat.

He'd punish them right up to their hidey-hole.

Splashing and churning all around the boats—the crocodiles were having a hell of a night. Dark blood foamed and limbs were seen occasionally before disappearing under the wake.

Another hail of crude iron slammed into the boats. None of them hit flesh. The Shemsari weren't unaccustomed to being shot at. They fired back with arrows of their own.

Rooster was beginning to question why he hadn't thought of constructing a more defensible craft.

The barges ahead were sluggish but making slightly better time. Perhaps this was the first taste the pirates had at anything tougher than cow-eyed merchants with potbellies and cotton to plunder—losing the stomach for a fight.

Too bad.

They had Antonius.

One of the cigar-shaped canoes carrying Faari riders was getting within boarding range of the pirate craft. The Shemsari cheered them on, whooping and hollering.

Moonlight illuminated a single figure leaping to the reinforced castle on the top deck to face them. Sheathed head to toe in croc skin painted a deep crimson. In his hand was just a sword—at first. Which then burst into red-hot flames. The raider with the namesake swung the fire sword in a merciless arc and raked the boarding craft with a twenty-foot spear of what fools would mistake for drakefire. It had the same effect.

Faari screamed and burned even as they hit the water and floated lifelessly on.

"Honest godfucking balefire," Big Mug swore.

The Flameblade swung the sword in a smoldering challenge for anyone else to near.

Pirates began to whoop and turn their big barges. There had to be hundreds of them stuffed wall-to-wall.

"Someone get me that big bastard. The Faari one. Bonesmasher or whatever it is," Rooster shouted.

The giant Shemsari lumbered up, grunting what could have been unintelligible language. Quickly Rooster told him the new ploy. If any or all of it made it through those ears, it was impossible to tell.

A dark grin showed filed teeth and the giant took off with a few of his comrades.

Squinting, Big Mug asked no one in particular, "Where's he off to?"

The pirates were using their barges to form a bridge made of wood, choking off the wide delta. They foolishly even dropped anchor. All they had to do was wait for Rooster and his company of Shemsari to smash into them and sink.

Another dark shape neared the middle craft with the Flameblade. The prince of the raiders must have been laughing madly up there—thinking they were trying the same trick twice.

The long curved sword burst into flame once more and

began its dreadful arc down.

But the little boarding canoe hurled something up at the aftcastle that shattered and exploded something liquid.

"Drakefire, meet hellfire," Rooster commented.

A wall of unnatural red and orange raced up the side of the barge and consumed the hide and wood of the top deck. Like the air was alight. The Flameblade was hurled backward and fell from view. To either side, the other pirate barges panicked and turned their craft away to avoid catching afire.

The self-proclaimed Bandit Prince might have had bigger fleet, three times the manpower and knew this bug-infested hellhole better than anybody.

But boats and fire didn't mix.

Flameblade would think twice before pulling out his little magic trick-sword out again.

Rooster spat, feeling rather vindictive.

The wall of barges collapsed inward as the pirates renewed their hasty retreat. Leaving the hazardous burning hulk to cover it as the Floodplain Raiders retreated.

It wasn't a victory yet—the pursuit was called off until the bonfires went down.

By the time the barge drifted harmlessly to the banks, the distant dark shapes in the fog crossed a great pool—a secondary and far greater lagoon—and entered under a titantic stone gate. A square seven-story tower of ancient make connected to a great archway that spanned the width of any mast, connecting to a ramp-like wall that dove right into the water.

Suddenly it became evident what they were looking at.

Nemset, the bedeviled city, was half-underwater.

Rooster saw no streets, only monolithic silhouettes of the city's construction trapped behind an even thicker fog—so thick one had to slice it with a knife. Not even the light of the rising sun could be seen here, trapped behind what appeared eternal cloud cover. Verdance looked dark green, almost black as it clung to stone that was over a millennia old.

Wicked ambience dribbled out from the depths of the place.

No sane man would cross that boundary except for the promise of untold riches.

Rooster felt shivers seeing formless shapes appear and disappear on the blocky shelves. Like the spectres of who once called this home.

"Hold. Hold damn it," he ground his teeth as some of the smaller craft started to run right to the gateway, "They could be laying up for us in yonder water. Keep your damn heads on. Talons, on me."

The Faari were reluctant to pull back—blood was in the water and they smelled it like sharks. They pulled at the leash, snarling and yapping.

"Bahram does not visit this place," Jhamon muttered quietly.

"It is not natural," Yhuuf commented, hands gripping his bow tightly, "We should kill them and leave quickly."

But it was Carver who spoke up the most eloquently, "According to legend, it sunk when the gods died."

"Who told you that," Big Mug accused.

"Everyone knows that, oaf."

"I ain't never heard of that."

The scarred man scratched his chin with a dagger, mock-shaving, "Remember the lepers who called themselves knights? They came here when the city wouldn't take them. They saw some crazy shit in here. Shit you wouldn't believe if you saw it yourself."

There was no other waterborne entrance into Nemset besides the archway. A perfect chokepoint.

Rooster had the barges brought alongside the tower and got to work.

First, the towers were cleared. Using skinwalkers to scope the high points of the more intact ruins. In the tower above them, a group of raider sentries who hadn't seen their entrance were dozing off and promptly dispatched. They swept all the scouts before they could croak. They wouldn't be reporting to their master anytime soon.

Earthenware was rolled out from the backs of the barges while Birds of Prey and Shemsari were tying chains of rope-like hemp spiderwebs. A Faari holding a torch mistakenly lowered his flaming stick next to one of the jars bearing dark smears on the lid. Lancer almost catapulted the man into the crocodile-infested waters, dousing the torch immediately.

Daisy chains of firepots were strung out and placed in a minefield just outside the archway. Any boat that went out would get hooked and even one good fire-arrow would send it down to blazing glory. For good measure, Rooster had a few of them placed at the base of the tower, having blocks of stone knocked aside and replaced with wood beams. If timed right the tower could be collapsed and cut off the pirate's flotilla in half while the rest burned.

All plans were bullshit anyway. Life had a funny way of sticking its foot in everyone's meticulous sandcastles before it was washed away by the tide. Didn't matter how well it was built, or how sturdy its foundations. Sand was sand, just like plans were only ideas. Ideas when birthed into reality never accounted for the random errancy outside the fabric of imagination or man's simple fuckery.

It had to have been midday by the time preparations were done—judging only by their exhaustion. There was no other way to tell out here what part of the day they were in.

Everyone was getting weary-eyed so Rooster ordered a quick break to be fresh by dusk.

Just a little moment resting on a wooden bench would rest him up for the next engagement...

There was no rest in sleeping here.

No dreams—only vague nightmares that banished hope and chilled the bones.

The man who did not know who he was walked through a pale sandstone labyrinth. It was seamless and advanced beyond his mortal knowledge of architecture. At times it reminded him of a city and others a mausoleum.

Alcoves dripped in oily black shadow and quivered like disturbed pools. Reliefs of primordial imagery—men with unnatural proportions, beasts that he had no name for—that stretched hundreds of feet into a shrouded void of a sky. Whispers and cries came from formless geists who blew cold death as they passed through the walls.

No matter how far he traveled, there was never an end to this labyrinth.

It was a walk of eternity and the kind of deathlessness that no one would ever beg for.

Something kicked a rock that echoed behind him. The sound of wisps of sand blowing over tile.

The man spun to look over his shoulder. A shadow waited there, almost formless. Its claws reached toward him—towards his brain...

Rooster jerked awake, soaked in sweat.

He'd fallen asleep and hadn't realized it. The nightmare was fading but burned in the back of his memory. Whatever and wherever it was did not yearn for a revisiting.

Something splashed. The millions of croaks and beastly yawns were almost deafening, echoing off the walls of Nemset.

A sentry boat was making the rounds, guided by lamplight. It was dark again. Dusk maybe. The witching hour.

The fog here was like a green-gray soup—heavy and ancient. After a certain distance, the shapes began little more than blobs of darkness. The evil in this place was ambient, it did not have a single entity to attribute to. Mistaking the lushness of the swamp was a grave mistake—nothing here seemed untouched by the unspoken and intangible spirits.

Up north, Rooster had doubted the idea of cursed places.

Nemset was becoming the antithesis of that philosophy.

So many snored. They too were tossing and turning.

Were they living the same nightmare as he had? Rooster tiptoed over the masses, navigating his way to the back of the merchant's junk.

Jhamon was leaning against the rear-most mast, wrapping his knees. Shivering.

"Anything?"

The boy didn't startle—he was a damn hawk, alert when most could barely keep their eyes up, "Something watches us from the sky. I saw it roost over there, near the tower."

"Hazair?"

A shake of the head, "Larger. Black. It moved strange. That's all I can say."

"Keep a weather eye then. Where's your brother?"

Jhamon grunted, lifting a finger high. From here all that could be seen was a small shadow perched on the mossy ruins, an arrow and bow leaned against an eroded slab.

"He waits for the Flameblade to appear."

"And if he misses?"

"I know Jhabari well. He'll jump in and ride a crocodile if it gets him a killing shot."

Rooster understood the sentiment—it was still foolish, "Why aren't you with him? Don't you want revenge too?"

"I want to avenge Father too," Jhamon said quietly, "But this is in Bahram's hands now."

"Seem confident your god will deliver eh?"

"He's your god too now Rooster. He chose you. We all saw the vision."

"I don't know what I saw," Rooster said.

Jhamon frowned and turned away, "The longer you deny it, the harder your path will be."

Rooster had every reason to be skeptical. In the stories, gods gave men purpose like plants ate sunlight. If Bahram was real and wasn't a hallucination, why were his only manifestations cryptic dreams that made no sense? Why wasn't there a reason behind the motive? Surely a god—banished or not—could at least give a little sign, anything to move the needle?

Perhaps man invented gods to disguise their plots for power as veiled religiosity.

That sure would explain the Beyik Alghasan's desire to let go of his failing position as chieftain.

Rooster had his doubts and would remain doubtful until proven otherwise. The clans would either accept that or not.

"Everything you do now will hinge upon J'awed."

"Maybe. Maybe not. I might have to write a line or two of my own Jhamon. There's a frightening lack of tactical sense in the J'awed."

The boy smiled and looked like he was going to crack a joke when his eyes darted sideways. In a blink he had his horsebow drawn at a perfect shot, "Someone's coming."

It wasn't one of theirs. A thin craft with a single passenger was emerging from the mouth of the sunken city. Holding a small stick bearing a torn piece of white cloth in one hand and, a lamp in the other.

"Hold. It's a messenger."

It wasn't a pirate. A child of sullen expression, dressed in the rags of a Nefaran urchin. Hoisting the white flag high. The boatman was ropey, with skin stretched taught over his bones. More corpse than man. His little smile was nerve-wracking.

"Who goes there?"

The child threw something over the railing; a desiccated hand. It seemed freshly cut, despite it had to have come off a long-dead corpse.

"My master wishes to speak with you. He has hopes you might come to an agreement," the child said flatly as if this was something an ordinary child would do and say.

The boatman's voice was gravelly, "If I may, the day has already seen so many dead. So many to wrap and offer to the gods..."

Carver was awake and snarling, "You shitting me? You think we're dumb as rocks? It's a trap."

Others were woken. Echoing similar sentiment.

But Rooster stared at the hand, realizing he'd been

played once more. It was a feeling he was growing ill of.

"The spy in our ranks. Was your master behind that too?"

The child stared back impassively, "You're allowed one other, if you wish. My master does not have infinite patience."

"Everyone listen up. Treat whatever Jhamon says, act like it came from my mouth. If I'm not back in two hours, you get ready to light this place up like a festival," Rooster announced.

Carver wandered off muttering about sewing back together captains without heads.

Picking Ahffan as his second they stepped aboard the little craft.

"Don't worry now," the boatman said, offering a purse, "Should you expire, my companion and I offer a service. A gold leopard will secure you a proper burial of your choosing."

Even the morticians here were shameless extortionists.

"That's blatant robbery."

A splash that pushed the boat was a grim reminder of how little wood stood between them and a reptile's next meal.

"If you should change your mind, ask for Petiri," the boatman grinned again, beginning to paddle.

The child handed them sashes of dark cloth to bind over their eyes. Ahffan grunted something sarcastic. Immediately and unnoticed, he passed into the skin-dream. Rooster heard rustling to the side and a pantherine shadow.

Blindfolds were ripped off. They were inside a sepulcher, backlit alcoves that oozed candlewax. Tomb raiders had been busy here then. This had to be deep in Nemset—there was only ambient light here besides scant spears of foggy moonlight that revealed the abundant dust.

On the dome's underside was dilapidated imagery and half-eroded carvings. It evoked something primitive in

Rooster. This was older than any civilization back home. Looking upon it, knowing it was crafted by man's hands once felt jarring.

There were dozens of others here. Thieves who were perusing over items on stone tables, inspecting them by candlelight. They were unbothered by the interruption. Or that they were surrounded by dead bodies—bones stacked neatly in piles, dislodged from their eternal rest.

Ahffan did not seem to be doing well here. He shivered as if ice water was running down his spine. Losing all his color.

The child led them to the central dais. A moat of crystalline water encircled the fully enclosed inner chamber of the sepulcher. Home to some funeral rite, ages ago. Candlelight glowed will-o'-wisp within.

"Welcome to the Sunken Reliquary," a familiar face appeared.

"Hello Amir."

Rooster took note of the wardrobe change. This time the teenager was sheathed in dark hide, onyx robes and fine boots. Not at all the peasant's garb. Something told him this was the true form of Amir.

"Always keeping us on our toes when we meet, don't you Amir?"

The boy indicated towards a stone bench, "Caution is the friend to thieves, Rooster. Or do I call you chieftain now?"

"I have a feeling this will be a short meeting."

"It can. If you want it to be."

Rooster did not have time for this, "What is the meaning of this?"

"I could ask you the same. You've got a small army knocking at my door. Why have you come for the Flameblade?"

"For whatever reason I like. He's a nuisance and someone will pay me a big chest of gold for his head. And he killed the father of those Shemsari boys you met before. What's it to you?"

Amir was inspecting Ahffan, the ram skull and fetishes, "That depends on your answer. Who's the one with the chest of gold?"

"Stop playing games boy."

"Have you considered that you're just a piece in someone else's?"

"Crossed my mind a few times. Get to the bottom of it."

The boy faced him, "This meeting only works with total transparency."

"That right huh? Tell me about the spy that was stomping around my camp wearing my face."

Rooster wasn't much a card player but he knew the psychology of how others gambled. When someone was bullshitting and when someone was holding onto a heavy card that could flip a table.

And Amir had his poker face on, "For my safety, I cannot say."

"Then why in the hell should I be frank with you?"

"Because your friend is alive. Kizzuran holds him hostage in this very building," Amir said eyebrows lowered, "My mission here is to broker peace, Rooster."

"Says you."

"Kizzuran is one of my oldest allies. Because of him, the Dead Hand lives. Much has occurred since your hasty departure."

Rooster asked, "So you're in league with the Ivory Queen as well?"

The scroll bearing the promise of riches hit the stone table. The thief scanned it quickly. Eyes widening with every moment. Amir let it fall from his hands.

"Tell me something Rooster. Who else has seen this?"

"Our mutual friend Tariq. The Vizier. Half of Nefara's finest."

Amir considered, then spoke, "This is the first time I've seen this. I doubt that Kizzuran is aware of its existence."

Rooster felt dumb.

"To my knowledge—and it is vast, I assure you friend—Kizzuran Flameblade has never spoken with the Ivory

Queen or her agents, let alone work for her."

"So this..."

"Is a forgery. You said Tariq gave you this?"

"It was intercepted by the Serpents by smugglers."

The boy frowned, "Would their names happen to be Skulk and Sable?"

"Yes."

Amir paced about the room like a caged tiger. A flood of emotions was flashing across his face. The boy was holding it back behind a stoic mask.

"Two weeks ago, one of our safehouses was raided. A decoy headquarters with its location leaked to potential rats. The personal guard of the Vizier on orders from the Qadi himself. The next morning? Tariq was back in the palace."

He continued, "Days later guards on the docks, pulling apart every boat larger than a dinghy looking for Skulk and Sable—also our allies. Kizzuran is nearly poisoned by a 'gift' from one of his men, a bottle of wine stolen from a beached Shalmanisar junk."

The facts were damning.

Rooster wanted to kick himself.

"That lying sack of shit..."

"This is no mere lie," Amir abruptly stopped, looking as if he'd received divine revelation, "And on the northern road. Did you happen to meet the other Bandit Prince? Azim?"

"He's on his way south."

"And Tariq knew of this?"

"It was his servant who delivered the same offer to Azim to take the Flameblade's head."

Fear laced the demand, "Call your men off."

"Why?"

"Either someone is faking us all out or there's a giant storm about to hit."

By his own admittance and the revelations discussed openly, Rooster knew that his part had not been a mere pawn in a political game. He began to reexamine every detail from that meeting with Tariq internally, racking his head.

The same thought began to repeat in his head; they should have never come back to Nefara.

Amir reappeared in the Reliquary after the space of an hour, looking drained, "Kizzuran might behead me before the night is through. You earned his vitriol for a lifetime from the river."

"Good. Maybe he'll learn what 'fight fire with fire' means."

"Kizzuran is crazy. You underestimate his talent for violence. And his short temper."

"Listen. If I expected to deal with reasonable, sane individuals in this fiery godforsaken sandbox, I'd have run north a long time ago."

The boy took an exhausted seat, cocked his head as he noticed Ahffan was in a comatose state. He kicked a sandalled foot with his boot—the skinwalker didn't react.

"So these are the Shemsari wizards?"

"Something like that."

"You're catching on. To our culture here," Amir said.

Rooster snorted, "It's the tattoos on my face, isn't it?"

"No. You say one thing but mean another. You obfuscate and swap the truth like shells under a cup. It's the trick to live long here in the desert."

"So where do we stand? Looks to me like a real debacle. I'm getting rather tired of the lawyering here."

Amir leaned back, deep in thought. Flipping coins between his fingers must have been a subconscious tic for the thief. Ancient ones plundered from very old places.

Those weren't the only old things on Amir either.

A pair of daggers encrusted with skeletal hands of bronze could have been more than centennial—multi-millennial even. An ornamental sundisk collar that could have belonged to any old kingdom pharaoh, studded with lapis, rubies, and a screaming skull in its center.

But what caught Rooster's eye was the oxidized bronze

mask on the shrine shelf, nestled between candles. The longer he stared at it, the more a mirage-like trick would hover over its surface. As if his eyes wanted to scry it but couldn't focus.

Details, details, and details. Things even a cautious cutpurse might overlook out of habit. Not him.

"One thing is certain; the Serpents are in control of a great deal of Nefara. They're going after and disposing of every rival or challenge to their rule. Capturing Tariq was their first move in the open," Amir stated.

"Impeccable timing with The Boy King is on his way with a grand army."

"Not impeccable—it's unusually prescient. For months they're working deep in the shadows, out of our sight. Then the Shah dies and we can't keep up with their moves. Their coordination is lethal. These are not self-interested thugs Rooster. There's something more to them that I can't see."

It was clear that the thief was not used to being outmaneuvered and left confused. The aggravation was palpable.

But Rooster had bigger fish to fry at the moment.

"How I see it, we can withdraw and bury the hatchet. But I don't think the Flameblade or Azim will be particularly satisfied with that outcome."

"No. Kizzuran won't ever be. He might be an ally but he's a madman. After this business if you ever cross him, best be ready to cross swords."

"I don't think either of our bandit princes will come to peaceful terms."

That was putting it lightly.

If Azim or Kizzuran found out they'd been tricked into peaceful terms, there wouldn't be enough heads to lop off to satisfy either madman. They were not mundane men who could ever retire to lives of gardening and netting fish. Not unless they got to plant the limbs of their enemies into the ground like carrots.

Even the Serpents might find an excuse to stay uninvolved between those two.

Rooster grunted. Thinking of anything that could work. And an errant impulse did come to mind. One of those paintings on his father's father's walls in his keep depicting ancient half-naked warriors duking it out with fantastically large swords over a field.

"A duel."

Amir wasn't paying attention, "What?"

"What if we had them duel? Forced them to confront each other as they should have?"

An unreadable expression crossed the thief's face, "So you'd leave it up to chance?"

"Not chance. They both call themselves the Bandit Prince. They want each other's heads. We give them what they want."

"And the outcome?"

Rooster didn't like gambling always. This wasn't a blind bet though. If the Serpents were truly in control of Nefara, a shakeup in the bandit hierarchy when the king was riding into town would be a disruption no one would expect.

A little earthquake here and there let things slip into the cracks.

"My condition; Antonius is released."

"I'll see what I can do."

"He's released or that chickenshit with a flaming sword will have to learn to talk crocodile. Then these drug-dealing thugs win."

Amir looked down at his boots as if they might offer guidance, "You would not joke about that if you knew what they're capable of. I swear to you Rooster. They are evil beyond anything I've ever seen."

"Everyone is capable of evil Amir. I've done plenty of it. I can happily bury my good nature if Antonius isn't released, unharmed."

"After this duel, we shall speak of it. And then you might think differently about how much wickedness you can stomach."

Age had diluted the innuendo of morality. It was a feat of impossibility to be a principled man and hold power.

Good and evil were the sugared decorations that justified any expedition towards conquest or control. When one got right down to it and the souls of men were bared for all to see, it was always the same base, primitive impulses that glistened like guts.

What separated the weak from the honest was that the latter could live with their spurs.

سوداء واحة
Black Oasis

Six hours until the face-off.

Rooster hoped he appeared far more imperturbable on the outside. Because on the inside his nerves were shot to hell.

What did you call a group of marauders, bandits, pirates, cutthroats, and wannabe warlords gathered under the pretense of peace? With each backing an egotistical raving lunatic of a champion who would try his damndest to kill the other? Better yet, being a schemer pitting these untrustworthy groups against each other?

Pure profligation.

They gathered at a plateau oasis, golden sward making a crescent about a forest of dry palms and a pool that ran right up to the ochre cliff face. With the grim standard of the Birds of Prey stuck at the mount for all below to see, they set about licking their wounds and resting.

It was short-lived.

A leopard ran alongside the cliffs and a ram skull hovered just outside Rooster's periphery. Followed quickly by a dust cloud from the north. A red and brown eagle skirted the dunes to the west and skimmed over their heads, with another cloud joining from the south. Skinwalkers were going haywire as they scouted the hosts that closed in on the oasis, beasts and suntanned wizards running among with new reports.

Something was up.

The bandit princes were told to bring only ten of each of their warriors to act as witnesses to the duel. Instead, they had brought their entire hordes. Every single Floodplain Raider and the Black Rider of Altaruk was present.

When the sun hit high noon, nearly five hundred

cutthroats packed the small oasis with eyes full of hatred and a hunger for murder.

Sitting on the colorful horsehair rug that had once been the old Beyik Alghasan's, Rooster did not feel like a mediator and judge presiding over the duel. He felt an imposter in both his mail coat and chieftain robes.

The small circle of concord had been designated at the center of the palm grove. On either half of the circle were the opposing raiders. Not too long ago they had once been part of one big happy bandit family—their looks to one another were anything but friendly.

Didn't help they were all armed to the teeth either.

The crowd murmured as Amir arrived, with him Antonius in tow. The Teridian looked unscathed if only a bit weary. They joined him on the rug.

The thief gave Awakener—naked blade stuck in the sand—the side eye, "Don't you think you should be unarmed? Given the circumstances?"

"As chieftain, I'm afforded a ceremonial dagger," Rooster said dryly, "Nobody said how big it could be."

Amir clicked his tongue and sat down.

Antonius grinned wide. Hands still bound. He was missing a molar, "How the hell are you captain?"

"I've had easier days. They try pulling teeth?"

"Nah, my shield. You should have seen their guys. I gave them a real pounding, eh."

Captivity had done something to the younger man. Livened up his spirits. Maybe the thought of death inspired Antonius.

The crowd was becoming more untenable. Then grew still, shifting their gazes up at the cliffs at Rooster's back. He turned.

Jhamon and Jhabari both descended. Sporting fresh war paint in bone-white and eagle feather crowns. They took a seat at Rooster's right hand.

No point trying to read Jhabari's face, "Whatever happens, you stay put."

A grunt back was not reassuring.

"Uncle's fate is in Bahram's hands now," Jhamon stated, looking at his brother.

Jhabari didn't seem confident in his god today.

The oasis simmered down beside the wind that tossed the palm fronds.

"Well, well. This looks like a suitable location for someone to die," Carver stated.

Suddenly everyone was standing on both sides. Azim had ridden in and began to walk the gauntlet. He spat in the faces of the Floodplain Raiders and taunted them by name. Jeering as he danced like the mad bird he was.

He arrived at the carpet, looking at his nephews first then to the Rooster, "This morning I threw one of my oracles off the cliffs. She said you would bring me the head of my nemesis. Isn't it such a disappointment—trusting in the words of your servants?"

"Wasn't my fight Azim. You ran when the White Dervish fell to Kizzuran. You should have stood and fought him then and there."

Hilt of the black-bladed saber was pulled out. Azim looked bloodthirsty but stalled—Hazair swooped down and landed on the hilt of Awakener. It squawked at the bandit prince. He recoiled slightly.

"Yhizzir was a gharib," Azim grated, his eyes narrowing, "Didn't you know?"

"Are you going to keep talking or are you going to duel?"

Behind the crowd roared again.

Kizzuran had entered the gauntlet. Who was much taller up close than far away on a boat. There was no decorum or derision in his approach. Raw enmity oozed from the pirate with the half-mask helmet that resembled some horrifying maw of a dread lizard, horns, and teeth sewn into the crocodile skin.

Both bandit princes realized how close they were, sidestepping as two panthers might—shoulders hunched, necks tensed.

"He cannot be the judge," Kizzuran snarled, addressing Rooster directly, "He is my enemy. I will slay him first."

"That was not our agreement," Amir stated cooly.

"You did not say the waterbird would be presiding. This duel is a farce."

Water bird? Rooster found it amusing, all these nicknames.

The Flameblade sniffed and walked back down the gauntlet.

"Aha," the half-laugh from Azim was barely noticeable.

And yet it rippled over the red crocodile skin like a chill wind. Kizzuran spun and gave him the side-eye with an intensity that could freeze hell over twice.

"What was that?"

"You're hearing things Flameblade. The ghosts of your past maybe," Azim snickered.

"I have no ghosts."

"Oh? There's one with us here now. I can see him now."

"Your wit will not save you from my culling."

Azim's eyes grew wild, "Oh? Here I thought you would slither back to that swamp of yours. My crones tell me you sleep with the dead, on a festering throne of slime. How fitting, for you."

Dead quiet.

Unburdened hate glared from behind that draconic mask.

"Your brother begged for mercy when I cut him down."

"Men who are stabbed in the back can't breathe," Azim fired back, "You toothless liar."

The heat in the empty circle of sand began to boil.

Kizzuran didn't turn to speak, "I accept the terms. I will have this one's head."

Who then drew his long, curved saber.

Azim answered it by drawing out his black-bladed one, "Go on. Run away again, little lizard."

Kizzuran looked like death on legs.

Rooster did not rise. Apparently a Beyik Alghasan would not—not even at the threat of death. That tradition was such a subtle dig, making everyone get down to his level, it was too much his style to let it go.

"The terms are simple. The fight is to the death. No quarter will be given to the other. Are both challengers ready?"

Azim raised his black saber and a buckler of the horse-raider fashion.

Kizzuran hissed something. Sorcery flashed. A fiery jet raced down from the handguard of his two-handed saber. It ignited like a blazing torch.

Rooster let his hand cleave the space between the two.

The death dance began.

Low drums rolled from the side of the pirates.

There was a brief moment of pacing in a slow counterclockwise circle. Both combatants felt out their range, their room to maneuver. Watching the other intently.

Flaming sword held high Kizzuran flew in with a rage. With terrible speed, he unleashed a series of blows like a windmill of fire—sparks arcing each time his steel bit the buckler shield. Wielding hell's hammer. The black robes of Azim smoked and were rent by a glancing blow, threatening to catch afire. The bandit prince dodged and flung a parry that would have severed both arms.

Steel aimed for flesh. Each matched in swiftness. The bandit princes gave everything they had, bitter and deadly.

One wild flaming swing would have cleaved Azim at the clavicle—instead, he deftly sidestepped and black flashed. Kizzuran howled as his belly armor was sliced open. Sweeping back. Azim stumbled back, holding his calf.

Both retreated for a brief respite.

The entire oasis held its breath.

The fraternal anger emanating from both princes wasn't metaphorical—it could be heard with every blow.

The bandit princes leapt once more into the fray.

Azim was a madman but he fought like a wasp slipping through smoke. Kizzuran like a coiled python striking with sheer force. Their clashes were nearly exact in skill and precision. Not like bandits at all but master swordsmen whose steel was an extension of their flesh.

The first bad strike landed when Kizzuran went for a lunge to hit Azim's bleeding leg. Azim smashed the buckler on the draconic helm and followed it with a sharp swing that missed the Flameblade's exposed neck by a hair.

The flame puttered and almost went out.

Azim swung wildly to cut off the hand that held said sword.

Kizzuran fell to a knee and rammed his horned helm into Azim's chest.

The bandit princes rolled in the sand, a frenzy of strikes and grappling. Dusty black robes unfurled as Azim managed to get up first—he didn't rush to strike Kizzuran, instead twirling for effect and soaking up the crowd's jeers.

A grave mistake.

Not a breath later the Flameblade was on his feet and delivered a series of burning slashes that cut Azim deep on his shoulders and chest. Leaving half-cauterized lacerations.

Flesh and cloth sizzled.

Azim tried the buckler trick again—Kizzuran ducked. Both panting and bleeding heavily, rushed in for the third and final time.

In a lightning-fast feint, sidestep, sidestep, and cunning slash Azim struck Kizzuran's stomach once more. The sand below drank deep of blood. The Flameblade staggered and looked as though he'd collapse.

But.

The burning spell of the sword intensified.

Kizzuran roared and raised it.

Azim spun his sword and answered the challenge, taunting.

Only Kizzuran grabbed the black saber in his gauntlet and headbutted Azim. Ignoring the pain of his hand, he pushed off the black-robed man and swung the flame-kissed sword in a lethal, lateral arc.

Once. Twice. Three times as savage as the last. And on the second strike, Azim's black sword was knocked aside.

The third took off his head.

A dull thud fell like a funeral dirge in the oasis like a coconut had been felled from a palm tree. The black turbaned head rolled right to the foot of the carpet.

And then there was one Bandit Prince.

The decapitated corpse of Azim managed to stay standing for an uncomfortably long time before it collapsed. To which Kizzuran reached down and grasped the black-bladed saber. Looking over towards the carpet and recognizing Jhamon and Jhabari for the first time.

The Flameblade began to walk right to the carpet, fiery sword still in hand.

Amir was cursing under his breath, leaping to stop whatever was about to happen.

But an eagle cry stopped Kizzuran in his tracks. Frozen like ice by the sight of Hazair, who was crying at the sight of the headless Azim.

Jhabari stood. Rooster tried to yank him down but Jhabari ripped his hand away.

Kizzuran menaced, "Come on boy. Come and die like the rest of your bloodline."

Rooster grabbed Awakener's handle.

This blood feud was nothing like he'd ever seen. It was confusing. And yet so visceral it demanded no explanation.

Jhabari was staring at Azim's corpse for a while before speaking, "I will kill you."

"Why not now? Why wait?"

Jhabari was fast. His hand grabbed the black saber right out of Kizzuran's grip. But not before it bit his palm as the Flameblade let the steel slice it open. Jhabari flipped it and snatched the handle out of the air. His blood seeped down the handle and onto the sand.

"One day I'll cut your hands and feet off and let the birds feast upon your flesh. Without glory to your gods, you'll die as a slaughtered cow. Bahram as my witness."

Kizzuran's laugh was pure mirth.

It was entirely possible that another duel would begin.

And yet the Flameblade staggered back, holding his

bleeding stomach as he walked down the gauntlet, making it halfway down the path before collapsing. The Floodplain Raiders roared at his victory. Their counterparts in black watched in sullen silence.

"It's over," Amir breathed in relief.

"No," Rooster disagreed, looking sideways to Jhabari, "This war was merely postponed."

The sunset was beginning.

The oasis was abuzz. The riders of Azim Altaruk were splintering already. Self-elected captains were holding fierce delegations while some of the black riders were already readying to leave. It was pure chaos as the Floodplain Raiders looked as though they might slip daggers into their former allies' ribs from behind.

"This is getting ugly," Antonius commented, chewing on some smoked lamb, "How is this going to shake out?"

Rooster watched, "They're bandits. The only thing that held them together were the antics of a delusional madman. They can't hit caravans with the Boy King coming—too dangerous. Who knows?"

"Shame we can't recruit them."

"Yeah."

An outfit like Azim Altaruk's was like a rabid dog. By not feeding it regular feasts of larceny, it would rear its toothy head in some town not far from here. Nefara was too protected. Other outposts in the desert were not.

Jhamon and Jhabari were discussing something heated beneath the palm trees. In Shemsari. The argument ended with a shove absent of brotherly love. Jhamon stormed off towards the Ramali.

"What was that about?"

Jhabari wore a mask of confusion, "He refuses to go after Kizzuran."

"Then he's the brains between the two of you. Flameblade will turn you into hyena food in his sleep."

Anger, then resignation showed in the boy's face.

Rooster could only imagine what he was going through.

"Azim..." Jhabari began and couldn't finish.

"Azim was a fearsome warrior aye. But his madness ruined any chance for glory. Do you think his men wanted to be hiding in the rocks their whole lives? His purpose died with your father."

It must not have been a reassuring answer but it was the bittersweet truth.

The bond between Jhabari and Azim might have been fractured but it dug at the soul. The kid had been holding on a hope to impress his uncle—win back his favor. Rooster wasn't inexperienced in that field of familial regret.

"And yet you let his killer live."

Rooster snorted, "Life lesson boy; there's little that you or I have control over. It gets easier once you figure out that we're all ants playing at god."

The sounds of horses being readied to be ridden reminded him that they were still embroiled in a shifting power dynamic. There was no sign of Amir. Maybe the thief lost his taste for politics when he saw what he'd sewed.

One of the black riders was approaching from the group. With an exaggerated swagger indicating he'd been recently promoted or elected to lead the bandits, swinging large in his boots.

"She belongs to me now," the bandit grinned wide, extending a hand for the black saber, "Hand it over boy. Hand it over now."

It was known now that the sword was called Eclipse. It had many owners. According to questionable lore, it had never been won without the killing of its previous owner.

Jhabari raised his eyes to the bandit—gaze frosted over, "Rooster. What do I do?"

"Be a better man than what your uncle wanted you to be."

The kid nodded.

The bandit lost his patience and reached to seize Eclipse.

Jhabari suddenly snapped it breakneck and decapitated the bandit in a single stroke. Cleaned the blade off on the robes of the headless corpse, then walked towards the rest of the black riders.

The oasis caught on there'd been bloodshed and there was a great deal of squawking.

"Here I hold Eclipse. Mine by right," Jhabari called out defiantly, "Who will try to claim it?"

There were no takers.

A group of bandits delivered a black bundle at his feet, to which the Shemsari boy wrapped the sash over his forehead. It was decided unanimously and without deliberation.

Jhabari turned back to the oasis—to Rooster. Words were not easy. The boy was wrestling with a mountain behind that face.

In Patina, the boy spoke, "Tell Jhamon that we'll speak again."

"You will."

"Don't let anything happen to him."

"Like he was my own son."

Jhabari stopped himself from walking off, glancing over at Hazair. The eagle flapped a wing and tilted its head. Damn thing wouldn't leap off the sword.

"We are Rooster. Don't ever forget that."

The bandits were growing restless, calling his name.

The day was done—destiny had come and gone.

Rooster even felt the shift in the wind. A small fire had been extinguished. A blazing wall was just over the horizon.

The Shemsari boy wiped the dust trails from his face and threw himself atop his horse. The bandits let out wild whooping and Shemsari shrieking as Jhabari cantered through their side of camp, each raising his blade in the air. Black and tan rippled through the oasis as their voices grew into a single hair-raising ululation.

The raiders had lost and found a new captain.

They rode out as an exultation of vultures taking flight.

Unaccustomed to the proclivities of thieves, Rooster felt very inept in the guise of a shepherd. The gaggle of goats he was driving down the streets of Nefara were bound for the market.

Jhamon, Antonius, and Goshawk were having a hell of a time of it. Though Jhamon had said little more than a sentence since he'd been parted at the oasis from his brother. There was nothing to be done about it. Best to keep the kid preoccupied for the time being.

Rooster himself was feeling antsy.

The herding mutt rubbed alongside his leg, snapping at the back of the goats before herding them down an alley. To a bystander it would have appeared like the dog was trying to round up stray beasts—while it was anything but the opposite.

"Hey," he muttered to whoever was within earshot, "Somebody kick that skinwalker. We're going to be spotted."

Goshawk shoved a stave into the handcart shepherds used to carry their livelihoods on. A little muffled grunt from within.

Yet nobody in the tenement-filled slums of Nefara's backside looked at them twice.

Come to think of it, there was a whole lot more beggary wherever Rooster looked.

Smoke-stained walls filled with city-dwellers who seemed to be very unoccupied. Their gaunt faces gazed vacantly towards nothing.

Rooster tried not to stare to draw attention.

"Lotus-eaters," Antonius commented, pushing aside a throng of peasants who didn't part out of their way, "Can't believe I almost got hooked on this stuff."

"You got lucky. They didn't."

'They' was not an insubstantial amount of Nefarans. They'd passed a hundred damned souls already and they hadn't been here longer than a half hour. And moving in gangs among them were enforcers and dealers—drug pimps. Amir had called them 'Coilers'. Indicated by the small badge they carried on the inside of their robes. The guard ignored their presence as if they were pieces of furniture.

The cerulean lotus and its lotus-eaters were looking more like an epidemic every day.

Into the market square they went. Where they posted up and pretended to be selling goats. Anyone who tried to buy was hit with a ridiculously high number, followed by colorful gestures that would make a scalper blush.

Just your regular market activity at midday.

"Look alive people," Antonius muttered, "On your right, Rooster. Yellow robes."

A saffron turban bobbed into view. The Qadi's head bobbed behind a group of baskets. Accompanied by a royal retainer and a sharp-looking fellow—a merchant lord well-known at the Caravan Court.

"Follow at a distance. Except Ahffan. Wherever he is."

A cat shadow crisscrossed the rooftops ahead of them.

They four began to move goats in the same direction as the Qadi's entourage. Following right up to the feet of a squat sandstone granary-turned-warehouse. A fortuitous patch of greenery gave an excuse for their cover—the goats happily munched as they spied and waited.

Rooster knew he should distrust Tariq now. Compromised and likely a puppet to the thugs, nothing he said could be taken at face value.

It was the why Amir had them in disguise and chasing the nobleman around was what was bothering him.

Sure, the Dead Hand had paid them a vase of tomb treasure.

But was the commission worth the unseen risk? What true good would they accomplish, running around town like this?

"Captain. They're coming out," Goshawk spoke into his robes like he was coughing.

The entourage was leaving whence they came, sans the merchant lord. Tariq was visible, well-manicured hands clutching a jacketed scroll. Impatiently moving to his next appointment, barking at the retainers for wine.

Rooster was about to pull them back to pursue when

the herding dog practically yanked his robe off, "Git. What's your problem?"

A low whine, the dog pointed its nose elsewhere—back to the warehouse.

He almost missed it.

A blob of saffron appearing and disappearing.

What the hell?

"Is Ahffan seeing this?"

Whether the skinwalkers could communicate with each other while in the skin dream as efficiently as Rooster wanted was one thing. Their talking trick was however infinitely valuable.

Fog of war could kiss his ass.

A pebble clattered off a nearby roof—the cat shadow was heading back towards the warehouse. So the skinwalker had seen the illusion.

They followed. Apprehensively. Shadows on sandstone grew long even at this time of day.

Rooster thought they'd been duped when the saffron appeared again. The face of Tariq once more.

Impossible.

A body double?

The pathway the doppelganger led them down grew labyrinthian. They had crossed from the core of Nefara into its southern quarters. Not quite the docks yet. Archways led into a dim tunnel where the streets were covered by dark red shades, opening into a yawning blackness. Once an ancient quarry dug straight into the earth now converted into an open air-pit with corridors etched into each level. Stoops where pensive business was conducted by anything but savory characters.

They said the Black Oasis was a place where anything could be bought. It was not a place for goatherds. That fact was obvious when a vagrant tried to snatch one of their errant flock—subsequently sent scampering by the rabid attack of their skinwalker herd dog.

Rooster delegated quickly, sending Antonius and Jhamon ahead to tail the doppelganger. They disappeared into the shadows.

It was a long hour when they returned from their haunt.

"We got as close as we could without him spotting us. I could see it Rooster. It's him."

There was no way. How could Tariq be in two places at once?

Nor was it a shapeshifter—Rooster knew only of one and it served another side.

"You're sure."

"I'd bet the farm on it."

The other lingering question was why Tariq was so publicly wandering the Black Oasis.

A sniggering ghost was pulling on Rooster's goosebumps on his neck.

The thief boy had been right—to a point.

"Did you see where he went off to?"

"He melted into the darkness," Jhamon said, "It looked like black magic."

"That's impossible," Rooster said, despite the fact he doubted his convictions.

This—whatever the Serpents and their new puppet Tariq were playing at, notwithstanding the paranoid Dead Hand and their teenage leader Amir—was all too muddied to see through. Webs of ever-thickening plots that covered even the most perceptive of eyes. All while Rooster and his crew were stuck in the middle. It didn't take a genius to figure out that the sorcery and the artifices that both parties employed would lead to something nasty.

Perhaps it was time they returned to camp and reassessed their commission.

Rooster knew his capabilities as well as when he bit off more than he could chew.

This was someone else's turf war now.

"We're pulling out. Everyone back to camp."

Antonius tugged at his fake beard, "What about our job?"

"Fuck the job. I'm not letting any of you die for

whatever Amir wants. We don't have the tools for this kind of work."

Goshawk nodded. The Ophi had strict rules against magic. They didn't mess with deviltry, even the mildest kinds.

"So Azim died for nothing," Jhamon threw his lot in the mix too.

Their voices were carrying and would bring bad attention. So the goats were moved so the conversation could carry on, en route to the gates.

"Azim died because Azim was more prideful than he was pragmatic. We, on the other hand, are not."

They got lost several times on the way out of the Black Oasis. Took a detour when guards were throwing merchants to the wall and interrogating them. Maybe it was the cult activity getting them paranoid. Rooster didn't feel like being questioned and moved them into a safe quarter before moving on.

It was dusk before they hit the road to the last square. The journey was proving much more packed than how they left it. Odd. Why were so many Nefarans flocking to the great archway?

And so many flies?

People were shouting, pointing up at the Medean-built architecture that stood ten men tall. There were shapes that were dangling from a score of ropes secured to freshly nailed spikes. Ropes that ended in nooses.

Pushed by the gentle and warm breeze were the corpses of children. And not just a handful. Dozens. Each clad in the smocks and dress of the silent caste of servants, lamplighters, and streetcleaners. The corpses were so fresh they had yet to go purple.

Which meant this was a message.

Goshawk almost fell over, praying in his native tongue. Jhamon emptied his stomach.

Rooster felt only anger.

The horror of the scene was not in their presence but in

the emotionless addicts who looked upon them with abject curiosity. These lotus-eaters might have been the parents but their addled minds were long rotted away.

For them to return to camp, they were forced to go through the archway. Under the lifeless gaze of the dead children, Rooster got a better look.

He noticed that every single one of them was missing their hands.

Which had been stuffed into their mouths.

At night they came.

Dark-shrouded assassins who stole through the nomad camp—quiet as the summer's wind. They alerted no animals and beggared no attention from the pickets placed on the outskirts of the hillocks.

They slid into tents with evil intent.

What they found was that they'd been expected.

Almost every single one was riddled with arrows or cut down by Shemsari who had been waiting in darkness with bent bows and murder on their breath. The remaining infiltrators were hogtied and hauled off to the tent of Carver.

Their tortured screams went well into the early morning.

Blood still painted the scarred man's arms as he exited the dome tent, shaking his head, "Didn't go well as I hoped."

Carver spoke as if he'd been performing emergency surgery on a complicated pregnancy and not pulling apart the bodies of the enemy. And so casual about it.

"Anything?"

"Like the others. They're in a trance."

Rooster cursed.

They were Serpents. The ones called Fangs. That wasn't the question. But why now? Why not earlier? Where was the motive?

"Shall I continue?"

Rooster waved him off, "No. We're getting diminishing

returns. Get some sleep."

Carver looked disappointed, heading back into his tent.

The camp was a mess. Everyone had dark bags under their eyes. More than a handful claimed they'd had haunted dreams again. A remnant from Nemset perhaps, combined with the nocturnal activities of dispatching killers.

Rooster rubbed his eyes. He needed one of those coffee-pot men. He wondered if he could train a Shemsari in the art. They were probably too prideful to lower themselves to such a task.

A disgusting patchwork of arachnid memorabilia crawled from behind the horsehide walls—Rhuïma finally returned, "Chieftain. We found a trail. But it ends suddenly. By the farms."

"Show me."

The small entourage trooped through the wild grasses on the western embankment where earth had been piled up against sandstone to guard against flooding from the river. Stains of human waste and other filth ran along the battlements—the farms came right to the corner of the White Kasbah's shadow.

The assassins hadn't climbed over the wall here. This was a fruitless find. They may as well have walked right through the gates for all the wasted effort.

"You couldn't sniff them out beyond this?"

Rhuïma recoiled, "This is not what a normal chieftain would ask us—"

"Are you lazy or incompetent?"

Threats of witchery and mutilation were thick on the skinwalker's breath as he began to stalk in the grasses. Peering back at the group, narrowing his eyes, "Go away now. Let Rhuïma do his work."

They bugged off to one of the farms, inspecting the abandoned windmill for any clues. None were to be found. This place wasn't fit for cockroaches.

Rhuïma returned, dripping wet, "Blech. We found something."

Rooster didn't dare ask who the other half of *we* was.

The assassins had been prudent.

But not infinitesimal.

Padded footprints disappeared then reappeared on a silt bank that pushed right up to a sluice gate—an overflow from the canal in the case the river flooded. By the look of it, the thing hadn't been used for ages until very recently. Drips that echoed hollowly from beyond in the wet darkness suggested a cavernous tunnel system. A rank smell of ancient misery that was buried under the sandstone floor of the city.

Rooster thought back to the myths Tariq had once told him months ago.

He sent the skinwalker to investigate.

Rhuïma was a serial whiner but he was the best of his kind. That kind of talent would not go unused while Rooster was chieftain.

When he returned to camp a visitor was waiting for him.

It was a morning of surprises.

"My master sent me to ensure you were unharmed," Nazsif sounded anything but concerned. The dark-clad servant flexed his fingers, "There was word of an attack last night."

"Word?"

"I would not have risked coming here and avoiding the spies of the Serpents had it not been deemed a legitimate fear. Was there an attack?"

The creature of Tariq was impossible to read. The sallow servant had mastered the art of stone-facing. No matter how brunt Rooster was, the man could not be undermined to reveal anything he didn't wish.

Even Carver might have a rough go trying to extract secrets with a knife.

"Run back and tell your master to find another errand boy to fight his wars for him."

Nazsif looked askance, "Why the change of heart Rooster?"

It would not be prudent to reveal too much here.

"My time is better used elsewhere."

A small scroll was conjured from one of the servant's dark sleeves, "Certainly. My master would insist you read this first."

Rooster sustained temperance and unrolled the scroll.

The contents of which were all but damning. Sentences that if uttered aloud would have cost the Qadi his life. There was no way even on a cold day in hell the Serpents would have approved this.

Tariq was begging for help. He was a prisoner to the Serpents—as had been suspected all along—but was a puppet subject to their manipulative devices. They had Nefara by the balls and anyone they couldn't get on their payroll was either disposed of or buried with the key thrown away.

Tariq was the last evidence of the coup—yet too valuable to the Serpents to be rid of. The thugs were using him as leverage against all; Shalmanisar, sellsword companies, and even the Caliph himself. In due time the Serpents would spread their cancerous influence everywhere in the Caliphate—piggybacking off the South Road and Nefara's port as their central infrastructure. Tariq hinted they all but controlled the Black Oasis, now that the Dead Hand and Shalmanisar had been kicked out of the black market; blind, deaf, and dumb.

So the gangsters wanted the city.

Rooster could have cared less.

Everything was junk to his ears save the last sentence of the message; the Serpents needed enforcers. The assassins last night weren't meant to succeed. The underlying message was that the Serpents demanded respect out of sheer fear.

They'd send a score of assassins every night—without fail—until they got their way.

"Where is he now? Tariq?"

"Confined to his chambers. They will not let him leave until the Boy King comes."

Rooster wanted time to deliberate on this. To confide in the Talons and consider how they could maneuver here. But time was of the essence. Meditation was a luxury they couldn't afford right now.

"Five thousand golden leopards."

Nazsif allowed himself a low, mocking chuckle.

It was an obscene price to name. Even for a nobleman's rescue. A king might hope for such a price for a ransom.

"Be reasonable Rooster."

"I am. Five thousand leopards is the annual value of the Shalmanisar trade in Nefara. Give or take."

"What kind of bearing does that have to do with my master's deliverance?"

"Let's put it this way, shall we? The merchants already got burned before Tariq was an instrument for the Serpents. But how pissed do you think they'll be when they find out that they're slated for slaughter—when I *inform* them."

Nazsif stiffened, "Tariq will never agree to this."

"Yeah? You willing to bet his life on it?"

As far as nobody was concerned, this was Rooster's only leverage. The trade wasn't the sum but in the long run it was far more. Losing a high-earner like the Shalmanisar meant losing all the future bribes and bags of coin that fell off the wagon that went right into a bureaucrat's pocket.

Rooster had worked it out; why they'd been hired by Tariq in the first place. Being the hatchet man keeping the Sabeans in line and the coin flowing. It had never been about the Shalmanisar leaving—merely flexing outside the boundaries of their agreements with the Qadi had resulted in them having to be reined back into the fold.

Which now were null and void, now that the Serpents had conducted a hostile takeover of all commerce.

"I risked my neck to come out here. My master will not be happy if this has been a fruitless meeting."

"Well, the nice thing is that you're just the messenger and I'm not asking. This is a demand, not a suggestion. Go on. Fly away and tell Tariq what I said."

Nazsif did not even attempt a benign outro. The servant buggered off with anger contorting his gaunt face, flapping out over the sands like the craven buzzard he was.

With that out of the way, it was time to find out if Amir was still breathing.

When Rooster departed the tent into the young sun's heat there was a great sense of urgency in the air. All of his Talons were waiting at the ridge of the shelf that the shepherds had used as a grazing ground. They watched a sandstorm that was smearing the horizon.

But it was an illusion.

The storm of boiling dust blotting the north and eastern ridges was not borne of nature. It flowed down from the Crownlands and the bandit roads, leveling off as it descended to the Ptahira. A single figure emerged from it—radiant light catching his mail amidst the sandy air—carrying a giant red banner. Behind him, a tsunami of thousands swelled over the hills. Tens of thousands. Heraldry of war fluttered over a sea of pikes and horses and camels.

Just as the morning prayers of Nefara moaned over the sands, the army of the Caliph had arrived at her ancient feet.

Part III.

اللؤلؤ ملكة
Pearl of Tyhri

Bestrode the ordinary anxieties that kept Rooster on pins and needles this night was a nagging sense he was being stalked by something. Or someone. Even as he sheathed himself in the garb of the Ramali chieftain and his captaincy there was an overarching sense of otherness that stabbed a cold little stinger into the back of his mind.

Candle flames blew ever so slightly, despite the tent flap remaining closed. There was no chill. No indication that anything had happened but a fluke.

Experience taught Rooster that nothing was as it seemed.

It also enlightened him that it was preferable to appear ignorant to those who believed they had the hand of surprise.

He went about fussing over the details of his ceremonial attire.

The tent flap was thrown open this time, admitting a Shemsari girl with his dinner and an herbal elixir of boiled roots and herbs that the nomads enjoyed. It had an earthy, tangy taste that he'd not quite got used to.

She invited herself to fasten his armor from behind. The Shemsari before her were very traditional about the fact he insisted on armor—their polite way of disapproving. A Beyik Alghasan was supposed to embrace the fact he could catch an arrow to the stomach—that was Bahram's way of proving destiny.

It was a tradition he had no intention of obeying.

She finished the loops on the armor without so much as a whisper of complaint, gave a smile, and reminded him that he was without a wife.

The Ramali and Faari were starting to talk.

Nobody questioned the providence that had given them

a gharib for a chieftain. But some customs were ironclad. Ignoring age-old traditions would only dishonor him in their eyes. A chieftain of two clans should have more wives than officers. Eventually, they'd stop dropping hints and they'd start trying to force their daughters on him.

The Shemsari girl was very ritualistic about cutting candlewicks, polishing his cutlery, and tidying his tent in the time it took him to eat and drink. He'd barely made a dent in the elixir.

She smiled and took off.

Leaving him alone to his thoughts and apprehensions.

Everyone was dressed in their best. Tonight was not one for poor impressions. With eagle feather crowns, tattoos touched up and armor polished black the Talons looked a mean bunch. Even the Faari looked a hair less feral.

As they saddled up Hazair flew down and perched himself right on Rooster's vambrace. Squawking when he tried to dislodge the bird. It insisted by digging its talons into his arm. The eagle fixed him with a stare inches away from his nose.

"One day, I'm going to turn you into a headdress," he told it.

Jhamon watched in awe, clutching their banner. Now that Jhabari was gone, he wouldn't let anyone else touch the thing.

With that, they were off.

They crossed the moonlit dunes quietly.

Rooster was reminded of his first crossing of the South Road. Only the hyenas were nowhere to be seen or heard. They'd scattered at the approach of the army.

The Caliph's pickets were professional. They were spaced out three layers deep, several hundred paces from the tents, and boasted a mixture of archers and light lancers. They were alert and they ran a tight operation.

The Boy King had some not-so-inexperienced advisors.

Standing torches and a wide war tent beckoned like a

warmly lit beacon. But cold iron faces appeared—two dozen mamluks who encompassed the entire tent. Faces entirely veiled in chain, they collected the arsenal of Rooster's party on a rug outstretched.

One outstretched a steel gauntlet, "Your pets wait outside."

Rooster realized it was Hazair they referred to and smiled, "My advisor? Fair warning; you can try."

The poor bastard tried.

The bird shoved its talons into his armored face and danced up to the standard, flapping its great wings atop the werehyena skull. Laughing in eagle.

The mamluks conferred with each other silently and waved them onward.

Jhamon entered with their banner first, followed by Rooster. Barking out all the titles and achievements that befit a warlord and chieftain of much grander status.

Rooster got a good look at them all while the boy rattled off the ridiculous and lengthy intro.

Firstly, the majority of the faces were not Medean—they were Shemsari. The Confederated Clans. Among them was Shalsem, who bowed his head. The others did not. Their expressions ranged anywhere from vexation to incredulity. So they hadn't been forewarned. That was interesting.

Immediately they chattered in Shemsari about the offensive nature of the prank and if the Ayubin would be insulted if they disposed of a white demon. Rooster grinned. They spoke brazenly of mutilation in front of his face. Clearly, they were used to Medean bureaucrats who didn't bother to get translators.

Even Antonius looked amused. He was beginning to pick up the language well.

"I am Beyik Alghasan of the Ramali and the Faari. Any chieftain who denies my claim is welcome to cross his knife with mine," Rooster spoke in Shemsari.

The Confederation went ghostly pale.

"I am no demon though you will certainly wish I was.

My coming is marked by the burning horse that rides into the long black night. I walk the great circle of J'awed as no other has before since the White Wastes. You will be gravely wrong to underestimate me."

It was part fluff, part bullshit, and the rest superstitious nonsense that everyone else said about his chiefdom. But the intended effect had nothing to do with Rooster's belief in them.

A long slow clap from the mostly salt and little pepper man in the back who was surrounded by scholarly-looking advisors. He was moderately dressed and yet his emerald and ivory tulwar at his waist was nothing of the sort.

"Very good. You are well met, Beyik Alghasan of the Ramali. Or do you prefer Rooster?"

"I've never been one for titles."

Salt and pepper nodded, "I am Ayubin Fadin al Hakim. Please call me Fadin."

A Medean boy slave appeared with a tray bearing wine. Rooster waved him off.

Fadin tilted his head, "It's not poisoned, I assure you."

"We of the Ramali do not partake in spirits."

The Confederation—who had been quietly quibbling for the last few moments—became rather waspish. Any tolerance that could be seen was draining from their faces.

"Ayubin Hakim we ask you to remove this devil from our presence. It stains this gathering and troubles my fellow chieftains," one boldly stated in the Medean tongue and not well.

"Oh?"

This was not the reaction expected, "The Ramali are elder and have not left their oasis for generations. They have no reason to journey this far south."

"Had," Rooster corrected.

The Confederation ignored him, with the same chieftain continuing his case, "The Ramali were once the pride of our people Ayubin. No longer. They've dawdled in the hills and become forgotten to themselves. We should not waste time with this pretender and demon."

Fadin pursed his lips and looked contemplative, "I see Chief Bharazin. Do you have proof of this?"

To that the Confederation leveled a whole host of inventions and speculations. It was clear they were irked more by the existence of a gharib chieftain than anything else.

What made Rooster laugh was how bureaucratic these so-called nomads were.

"How the domesticated dog yaps until it is fed from man's table. You are not wolves," he growled.

The Confederation began to raise their voices. Shalsem sipped wine and enjoyed the handiwork of the tent stitching.

Yhuuf fixed the chieftains with a wild eye and didn't bother to whisper, "Should I have them spitted like goats Rooster? I cannot stand this insult any longer."

Scorchhide pulled him back from the ledge of violence.

One of the advisors looked as though he was going to grab the mamluks. Fadin rested a hand on his forearm, gently shaking his head.

"No," Rooster let his voice carry as well, "I want this to be an educational experience for these and any Shemsari. Hazair. Show them."

From out of his robes he pulled out the Blue Eye. It wasn't premeditated—it just felt like the right thing to do.

The eagle swooped down and plucked the great blue diamond right from his grip. It hovered there at the ceiling of the tent above their heads, snapping its beak and crying out. The light from the candles seemed to be draining into the Blue Eye as it glowed with icy radiance.

"Behold, you sniveling cowards," Rooster growled, "And weep."

The Confederation recoiled as if Bahram himself had jumped down from the heavens and spanked them.

As the diamond was dropped back into his palm, Hazair returned to his perch.

"Now. As we were saying."

Ayubin Fadin al Hakim was once an up-and-coming officer during the reign of the last Caliph in the bush wars, the advisor to the White Dove for the long reign of peace, and now the same for the Boy King. He claimed no glory and spoke little of his accomplishments. He listened well and seemed more interested in history than prestige. His desk was a mountain of scrolls and manuscripts that had no bearing on the task at hand.

Rooster saw right through the veneer.

This here was the military brains of the Medeans.

A cold and utterly ruthless tactician.

Fadin al Hakim did something that he'd seen only the most accomplished leaders do—there were no plans anywhere to be seen. No maps with pieces. They existed, no doubt. But would never see the light of day or by those other than Fadin himself.

Hard not to respect the subtle tenacity.

The hour had grown late, most of the fair-weather warriors had long fled the tent for more riveting entertainment or sleep. Which left but Rooster, Fadin and Antonius to deliberate.

"I hope this night has not been a waste of your time with all this court banter. You are after all, quite far from the Ramali homeland as I understand it," Fadin seemed to have an endless reservoir of stamina.

"War moves us all like the tides."

"Yes, it does. I have not seen my estate for months and I fear I will not for many more. This business with the usurper Queen requires the aid of the entire realm. The death of his Grace Shah Anwar Albayda, the White Dove, will not go unanswered. Did you know that he was my brother?"

Rooster must have looked astonished beyond words.

"I preferred to remain rather anonymous and in my brother's shadow. And he casted a rather large shadow."

"So this is personal then."

"What war isn't," Fadin scratched his beard, eyes shadowed, "So which one is yours? A gharib from the north, now chieftain to two Shemsari clans. I wonder what war you are waging, Rooster."

Too many to name would have been the honest answer.

"As you are well aware, we are little more than a warband now."

The older man poured his own tea, delicately and precisely, "Warbands are as dangerous as any army. Even more so in many ways. They are easy to feed, can slip into gates unnoticed, and can wreak havoc inside a fortress all within a night before disappearing. With the right captain—or chieftain—a warband can punch high above its weight class."

Antonius was trying to keep up with the banter. Only it wasn't just talk. It was a proposal.

"Sixty thousand can make even the most fortified city weep."

"Yes, but without a fleet to blockade her, Tyrhi can easily keep supplied."

"So throw bigger rocks at her wall."

Fadin smiled wryly, "Are you always this hesitant to fight someone else's war?"

"That depends on whose asking and how much they're offering."

"How does twenty-five thousand hectares of arable, green land north of the Wall sound to you?"

"Where?"

"The Jewel Valley, al Jawhara al Wadi. It once belonged to Ayubin Umar al Jalil. Who is now al Ihrab."

Without a map and an expert in the region, it could have been the promise of a dusty field with a lame donkey and rusty farm tools. But Fadin's tone was not that of a shyster. And something told Rooster this was not an offer that had been lightly offered.

"I'm assuming this is good land."

"The most lush in the Caliphate. You could not find better. My estate runs parallel to the same rivers that flow into the Jewel Valley. You, the Confederation, can have it all. It's large enough that your clans could occupy it and never run into each other for years. And you won't need to—many wild horses call it home."

It wasn't offering a bounty of land but paradise.

No reason to question the why. It was all answered in the history of the Shemsari that Jhamon had taught him.

"Who does this offer extend to all, exactly?"

Fadin's eyebrows raised ever so slightly, "Any Shemsari that wishes to pledge loyalty to the Caliph. You see his Grace is quite interested in the clans. The future of the Caliphate relies on our good dealings with the Shemsari."

That was one way of putting it.

The other was that by offering the Shemsari this land, the Caliphate could put the only enemy out to pasture that ever got close to wiping them from the earth. Planting them right in their backyard to be domesticated. It was ingenious.

"What exactly about the clans is His Grace so interested in?"

"Ah. I've wondered that myself. However, it is undisputed that there are no better bowmen in any saddle. Or horsemen for that matter."

"Sure. And now you've just insulted clans with five thousand riders under their command by inviting me in. I have but sixty."

Fadin al Hakim interlocked his fingers and thought quietly.

Rooster did not dare presume any further.

Outside of this tent was an army larger than any he'd ever seen. More than half were professional soldiers who'd seen conflict before this one. The other half were levees that had cut their teeth already fighting their way out of the Sunstones to join the Caliph.

If the Ivory Queen was wiser than prideful, she'd come to terms quickly.

If not, this was going to be an interesting few weeks.

However grand this army was, would not find these sands to welcome it. Summer was here as was the intensive heat. Soon even the most supplied host would suffer the scavengers.

And the opportunistic. That was the catch.

Fadin seemed to read his thoughts, parsing over a scroll bound on ancient horsehide, "I am not unaware that the Confederation makes up the smaller portion of the Shemsari clans. They do not even compare to the Ad Daal; those without a clan."

"You have nothing to fear from them. They are scattered and seek nothing of the Caliph."

"I disagree Rooster. The past is the greatest predictor of the future. Did you know that Dhaban, Chieftain of the Zadrawi, was an Ad Daal? The clans could not rein him in or keep their warriors from leaving their ranks to join his. And Dhaban was a fiend. We Medeans have names for him. Even these days. Our war with the Shemsari would have ended differently had he been allowed to live."

Fadin wasn't thinking of who he had to fight today but tomorrow. Never comfortable with the distraction of court intrigue and the red herrings of political spats. Rooster suspected the tactician much sharper than he gave on.

"If I were you, I'd be a lot more concerned with the state of Nefara."

The older man sipped his tea, "We agree. I've heard of the bandit armies that have frequented her in my brother's absence. I'll be taking up al Khandaq Keep until the Caliph returns from Tyhri."

Was that wise?

Fadin sipped with the slightest mirth, "So. What would it take for your loyalty Rooster? If land doesn't interest you?"

"I'm afraid my mercenary instincts have overtaken me Ayubin. The best we could do is take a commission for our aid."

Rooster wouldn't have been surprised if the mamluks had been called in, dragged him before the Caliph, and summarily executed. Asking for a sellsword's commission was a clever way of denying fealty. And Fadin was too smart to miss that.

"Ah. Certainly," the old fox said without missing a beat, "A bounty we could oblige."

In other words? They had just established a compact that they were neither friends nor enemies. One that could be voided at a moment's notice.

It was a risky maneuver but it was the only way to make this work.

Given of course, what Rooster was planning and dared not utter to anyone aloud. Not even the Talons knew what he was cooking.

"Well, I think we've hammered all the useful hours at night. I must rest. An envoy will be sent to your camp in the morning," Fadin stood.

"I agree. Thank you for this meeting Ayubin," Rooster gave a light bow.

"Oh, I think it was rather productive. We'll be meeting again Rooster. Of that I'm sure," Fadin bowed back.

They stepped out into the night air. It was like stepping into an oven. Roasting in darkness. Already he yearned for temperance of winter months long gone.

The Talons rose to join him.

All save for Scorchhide. The skinwalker was nowhere to be found. Everyone was more exhausted than anxious to care.

"Go back to camp. I'll find him," Rooster volunteered and wouldn't take no for an answer.

They were too relieved to notice his demeanor.

A quick scan around the big war tent did not show any animal signs but human tracks. Which would have been odd, had he not had suspicions from earlier. Little peculiarities that no one but a handful would have picked up on.

One of the mamluks sauntered up, "Is there a problem?"

"We're missing one of ours. A short Shemsari. Yea tall. Arms covered in tattoos. Bone jewelry in his face. Wears a wooden mask. Can't miss him."

With torches in hand, the mamluks began to look. They

were just as eager to find someone who was wandering where they shouldn't.

Rooster was starting to fade when soft steps hit the sand behind him, "Chieftain? You're still here?"

It was Scorchhide. Looking perturbed.

"Waiting for you. Let's move."

In the vacant stretch of sand between the two camps was a walk of silence.

The moon was barely a slit in the black belly of the sky.

Scorchhide was right behind him, muttering to himself. Fidgeting with his mask. All the things the ropey skinwalker did when he was nervous.

Rooster paused, squinted at the shadow of a dune, "Hey, you see that over there? Is that one of ours?"

"Huh what," the skinwalker pulled up his wooden terror mask so he could get a good look.

The distraction stumped Scorchhide.

Which gave Rooster enough time to spin and reach for his face—that when his fingers touched, did not feel like flesh at all. They found the edge of cold metal. He ripped free.

Scorchhide faceplanted into the sand. Rather a perfect clone of Scorchhide that swiftly dissolved away like grains of sand.

In his fingers? The same ancient patina mask that had been sitting on the stone shelf in Nemset.

"Goddamn I hate it when I'm right," Rooster grunted.

A teenager in all black sat up. Gave him the evil eye.

"Amir."

"Very clever Rooster. What tipped you off?"

"The real Scorchhide would have never pulled Yhuuf from a fight. Nor would he be out stalking in his flesh when he could be in the skin dream. Now I'm owed some explanations. Where is the real Scorchhide?"

"Asleep like a baby. He's unharmed."

Another memory prompted Rooster, made him even angrier, "That was you too. The serving girl in my tent tonight. Of course. Old servant habits die hard eh?"

"Yes," the boy begrudgingly admitted.

"What the hell are you doing walking around like one of us?"

Amir reached a hand out for the mask, "Please. My friends died for this artifact. I cannot bear to lose it."

"Yeah? When were you going to tell me that you're the Prince of Many Faces?"

With his back to Rooster, the boy faced the dunes and distant Nefara, "For the safety of my friends, I saw no reason to divulge it. Don't take offense. But we didn't have reason to trust you until recently."

"That's rich kid. You had us risk our necks to chase after Tariq. Who is also tricked us real good with a doppelganger of his own. How many masks are there?"

Amir heelspun, "Only one. You're sure?"

"We chased one right into that black market pit. I'm sure."

"Then understand this Rooster; the game has changed."

"Enlighten me. I want to know everything. Spill your guts and I might be merciful."

"It's late," the boy said wearily.

"I don't sleep much these days. Try me."

And so Amir sat down crosslegged, indicating Rooster to follow suit. In the small space of sand, he began to draw a biography. Who Amir really was.

A boy born to slaves parents he didn't know had been picked up pickpockets in the Jewelport of Qamar. Ran with that bad crowd until he wisened up and went into hiding after faking his death. Hitchhiked to Nefara where he started back up again, only this time under the protection of a man called the ferryman who was one of the few souls to frequent and have intimate knowledge of Nemset. Together, they began to collect the rejects of the city; orphans like him.

But the treasures of Nemset weren't just there for the plucking, the boy explained. He and the crew of thieves who had once been window snatchers and merchant robbers were in a symbiotic relationship with the sunken city. As if it was a living thing. The conversation took a turn of the spiritual as the boy rattled off the name of gods as if they were living in the walls and speaking to him. The Sunken Reliquary as some kind of protected sanctum on the boundary of ancient darkness.

The thieves began to discover places within the vastness of Nemset that were not fit for humanity. What had been left there were items of untold value. So the thieves did what they did best; they sold them to the highest bidder. Cashed them in without a thought for what they'd be used for. Relics of the ancient kingdoms were suddenly being offered through legitimate channels of the college of the Kashar. And there were buyers. An anonymous one in particular who claimed to be a wealthy lord from north of the Wall was suddenly buying everything that flowed from Nemset.

It was then that the White Dove had decided to claim Nefara for his own. Shortly thereafter the thieves went into hiding, teamed up with Kizzuran and his newly formed Floodplain Raiders, and avoided the political turmoil. Then the buyer in the Kashar was more demanding. Wanted to meet Amir. Offered him a substantial hoard to work directly for him. Which scared the shit out of Amir. They were finding things—big magic things. The kind of boogeyman relics that kept the sorcerers up at night. The thieves grew a conscience overnight.

The day that Amir found the mask, he decided to end the tomb raiding.

The moment they stopped pawning, the thieves were finding themselves hunted. Outlawed. Punished and tortured whenever they were discovered. They got craftier and their pursuers got more diabolical. Hiding out in the swamp wouldn't last forever. So the Dead Hand was born out of desperation. They took up the guises as the lowliest of servants; lamplighters, street cleaners, fish-gutters, and ratcatchers. Which worked for a while.

Until the Serpents showed up.

"My instincts tell me that they're behind it all. I had my run-ins with gangs affiliated with the Glasslands back in the Jewelport. They're nothing but nefarious. They crawl inside a city like a parasite and drain it until there's nothing left."

"That's all interesting but why are you *here*?"

"I needed to see for myself—what the Caliph is planning. What you're planning."

That wasn't the whole truth.

"For a thief, you could use a lesson or two in lying."

Amir took a deep breath, "You saw what the Serpents did in the square?"

Even thinking of it made his stomach turn, "The dead kids?"

"They came for us—for me. Wasn't like the last time. They must have figured out we were going to be at the docks. Dozens of Fangs jumped us," Amir looked like he was going to break down, but calmed himself, "Kizzuran was there. Made them pay for every kid they grabbed tenfold. It was worth it."

"*What* was worth it?"

The boy switched to something furtive, "The day you saw the Qadi's body double?"

"What did you do Amir?"

"It's better if I show you."

The thief led them to a dilapidated ruin at the edge of the old farms. Weeds and sand overtook its tan bones. It was so buried the next sandstorm that blew through would bury the thing.

Amir lit a small lamp and handed it over.

Rooster took it and inhaled before he went in.

Expecting to find perhaps a shipment of drugs, a crate of jewels, perhaps even a damning stack of ledgers that could sic the Caliph on the Serpents. None of the above. He almost dropped the lamp.

Hogtied, gagged, and shivering in the corner was Tariq.

Morning came with cruel beauty and reminded Rooster that he was a dead man.

Flamingos and cranes from Nefara were flocking over the Ptahira—a burning orb, the king sun rose in the southern horizon, turning the river into a writhing bloody snake. Everything in the desert was moving westwards. Even a great cloud hung above the Caliphate army as a battalion of scouts were readying to ride.

The thought of a likely and immediate death was always the best incentive to be bold.

A flame-colored scorpion scuttled from a group of bushes and up one of the palm trees that swayed at the river's bank. It looked like a monster compared to the little brown dots that were floating down the river their way.

"This is insanity," Big Mug was saying, washing his face in the water, "Ain't no way this is going to work."

Antonius rounded on him, "You swore an oath to the banner. What the captain says goes."

"Ah yeah but this was your stupid plan, wasn't it?"

It was in fact, the Teridian's idea. And it wasn't half bad.

"Face it, kid's got stones," Carver muttered and earned a dozen shocked expressions, "What? Wipe those stupid looks off them faces. I say it how it is. Doesn't mean I like the kid."

Antonius snorted and went back to unloading his horse.

As did the other dozen plus that had come down to the river.

The barges from Nefara crawled up to the shore. With holds bereft of cargo. They'd barely be able to fit a hundred souls, plus the empty barge in tow for what they'd be bringing back.

If they came back alive.

Amir hopped off the first craft and legged his way over, "You're still going through with this?"

Rooster could only laugh, there was no other way to express his apprehension, "What? You think we're all about to hop on the boats for a tour of the countryside while we sip chilled wine?"

"It's never too late to back down."

"Should have thought of that when you kidnapped the most powerful man in Nefara."

"We still could try to hand him over to the Caliph."

"How do I know Medean law better than you? It's an offense punishable by death for putting hands on him. Let alone bagging him like a turnip. The best we'll get is a trip to the dungeon. Where the Serpents will put poison in our water. If we're lucky."

"What of your compact with the Boy King?"

Rooster looked at the war camp, and shrugged, "Who said we're not doing our part?"

"I count twenty."

"Fifty will go with the army. Don't worry. Jhamon has it covered. He'll make it look like there's a whole bunch of us on the northern coast, raping and pillaging our way right to the walls."

Amir's mouth hung open ever so slightly, "What does that accomplish, exactly?"

"The Ivory Queen will have even less reason to watch the river."

"But we're going after the gates to help the Boy King take Tyhri, no?"

"Is that what you thought I brought you along for?"

Rooster allowed a little catlike grin. The shit-eating kind that his brother used to do when he stole cake from the kitchens on a holiday and it was smeared on his fingers and mouth.

Even before the events of yesterday, this plan had been in the works. The bounty to rescue Tariq would have never been paid out. Rooster knew that from the beginning. And yet it was precisely that amount of coin that would secure them whatever they needed; sellswords, horses, ships, bribes, whatever the future would demand.

The truth was that they lived in uncertain times that might soon turn into deadly ones. It was in those days that a little gold went a whole long way.

And Rooster was done waiting to be offered any.

As Amir was trying to rack his head trying to piece

together the unspoken goal of their mission, Lancer was hauling a wriggling potato sack onto the first boat. Tariq's muffled yells earned a round of laughs from everyone.

They were fools to laugh.

"Tell me, Prince. What's the last thing that anyone expects during the first hours of a siege?"

"I'm afraid to ask."

"Antonius? Elucidate."

"Simple really. City like Tyhri is worried about food. Thieves start hoarding it, stealing it, whatever dirty tricks they can pull to make a killing. Longer the siege, the better the payout."

Amir shrugged, "And?"

"Food, water, wine—that all starts becoming more valuable than gold. So the Ivory Queen is going to be guarding her stores like they're treasure."

"And?"

Antonius leaned against the bulwark, "And not guarding her actual treasure."

"Wait..."

Rooster pointed to the proverbial city, "They say the Ivory Queen has a vault carved purely from pearls and sapphires. I imagine those are rumors spun up by morons who call themselves poets. But the truth has to be somewhere in the middle. She isn't the Queen of Pirates for nothing."

"You want to *rob* her?"

"No, Amir. *You* are going to rob her. What I'll be doing is using said riches for what comes after. You wanted help with the Serpents? This is what it looks like."

There was a long list of expletives in a language Rooster didn't understand. Amir aged decades in minutes, rubbing the bridge of his nose.

"And they called Azim mad."

"Who knows? Maybe a bit of it rubbed off on me."

The boy looked him down suspiciously, "Even if we do pull off this heist, the Boy King will find out you were behind this. Are you trying to become the most hated person in this corner of the world?"

Rooster whistled.

Ahffan and Rhuïma appeared looking rather mischievous. Onto a small horsehide, they dumped a series of articles. Personal effects that had once belonged to the Fangs of the Scorched Serpents; badges, sashes, even vials of their wretched poisons that gave off the metallic scent. How they were obtained was hidden away behind the evil grins both the skinwalkers bore.

Truly, there were no heroes when it came to war. Everyone was a villain with their own misbegotten sense of justice.

"Feel like eating crow yet?"

Amir picked up a Coiler badge, "They'll deny it."

"To who? Without Tariq, they're a faceless cartel. They don't exactly have emissaries."

"I must admit Rooster. I didn't think you capable of this kind of guile."

"Don't kiss me yet. We still have to pull this off."

The compliment of troops had boarded the second craft and were making it their new home. Last to hop on were Rhuïma and Ahffan who almost had to be dragged aboard. The Shemsari still weren't keen on traveling on water.

From the hills rode in Jhamon, Big Mug, and Lancer to collect the horses.

There was one more detail before the send-off.

In a few moments, Rooster had his chieftain robes and armor in a neat pile. Big Mug was roughly his height and weight. Maybe slightly on the heavier side. From afar he'd look the part.

They began to trade their garb and kit. The final piece—and with great hesitation—Rooster handed over the bastard sword.

Big Mug belted it to his side and gestured, spinning around a full circle, "Eh? How do I look?"

"Make sure they paint your face good. Do I lean that hard on my left knee?"

"No offense captain, but you're starting to hobble."

Rooster looked at Awakener, reminded of the last time he was parted from it.

"Don't take any risks. The moment you get the whiff of a chase you pull out. You're not there to fight."

Big Mug beamed, throwing on the chieftain hood, "Keep your pants on. We got a campfire scheme we're going to pull on them. Good luck captain."

"J'awed guide you," the phrase came out so naturally Rooster didn't realize he'd uttered it.

He really had gone native.

In five days and four nights, they reached the mangroves that bordered the sea. On the pink glow of dusk, beheld the jeweled pearl of the west; Tyhri, the coastal throne to the Ivory Queen. Her walls that stretched onto land and sea made Nefara's look like ramparts of sand. Even on the eve of battle, hundreds of white triangles of ships from afar were wandering into her bosom.

Even the apocalyptic army of the Caliph would find victory against her pyrrhic.

It was a calm evening as the pastels of pink and blue faded away.

The boats peeled off into the spiderwebs of roots where the river met the sea, tucking themselves into the foliage. They lit no torches or lamps.

Skulk and Sable hopped along the gangway from the pilot barge to the second, making sure everything was ready. Funny creatures they were; Sabean twins with wide conical hats who had an affection for little black birds in cages they kept onboard.

"They're spies," Rooster noted as they walked past, "Hey. Who are you sending those little scrolls to?"

The smugglers smirked and kept walking.

"They don't speak Medean," Amir offered.

"No? Well, they clearly understand it."

Something splashed nearby, a tropical bird flashed as it escaped perhaps the teeth of something. Gentle lapping of waves rocked the barges and all that could be heard of

Tyrhi were the bells that tolled the closing of the gates.

Rooster wondered what their thoughts were, seeing the vastness of the Caliph's army.

Whether this entire conflict was one giant quagmire. A political disaster inspired by information that no one quite could prove. If the Ivory Queen intended to rekindle the flame of rebellion by slaying the White Dove, she would have done so in a position of strength. By all accounts, she was nothing but a shrewd and calculated leader. She would have known the Caliphate would rise like a cobra from a basket and strike viciously—that they could levee such a force.

The story of this war was missing the heart of it; the why.

"I'm going below," he warned Amir and proceeded down the hatch.

The total darkness of the hold allowed for a small lamp. In the dim light their prisoner was waiting with a not-so happy expression.

"Hello Tariq. How are you faring?"

The bureaucrat sniffed, "I don't suppose you brought food."

"We can scrounge up something."

There was no need for chains or ropes. Truthfully this was a rescue more than a hostage. Besides the fact there was nowhere for Tariq to go if he did want to try to run.

"Why the long face? You didn't have to pay me a single leopard to drag you out of there."

"The cost for this little stunt will come at a price far greater than gold my friend, I assure you."

Amir came down and took a seat, saying nothing.

"Got nothing but time to kill. Why don't you fill us in on why you're so upset about us keeping you alive?"

Tariq looked out the little gap in the planks, "Your sneaky friend here knows why. The Serpents will tear the city apart for his gang. Brick by brick."

"Rest assured, they'll never find us," the thief said.

"Ah. So you say. Nevertheless, the devastation will be

chilling."

"Help us end it then. Put a dagger in the belly of the snake."

"If only it were that easy," Tariq craned his neck, fixated on Amir, "I've been sworn to silence. Bound by oaths older than this world. The Serpents are devils. I was forced into a contract when they took me."

"What kind of oath?" Amir was on the edge of his seat.

"One only the gods can break."

Intuition told Rooster that this was no small detail to blink away.

The posture of the thief confirmed that.

"Gods-oaths are no small things. If this is true then you could not help us defeat the Serpents under any level of duress. Even death."

"I had no choice. I was locked in a room without food or water for days. I was drugged and poisoned, promised an antidote only when I would capitulate," Tariq almost whispered.

"What are the terms of your oath?"

"Anything I say or do that would betray the Serpents and I choke on my tongue."

That was convenient.

Amir kicked over a nearby bucket. The kid had this figured wrong. Traded the lives of friends for what must have felt a waste.

"My apologies for being so useless."

Rooster chimed in, "Not useless. You're being here must be crippling. Now there's only one of you to pretend to govern."

Tariq twitched, eyes darting sideways, "What?"

"They've got you cloned. You didn't know? Another Tariq is wandering around."

"Until very recently I was drugged on the lotus and propped up like a doll in the Vizier's palace. Figured out how to trick them into thinking they were double-dosing me when the lotus wore off. Had I not learned how to do that, my mind would have long melted away. I wouldn't put it past them to find out how to create an illusion of me to further their plans."

The thief boy looked incredibly vexed, "If this is the case, we can't afford to wait any longer."

"Your band of thieves may be cleverly hidden but the Serpents are more nefarious than either of you realize. They wanted the Boy King to come."

"Why?"

Hand-wringing, hard swallowing. The bureaucrat suddenly got tongue-twisted and began to cough violently. Quite literally strangling himself—the oath wasn't metaphorical at all.

Tariq recovered after the violent fit, shaking, "I can't say it if I wanted. But yes my furtive friend. The hour grows near. And when it does arrive, not even his newfound god can save you. Any of you. A blight of shadow and death will fall upon this land like a pestilence of locusts for a thousand years..."

A premonition too far, Tariq could not finish the sentence. He clawed at his throat and gasped for air, choking on the oath.

One by one, lights blossomed in the darkness. Hundreds, then thousands. Fiery twinkling dots that quintupled every breath across the bleak void of sand. That suddenly lifted to the sky in a hailstorm of fire. Followed by burning comets that scorched across the night, racing towards the walls of Tyhri.

An invisible force held its breath, bracing.

The volley exploded across the roofs and battlements, sending showers of sparks and flame to the city below. Blackened marks on battlements already appeared. A secondary salvo was otherworldly in color, creating white-hot shapes of phoenixes that glided and ensorcelled Tyrhi's finest with a hellish flechette of fiery barbs. Which were dispelled by gusts of ethereal wind—the war-casters of the Ivory Queen had been ready.

The Boy King unleashed his fury—again and again.

It was a hell of a fireworks show.

Dong-gong-dong-gong. Bells raised hell all over Tyrhi. There would be no sleep on this night.

The siege had begun.

Skulk and Sable may as well have been raccoons in the henhouse. They deftly stole the barges right up to the walls and into the bay of the city between roaming patrols crossing the catwalks above, sidling up to the jetties that fed right into the heart of pale stone. Inside the safety of the harbor, no one would have ever suspected them as imposters.

Just another group of barges.

A leopard shot from the boats and disappeared into one of the alleyways. As always, the beastly form of Rhuïma was ominously absent.

"From here we're on our own," Amir had taken the guise of a nobleman of azure robes, "If we're not back by dawn, leave us."

Rooster regarded his troops.

All in the black of the Serpents, they looked like Azim's wayward bandit cousins. Like death on legs. But behind those veils, he could see they were unsure.

Their morale could not have been high.

That was his fault.

"You two. Smugglers. The guy we have stuck down below? Watch him like you would your own sister. Don't let him off the boat."

Skulk or Sable—he couldn't tell them apart—cackled and dipped the conical hat.

"What's this," Amir's voice was gruff and alien.

"What kind of commander would I be, sending you all into the lion's den like this?"

Antonius shook his head and tried to stop him.

Rooster would have none of it.

It took moments to doff the assassin getup.

"It was my harebrained plan," Antonius hissed, "Not yours."

"Good. Then it's your fault if we all die."

A rope ladder was thrown down and the troops began to file off. Sacks over their shoulders, daggers stuffed into their sashes, dressed like the night. Something right out of those books about noble thieves that tiptoed the edge of sandy rooftops, plundering the gluttonous palace princes.

Except there was nothing noble about this.

The din of the siege rattled the loose stones into the water, repeating ghastly echoes across the restless city. Women cried for their men who wouldn't return home. Glow from fires started by the constant bombardment from siege engines.

The first patrol didn't even see them coming.

If the night kept up like this they'd be rich without a scratch.

Just as Rooster was thinking about that, he made a corner and came nose-to-nose with a steel-faced henchman. One of the infamous Immortals. Who raised his bladed spear and drove it right at Rooster's heart.

He was saved by throwing himself at the wall, rewarded with his knee erupting in pain.

Shouting up ahead.

Rooster cursed.

A whole squad of Immortals rushed in from the alleyway, drawing their swords. Sealing off any hope for escape.

Rooster leaned against a wall to catch his breath. Checked for blood. Surveyed their troops.

Twelve of what had been twenty. Some had retreated to the ships to nurse their wounds. Two Ophi and four thieves were left on the cobblestones.

The Immortals were lions among men.

If it hadn't been for Amir catching them off-guard…it was too dire to consider the consequence.

In an alcove below a defaced marble conqueror, they recuperated before pushing ahead. This was not the Ivory Queen's work. She was merely the most recent of the occupations.

Through tunnels unmanned and across squares abandoned. With the aid of the disguised Amir, those guards they did come across were too busy aiding a frail nobleman to look over their shoulders to the blades that passed between their ribs.

They crossed the last threshold before the storied palace.

And it wasn't all fiction—the tales from the poets.

Walls of turquoise and flame-tinted sea glass made a warped tunnel diving down a wide spiral staircase. Leading to a door at its feet that appeared as a golden seashell broken in half, studded with gems of all shades.

The troops whistled all.

Amir worked his magic on the golden doors. With time and elbow grease they gave inward, and they yielded. Their target; an octagonal room, pillared at every corner of the same sea-glass. The Opaline Vault. In the flesh.

Some of the men fell on their knees and wept.

Glittering, tantalizing, and beckoning to them—a hoard of a thousand pirate captains. Who all had been subdued by the cousin of the Caliph, a Medean noblewoman who called herself the Ivory Queen. The vault of Tyrhi was everything and more than any fable could have hoped to sing of. A dragon would have eaten its children at the chance to sit on this hoard.

"Bitch was holding out on us," Carver laughed manically, scooping a handful of coins, letting them fall to the floor.

"Good work Antonius," Rooster slapped his back.

But the Teridian was too dumbfounded to say anything, just giving a sheepish grin.

Not with a hundred men and double the sacks could they hope to cart away the treasure in this room.

Amir walked up and plucked a bronze lamp in the shape of a woman's body, stretched and ending with a siren's head, "We shouldn't linger. Places like these always have traps."

"You heard the man. Move it all of you. Double time."

Gold, jewels, scrolls, whatever looked valuable were stuffed into sacks. Took serious willpower for even Rooster to busy himself with merely fist-sized rubies and priceless trinkets.

Poor Ivory Queen.

This oversight in security was going to cost her.

In five minutes they were sewn up with treasure. Enough that it would be a bitch to haul it out.

"Whoreson," he cursed himself, knowing he overlooked this detail.

If no one saw them dragging this hoard to the ships, it would be a miracle from Bahram.

At a decent pace, this would take them all night.

The thief boy snatched a few more things off pedestals, turning, "Time to leave."

Articles of the Serpents were carefully strewn about. Made to look like they'd fallen out of careless pockets. They'd be easily discovered.

A few of the troops dug their heels in. They wouldn't see anything like this again in their lifetimes. It took a few threats of throat-cutting to make them see reason.

Just then a sandal stepped on the wrong tile. Acid started to flood the chamber from the depressed piece of stone. The thief responsible yelped as his flesh sizzled. It ate flesh and didn't touch gold.

A healthy sense of fear overrode greed.

Like bandits, they stole out in style.

Fattened rats fleeing a burning ship, the three boats slunk away from the travails of the besieged city.

When the coast was clear dozens of heads popped up and everyone gathered on both decks. Getting one last look at the carnage before they'd have to grab an oar and make upriver. It would be a long sail to Nefara, moving upstream.

The morning air was ripe with victory.

Rooster didn't feel like gloating. Leaning against the bulwark of the enclosed aft, watching Tyhri's failing attempts to hold back the overwhelming firepower of troops.

Catapults had not ceased their volleys in more than twelve hours.

The Boy King had an endless supply of hate to fling at his enemy.

"Congratulations should be in order," Tariq had ascended from the hold, looking rather weary, "A toast to the victorious thieves."

Rooster grunted.

"You're as rich as I ever was. You're not happy? Pray, tell me why."

"Him."

Amir, the thief boy and Prince of Many Faces, was sitting on the point of the stern. Letting his sandalled feet drag in the water. Not a word was spoken since the vault.

"I never count my eggs before the day is through. Do you think he is? Capturing you cost him dearly."

"He's not a hen and neither are you. Do you fear what awaits you in Nefara?"

Rooster didn't fear the threats they faced but the losses that would come with it. War had already taken his family, his namesake, and home. The thought of losing it all over again was gutwrenching.

Part of it willed him to take the treasure and find a nice island somewhere.

But that wasn't J'awed.

"I'm father to two families now. I fear for my flock."

Tariq took a seat, "Suppose I've been an orphan too long to recall the feeling."

"Don't you feel responsible for the people of the city? For Nefara?"

"Truthfully—and I do mean it with my whole heart—no. My life is a paradox. If I am capable of improving the lives of those of a city that predates our very language in my brief reign? Then that is good. If the serfs and slaves go on with their existence without any loss or gain, then that is fine too. I am what I am, Rooster. I live under no pretense that I am a benevolent servant. By my hand, Nefara functions well and will continue to flourish despite its antiquity—despite its want to return to its misbegotten ascendancy."

Rooster accepted it. What else could he do? He had no ideology outside primitive tribalism. In his years nothing supported the notion that utopia could exist nor did those who claimed to represent the benevolent spirit that created one.

Behind on the deck, the men were ruckus. They wore crowns atop their heads and waved jeweled scepters, dictating to the croaking frogs that watched them from ashore. Dancing and tossing gold coins without care if any fell off the gunwales. They were overcome with that giddy laugh that lingered at the top of one's throat from sheer excitement after narrowly escaping danger.

"How simple their lives are; the unlearned. It's an enviable existence—never worrying about the invisible, the words on a page," Tariq muttered.

"You have your free will. You could join us. Abandon the games of politics. Live by the saddle."

"If only you knew Rooster, why my path is set before me."

"Do you know that a sheep trained to obey a fence will continue to stay inside its boundaries—even if the fence is removed?"

The bureaucrat touched his eyepatch by habit, "Pleasant as your notion is, I would be doing a great disservice to myself. My great life's work is in Nefara."

"Have you given it any thought? How we can aid you?"

A contemplative nod, "Yes. Unfortunately, I am stumped."

It was a frustrating conundrum.

Rooster thought long and hard, "Even in a roundabout way, you can't divulge critical details."

"Afraid not. Lest I wish the grave."

Hazair appeared, gliding parallel to the boat. Ever the prudent watcher and follower. The bird was like his third eye. A silent servant.

Which struck him with an inspiring thought.

"Wait. Nazsif. Your servant. That's it, damn it! Did he take the oath?"

Tariq frowned, "Not that I'm aware of..."

"And does he know these incriminating and sensitive details of the Serpents? Could he speak where you could not?"

The bureaucrat's dark eyes brightened, "Aha. Clever. I didn't think about that at all."

Neither had the Serpents, in their infinite wisdom.

Troublesome to the powerful were the little people, the candle-lighters, and the rat-catchers. They were the ones who saw and heard everything. They were greater informants than even the most cunning spies.

The downfall of every empire was always hubris.

Hazair cried across the waking river, peeling off to chase something dark that raced over the dunes. The bird came back with another, leading to a skinwalker eagle-talker who whispered something intriguing in Rooster's ear. One that had flown all the way down from the Wall.

"What is it," Tariq cocked his head.

A development that didn't directly involve present company, he decided to keep a lid on it.

الأوبيليسك حصن
Hemopolis

Preparation took a mental toll—Rooster found himself in need of moments of thoughtless riding or walking. It was far too hot to push Nereel out into the sands during the day, so he ventured into the city where he could be alone with his thoughts. There was never traffic in the Maze besides the vagrants who lingered on its exterior.

Of course, there were hordes of urban filth everywhere in Nefara now.

None of the lotus-eaters bothered him. He was draped in their same fineries to pass into the city. They were harmless, besides the mindless dronings and ramblings.

Rooster felt pity when he saw one, stroking the corpse of a dog that had begun to rot. He tossed a handful of silver crescents into the pot and turned away. Feeling disgusted.

Cities were rife with downtrodden by nature—but this existence was becoming too bleak to stomach.

Something *had* to be done.

There was talk in the Sword Row that bodies were beginning to pile up. Casualties of the drug were stacking. Flies and disease were beginning to spread, which only fueled the fire of the cultists who took them as portents to whatever spiritual uprising was taking place.

Summer and its heat had only just begun. These problems would only compound when it was too hot for bodies to be carted out. More would pile up. The squares would become open-air mass graves. A siege would be more humane than what would start to happen inside these walls.

He thought about leaving and nearly kicked over another vagrant slumped against the sandstone. The bundle of rags wheezed, grabbing at his ankles.

"Sorry," he grunted in earnest, trying to walk away.

But the grip was like iron, refusing to release.

A hoarse prattling that was long and drawn out, "*You*."

Rooster flipped a coin but the vagrant didn't budge, "Let me pass friend."

"I know you. *Gharib*," the last word enunciated in recognition.

The turban was faded. The eyepatch was missing, leaving an empty socket. Skin gaunt where flesh receded into the skull. But there was no mistaking the hillman's sharp gaze.

It was Darwish. And very much alive.

"This is fortuitous news," Tariq glanced up from his papers at the disturbance of the door opening. The man had insisted on continuing his work as secretary to the Vizier, even in captivity.

The candlebra in his hand teetered and Tariq cursed as wax dripped onto one of the scrolls.

Light was scarced in the Sunken Reliquary but it was the only suitable hiding place. The location made Tariq veritably untouchable—only the Dead Hand knew its depths and location, according to Amir.

Rooster agreed, but that didn't make him any happier, "You lied to me."

A shake of the head, "My servants are not surgeons nor priests. How would you expect them to know any better? He had all the appearances of the dead."

Had he been discovered perhaps even a few weeks from now, there was a chance Darwish would have been. The man was barely skin and bones. It was a miracle he'd survived.

"How is he?"

Rooster sat on the stone bench, "On the mend. I think. Carver thinks he's half braindead. This lotus stuff isn't like anything he's seen. It will be a godsend if he regains half his intelligence."

Tariq grunted as he returned to his work, "Indeed. If there's anything I can do..."

"You could. Where the hell is your servant? It's been five days."

"My guess is as good as yours Rooster. Without my usual channels," the man indicated to the stony surroundings, "It's a matter of time before he shows up."

"*If* he shows up. If the Serpents didn't wisen up after our little heist."

"Paranoia doesn't suit you, my friend. Be patient. Nazsif is a prudent creature. His talent at evasion is as adept as your young friend's there," Tariq paused to jerk his head over at the thieves in the inner chamber.

"He better."

Rooster stepped over bedrolls scattered around the mausoleum. Some were occupied. Few thieves here were above the age of twenty. There was too little work that was too dangerous for them in the city. Now that the Serpents knew how the Prince of Many Thieves operated in the city, the anonymity once bestowed on the faceless caste of servants had become a target.

According to the rumor mill, dozens of children were being thrown into the dungeon below the White Kasbah daily. Most were urchins without families to weep for them.

But the Dead Hand wasn't waiting around with idle hands.

On a long stone table once used for embalming, the thieves had a working spiderweb—a hit list. Illustrations of faces in charcoal atop a chalk map of the city, corresponding with where they were seen last. Coins were placed on their eyes if they were dead.

Amir consulted with a familiar face; the oud player from months ago. They held a quiet conference away from the table.

"What's with the old guy," Rooster asked no one in particular.

The teenager who answered whispered in awe, "Dario the Master?"

"Not a lot of other gray hairs in your ranks. What's his deal?"

Another teen chimed in, "Fool. He is father to us all."

"How?"

The first, "Without Dario the Master, there would be no Dead Hand."

"I thought Amir was your leader?"

"He is. By notoriety. But he was one of us once."

Like an advisor to a king, the oud player placed a gentle hand on the boy's shoulder before taking off into one of the dark archways. Into one of the seven tunnels in the circular Reliquary that led to who knew where—the mystery of the dead city.

Amir strolled over with a vacant expression, clearing his throat, "Rooster."

"Something I should be aware of?"

"A personal matter. Dario is in many ways like a father to me. I heard you recovered a friend from the Maze."

"Whether he recovers remains to be seen," Rooster bit down and swallowed his regret.

"For both of our sake, I hope he does. What of Tariq's servant?"

"Still missing in action. The skinwalkers are on the prowl and have seen nothing."

"This worries me."

"It should. Every moment we spend wasted here is one the enemy plots against us."

Amir nodded back to the table, "We've had a windfall which should buy us time. Those cults in the city? They're starting to cause problems."

"Eh?"

"The disappearance of the Vizier has caused a religious outcry. It's one of their signs of an apocalypse."

"Wait, what?"

"I only received news of it myself this morning."

There could be no coincidence. News had started to leak out about the siege, reported by traders who'd escaped the Boy King's outriders.

The issue wasn't that the Vizier was missing—the man was a poof, an imbecile, and a very obvious figurehead. It was the meaning of his disappearance. What was the point?

"What about our second Tariq? Have you seen him?"

"Locked away in the palace. Using the riots of the cults as justification to seal it away."

"What's the Medean policy for interregnum? If the Vizier is gone too long?"

Amir thought, "The secretary until a replacement can be found or a military coup is declared."

Which was nice and convenient, except the doppelganger Tariq already had those powers as the hidden governor. Unless the purpose was to forestall a military occupation electing Fadin al Hakim, who was garrisoned at Al Khandaq Keep at this very moment.

Rooster explained the thought process.

"They're hastening their plans, whatever they are. The Serpents can't afford to wait for the Boy King to return," Amir realized quickly.

"Precisely my thought. When will they end the recess in the courts?"

"Tomorrow morning after the call to prayer."

"Tonight then."

Amir stared off towards the edifices of old before nodding, albeit hesitantly, "Tonight. We need that servant."

The truth was they weren't ready. Too many critical personell in the ranks of the Serpents had yet to be identified. Only one potential location for their operation had been discovered.

But the timetables had shifted in their favor.

Later as Rooster was doffing the shepherd's robes and adjusting the sash, there was a cry of elation from the center of the Reliquary. Tariq was holding up a scroll as if it were a lost treasure.

"What is it?"

"Nazsif! I must have overlooked it the first time in my correspondence. See the encryption in this harvest report? It's spelled out here; the first two letters staggered on the third sentence from the last."

"*AT.SC.OR.PI.ON.PI.TH?*" Amir scratched his head.

Rooster was already moving to the archway, "Blindfold me. Get me the boatman. I know where he is."

In times of both feast and famine, taverns were always occupied. An empty one indicated a ghost town or more pressing matters were keeping its patrons away from drinking. And right now The Scorpion Pit had a bored, vile air about it. Which drove the guards and decent folk away.

Nazsif had hidden himself well in that ideal and dirty nook, just another vagabond riding out the storm.

The servant happily spilled his guts on everything he knew.

Every piece of intelligence was ripe and warm.

Not one moment after his lips sealed Rooster was already on the move to act on them.

Back in the Reliquary the air was electrified with anticipation. Knives were being shoved into sheaths. Cowls thrown over shoulders. Candles and offerings made to those pagan desert gods while praises to Bahram filled the hallowed ground.

The night was young and promised much.

Two hundred of them stuffed between the cold walls, crowded around that long stone table. Armed to the teeth. Coiled like springs, ready at a moment's notice.

Only once in his life had Rooster been here before.

It was the night before a pitched battle. He'd never been so terrified, so alive.

A prophetic silence ushered—Amir had entered, the bronze face masking his own. Walked down the aisle to the edge of that stone table that had once prepared priest-kings for their eternal burial.

"Everything ready?"

"I was waiting for Dario. Must be on his way back still from the drinking halls," Amir looked calm but his hand slightly shook.

"Nervous?"

"I'll manage. Go on."

All eyes were on them. It was time they unbagged this cat.

With a silent prayer of gratitude to Nazsif, he shuffled forward.

"Good evening gentlemen. As I'm sure you're aware, the gangsters known as the Scorched Serpents have made it abundantly clear they are in charge of Nefara. All trade and communication have been supplanted with their spies, public office as well as the city guard. That said, what you may not be aware of is the fact that they are in the middle of contaminating the wells that the city relies upon for clean water. In other words; poisoning it."

Shock rippled over the faces of those gathered.

"It is my and my cohort Amir's belief here that the Serpents are poisoning the water for the sole purpose of controlling the inhabitants of both Nefara and Tyhri downriver at best and to eradicate some level of humanity. For nefarious reasons that have yet to be determined. Needless to say, the eyewitness who has seen the foundry of this poison—a subterranean laboratory located in the old Hemopolis—indicated they are nearly complete with this project, as they round up competitors and rivals they deem as a threat. In other words, everyone in this room."

Skulk and Sable both grunted, leaning over the table.

"We have pinpointed the location of this alchemical foundry, along with key warehouses where those known as Coilers distribute their cerulean lotus. Without these hubs of operation, the Serpents will be cornered and likely to lash out in retaliation. We have measures prepared for such a contingency. Are there any questions?"

No takers. The room was still chewing on the information. Perhaps boiling over in silence.

Amir lifted his head, "Our patience for this cartel is at its end. They invited themselves to our home and tried to push us out with the tools of cowards and liars. No patch of sand in this city will be safe for their kind. We will punish them bitterly for every life of our friends they have taken and tenfold for the misery they've wrought on the helpless.

Tonight will be one of their reckoning."

At that, there were several hear-hears.

"This enemy is not made of giants. They're not master swordsmen or good in the saddle. They operate in the shadows because in the light they're nothing. Remember that. Keep sharp and swing hard. If you can take on this enemy at a distance, do it. Water the sand with their blood. Kill and kill and don't stop until they're dead."

A war-like cheer repeated the phrase.

Gravitating from the outskirts of the crowd was the hovering face of Tariq, deep in thought. Animated as they were, though reluctant to say anything that could incur the curse.

His nods were affirmation enough.

Rooster reined them all back in, "As it stands currently, we hold the element of surprise. The Serpents won't know what's coming. A diversion will take place sometime in the next few hours—that will be your signal. Talons, you have your instructions and orders that you will disperse to your squad. Each Talon will be assigned an eagle-talker as your line of communication with myself and Amir. If anything happens, you tell your skinwalker and they'll get the word out. We anticipate the Serpents will counterattack. A reserve squad will be on standby to repel said attack wherever it pops up."

Rhuima and Scorchhide locked gazes with each other. Their sneers suggested an animosity that Rooster had not picked up on yet. The skinwalkers were all a little funny in the head anyway.

"You'll have ten minutes to get your shit in order. After that, listen to your Talon, they know what to do."

It was redundant. The whole room was jittery and ready to go.

Antonius stepped forward and rapped his shield with his fist, "The Birds of Prey are with you Rooster. Whatever enemy. Whether they stand in rank or hide in the shadows. If you march we will follow you until our flesh is eaten by the sun and we are but bones."

Shields were beaten, spears rammed into stone and a raucous shout filled that crammed room. The morale would have seduced the dead to rise and join in their frenzy.

Rooster looked at them, prouder than he could remember for a very long time.

"You are our river chieftain," Jhamon added, "We are all richer for it."

It was all very fine speech. But words meant little while the enemy gathered in strength, readying to get them dead with bated breath.

In very Northern fashion, Rooster put his fingers in his lips and let out a high whistle, "That's your warning. We depart in ten. Let's stomp out these assholes."

Flapping in the dark overhead. Hazair ignored the normal nocturnal behavior of his kind and kept close.

Rooster didn't mind the extra company.

He stepped off the boat onto the ledge, grabbing onto the grate. The entry from the canals to the layers of the city under the sand was guarded now by Yhuuf and Big Mug. Blades dark and wet. The previous sentries were floating facedown in the water.

According to the servant, this was the main artery that fed into the Hemopolis. Three squads led by Antonius, Amir, and himself would venture in. The goal here was to capture Black Nizzar and a half dozen key officers in the gangster's ranks, level the foundry to the studs, and scour whatever intelligence they could on the rest of the Serpent's operations. Once they'd made contact, Ahffan would get word to signal the other squads to commence their operations.

No ambience beyond, just the lapping of water against ancient stone.

Ahffan pitched forward, eyes rolling to the back of his head. The skinwalker would be woken up only in the most pressing need.

The group at the tunnel waited for his command.

Air bristled and then a bundle of feathers smacked

Rooster right in the mouth. The damn eagle was doing passes on him, squawking. It was going batshit for no evident reason.

"Need a bag," Bonechewer offered, grinning with sharpened teeth, "I've got a bird bag for crunching."

"Give me a minute."

Antonius stepped in, "We've got this captain. We don't need you going facefirst anyway. Bring up the rear and maybe there'll be some killing left for you."

Subdued chuckling by all the men.

Rooster swallowed his pride, "Go on then."

They raised shields and shuffled into the tunnel, leaving him and Ahffan. Who grumbled and twitched in the skin-dream.

Wind whoosed. The eagle came down again, striking this time with his beak. Getting Rooster right beside his cheekbone, drawing blood. He nearly fell into the water.

What the hell was the bird on about?

Rooster tried to bat it away with the hilt of Awakener—talons dug into his shoulders, helmet, anything it could gain purchase.

"Gah. Quit it bastard," he hissed but there was nothing he could do.

Hazair grabbed onto the Blue Eye and pulled it right off his neck. The bird flew down onto the ledge and began to hop like a little person, cadence a mockery of a bigger one.

Rooster tore after it.

The eagle kept the blue diamond barely out of reach, leaping at the last second out of the tunnel and into the moonlight.

Rooster continued to follow it.

No way he could let it get away with this. He knew it was trying to bother him. Maybe it was going insane. A man's soul trapped in a bird's body for far too long did not bode well.

They were up in the market district at the edge of the wharf. Dead quiet up here at the top level. Besides the stupid eagle. It landed atop a canopy stretched over an alley.

He climbed, "Give it up."

Hazair twisted its neck and chirped in mockery.

Rooster lost his footing. Felt gravity push against him, flop him head over heels in a dogged tumble. Something hard smacked him in the temple—a wood beam.

Knocked him out cold.

Ice claws dug deep and yanked the man from blackness to another world.

A frigid dream that could not be banished awaited him. Pale ash and rubble amidst a dreary gray ruin. It was the same empty metropolis dream again—the endless maze of stone. The wind howled through gaping teeth for shattered walls, over stumps for pillars.

Why did this place yearn to be known? The man who dreamt did not recognize it as fiction—it was too vivid, too detailed. The uncanny microscoping spiderweb cracks in the decrepit stone beggared an explanation that he did not possess.

As before, he began to walk aimlessly down its corridors.

Nape began to prickle with that static tickle—the sense he was being followed.

The man stopped and twisted his head.

Dark grains of sand were swirling behind his heels, formless and moving against the wind's caress.

Strange; there hadn't been black sand before.

He pressed on. Trying to remember how he arrived here.

Shivering as there was no warmth in this nightmare. The flesh felt waxy and rigid. The man feared he would perish if he ceased his walking.

He turned a corner blindly.

At the end of the corridor was an archway that pooled oblivion under its keystone. Warping light and color within a strange oblong fire. The man moved towards its mesmerizing pull.

Wind intensified, hissing as it stole into the long walk.

A voice was being carried through the wind, speaking softly, rapidly. In a harsh and alien tongue, the man didn't understand.

Black sand was gathering. Forming a column that split into a walking man-sized mass of glittering soot. A bipedal form emerged. A ghost wearing the skin of sand.

Dozens of voices began to add and compound to the first. They were chanting in unison, that same language.

Gales were tearing at the man's flesh. Rendering the sky an abyss of night.

The black sandman lurched, grasping at something—towards the dreaming man's chest.

His heart began to pound, threatening to break from his ribs. Breath ripped from his lungs. His feet became glued to the pavement. Pure terror stabbed his gut.

And then the dreaming man saw it.

Behind the sandman trailed a wisp of darkness that tethered it to the heavens. Boiling clouds of ash where something monstrous lurked in silhouette. Devouring what appeared to be sunlight.

Amid doom, the dreaming man noticed the single orange orb where the sand man's eye should have been. Back in the mortal world, little details like these were irrepressible.

The sandman halted.

Blue light suddenly burned through the heavens and seared the gray murk. Banishing the sinister shape in the clouds. As the tether was severed, the black grain of sand swirled, tumbled, and shed into piles that seeped through cracks in the stone. The sandman flailed before disappating into oblivion.

The nightmare was over.

For now.

Golden eyes hovered inches away from Rooster's waking ones.

He felt the cold weight of the Blue Eye in his palm.

Hazair squawked softly, nudging him with its beak.

"Apology not accepted," he groaned, feeling something strained in his lower back. It would take a good week to recover from a fall like that.

Had he been dreaming? If he had, the contents were seeping through his fingertips like sand. Unable to grasp at what had all transpired in the dream as his mind had erased everything.

Except for a feeling of chill dread.

That had yet to desert him.

Rooster shivered and looked around. It was still night. Dead quiet even for Nefara. This city had changed since his first arrival. Never used to be this inanimate, even when the sun had fallen.

"Where are we?"

The eagle took to the sky and began to guide. Patiently circling while he rose and got his bearings.

Not a few moments of walking through the empty market stalls when something began to shake the ground—another earthquake. Rooster grabbed onto the nearest sandstone pillar. But the quake abruptly ended, leaving susurrations.

A glow like the moon was rising, blocked by buildings.

He knew something was deeply wrong.

Earthquakes usually lasted much longer.

When he finally found a staircase and a balcony overlooking the city from a high vantage, the clarity punched him in the gut.

A sinister plume of green smoke cast by a raging yellow flame curled its way into the night sky, an unnatural hue that cast a ghastly glow. The plume twisted and coiled, visible from every corner of Nefara, a signal to all who had ears to hear and eyes to see that something terrible—and deliberate—had occurred. The fire alarms should have been screaming by now, the guards at least rushing to see what the disturbance was.

Nothing.

Flames continued to wreathe the dome of the sealed

Hemopolis and not a soul tried to douse it.

At first, no one came out. The lapping of the canal water grew odious as the moments stretched. Then a shadow cast against the tunnel wall; a monkey, staunching blood from a stump where its arm had been. It hobbled sadly onto the barge, whimpering. Behind it came injured men, many leaning against each other. Far too few had returned.

Rooster knew something was deeply wrong.

The leopard came out, dragging Amir by the scruff of his cloak. The boy looked bad. Blood oozing from gashes everywhere. Alive or dead, it was impossible to tell.

Bonechewer dragged the last litter before heading back in.

The next that came were bodies. Quail and Songbird of the Ophi. A few of the Faari who he didn't know their names. Many thieves were far too young to be gazing into the abyss.

And then lastly, Antonius. Burn marks had scourged the young casanova's once-chiseled face, melting his armor and flesh. He looked peaceful on his shield. Never again to march or sing or laugh.

Rooster closed his eyes and felt his knees threaten to buckle.

The carnage was too much to bear.

He loathed himself.

The only thing that kept him from breaking down was the hate that began to bubble up from within. A seething darkness that heated his blood with every moment of realization.

His troops hadn't failed him.

They'd been betrayed.

Ancient doors nearly broke off their hinges as Rooster kicked them in as he stormed into the Reliquary. The lone figure bent over the table glanced up, very much shocked at his arrival. Single eye bulging out of its socket.

"Tariq. You look surprised to see me," he said blithely,

crossing the threshold with speed.

The bureaucrat stumbled back against a wall, babbling, "Rooster. I did not...I did not think you'd be back before dawn..."

On the floor of the mausoleum, Rooster noticed there were thieves strewn about. Writhing in agonized sleep, muttering as they convulsed. Under some kind of spell.

"Did you poison them too?"

"Did I...?"

Tariq croaked as Rooster rushed him, seized the smaller man's throat, and began to squeeze. Hard. The Qadi began to choke, fingers clawed desperately.

"What's wrong Qadi? Choking on your words?"

Tariq was going purple.

Rooster didn't care. All that raced in his head was the sweet vision of strangling this vile little worm. Squeezing the politician's throat until his eye popped out. Tariq started to weaken, arms going limp.

"Die. You. Fucking. Bastard," forearm shook.

And Tariq would have.

From the threshold came cries, "Stop! Wait! He needs to live!"

It took all of Rooster's willpower to release his grip. Tariq collapsed under a fit of hacking.

Amir hobbled in, aided by a skeleton of a man. The creepy-looking boatman, Petiri.

"Give me one good reason. One."

Petiri approached the stone table and placed a little wooden box atop with a grimace, "This might. A gift from the Serpents. It arrived just after you returned."

A simple little thing, carved from palm wood and perhaps meant for collecting loose coins. It might have fit on an old mantelpiece save the rooster's head that was nailed to the lid. He creaked it open. Inside was another grisly trophy. An old man's right hand. Clutched in its waxy grip was the handle of an oud.

Amir quaked.

A message came from one of the eagle-talkers. That same one who Rooster assigned to keep close tabs on the development near the Wall, which had now moved southward. Nearing the Fists of the Shemsari. He poked around, asked questions about it, nobody else knew what was going on up there.

That development had a message for him; it demanded a face-to-face meeting. A gigantic risk with the potential to be an even greater reward.

Pretending like he was going off to visit his clan, Rooster found himself on Nereel and stole into the dunes on his private crusade. With Ahffan as his only guide. They rode into the night and day like madmen.

They returned with a third, who slipped into their ranks without any notice. Their alibi was that they'd been a wild antelope hunt.

No one was the wiser.

The air hung heavy with the weight of ages, dry as old bones yet thick with the scent of ancient dust. Pale shafts of light slanted through the cracked skylight above, catching the haze in the air like a ghost's breath. Beyond the tarnished brass door, its surface green with age but still firm in its frame, the corridor stretched in solemn silence.

A rough-cut of a pirate who went by Zaref stood guard, alongside six other cutthroats. Hands on the hilts of their swords tucked in silk belts, eyes tracking every movement.

It was understandable why Amir wanted the Floodplains Raiders to hold down the fort. The pretense of safety had all but vanished—even in Nemset. But all it accomplished was adding unnecessary tension to an already edgy climate.

Rooster dusted off the orange that clung to his robes.

Footsteps scraped against the stone in the room beyond, and low voices murmured beyond the threshold. That and the soft rustle of insect legs somewhere in the buried mausoleum.

The conference ended with the door opening. Kizzuran

stepped out, fully kitted out as always. His eyes locked Rooster's. The pirate took a step forward, more ambush predator than man.

"The gharib who thinks he's a rider," the man chuckled low, "We meet again water-bird."

Rooster wasn't in the mood, "I'm not here for you."

"We have a score to settle still. You and I."

"Do we? Burning one of your ships wasn't enough? Shall I burn another one?"

The clasp to the sheath clicked, the slow rasp of steel, "You like fire gharib? I'll show you *fire*."

Interrupted as the bronze door opened and out came Amir. Who looked perturbed and not by the sight of a duel that was about to begin, "Rooster? It's time."

He walked to follow but not before patting Kizzuran on the pauldron, "My food is getting cold back there. Why don't you be a dear and use that sword to heat it for me."

Into the cold cell, he went, closing the door.

Amir turned, "Please don't antagonize him. Please. I can't afford to lose any more allies now."

"Keep your dog leashed and I'll consider playing nice."

"What's with the dust," he indicated at the sand Rooster was tracking in.

"Just a little light riding to calm the nerves."

Faint shafts of light illuminated the cramped cell. Across on a stone bench was Tariq. Rings clinking of the chains that bound him. Neck still ringed a deep and ghastly purple from the near-strangling.

"Traitor," Rooster said gruffly.

The man looked up, "I did warn you. I told you there'd be a price for kidnapping me."

Amir began, "Tell me, Qadi, does it give you comfort to know the chaos you've unleashed in the city? Even as Black Nizzar lies dead and the workshops of the Serpents destroyed in flames? All your friend's work in smoke?"

Their prisoner hung his head and said nothing.

"Speak now and speak plainly. Your intentions. What your gangster friends will do now? Perhaps your words can begin to mend the shattered pieces of trust between us," Amir's voice lowered, a subtle edge creeping into his tone, "Or perhaps not. Either way, you will answer for what you've done. The question is whether you will meet that moment with dignity. Or despair."

Tariq glanced up with a wry smile, "Why, have you come here to gloat, thief? Or should I call you the Prince of Many Faces?"

"Do not be coy with me, slime."

"Tell me Rooster. Have I not treated you fairly and equitably these last months?"

He had no words to retort.

The bureaucrat shrugged, "Here I am bound and helpless in your care. You wish me to yield the secrets of the Serpents? What guarantees do I have—what kind of deal will I receive?"

"One that might grant your miserable life," Rooster growled.

"Ah, in that case, I will seal my lips. Tell me, did you lose friends in the fires last night? Any that I would know?"

The sly, mocking look on Tariq's face was all too much.

Rooster saw red. He'd thrown a jab and crumpled the bureaucrat before he could think. Amir was grabbing his wrist, pulling him back.

Tariq howled in laughter, blood coating his teeth, "Don't stop. I'm game. Show me your *mercy*."

"We kill him and we lose everything."

"You lose your friend. I've already lost mine."

Amir snarled, stepped back, and became lost in the mire of his predicament.

Lying on the bench Tariq wheezed, "Did our gift find you well? Good. Then you see—both of you—we are reasonable people. Amir's father is perfectly healthy and alive. Except that one hand of course."

A knife flashed in the boy's palm and he stared death across the room. Now it was Rooster's turn to keep him at bay.

"This can all go swimmingly in your direction, so long

as you obey. No one *has* to die," Tariq said.

"The promise of a liar and a traitor."

"I'm afraid that's all you have to go on, isn't it?"

"Or we can burn your friends to the ground. Branch, trunk, and root. With nowhere in the city to hide."

The bureaucrat grinned, "Oh yes Prince. And you might even succeed. But Dario—his name is Dario, I believe—will be dismembered, flayed alive, and left to dry in the sun before then. Is that the cost you're willing to stomach?"

Amir faltered.

"Or shall we broker a deal?"

Rooster asked, "And what kind of deal would that be?"

"A pact of the gods. A binding one that cannot be easily revoked."

In the heat of the discussion, there was something that could not be unseen in the visage of Tariq. What had been hidden away, deep behind the mask of a courtly nobleman obsessed with finery and politicking. Underneath the persona presented to the outside world was an ugly and sinister being.

Someone fully capable of immense cruelty and plotting with little care for the casualties. Bordering an inhuman revulsion for social engagement. Like watching a caterpillar slip from its cocoon a gangly, spidery thing with no relation to its past iteration.

The longer Rooster looked, the more he realized that he did not know who Tariq was.

"No more deals. We trade you. That's it," he said at last.

They worked out the particulars of the hostage negotiation, which felt more like teeth-pulling than diplomacy. Tariq seemed disappointed realizing there was no torture in store for him, going dull as they ironed out the time and place for the exchange. Agreeing to the release of Dario and saving his skin like it was a chore.

Tariq only requested a small list in his imprisonment; a mirror, brought to him from his quarters, as well as his finery so he might keep up appearances. The man's narcissim had no bounds. They denied both.

What was the point of handing him over to the Serpents, now down to one leader and devoid of any way to manufacture their narcotics? The Hemopolis had been a pyhrric victory for them but a victory nonetheless. They had the Serpents on the back foot—reacting instead of plotting ahead.

Weakness would spare them. Inability to do what was necessary to destroy the cartel and their conspirator.

Amir could not let go.

The boy had not lost enough in life to make the harsh and necessary decisions.

Rooster ground his teeth and sucked in air and pretended not to be furious.

This was war. There was a reason wives and children weren't brought to the front lines.

Right as they were leaving, a shadow darkened Tariq's face as he chortled, "Do you want to know something, northerner? My greatest mistake? You. Such a worthless investment. All my faith and coin to turn you into my right-hand blackguard—wasted! Look at what you've been reduced to; an aging fool to a band of savages who ply a futile existence in the sand, divining prophecy from crude circles they carve with sticks in the sand. What a pity. You could have been so much more."

They slammed the bronze door shut and left him to rot.

For the time being.

Amir had something else to show him. A deeper level than the Reliquary yawned. Nemset's storied and endless subterranean foundations. Where the cobwebs were fossilized and darkness stained the walls. Whispers came from a stone door, flanked by guardians of bleak limestone.

Rooster had questions but the boy indicated reverence, pushing the stone aside.

Trembling shadows dodged candlelight. Antonius was lying on a smooth block of marble. Over his corpse stooped the creep boatman Petiri and a smaller dark-clad associate who had an equally unnerving aura. The room cloyed with an aromatic funk. It was far colder than it should have been.

Words that were being spoken from an elder age came to a halt.

"Where are we?"

"It doesn't matter. Norulo and Petiri must ask you something."

The pale-faced associate was first, "His last ember is fading. Your friend is at the threshold of the great beyond. If we are to spare him…it will come at a price."

"But he's already dead?"

Petiri's ancient, raspy voice croaked, "Not quite. Last night a veil between life and death was torn; a rogue god, a wrath of spirits, we do not know. This one fell from mortality into that tear at the very same moment. He walks it now, knowing neither the world of living or dead."

Candle flames blew sideways, threatened to dim.

Rooster was reminded of the feeling of the nightmare if only the dread.

The associate stared around at the shadows with trepidation, "Thief, you know as well as we that Nemset does not suffer our entrances or taboos. Either we intervene or allow the gods to take their pound of flesh."

Amir tugged on Rooster's sleeve, "You must act quickly."

"What does intervene mean? You can bring him back to life?"

"No," Petiri swiftly corrected, "Not rebirth. The Black Amenta—its shards—do not grant life. They only bind the soul to the body, a body that is no longer alive. What has been wrought here is beyond my understanding, but the will of whatever power created this tear is not to be trifled with."

"This is no mere necromancy," Norulo added.

Possibility gnawed like a feral beast.

Rooster was stunned. He'd already begun to grieve Antonius in his way. Now there was some third pathway? Impulse began to writhe its way into his jaded heart.

"I can't…."

A shadow leapt from the wall. An idol crashed as it was tipped over. Tools sent scattering everywhere.

"Now or never," Norulo clenched his teeth.

Reluctantly, the answer was given.

Rooster watched.

The boatman's face was a worn tapestry of age, his skin drawn tight around the hollowed pits of his eyes, his lips muttering incessant prayers that only the dead would understand. Allayed by something more than a mere fascination with the preservation of bodies. He and Norulo worked in perfect, quiet unison as they prepared Antonius for whatever came next.

Petiri lifted a melon-sized shroud and peeled it back. A seamless orb of black glass. Strangely it caught no reflection, nor shimmered at the candlelight. As if the thing was an aspect of darkness itself. Staring at it produced a humming in the back of Rooster's mind.

"Leave us. This next part is not fit for the living," the boatman warned.

The last thing that could be seen was the wrapping being removed and the orb placed directly on Antonius' chest. A bestial sound escaped from the lips of the corpse that did not belong to the departed. Shadows that flew from the wall were sucked into the depths of the orb.

They fled and wheeled the round disk door.

Stone entombed it all.

فاتحة قلعة

White Kasbah

Skinwalkers were just too good at smelling people out. They detected humanity in devilish ways no one else could. In their soulbound beast, they were the perfect spy and scout. They blended in almost any surrounding—even in plain sight. The enemy had not yet figured out that the eagles, leopards, and jackals weren't what they appeared to be. And they paid the price dearly for it.

As the days came after the Hemopolis, spies of the enemy who wandered too deep into the delta became a permanent addition to the swamp. Their bodies or what was left of them would never be discovered by their masters—whoever they were.

One of the skinwalkers in the form of a crocodile reported that a group of three spies had overshot the entrance and attempted to find the Reliquary by entering the dead city another way. They were found hours later impaled onto spikes several stories above a plaza wreathed in mist, eyes gouged and their tongues pulled from their heads.

No one claimed responsibility—none were capable of pulling off such acts.

Nemset had, silently. A chilling reality permeated the talk in the Reliquary that the dead city harbored things that did not belong in civilization.

Things that did not tolerate the existence of man altogether.

The Scorpion Pit suffered a random bout of arson recently that reduced the place to scorched rubble. The proprietor's throat rumored to be slit in the alleyway behind by another equally random act of desperation by a vagrant who mysteriously disappeared. To the passerby who relayed the story, the series of misfortunes befalling the sellsword's tavern was just yet another thread of chaos sewn into Nefara's current fate.

Rooster knew differently.

He stepped off to seethe in the alleyway.

"Clear as fog and quiet as frog croaks," he muttered an adage he'd recently recalled.

The Qadi was no spring chicken. Leaving no loose ends. Not even small-time merchants who might have had a conversation with Nazsif. The whereabouts of his servant were proving an easier find than a snowstorm in the dunes.

Behind Rooster, his shadow gave a gruff I-told-you-so grunt, kicking over a piece of rubble.

"You shouldn't be out here. A light breeze could blow you over."

Darwish glared, "I was taking ears for trophies when your old man was a twinkle in his daddy's eye. You keep your advice to yourself, boy."

More skin and bones than flesh, the old warlord refused a crutch. Instead, using one of his sheathed swords to hobble around, comically.

Why—Rooster didn't dare ask—could that be any less humbling than a walking stick.

"What are we supposed to be looking for here?"

"Anything."

"When are you going to admit you're not half as smart as you think you are?"

"Anything else?"

"You're two steps behind and he's two steps ahead. You're playing catch with a cobra and you're pouting about fairness. I can keep going all day boy."

Rooster licked his teeth and began to walk towards the next location, "Go back to the boat Darwish."

Ignoring him, the warlord pressed, "Maybe you need to come down to earth with all of us other dirt grovelers and realize you don't understand this man you got in chains. He's playing you like an oud."

"The real enemy is the Serpents. Tariq's just a good-for-nothing charlatan. Perhaps a mastermind in the political sense. But he's out to save his skin. He's as desperate as we are."

"Says you."

There was a decent place to rest between plazas, in the shade. The other locale that Nazsif was seen to frequent was a merchant who peddled vases, occasionally decorative trinkets. An odd duck, the servant. Perhaps a front for Tariq to fence off Shalmanisar goods?

The heat even in the late morning was blistering. Frequent stops with the water skin were necessary now. Most of Nefara did not expose themselves to the direct sunlight except in short bouts.

"Go on then. Give me the earful," Rooster wiped the sweat from his brow.

Darwish was less fazed by the heat. Acclimated from his time as a vagrant. His one saving grace all this time was that he'd rarely touched the lotus, drowning in wine instead.

Darwish sat and drank from the offered waterskin, wiping his mouth, "Back in Ghazwala, there was once a spring that bubbled up after a rockslide. The valleys around it had gone dry, so the tribal chieftains of each went to the spring to claim it, seeing it as a good omen. On their journey there they found a man who offered to fill their waterskins, in exchange for a blanket, a sword, and a hat. The chieftains were tired from their journey and trusted the man so they gave him what he wanted. In the night the man slit their throats with the sword, took the waterskins, and went down to the valleys. He told a story of how the chieftains fought each other over the spring and perished."

"Days later, a shepherd found the place in the mountains where he saw an idol that wore a hat, a cloak, and a sword. And there was no spring. The chieftains had all been tricked, clouded by their desperation. No one could say if the killer had been a devil from the mountain or a clever hillman. What could be, was that the chieftains were blind to trust a stranger so willingly."

"Why are you telling me this?"

"Because you've trusted this secretary far too long. Even as your enemy, you believe his actions match his words. That he's an agent of greed like every other enemy before him. For that, you've gravely underestimated him."

The route to the peddler wasn't a walk in the park. Cultists had enshrined the street to a deity from their ever-expanding roster of gods. An apocalypse shrine, choked with flies so thick they made a black screen in the air. There were overturned carts filled with putrefaction. This god seemed to like dead things because the entire street was filled with them. Mostly rats. But there were larger things that rotted there too.

Walls of sandstone had become canvasses for the ramblings of the insane. They said the old kingdom languages were dead ones—no one spoke or wrote them anymore. And yet here they were, scrawled in drying filth that blackened in the sun, invoking the obscure.

A gore-smeared cat regarded them from atop the stone pedestal—the shrine's four-legged priest.

The world was getting stranger.

Darwish banished it by kicking a rock over, "You got lucky the last time. If the Qadi didn't know about your magic bird then, he does now. There won't be a next time."

"Amir won't let his father die. The hostage exchange is happening whether we like it or not."

"And when it does go down, this secretary has a plan to bury you all boy. Six feet under."

"Just how do you think I'll be able to shake that?"

The warlord tugged his mustache and grunted, "Well you got one advantage going your way."

"What's that?"

"Take it from me, I've been on this world a little while. That secretary is suspecting that you're desperate, that you're going to fall back to the same tricks you've been doing these last months. Because you are. That's predictable behavior. If I was in your boots boy, I'd exploit the hell out of that."

Six hours later, they gathered once more at dusk to step off to Nefara. The spirit inside the Reliquary was nothing of the glamor and amity of before. As they got their kit ready, a grim silence fell upon the cold mausoleum. Barely a word was spoken between them. If anyone was fired up about what they were about to do, they hid it well.

When the time came there was no briefing. Far fewer faces than the last time. Even with Kizzuran and his cutthroats.

Amir drummed up the basics; this was an escort mission. There would be no hard targets or confrontation, unless they were attacked. Which was expected. The anticipation of said attack was an unnerving concept—the Serpents excelled at assassination.

As he talked, Rooster watched Jhamon and felt a pang of fear. Especially when the kid made an unconscious turn of the head where Antonius usually stood, replaced with Lancer now.

The absence was felt by everyone—all the itinerants. There was no sellswords and Shemsari anymore—what remained was a brotherhood. The Birds of Prey encompassed something that threatened longevity. Every victory and loss was shared. They had their gripes and animosity flare ups but the barriers between them had shattered. They were one, forged by the ugly kiln of war.

Rafe, Vulture, Heron, Quail, Songbird, Gamba, Antonius. The blood price paid so they might have a future. The dead names lingered and haunted the living. Their names carved into the shaft of that monstrous standard.

Rooster worried how many more would be added after tonight.

If they failed, it wouldn't matter.

Dust to dust, their legacies would all be like a bad dream.

They began to file out of the mausoleum, bringing with them Tariq, blindfolded and head bagged. The Qadi was chuckling the whole time they loaded him on the boat.

"I always win," he gloated, muffled.

Kizzuran guided them out of the swamps. Atop the barges that Rooster had once been hellbent on burning up now safely escorted them to the docks.

Life was funny that way.

Nefara's harbor did not raise a bell of alarm. There was a frightening and intentional lack of guards ashore.

Tariq knew they'd made it to the stone jetties, "Don't worry. Musha won't lift a finger so long as you honor the bargain."

Rooster stepped off, along with the men. They formed a simple box formation with Amir pushing Tariq in the middle. And began to march.

He turned back ever so slightly.

The red-armored pirate was pushing off the barge. Pirate shadows were sliding from the gunwales into the water. Only the most careful eye would have spotted the disturbances that slipped into the canals with reed-tubes poking the air.

Then they fell behind a wall.

The band was walking for some time before they reached the dim plaza. Without hazarding any kind of surveillance—far too many angles and shadowy crevices for danger to lurk.

Amir ripped off the bag and slipped off Tariq's blindfold.

The bronze mask did not wear another face this time. The Prince of Many Faces pretended to be no one tonight.

"Ah. We're here. Almost there, little thief. And you'll be reunited with your father…"

The flapping of wings interrupted. The eagle squawked above, circling the group.

Tariq eyed the bird with the slightest smile.

A dark shape far larger and too fast to track suddenly smashed into the eagle. The eagle cried desperately. Feathers tumbled to the sand, droplets of blood too. The pair disappeared over the rooftops.

"What's wrong Rooster? You look rather disheartened."

Another rumble in that general vicinity—a yowl of a large cat, honking of a distressed bird, then a meaty crunch of bones.

Tariq's eyes narrowed.

Moves were happening faster than anyone could track.

The box began to move again, deeper into the plaza. It was alive as a graveyard. Not a soul to be seen, not even wandering drunkenly from the halls or smoking hash from a rooftop.

When another disturbance came upon them. Another eagle, crying out and circling the group. This time it landed on Rooster's shoulder. Pecking at its missing tailfeather and shaking its head.

It was unharmed.

He said, "What's wrong Tariq? Cat got your tongue?"

The Qadi's lone eye bugged, began to dart around the plaza. Man's demeanor shifted to something anxious, all the confidence washed away. Like something had gone wrong.

Bastard had been betting on some guarantees that just got snatched out of thin air. And he was just starting to figure it out.

"This is the place, isn't it," Amir's voice behind the mask was gruffer tonight, likely from the stress, "Where's your friends?"

"I..."

A hidden man screamed, toppled from a rooftop, and landed bent in the wrong places. Pushed off by something that deftly ran along the domes of the surrounding buildings.

The air in the vast mezzanine was changing. Like it was becoming self-aware and everyone in it understood what kind of sandpit trap it was.

There could have been—and likely was—a hundred assassins poised to strike throughout the square. But the night and the darkness were no longer their advantage. The tactical ground was being ripped from out underneath them.

"This was the deal, Tariq, wasn't it?"

The man surveyed the area once, then inhaled slowly, "Take me to the White Kasbah."

"Why?"

"Because your father is there. If you want your father back..."

"You're altering the deal," Amir stated coldly, knife in hand, "Why?"

A smile that did not reach the eyes, "I underestimated you."

Rooster didn't feel it necessary to correct him.

It was poor form to bully an enemy who had all but surrendered. Until they won, at least.

The order was given and the formation loosened, this time moving west. The streets were still hauntingly clear. Not even the cultists were poking their heads out of their rabbit warrens to see what the fuss was about.

A vagrant was moving parallel to them. Perhaps to beg for coin for their empty stomach. Except this vagrant hobbled on a sheathed sword and looked rather menacing for how skinny he was.

Lancer left the formation, hoisting the large sack he'd brought from Nemset. The bag clinked within and was inordinately heavy. Bonechewer carried one similar. Together they split off and joined the vagrant, who gave Rooster a single-eyed salute and peeled off towards the Sword Row. Another step of the plan in motion underway.

Tariq didn't notice any of this, focused on the road ahead.

The tall wooden gates to the White Kasbah were opened and entirely pregnable. Word had somehow traveled this quickly, or the contingency was in place. Now the palace stairs did have guards stationed—every one of them was slumped over, crumpled on the steps.

Carver checked one's pulse, "This one's breathing. Drugged."

"Your escort will have to stay behind," Tariq warned, "There is a limit to our hospitality."

Jhamon, Goshawk, and Yhuuf drew back. They all but winked at Rooster, fading back into the buildings.

"And your bird."

Hazair leapt off of his arm and flapped away. Not south like the rest, but north. It would take him minutes to cross the desert plateaus. Hell, the bird was already there.

The Qadi raised his chained arms, "I'd feel far more comfortable if I wasn't in this state."

"Lead us to your masters."

A flicker of anger, then, "Very well. Wait. What about him?"

Rooster looked back at Ahffan in the ram skull, "He's my witchdoctor. If the boy's dad is poisoned, we'll know."

"Clever, trying to sneak in one of your Shemsari sorcerers..."

"Skinwalkers can't walk and enter the dream at the same time. He's here to ensure we're not being screwed. We don't go in without him."

It was in fact, the truth. No point in lying at this stage. Unless they wanted to compromise all they'd burned to achieve this.

Tariq sucked his teeth in annoyance, "Very well. I'll be watching closely."

Inside the palace walls, the cushions and their denizens were also drugged. Luxuriously dressed noblemen and women contorted in the most awkward of poses, captured by a coma-like state. A few face-downs were choking on pools of their vomit. The guards who would have rescued them were too, drugged.

It was all too poetic of who was in charge here.

How much further could this city devolve?

Rooster passed by a woman, bejeweled and draped in the finest silk—Shalmanisar woven, no doubt. A beautiful creature, likely belonging to some Medean dignitary. Drowned in her own puke.

Tariq sneered at those sleeping and dead, entering into a doorway that seemed like an innocuous servant door. It was. A brazier activated a switch that revealed a steep staircase down.

"After you."

Torches barely illuminated the narrow descent into the belly of the beast. Subterranean complexity hollowed out what was supposedly the oldest construction of Nefara. It looked like what Rooster had seen the prisoners working on, only this construction was far older. Reverberations from a pin drop above their heads would echo down here into a twisted, deafening drum.

A stone archway fed them into a series of intersections that went in all directions. Labrinthian on purpose. There was recent foot traffic here but impossible to know which way would venture where.

A servant from the Kasbah who got lost here would never find their way out.

They traveled together in silence. Ahffan especially, was more inquisitive than talkative. Brooding. Shivering and shaking from the effects of the roof over his head.

They reached the end of the journey; a grand relief featuring the grotesque head of a serpent looming from floor to ceiling. The stonework was immaculate and looked recently made. Tariq pressed his chained palms to the stone eyes—sinking in, they began to recede, as did the entire maw. Revealing a hidden stone doorway, narrow for but one to enter at a time.

Inside lay a vast and tall chamber illuminated by a single shaft of light from the moon. And Dario was sitting on his haunches there, like a damned man awaiting execution.

Tariq stopped, and turned, "My shackles."

They denied him, "Witchdoctor first."

From the shadows emerged two figures. One was a black man sporting a fresh and ugly scar that started at his eyebrow and ended at his collarbone. The other was Tariq—or rather a doppelganger of the Qadi. Both smiling.

They did not seem bothered by Ahffan scrambling over to inspect Dario, barely casting a glance.

"In good health I see, Black Nizzar," Tariq said, dubious, "At what cost I wonder."

"Never mind you that, Qadi. You're going to owe us far more. A lifetime of debt, I think."

The reality of the cartel's relationship was becoming much more poignant. Born not out of mutual respect but of greed perhaps. Maybe even fear.

It was the doppelganger's turn, who faded back and returned an innocuous desert wanderer, bearing a small resemblance to Tariq's true form, "All will be forgiven."

"Forgive me Malakai, if I am not feeling trusting tonight."

Ahffan finally returned, nodding.

"Everything seems to be in order," Rooster declared.

Black Nizzar spoke, "Against our better judgement we'll allow this hostage exchange to take place. The Qadi in his position is barely worth more than a beggar with an oud."

"It is unfortunate, the entanglement at the Hemopolis," Tariq widened his palms, earning daggers from the chemist.

So the trap hadn't been just for them but Black Nizzar—very interesting.

"You tried killing all three of us that night. Why?"

"Unshackle me."

Rooster produced the key. The heavy iron manacles hit the stone floor. Tariq breathed a sigh of relief. Malakai was lifting Dario from the floor to begin the exchange.

Black Nizzar took a step forward, "What is this? Explain, dog!"

The Qadi walked and entered the moonbeam, "Must I repeat myself Rooster? You ceased being useful to me a long time ago. I abhor useless things."

But the end of that sentence wasn't directed at them—it was at Black Nizzar. A sleight of hands between Malakai's sleeves and suddenly Tariq had a shining blade in his hands. The chemist didn't see it coming until the last second—when that dagger rammed home into his chest, over and over. With a wet gurgle, the leader of the Serpents collapsed.

Meanwhile, Malakai had become Tariq again, doing something with his hands. A crackle of sparks. Energy arced from a dark rod produced from the robe. The spell would have hit Rooster but Amir threw himself sideways and absorbed the energy. Fried flesh sizzled as the bolt seared right through the thief, sending him flying like a ragdoll. A smoking hole blasted right where the heart was.

"No," Dario screamed and bolted to the fallen boy.

"Thank you," the Tariq with the bloody knife said before bolting into the dark, "I must be going now."

High above their heads a surfeit of groans rocked the chamber. A great exhale of dust. The moonlight blocked for but a heartbeat by an enormous shape moving.

Meanwhile, sorcerer Tariq lifted the rod once more and aimed it at Rooster. Crackling built up at the end to deliver another deadly spell.

He grunted—suddenly sprouting a dagger from his forehead. The rod clattered and shot wild, ricocheting off the walls before dissipating.

Slain by Ahffan, who already had a throwing knife at the ready.

Dario shouted a futile warning right as the ceiling fell on him. A mass smothered the center of the chamber, crushing the oud player like a rat under a wagon wheel. Gore raced outward from the giant black mound that appeared—a mound with a face to match the carving, with glittering eyes and teeth that could have swallowed a cow whole.

Scales began to ripple as the serpent unfolded.

The monstrous black head turned and eyes fell upon him.

Rooster was frozen. Locked in hypnosis. He could not escape their spell. A soft voice of a woman filled his skull, seduced his hyperactive mind. Faintly in his ears a monstrous, grating one was speaking at the same time.

That giant cart-shaped head was rising from a long neck, hovering over him. Jaw unhinging to reveal an abyss framed by sword-sized teeth. Yellow-green acid beginning to drip from glands under its enormous forked tongue.

A lance thrust right into its soft gullet.

Bestial wheezing shook the chamber—the wyrm flailed and began to cry.

It had been thrust by Amir— somehow on his feet despite the scorching hole in his chest. The thief was rushing the giant serpent, trying to find purchase in the missing scales off its melted hide. Deftly moving past the snapping teeth.

Rooster drew Awakener and joined him.

"Flee little rats, before dread Zalgurak," the woman's voice hissed in his head simultaneously as a beastial moan came from the wyrm's throat, *"Flee."*

A gout of acid flew in a stream towards Rooster and he ducked. It caught fire—yellow-green and wicked, burning the stone. Another one sprayed the corpse of Dario—what was left of him. An explosion of demented flames filled the chamber.

And then the wyrm shrieked once more as Awakener bit into the chink in its black hide. Rooster swung the big sword wherever he could. Wounds wept viscous blood onto the stone. It really started to scream when Amir drove his lance into its belly. The wyrm bucked and its wicked tail slammed into the thief.

Amir went flying into the stone wall like artillery from a catapult. Crushed into the side of it and lying still. Lance snapped in half.

Rooster knew he was going to die.

The wyrm opened its mouth to shoot more flammable acid.

A bow twanged, an arrow sailed, and struck the serpent right in a glittering eye. Ahffan had a bow out, drawing another arrow. Again and again. Arrows that hit the wyrm's mouth and scales. The viscous blood was pooling thick now. Enough maybe to put the big bastard down.

Bony tendrils extended from the thing's back—unfolding like a bat's. The wyrm gave its last enraged roar as it launched forward and took a cowardly flight down the tunnel. Leaving smoldering remains.

And silence.

Ahffan dropped the bow and fell to his knees. The ram skull had slipped off. The fake tattoo paint was smeared and left behind the face of the real Amir, who wept over the burning body of his father. Whimpers rang out throughout the room.

Bent armor creaked—the other Amir miraculously began to rise. The bronze mask had been knocked off during the fight, leaving behind the petrified face of a corpse. Antonius, in the guise of the thief, joined in silence.

Rooster let his sword clatter to the ground.

He didn't have the energy to feel anything.

The ploy had worked. At a price so invaluable, the thought of defeat sounded just as sweet. Inside—as Rooster watched the Teridian—felt repulsed.

What had he done?

What had been brought back from the grave wasn't even a dead ringer of Antonius. If any soul remained of the man, it was trapped somewhere very far away. What remained was a physical mockery of what Antonius once had been—muttering every so often with a rasping voice of a thing that was not his friend.

Antonius would never feel joy again, never feel love from a woman, or be more than a deathless revenant cursed to walk the earth. Nothing more than a shell filled with a void and denied the grace of mortality.

For that, Rooster was utterly responsible.

"I should have let you die," regret was starting to sting.

Antonius did not react. Face frozen in stoic indifference.

Amir wiped his cheeks, "We should go. Tariq will have started to raise alarms by now."

"No. He's a coward. He's going to run."

"Staying in Nefara was my fault..." the boy began.

"Don't. You start blaming yourself, you start going down a path you can't come back from," Rooster knew he was a hypocrite but it's what the kid needed to hear right now, "Mourning down here doesn't do us any favors."

The thief blinked and nodded.

Rooster picked up Awakener.

They had a lifetime to regret their decisions—they only had tonight to make sure it wasn't in chains.

Panic gripped the White Kasbah, swiftly dispatched and replaced with a primitive knee-jerk of defensive reactions.

The group of guards at the top of the stairs almost did the three of them in, cornering them against the pillared chamber. Swords and shields swung wild. Against overwhelming odds, Rooster came out of it with only a few minor scratches. Amir's suicidal fury was largely to blame.

No mercy for Medeans tonight.

The sounds of mail clattering and guardsmen shouting inside the palace almost drowned out the bells that gonged outside. So the deal had always been planned to be finished with martial law. Perhaps the Serpents had been bold enough to try an incursion into Nemset.

The thief returned through one of the windows, "Has to be half the city's guard upstairs. Tariq has a little army to protect his retreat."

Rooster kicked the last Medean off his sword, "Where's Kizzuran?"

"I don't know. He was supposed to rendezvous here."

Distantly, outside the Kasbah the echo of melee could be heard. A small group. Likely the Birds of Prey carrying out the next part of the plan.

"Where else would that bastard be?"

Amir stared off into the nothing, "Damn him. He's going after Musha."

"And where's Musha?"

"At al Khandaq Keep. Where Kizzuran was imprisoned..."

"Shit. You know him better than me. What are you betting on?"

"Revenge," Amir said.

Without hope of reinforcement, there wasn't any way

they could take the White Kasbah. It was too big. And now they knew the Serpents had infrastructure tunneled out beneath it. The palace was a giant death trap.

"New plan," Rooster declared.

He grabbed a table and braced it under the double doors that led from the salon into the central chamber of the Kasbah. Ripped curtains and pillows and tossed them onto the growing pile. Then took out the little oilskin sack he'd brought for a rainy day. Containing the agave tar. He threw it on the pile, tore a brazier off the wall, and threw it atop. A little bonfire started rather quickly. And grew at a frightening pace.

"What about the guards?"

"What about them? They chose the losing side."

Together they sealed off the main wooden doors.

Black pillars of smoke were beginning to rise from the pearly frame of the White Kasbah. Stone didn't burn easily. But everything inside of it would. Desperation could be heard pounding on the barricaded doors.

Rooster was indifferent. He posted up to cut down any guardsmen who somehow broke out and tried to douse the flames. Which didn't happen—the inferno was out of anyone's control now.

From the northern gates came a whooping of Shemsari cries. Silhouettes on horseback stormed through the barbican and rode down the fleeing guards who'd dared raise a spear. The uncoordinated defense quickly splintered away as the Ramali and Faari—hidden behind the hills of sand just beyond the city—rode behind Jhamon, savagely attacking anything that half-looked like a threat.

To the south came more bells of attack. Little spidery hooks were being thrown up at the towering Al Khandaq Keep, repelled by archers who rained hell down on pirates that attempted to climb her walls. While others must have been raiding and pillaging the nether quarters of the city.

A headless Shemsari horseman passed them by with a torch dangling from his lifeless hands, blood staining his bone shirt, steed trampling the unlucky who stood in her way. The pair carried on down the streets as an unholy symbol of what was about to happen.

As the palace burned, Nefara plunged into anarchy.

اختراقه يُمكن لا خندق

al Khandaq Keep

Sacking a city was a thing easily overdone. An army whetted by lust without restraint could damn themselves once they subdued whatever force was charged with protecting its walls. The undoing of many bandit armies was caused by the redress of a sacking. More enemies were created by the injustices of occupation in the short term—man was a short-sighted beast, especially the civilian.

Rooster never intended to pillage Nefara. Its storied history was full of such instances—even as recent as the White Dove. Sacking served no purpose. The plan had always been to eliminate the Serpents, remove Tariq from power, and restore the Vizier.

But he was Beyik Alghasan of two Shemsari clans, both of whom traditionally only entered cities for a single purpose. They engaged in that purpose the moment the gates were open, and they did it well.

The guards who remained under Musha's command did something foolish—barricading plazas and bazaars—by taking women and children as hostages. They thought the soft targets could buy them their freedom out of the city. Or maybe the horde would shy away from civilian casualties.

That belief was blackballed soon after Bonechewer and his giants smashed in the heads of guards and their hostages equally. They then ran down the fleeing Nefarans innocents without quarter. Laying waste to those who tried to protect their estates, throwing people from windows, and torching them without reason.

Barbarism enveloped the city like a black cloud.

Its hideous, terroristic glut did not cease as the first night grew long. Then came the second. And the third. The fourth.

By night those guards and troops tried to sally out—the

streets pulsed with the clash of steel and the pounding of hooves as the warriors of the al Khandaq struggled to hold back their relentless tide. Each skirmish a fresh wound and a reminder of how the city—once proud and secure—was tearing itself apart. The Shemsari, The Floodplain Raiders, the criminals loosed from the prison cells of the Kasbah were relentless. The gates to Nefara remained open and more Shemsari were appearing as if summoned like ghostly desert winds.

The endless cycle of violence built and built.

Only tempered by the calls to prayer on the shoulders of the days, the onslaught began again. The calls of the muezzin cut through the madness at the same hour—steady, constant, offering the briefest respite to those still alive in the streets. It brought the little peace Nefara knew now. By dawn, the bloodshed began anew.

Enough to turn the stomachs of men who were used to sieges and war.

Under the heat dome of summer's torment and with no identifiable signs of monsoon, the wind picked up suddenly. It flew into the bailey of the Kasbah where they were quartered, toying with the standard of the Birds of Prey. Sending the canvas of the tents flying up, threatening to send them to the sky. And then abruptly it ceased.

Rooster didn't like it, "I smell sorcery."

Darwish looked around, "You've incurred the wrath of many. It could be a god's warning."

"Divine bullshit."

A man tried to cross the large courtyard to approach the tent. From nowhere two Ramali descended on him, flattened him, and prepared to gut him, "A spy, Beyik Alghasan!"

"Why aren't you two out fighting?"

"For your protection chieftain. We will die before you are touched," the one who held the knife was more gray than copper.

Madness. Both were several decades his elder. They

were too old to be riding in the saddle. And nothing he would say would persuade them to retire.

"Fine. If you're going to be my bodyguards, screen them, don't stab them. This one's ours."

In turban and outrider robes, the only giveaway the Medean was highborn was how clean his fingernails were. He dusted himself off and headed over.

"Shihad," Rooster addressed.

"Why haven't we taken the city yet?"

Darwish snorted, "Learn some manners boy. That's the damn general you're talking to."

Shihad ignored him, "We're wasting precious time Rooster. You swore..."

"I swore nothing, except that I'd take the city."

"Six days and we are no closer to capturing Nefara while the Caliph is surely heading back from Tyhri. You've ignored all counsel," the retort reeked with condescension.

Darwish snapped. The one-eyed warlord started to wrangle the youngster. Rooster let it go for a moment before whistling Darwish down.

"That's enough."

Everyone was raw, letting their demons take over.

"Little bastard," Darwish glared, "Who do you think you are, telling us what?"

"He's the eldest son of Sultan Sulman Mastoor. Leader of the al Ihrab."

Shihad unruffled his robes and made an indignant sound.

"What? Since when was the Sultan of the Rock a rebel?"

"Since the Caliph declared my father an outlaw," Shihad answered, "And sentenced him to die."

Darwish chewed on that, "Where is he now?"

There was no point hiding the secret any longer, "A hundred miles north of here, in the Fists of the Shemsari. With the rest of the al Ihrab and their warriors."

All thirteen hundred of them. Waiting to see if Nefara fell first to a gharib, or to wait the clock out on the Boy King—swoop in and take it from behind. The al Ihrab didn't trust him, plain and simple. So they'd play it safe.

"So the tiny tyrant started a civil war before marching here too? Medeans never learn. So boy. Who else joined the Sultan of the Rock?"

A list of names that meant nothing to Rooster was uttered. Darwish was a different story. Wrinkles tightened, lips curled into a snarl, and a shadow darkened his brow.

Whatever that meant, they'd bridge the ugly history later.

On the map below they were using little wajiit pieces to represent allied forces and arrowheads for the enemy. The current status of a few were still to be determined. One with an X was pushed by Darwish, over to the Black Oasis.

"That Prince kid and his thieves just reported in a few hours ago. They're beginning their assault on the rat holes of those drug dealers."

Amir was on the hunt. The kid wasn't sleeping, wasn't eating. On a one-man crusade to purge the city of whatever cells of the Serpents still remained. A few of the blackguard had struck a nasty blow the night before last—attempting to make off with one of the pirate's boats. Enough of them were captured and squealed off about the rat holes. Leading to a brigade of children with knives who started going from drug den to drinking hall and making bloody work of the front-facing operations of the Serpents.

Even if they were destroyed, only one small fire had been doused.

"Where do we stand in our negotiations in the Sword Row?"

Darwish sucked his teeth, "Slow, but we have a commission ready. A hundred swords stand ready."

"A hundred? That's less than half of what you promised."

"If you asked me to find willing souls before you started torching the city, might have worked. Everyone wants to sit this out, wait for the dust to shake out."

It was disappointing news. The amount of gold offered was considerable.

"Hundred they may be but they're hard fighters. Your boys know some of them. They'll fight better than any goat-born Medean bastard."

The meeting went on a little longer before an eagle-talker came to interrupt, "It's Kizzuran."

Things weren't looking too hot for the pirates. Sustaining heavy losses after failing to crack into al Khandaq, the Bandit Prince was on a suicide mission now. At the expense of taking several wounds himself and overextending the siege, Kizzuran threw his men at the gates like some hunters did their dogs at a cornered puma. They had nowhere to run. By nightfall, there'd be nothing left of the Floodplain Raiders.

Which at another date, wouldn't have been a problem. Except that they were uncomfortable allies and as much as Rooster despised it, they needed the Flameblade.

"We'll settle the commission later. We need those sellswords now. Take the mantlets on our side of the canal and run them up behind Kizzuran. Defend his retreat, then seal up the bridge. If you need reinforcements..."

Darwish snorted, "Back in the Hounds we fared a lot worse back when you were a pup. We can handle it."

Shahid watched the warlord hobble out, "Why is a war criminal your advisor?"

"Because he's the second-best commander in this stinking spider hole of a city."

"And the first?"

The majority of the arrowheads were clustered at al Khandaq Keep. Trapped yes. On paper. But Amir spoke confidently that the garrison was equipped to withstand at least six months of a siege, in the event of riots borne from famine or hostile takeover. With six hundred professional mamluks and janissaries—some of the Caliphate's finest troops could wait out the clock until the Boy King could rescue them.

More importantly, was who was leading them.

"Fadin al Hakim."

Shihad circled the map, scratching his shaven chin,

"The old fox won't sally out to fight. He's too smart for that. They have no choice but to take the bridge."

Maybe.

Or maybe not.

The general had not grown long in the tooth, outlived two kings, and maintained an infamous battalion of hardened troops purely from luck. In more ways than he felt comfortable admitting, Rooster and he were similar. One factor above all was what was keeping him up at night.

Fadin al Hakim wasn't one to be predicted.

Sitting around a table wouldn't enlighten him on the general's next move. He needed some eyes on. Firsthand intelligence.

"I need my horse."

The bridge would have to wait a little longer. As soon as Rooster saddled up Nereel—Shemsari escort in tow, whooping foolishly as they assumed it was to fight—there was another distraction waiting just outside the Kasbah.

A familiar powdered face; the Shalmanisar heiress with the jade-green nails. Siege or not, she dressed to kill. Peasants would starve before the merchant lords embraced austerity.

"Lord Rooster," she bowed, "I must have a moment of your time."

"I'm busy. Whatever your name is."

"Ninsina, of the Qorchi. Be assured this is a matter of urgency."

Little servants bumbled up and tried to set up a table with tea. Inappropriately in the middle of the road, where the debris of death and siege was visible all around.

These funny people and their stupid, pointless traditions.

"Save your tea and get to the point."

"Wheat," she stated simply, "Is the backbone of Nefara."

"What about it?"

"Our grain stores have been depleted since you began sacking the city."

Of all the problems facing his force, supply was not one of them. Shemsari excelled at being self-sufficient. He explained it in short order.

Ninsina frowned, "Despite our complicated history, I did not come here to accuse you. If you have intentions to become Nefara's next warlord, understand our grain is what keeps famine at bay. Our stores were pillaged and need guarding."

"From who?"

"I am told it was one of the cults."

"Have your people do a better job. Mine are fighting to restore order."

She sniffed, "My people will leave and take our grain with us if need be. The cults are not doing this randomly."

"That's madness. Why the hell would they be attacking their own food supply?"

"If I was an insane person capable of following their logic, I would not be standing here before you."

Rooster wondered if it was a trap.

The woman had been in league with the Vizier.

She must have sniffed the trepidation, "If you think me in partnership with those drug pushers, you have me mistaken."

"What about Tariq? Did you have dealings with him?"

"...yes. I'm embarrassed to admit."

"Then you're right; I don't believe a word out of your mouth. Get lost lady. Guard your own grain."

She froze, lost in thought.

He didn't have time for this.

Before he could steer Nereel away, she spoke up, "I will submit to any questioning you can think of. Know my intentions today are pure. Do nothing and the city will suffer. The cults are a threat graver than you could imagine."

Those bald freaks? Unlikely. The Shalmanisar were capable. They didn't like the shake-up of power. If Tariq had been a partner, they would have felt the ground fall beneath them.

"The lion is loose. Ignore that at your peril," was her final cryptic message.

Drums growled and arrows whistled like angry bees.

One of the Ophi strutted out atop the stone bridge, challenging the Medeans to a duel. Of course they wouldn't accept it. A hailstorm of missiles pelted the spot right as he leapt back, did a mocking dance, and fell into cover. Followed by the back and forth from their side, as mercenaries and Shemsari fired back. The arrow-ports of the keep were narrow, so most of it was a waste of good arrows.

Mantlets—some burning—were left on the bridge from the maneuver. The narrow bridge spanning the canal ended at the keep and the Khashar bristled with an equal amount of wooden fortifications—a moat of sharpened staves. There were a few pirates still impaled on them.

Darwish looked at his handiwork proudly, grinning ear to ear. Someone said he'd knocked an arrow mid-air with his sword. As if the hillman needed any more hot air.

"How's our least favorite pirate?"

"Alive," the warlord grunted, "Almost broke the jaw of that big bear nomad you got, Bone-something."

"How many raiders are left?"

Another sucking of teeth, pulling on the beard, "Forty if the wounded make it. Thirty if we're being honest."

Barely a fraction. The retreat to save them was barely worth it. What was left of the Raiders couldn't be counted because pirates were cowards by default. If morale was low, they might just cut their losses and leave for Nemset.

If they kept losing troops like this, then Fadin had a chance to break out.

Rooster imagined the old fox was staring back at him through one of the arrow-ports, hatching that very scheme.

"Morons. They should have waited for my signal."

"We can hold them here for now," Darwish nodded to the sellswords who'd barricaded the canal and street, "Even if they tried to ride out."

"Not against six hundred."

Wind again. Arrows sailed wild for the span of a breath. It could have been mistaken for a fast breeze from the river. But Rooster saw a flicker of something on the rooftop of Al Khandaq—like a miniature dervish spinning up and dying suddenly. Goosebumps followed.

Fadin was up to something.

"Bahram," he muttered a brief prayer.

"Come again?"

"Find Kizzuran. Have him haul a few of those smaller boats up the canal. Bring them here, on the edge of the bridge. Then broken carts, whatever you can to burn. When the call to prayer starts, light it up."

Darwish looked at him like was speaking gibberish, "Lost your damn mind boy?"

"We're going to need smoke tonight."

An attack did come. Over the bridge, a significant force broke through their lines and engaged in some nasty melee. The smokescreen from the burning boats shielded it from arrow fire.

When word reached Rooster he was prepared.

A relief force of Faari led by Jhamon and Lancer harried the Medeans and prevented any further ground taken. By morning, the mamluks steadily retreated to al Khandaq, having taken a few dozen casualties, inflicting just as many back.

Fadin was testing them.

Whatever the old fox had hoped to learn, Rooster had a gut feeling that it was successful.

Sleep was torture. Though it was without dreams, Rooster felt those icy claws try to dig their way into his mind. He tossed and turned and when the disturbance of light woke him up, felt like it was still midnight.

Groggily he went to the lamp that dangled just outside the tent. An unbidden shadow, Petiri was waiting. The tall, gaunt boatman looked like a corpse had been propped up and the only giveaway was the subtle, harrowing sound of breath moving through that ancient body.

"What hour is it," Rooster demanded.

"That is irrelevant," Petiri seemed more interested in him, scanning over his face, "Have you dreamt tonight?"

"No. What the hell is going on?"

Then he heard it.

Faint pleas were filling the Kasbah. Sleeping men crying out for their mothers. A melody of nightmares captured the entire courtyard. Its inhabitants were convulsing and begging for it to end. The boatman led him around the quarters were the men were sleeping—the haunted spell overtaking them.

Dread began to take hold, "I thought it was Nemset..."

"No," the boatman banished, "The realm does procure visions of the ethereal yes. Not take over your mind. You were misled. The invader of your dreams wanted you to think so."

"Why?"

A horrid, rasping laugh, "And the Prince assured me you were clever. Think warlord; at what eve have your dreams been haunted by this unwelcome stranger?"

The pieces were slow to form in this exhausted state but Rooster carefully recalled. The sandman. The lone eye. The timing of it all. When he got the answer it felt more like a punishment than a revelation. There was no bottom to the depth of their previous employer's betrayal.

How could no one have seen it before?

"Tariq," he breathed shallowly, "I didn't think...?"

"Deceived you all. The signs of his treachery were always there, you were just too blind to notice them," Petiri leaned down and placed a spidery finger on Big Mug's face, holding some kind of pendant. The mercenary faded off into a calmer sleep, "However. This power is beyond mere sorcery. The ability to steal into one's dreams and manipulate them is not something I've heard of."

A dark presence not yet announced, Norulo entered the light. The necromantic apprentice frowned at Rooster,

"How have you escaped this spell?"

At his neck, the Blue Eye was ice.

"It's a Shemsari trinket."

Norulo's eyes glittered with envy, "No. You're mistaken a second time. Perhaps it is now. But it hasn't always been. That isn't old kingdom—it's from before."

"Was this a warning?"

"An attempt. This deceiver thought he could infiltrate, capture your mind, steer your men to protect his last asset in the city," the assistant replied.

"The Prince has made contact with the last holdout of the Serpents. A lair in the depths of the Black Oasis. By dawn, they'll be finished. The deceiver and his allies will lose," Petiri stood, smiling grimly, "Or so the Prince thinks."

"Why did Tariq slay the Black Nizzar then?"

"I am impressed by darker possibilities Rooster."

They walked and one by one, restored the sleep of all the troops.

The Qadi had not been seen since the battle below. It was all but certain he was lying low with the assassins for protection, deeply embedded in their hidden places. The only other alternatives made little sense. Tariq wasn't the kind to just go belly up and accept surrender.

All while they walked, Rooster could not make heads or tails of it.

"If the Prince finds Tariq in their lair…"

"He cannot be allowed to live, you would suggest."

Rooster was baffled, "You'd let him live? We imprisoned him before. Look how well that turned out."

"A king might receive the gift of a lion cub and mistake it for a kitten before too late. You did not know what you held onto."

"He will subvert any attempt to negotiate peace."

"Ah. But now that you have seen the deceiver's true colors, what exactly are his intentions?"

There had to be one, but there was no point pretending he knew.

They were all in the dark.

Petiri leered and indicated to his assistant they were leaving, "Ponder this. Guard your thoughts. Trust no one in your mind but yourself."

Day came with a stillness—the final vestige before the storm. Shutters were closed, and the bazaars empty. The stray cats watched from the safety of rooftops. Even the cults had retreated into their hidey-holes, barricaded their shrines.

Nefara waited with its breath held.

The sun god shone brightly with the promise of a hot day as the armored man swung onto Nereel, big sword sharpened and polished. Hazair did not take roost on his forearm, crying down at the crowd instead.

Too smart for its own good—the bird.

If Fadin had spies he'd know the time had come. A Ramali rider with a scroll took off before the armored man and his cadre rode down the main artery of the city. First to deliver the terms to the old fox for surrender. And if that didn't work, then to besiege him.

The armored man signaled and his horde took off.

Left in the dust of the whooping horsemen, the small group crossed the street and began to navigate their way to the southern plazas. Dressed in the guises of rogues. They passed what had once been busy places, reduced to a ghost town.

Halfway to their destination, the wind began to blow through the streets.

One of the thieves grabbed his comrades and pointed to the sky. There were no clouds. Across the rooftops, however, he saw something and indicated.

Gusts were blasting out from the rooftop of al Khandaq. Figures like ants stood with arms uplifted. Dust and sand began to pick up with the ever-increasing speed of winds, torrenting in streams from the fortress. Within moments a funnel was beginning to build, surrounding the fortifications. A screaming wall of dust began to pillar into the heavens and darken their world.

Even the sun became hidden behind the building sandstorm.

"Habūd," a thief swore, "Bahram have mercy on us."

"It's Fadin. We need to move."

They delved into the Black Oasis—narrowly avoiding a cart that was picked up and smashed into a nearby wall.

If Darwish and his men could hold the bridge, it would be a miracle.

They ran down the pit, entering a shuttered shop. An old apocathery—perhaps an old front of the Serpents. It wasn't. Their guide peeled a rug from a wall, pulled a series of cleverly hidden levers, and then pressed in a brazier. The wall fell away into a dark tunnel, an ancient passageway. Their guide put his hand up to a skeleton who stood guard at another door. Some kind of sorcery? Clicking came within the wall and the door fell once more. Revealing a sepulcher of great size, converted to a living space for a hundred. This wasn't a small operation. It was impressive.

At the nave stood sarcophagi. Old kingdom reliefs were the only décor in the grim room. At its obsidian fulcrum, Petiri and Norulo were working under strange red candles, embalming a little body. That menacing dark orb on a pedestal nearby.

"The Serpents never discovered this?"

"No. Or Tariq."

A thief chuckled, "Those poor bastards. You were under their nose this entire time."

The guide replied, "Only those sworn into the service of the Dead Hand are allowed to see this and walk away."

Norulo lifted the giant black orb by a gray sheet.

They made the group place their hands on it and swear an oath.

The words came to them unbidden. The hum from before was infinitely more powerful. Provoking imagery, a dark sense of an abyss. Hours passed by before they lifted their fingers.

The group realized it had only been a moment.

"No grave can hold the Hand," their guide began to

chant, his bronze face masking his emotion.

All around the complex, thieves stopped their mundane work and stood.

"In shadow, we endure," they said.

"The law forgets," the guide continued.

"The Hand does not."

"Our breath the torch, the step of silence."

Children's voices like a choir, "Our bodies fall, our will persists."

The Prince of Many Faces finished, "Gold rusts, kings rot, the Hand remains."

Before the ceremony was over, the group already set their packs down and began to don their new guises; the mustard-yellow coats and veiled wraps of janissary officers. Tulwars and hooked spears in place of longswords. Their previous owners floated somewhere in the canal.

Then the Prince led them down another hallway that stretched a mile—the labyrinth of old kingdom burrows. It shed light on how the Dead Hand was able to move through the city so quickly. A foul stench wafted down the hall. The Prince moved into one alcove where a barricade was removed.

They crawled at the bottom of what appeared to be a septic tank. A well-used one. Slanted light above—and the ass of a Medean who was currently using it.

"al Khandaq is right above us," the Prince whispered.

Turds fell and the light returned again.

The Prince ascended a pre-nailed ladder staggering across the septic tank's wall.

The group followed, breaking into the latrine.

Commotion awaited the other side of the door. Hundreds were mustering. Steel banged and mail rattled. Platoon leaders were shouting at their Medean troops. A whole lot of action going on in the central hall.

And even in here, the howling wind biting at stone was still audible.

Prince peeked the door, "Shit. They're moving out."

They were too late.

"Any sign of Fadin?"

"No. Looks like cavalry then infantry."

The Medeans were trying to break out then.

"If he's still in here, the upper levels are the most secure. I'll take you there," Prince walked out.

Into the dark lion's den they went. They plied the vastness of Khandaq's central hall, where the bowls of slop were still warm. The Medeans had left in a hurry. A cluster of surgeons were setting up a field hospital.

Faceless mamluks in heavy mail were rushing down the steps, led by a bannerman of a stylized helm. The group barely got missed, pressing into the alcoves.

"Fadin's son," one of them said, "Wonder what he's doing."

The Prince listened, "Trouble up ahead."

"We deal with it. In too deep now."

Sentries of the general's retainer were guarding the second and third floors of the Keep. They looked ready to move out at a moment's notice—probably were. Dozens of mamluks who were no strangers to war.

The gamble was whether the old fox had already left.

Prince turned to them, "I can climb the window and get to the top floor."

"Do it. If we fall or get captured, you can still end this."

The thief broke the wooden bars and started to ascend. The group threw their rope ladders down and used a nearby torch to light the alchemical flare—an invention of Skulk and Sable, used as a signal for friendly ports for the smugglers.

Even in the sandstorm, the bright green fire would have been visible.

On the west end of the old farms, shapes were moving through the grass. Human and beast alike. They began to climb up the ropes.

Mamluks noticed the disturbance and were walking the long hallway down their way. Gruffly demanding what a group of janissaries were still doing, lingering where they shouldn't. Their mailed gauntlets yet to reach for swords.

The element of surprise was a bitch.

The group ran them through before either sentry figured out they weren't Medean. Blood splashed the stone.

Hell was raised and doors started to open up along the fortress. Mailed soldiers piled out and formed a deathly wall, pushing their way.

"Fall back," one of them called in Shemsari, "Stick to the plan."

They waited until their backs were at the stairways leading down. Two of the group produced javelins and hurled them into the mamluk lines—the throws of Ophi warriors. Mamluks took the hits and continued to press. Another round of javelins didn't bite. The spears of the troops were pressing them down into a deadly backpedal.

A Mamluk screamed—a leopard snuck up behind and tore the man's midsection in half, tossing him like a toy. Arrows from shapes that piled into the windows. Eagles, an ape, and a horde of buzzing black things joined the fight. Alongside them Scorchhide and his cohort of feral witch-men.

"Now," one of the janissaries roared and threw himself at the nearest Mamluk, swinging the tulwar with a hand used to a larger sword.

Fusillades of missiles almost took out the janissaries, who locked horns with the mamluks. One of the group took a spear to the chest and somehow managed to behead the Medean responsible, walking around with a spear in his belly. Antonius calmly removed it and pressed into the troop's ranks. They changed their strategy and tried to chop him into pieces.

Melee became vicious. Janissaries started to fall. A shorter one cried out in Shemsari, his bow snapped in half. The mamluk responsible went in for the kill.

A man in yellow screamed, "No!"

The soldier hesitated for enough time for the man to knock him off balance with his shield, then repeatedly beat the mamluk's helm in with his tulwar. It blunted the sword's edge but he didn't care—animal instincts in control. At some point, the mamluk fell. Skull cracked under the dented helm.

His name was called over the din.

A few of the soldiers tried to break free in the rear to alert the top floor—the beasts subdued them. An eagle was cut in half and the ape whimpered as it took a sword to the eye.

Then the skinwalkers started getting nasty.

The leopard started to drag injured troops and hurled them out the windows. Buzzing reached a frightening height, jamming stingers into any gaps in armor they could find. Some of the Medeans fell, venom swelling their throats.

Below, the central hall was getting loud.

Fighting and men shouting.

They had to end this soon.

The man grabbed the remaining janissaries and started to climb over dead men, taking up a spear and shoving it at anyone in their way. Mamluks fought but were pushed against the hallway's flanks, now on the defense. Giving them just enough room to squeeze through and past the stairs.

A gauntlet grabbed the man but dropped as the leopard snapped its jaw on the forearm and wrenched it aside. The big cat gave him a look as if to convey it could handle the situation.

"Go," the man roared hoarsely.

They broke through and up the stairs.

Barreled into the last sentries on the top floor that waited anxiously, having heard the fight below. There were too few to make a difference. The man took a deep wound in his shoulder and his bad knee. It might have broken but he punched the mamluk with his gauntlet. Throwing daggers flew over his shoulder, sinking into a sentry with a raised sword. More wicked blades somersaulted in the air and turned the remaining mamluks into pincushions.

The Prince stepped out from the pillar, nodding.

Surrounded by bookcases, leaning over a table where

an emerald-studded saber lay, and staring at the corpse of a princely boy who had bravely and idiotically tried to defend him, was Fadin al Hakim.

"Rest in peace, Umeir ib Khalid."

"Fadin al Hakim," the man ripped off his headwrap so the old fox could see him, "I wish you had accepted my terms."

"Rooster," the old fox smiled wryly, sadness still stinging, "I shouldn't be surprised."

"Surrender and we can end this bloodshed."

"Momentarily, I'm afraid. You are too late."

"For what?"

The old fox nodded to the window. It overlooked the bridge connecting the Khashar and al Khandaq to the city. The gates to the bardic college had been forced open—dead scholars were strewn, trampled by horses. Behind the Khashar, to the east was a dust cloud that raced into the desert.

"My son is already on his way to the Boy King. If he falls, twenty other riders have the same message. The Caliph will come for Nefara."

Rooster blinked, "You stayed behind on purpose."

"A trap to keep you bottled up in Nefara, yes. Blindly swinging at my walls. Not to take me prisoner. How did you do it—finding your way in here? A hidden tunnel perhaps. I always suspected the like," the old man said more to himself, amused.

"The sandstorm?"

"We took a few wild sorcerers prisoner at the Sunstones. They have a rather useful talent for imitating a habūd, don't you think?"

Jhamon whispered something under his breath.

"It didn't have to be this way Fadin. I never intended to take the city. I was forced to."

The old fox grew quizzical, saying nothing.

"Do you have any idea that the city was being run by a maniac? That the Vizier is missing, probably dead, and crocodile food now?"

"I did find it strange that we hadn't seen him for some time."

Rooster had to reorient himself. The situation was changing. Capturing Fadin to bring stability meant facing down an army of fifty thousand or so. This wasn't the plan.

"What will you do now I wonder?"

"I'm thinking about it. Will the Caliph listen to reason? That there was a criminal element running his city into the ground?"

Fadin considered it, "Do you have proof of this?"

Prince was there, at the edge of the table, "We burned the Serpent's lair. Besides the few we kept alive, everything's in ashes."

"Then I am sorry. The Caliph will not yield. Not even to reason."

A yellow-veiled janissary threw off his wrap, looking at the fallen boy. Then up to Fadin, "We'll see who is sorry. My father's mercy has its limits."

"Ah, Shihad Mastoor. I had no part to play in your father's arrest."

"Silvertongue. Will you act so devious when your head is on the chopping block?"

"Enough. He's my prisoner anyhow. And until we figure out what to do next, no one is losing their heads," Rooster growled.

Shihad snapped, "Twin Sons of Hijr al Nar flies above the Kasbah. Nefara belongs to the al Ihrab!"

Amir chuckled from behind his bronze mask, "Oh I don't think so. It wasn't the al Ihrab who just forced the surrender of the Caliphate."

With a steady hand, the old general grabbed his bejeweled sword by the blade and handed it outward. The act was a small one, but nonetheless chivalrous. There was no animosity in his eyes—if anything, humility.

"Indeed. I surrender to you Rooster. Nefara is yours, if even for a short time. I am at your mercy."

Satisfaction was short-lived.

They passed the hallway of what remained of the battle. Bodies lay everywhere. Few had survived. The ape was sniffling, one eye left, cradling an eagle with broken wings. Scorchhide was tending to many Faari, most were dead. In a pool of blood and surrounded by a knot of mamluks lay the wounded leopard.

Rooster didn't know why but the scene hit him harder than anything else. Punched right in the gut. The bond between skinwalker and their beast was symbiotic.

Rhuïma was there, squatting over the cat, "He may not make the night."

"I'll get the healers," Jhamon whispered, his yellow veil torn off, "Ahffan may live."

Too many good men dead and dying.

For so small a victory.

"We go where you go chieftain," Rhuïma mocked Jhamon, "How many Ramali will die for his pointless wars? All of us?"

There might have been another little battle played out but someone was coming up the stairs.

Kizzuran marched up like a bat out of hell. One hand clutching the naked blade. The other the head of Musha, still dripping. Judging by the expression on the trophy, the end hadn't been pretty for old Musha.

"I was looking for you both," he said, eyeing Rooster, "We business, you and I."

Jhamon acted very un-Jhamon-like and raised a spear.

"First, I'm going to slay your Shemsari dog. Then mount your head on my boat, water-bird. Every one of your heads I'll string up."

"Stand down Flameblade."

Warning washed over deaf ears. The crocodile-skin helm dipped. Sword ignited. Kizzuran began to walk right at them. Letting Musha's head roll on the stone like a melon.

Rooster pushed Jhamon aside, "Don't get involved."

Grabbing the boy's spear seemed a good option. Reach would help against that sword. Couldn't do anything about the flame though.

Then started to walk, "Some gratitude. I saved your miserable hide."

He didn't care anymore.

The Bandit Prince was halfway to them, his infamous blade burned like the devil's tail.

Amir swooped in and got in between them. Whispering words to the Flameblade, who barely came to a grinding halt. It didn't look like the fight could be stopped. But the thief had his hands on Kizzuran's wrist, hissing just barely quiet enough to not be overheard.

Any moment now, he'd be thrown aside—Rooster stood at the ready.

By some miracle, Kizzuran took three steps back and snapped, "This isn't over. I'll see all these birds dead. Fucking dead!"

Stormed out the way he came, snatching Musha's head along the way.

Fadin finally exhaled, "Not a very reasonable character, is he?"

"I'll deal with him," Amir put his hand out, "Blood's just gone hot. All his friends are dead now. Kizzuran lost a lot today."

Hadn't they all?

Shemsari didn't bury their dead in foreign lands.

A cultural artifact from a bygone age—perhaps a time where all bodies left in the sand came back to haunt their predecessors, the Shemsari burned their fallen. No wood was required. Scavenged bones were turned into scaffolds, horse hair mats used for kindling. Like everything they did, nothing was wasted.

Dozens of platforms skylined the plateau overlooking Nefara. The clans watched the sunset in silence after carving J'awed around each of the funeral scaffolds.

That beautiful Shemsari girl—the one Rooster had spied singing back at the waterfall—led the procession. She took him by the arm and together they began to throw burning ashes.

Pyres lit right as the sun was eaten by the southern horizon.

That same land that originated these people.

It occurred to Rooster that the White Dervish was obsessed with going south to the White Wastes of Death and had perhaps had a good reason for it. In his eagle form, he'd seen much. Maybe omens that were now just starting to rear their head in Nefara. The idea wasn't half-baked that Jhamon and Jhabari's old man knew something they all didn't.

The woman broke away and began to sing for the fallen. Just as she had for the wild horses to return to the Shobai Hamada.

At night he dreamt of the face of every friend who had died since he stepped foot in this land. They waved at him. They did not seem disparaged but rather encouraging—they wanted him to join them across the ghostly waters.

Worse than any nightmare, he began to feel the sense he was alone in the universe. The existential reminder that mortality was fleeting and a blink of flame that was extinguished too quickly for one to recognize they'd wasted their years. How many more would come before the great black nothing would close in around him?

Drinking had subdued these thoughts by dulling the pain of regret. Now in sobriety, Rooster had nothing to guard against the harsh reality that he'd wasted up his youth. All his best years burned away like ashes, pissed away in the wind.

Strange sounds woke him up; Hazair had flown into the tent and was sleeping soundly at his feet, a bundle of feathers emitting quiet cooh's. More loyal dog than eagle.

The White Dervish might have been trapped in a beast's body but his soul was free to soar. His own end had just been the beginning of a cycle.

Rooster stepped outside to get fresh air. There was no lack of it with this crew. Nomads and sellswords alike slept under the ceiling of starlight. For the first time in weeks, they had nothing to worry about but the wind in their hair and the horse to take them to tomorrow's fields. In the morning would be revelry in the Shemsari fashion—a steer would be smoked under the sand, friends from Nefara would join them, and together they'd find joy in the laurels of their victory.

He wished he could be so carefree.

One day, Rooster knew he'd come to terms with what life had been like before that prodigal boat ride. Stepping on these foreign sands under the pretense of a simple life. How very wrong he'd been on that one—played for the fool. But the past was exactly that. Days gone and done.

On that day he'd bury his sword.

But just like the dawn that would surely come with its warm rays and banish the night, he felt that existential fear begin to fade away. Replaced with a feeling that could have been Bahram's grace.

Or perhaps it was peace at last.

Rooster felt the white scar over his heart and snorted.

Death could try a little harder.

He kept on walking and the world kept bleeding to stop him. It might have been a curse. Or just fool's luck that kept away the reaper. No grave, no gallows—not for Rooster.

And even when death finally came, he knew one thing.

He was damnsure it wasn't the end.

Epilogue

The uppermost level of the palace had been spared the kiss of the flames and though it wasn't exactly a miracle, Amir treated the place with an appropriate degree of suspicion. He was well-used to the fouler places of this world. With gloved hands, he checked the exterior for booby traps once, twice, then a third time just to be safe.

Inside would be a different story.

"Paranoid today, aren't we?" Norulo chuckled, dusting ash that clung to his basalt robes.

Petiri's sidekick was a welcome nuisance for kicking around unwelcome places. In every other event, the macabre acolyte enjoyed being a shadow until someone knocked over a century-old coffin. Then it was a real pain in the ass trying to make Norulo shut up.

His being here would be worth it if Tariq had left them any nasty surprises.

Their third didn't chime in. Amir didn't expect him to. Wait until teeth needed to be pulled, as their middle-aged comrade liked to say.

Who speaking of which was quite late.

"If you have other business to attend to, I can manage the horse lord and his flies," Norulo snickered.

Amir realized he was pacing and stopped, "No. I can wait."

"Has anyone told you that you're starting to walk like him?"

The thief was getting irritated, "Sure. So are you going to tell him the bad news?"

Humor died like a candle blown out prematurely, "What? And earn the warlord's ire? I like my head where it's at."

"Someone has to, eventually."

"Truth is a dangerous thing, Prince. It makes even the

most sane of us go mad."

Both of them, sitting on an apocryphal fact like the pressure plate of a trapdoor. Neither wanting to budge, yet neither willing to live with the consequence of keeping it hidden.

"Rooster has to know. You owe it to him."

Norulo bared his teeth, "Owe? Fools can't bargain with spiders."

"If your head was any bigger, you'd need a wagon to carry it around."

"Bah"

"He's not as dumb as you take him. He figured out more than either of us did about you-know-who here," Amir nodded to their surroundings.

"You think that scares me?"

"I think you're scared of what you don't know about the Black Amenta."

The acolyte fell into a squat, muttering under his breath.

"Rooster has to know about Antonius."

"He'll know soon enough. When the dead begin to dream."

"What happens then?"

"The hell should I have a clue? We never tried the Amenta on a human soul yet," Norulo spoke before he could shove his fist into his mouth, "Shit."

Amir should have known better. Necromancy was too sweet an allure to some. Too attractive to those who longed to be reunited with their loved ones. All his fears were now confirmed.

But the acolyte made excuses, "Listen. It's not all bad."

"Really? How so?"

"The soul has a chance to return to the body. It hears the echo. It just has to make the crossing."

"And if he doesn't? If Antonius can't find his way back?"

"We keep a close eye on the body."

"That's a funny way of saying we wait for a demon to take possession," the thief started to say, but realized his companion's demeaner shifted to something conspiratioral, "Wait. I can't believe this. You wanted this to happen?"

Norulo looked away.

And here Amir thought that all his friends were being upfront.

"You're playing with a man's soul like it's a toy."

The acolyte yammered, "We've never had an opportunity before to try it. The circumstances were too divine—we performed a miracle! You even said it yourself—it was Rooster's call! We are simply the instruments that provided the means."

"The means to damn Antonius to an eternity of torment, you mean," Amir snapped.

A punishment that not even the Serpents deserved. And they deserved a lot of hell for what they did. Amir gave it to them—with extreme prejudice.

"Now that is being rather presumptuous..."

Footsteps on the stairs were their cue to shut up.

The man himself arrived. Limping ever so slightly. All the time he was complaining about that knee. He smoothed back the gray hairs winging at the temples, looking at the door.

"Damned stairs. Had to be the top floor. This is it, huh," Rooster made one of his overt unimpressed faces, turned down to their third, "Whose the bum?"

"A Fang that I kept alive."

"Whatever for? I thought you smoked them all?"

Amir opened the doorway like it was a basket with a cobra inside, "I'll explain. In here. Where no one can hear us."

They four shuffled in.

For a man of high tastes, Tariq's personal apartment was curiously spartan. Bare sandstone in harsh angles, cold stone floor, a mere cot pushed against one wall for sleeping. Besides that a simple wooden desk that was uncluttered, a tall mirror framed by slate, and a chest. That was it. The secretary of the Vizier lived a life a little less barren than some prisoners.

Another few minutes of ruffling and Amir cleared the room best he could of any traps. Then spent the next few utterly baffled.

"It's clear as far as I can tell," Norulo stared at the ceiling, "But my powers can only observe so much. Hard to say with a character like the Qadi."

A man of pure contradiction.

Up until a week ago, Tariq was simply a charlatan and an adept politican. An exceptional man of lowborn status who—despite all odds—triumphed in a way no other dhimmi had ever dreamt of. Crafty, talented and untrustworthy. But not *this* capable.

Rooster stomped around, did his thing looking wise with his thumb in his belt, and shrugged, "Maybe he's got a closet downstairs. Man loved his clothes."

"Didn't you say he spent two hundred gold leopards bringing iced wine down from Nahil?"

"Doesn't match, does it," the warlord craned his head to look up at the mirror's height, "This is a nice piece. Wonder who died for it."

So was the wooden table. Masterfully crafted. And was free of any clues, hints, or pieces besides a few grain reports and dock inspections that needed his stamp. Quills and ink. The chest was empty scrolls and the necessary writing paraphenelia.

Absolutely nothing that told them anything they didn't already know.

Even while on the run and exiled from Nefara, Tariq was having the last laugh.

There was a squirm out of their fourth and mute companion. The Serpent assassin was not enjoying their surroundings.

Amir ungagged him, "What, got something to say?"

The thug just gave him the side-eye and spat on the stone.

Rooster cursed. He'd run his finger on the slate stone of the mirror, cutting himself, "Damn. So. What's his deal?"

"Tell him what you told me."

The thug didn't want to talk.

"Or should I have Norulo *encourage* you?"

One look at the acolyte—spinning a nasty bit of magic between his fingers—and the assassin started to babble.

"Hold on. Slower."

"Ach. I see little, hear little. But this place—I know this place."

Rooster asked, "Why?"

"Black Nizzar. He was unhappy with the arrangement. With the partners. Nizzar was always trying to build…trying to make us whole. After the White Dove's death, it was impossible."

"What do you know of it? Who was responsible?"

Blinking, the thug looked around, "You don't know? The Qadi, the Shalmanisar, and us. We all did. It was the merchants who wanted it but the Qadi facilitated it. Was his invention. A special poison to the heart that no one could detect."

Norulo nodded.

They all suspected.

"It was good for a while. Everyone was happy. Coin was coming in. The merchants were making a fortune. But something happened. Nizzar wanted to end our agreement. Got cold feet. He sent Fangs here to end the Qadi's life but they never returned."

The words drove nails into Amir's gut still, even for the second time.

"We knew he was a sorcerer. We warned of his evils—to stay out of his way. Then…there were two of him," the thug wheezed, eyes bugging out, "The Qadi was everywhere. Everywhere you looked he'd be there. You couldn't even escape him in your dreams. We think he tried to break Nizzar but…"

Rooster let the man get some of the fear out, pacing, "What happened next?"

"One of the Fangs found his way in here. Found the others. Said they'd been flayed. Found jars. And heard sounds…"

"What kind of sounds?"

A whisper, "Voices. Dark voices."

The temperature in the room dropped and not in their imagination. The candles lighting the room even swayed. It was perfectly balmy outside the lone window.

Norulo grunted, "This is impossible, even for Tariq. Black Nizzar was old Saramish. Folk from the Glasslands. The Serpents came from there. They served him."

But the thug shook his head vigorously, tears from buried memories streaking, "You did not see it—the shadow that walked behind Nizzar. Eating his soul."

A flicker of darkness caught Amir's eye.

A trick of the light maybe?

In a breath he had a dagger in his sleeve, ready to throw. Scanning the room. Ignoring the sobbing thug.

He saw it again. In the mirror. Rooster was standing still, back turned to the tall silver glass. But in the reflection, the dark sliver was moving, creeping up behind him. A rogue shadow moved to strike.

Amir hurled the throwing blade at the mirror. It did not shatter as expected—crystal sundered, cracking like ice. Spiderwebs began to form around the impact, enveloping the surface. And there was a hissing as smoke suddenly gave inward—the shadow slipped into the crack.

Rooster saw it and kicked the dagger's pommel. The mirror broke then.

And an archway appeared in its place, into an entirely new chamber.

Norulo hissed, "Wait. I feel something in there."

They went when he gave the go-ahead.

Dust hovered thickly, smearing the darkness inside. It was chill and barren as the last but like the mausoleums of old. Lightless and sunken.

Amir illuminated the lamp.

Corpses were stacked inside like cordwood. Floor to ceiling. Dozens at least. Maybe a hundred. They all bore two similarities. First, they'd been skinned, leaving petrified flesh that was beyond the consumption of maggots. Lastly, they all had a gaping hole in their chest where the heart should have been.

A lonely stone table stood. Tools that belonged to a millennia ago lay scattered—dried blood still coating them, so recently used.

"Rooster," he gasped.

"I see it too."

The etching on the walls. Black markings in a language neither were privy to covered every scrap of bare stone. By tools or fingernails, it was impossible to tell.

What was that it was the byproduct of a mind consumed by madness.

A psychosis.

The warlord approached an inked skin that hung from the wall, face unreadable, "I know this one. Skinny. Funny little sorcerer I ran along with, back before Nefara."

But the thief found something else.

"Hey, isn't that the lamp we found back in the Opaline vaults?"

Amir went to grab it but Norulo's hand gripped his wrist like an iron claw, "Don't. It's been touched. Look."

What had been a brass lamp carved in the shape of a woman's body with her head at the spout was deformed. The neck twisted, the belly had been torn open, a gaping hole where the metal curled from it. If there had been anything in the lamp, it was gone now. Around it were strange dried droplets that looked ashy, translucent.

A ritual had taken place here.

Whatever Tariq had gotten from the lamp, it was long gone now.

"Devnawe. Djinn-eater," Rooster was muttering, his face darkened, "That ring any bells for either of you?"

It didn't.

When they stepped out into the sunlight, it barely warmed the bones. Amir reached for the ancient bronze mask, staring at the patina-riddled surface.

It was true that he wore many faces. But behind it, there was always the same one below. One of flesh and truth. The Dead Hand did not lie.

There was something else he'd learned from the servant Nazsif—too bitter a knowledge to share. In his final moments, the vulture had croaked a name out in an attempt to summon his master. It was clear who he was begging for.

Tariq Ashur wasn't even his real name. The White Kasbah had burned but its records remained. Amir took the time to pore over them, meticulously. There had never been an Ashur in Nefara. The last one to even visit Nefara was over a century and a half ago. Tariq meant road in Medean. Which just so happened to coincide with his title as the master of borders.

That discovery twisted the knife.

Tariq's entire identity was an invention. Everything they knew about him was a lie—the rest were artifacts of a ghost.

But that evil son of a bitch had taken Dario away from him. The music of life replaced with the empty howl of wind. Youth devoured by the wickedness of reality.

Amir looked at the dunes, eyes shining with rage.

If it took his whole life, he'd find Tariq—whoever, and whatever he was.

And make him suffer.

Norulo knew Nefara better than most. Even his cutpurse colleagues would have a hard time following his rat trails that wove through the ancient city's maze. Bodies didn't have the sense to walk to easily accessible places like plazas to be collected—they keeled over in dark and hard-to-reach places all the time.

The nose knows all, Petiri's first lesson to him. Next the flies. Then the vultures. Then the rats.

The acolyte donned what had now become the camouflage of the masses; the cult robes of the initiated. Believers could walk from corner to corner of Nefara and never fear molestation or interference.

They might have cried the morning and evening prayer, but the city still clung to old ways. It was in their blood. Like a beast without needing instruction, it understood the necessity of the priests.

Into the shadows, he plied.

Contemplating all he'd learned. Memorized it all. Then discarded it like the junk it was. Puppet or puppetmaster—whoever Tariq was, it was irrelevant.

The Qadi was yesterday. Today was much worse.

The others didn't know it but they soon would.

Just how very fucked they were.

Norulo snickered, feeling rather self-aggrandized. Slipping past the slums and tenements of the paupers who were all in the same boat.

Everyone ignored the signs until it was too late.

Not even an earthquake and a monument of the elders could sway them from their insipidity.

His nose went—familiar stench of death wafting from an alley nearby. The acolyte headed there. An impressive shrine that stunk like a mass grave. Its stewards had been busy. Very industrious in their efforts indeed.

As a corpse collector and embalmer, he should have felt reviled at this place—it was his archnemesis. The dead should not be left to rot in the sun like this.

And yet he was awed.

Medeans. Druglords. Warlords. Outsiders. All the meddlers grasping at power hadn't a clue. To them, all the cults were the same strawman. A revival of crazies that were shaken up from their political instability.

Norulo stifled a giggle.

Turned back to the shrine.

Of all the cults—and known only to the other sects—this one was gaining dominance. The gore painting of the monstrous lion who had been known as another god, in another time. But if he was manifested here, south of the Wall then something terrible was happening to the old pantheon...

A cult member noticed his trespasses, smiling, "Are you here to worship brother?"

"Yes. I'm ignited by the fervor."

"Join me."

In the woman's arms were weapons piled. And severed arms that had held them. There weren't enough soldiers to guard the dead. They expected graverobbers, not this.

He pretended to enjoy the next bit. Together they walked to the cart and made the grisly offering.

Norulo had seen other revivals attempting to resurrect long-dead gods. This wasn't one of them. This wasn't desperation—it was reverence.

"He comes soon," she whispered, bloody hands dripping, "The avatar of our savior. The White Lion approaches. His flood will bathe us all."

When she became lost in prayer, Norulo found his cue to exit. Looking back in shock. The woman wasn't an oracle, just another believer. Which meant the sermons were changing.

The Scavenger Gods had no avatars. They were purged, scattered into thousands of pieces, and cremated into so many fires. They'd almost brought the world to ruin—back before the wheel. If they were back, truly?

Apocalypse.

He staggered at the thought.

Norulo found his way back to the pit, to the door, where their black sanctum welcomed him in. Petiri made an impatient sound. On the marble slab awaited their next task; the grotesque corpse of a vulture that was frozen in mid-transformation back to its human form. Nazsif, Tariq's creature, had many secrets buried away in the flesh.

The boatman sent him to fetch the necessary tools.

Norulo made him wait just a little longer.

In the chamber adjacent he lingered. Where a dark rod stood on cool stone. Found on the corpse of Malakai—Tariq's secret apprentice. The sorcerer hadn't an idea what he possessed. The two had been collecting relics from Nemset, buying them from ignorant little Amir. The Qadi playing at his games, operating under an entirely different pretense than the forces at hand.

The acolyte handled the rod with cloth, careful not to

make contact with the flesh. The surface dark and fathomless, untouched by light. The same glassy obsidian material as the Amenta. As was the tablet out there, shaken loose by the earthquake. All built with a different purpose, by the same architects.

The Hollow Kings.

It was the sorcerer-tyrants who defeated the Scavenger Gods. Prevented annihilation. Their black magic constructing the Glittering Wall—trapping them from the outside world.

Or so the stories went.

The rod hummed with dark intent. Begging silently to be used. Norulo was tempted. Perhaps in the right circumstances, it was necessary to return to lesser evils.

He could not resist touching it.

His mind panicked as flesh became a lightning-rod for the dark glass.

Then again…

Stories could be wrong.

www.ingramcontent.com/pod-product-compliance
Lightning Source LLC
Chambersburg PA
CBHW022016050726
47499CB00004BA/1024

9798218710897